THE
GATES OF
EXQUISITE
VIEW

JOHN TRENHAILE

THE GATES OF EXQUISITE VIEW

E. P. DUTTON NEW YORK

Copyright © 1987, 1988 by Dongfeng Enterprises Ltd.
All rights reserved. Printed in the U.S.A.

Publisher's Note: This novel is a work of fiction. Names, characters, places, and incidents either are the product of the author's imagination or are used fictitiously, and any resemblance to actual persons, living or dead, events, or locales is entirely coincidental.

First published in the United States in 1988 by E. P. Dutton,
a division of New American Library,
2 Park Avenue, New York, N.Y. 10016.

Originally published in Great Britain
in somewhat different form under the same title.

Library of Congress Cataloging-in-Publication Data
Trenhaile, John.
The gates of exquisite view.
I. Title.
PR6070.R367G3   1987   823'.914   87-13630
ISBN: 0-525-24595-2
OBE

DESIGNED BY MARK O'CONNOR

1 3 5 7 9 10 8 6 4 2
First American Edition

For Mother and Father, who began it.
And for Pin Fan, who made it real.
With love.

AUTHOR'S NOTE

The People's Republic of China is mainland, or Red, China. It is not to be confused with the Republic of China, which is better known as Taiwan. Red Chinese habitually refer to Taiwan as "the other place," and vice versa.

Quemoy is the same place as Kinmen; Taiwanese use these terms indiscriminately. Mainlanders sometimes call that island Quemoy, but they refuse to say Kinmen, and their maps show it as Jinmen. This is in keeping with both sides' determination to be different at all costs, no matter what the price may be in terms of confusion.

For the same reason, Taiwanese never call Beijing anything other than Peiping.

The Kuomintang government of Taiwan has continued to proscribe the Taiwanese independence movement (called, by me, Our Formosa Now) ever since it first took power. But the movement does exist, and is not without friends both in Taiwan and elsewhere.

The unit of currency in Taiwan is the New Taiwan Dollar. Taiwanese refer colloquially to something costing, say, "a hundred NT," and I have followed this custom. The principal currency unit in mainland China is the *yuan*.

Chinese family names precede given names. Qiu Qianwei is pronounced Chew Chi-en Way, Qingqing is pronounced Chingching.

Mainland Chinese names and places have been romanized in accordance with the Pinyin system. Chinese spellings associated with Taiwan and other Far East locations, however, have as far as possible been transliterated to match prevailing local usage.

A glossary of foreign terms begins on page 373.

I'm extremely grateful to those people who looked after me so regally in Taipei and elsewhere in Taiwan, but who would probably prefer not to see their names associated with this novel. Special thanks are also due to Cedric Lee, who weeded the manuscript of many horrible errors and generally did so much to raise the tone. I won't forget.

In this book, some people express opinions favorable to Red China; others condemn it while praising Taiwan. This is an area where all the characters, disparate in other ways, do have this at least in common: none of them speak for the author.

The Government of the United States of America acknowledges the Chinese position that there is but one China and Taiwan is part of it.

—Joint Communiqué on the Establishment of Diplomatic Relations Between the United States of America and the People's Republic of China, January 1, 1979

I

MAY-JUNE

Bao Dao

(The Treasure Isle)

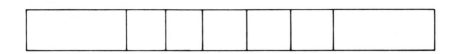

ONE

The evening sky glowed warm gold, as if its light had been filtered through finest-quality olive oil before bathing the crowded scene in Bangkok's Lumpini Park. Happy pandemonium reigned. Swallows screeched in the trees, traffic roared around the perimeter of the King's statue, food-hawkers cried their wares. Youngsters flew kites, craftily fashioned into the guises of dragons, snakes, or bats. In the center of the field, beneath the sparring kites, a raucous game of *takraw* was in progress: twenty or so men, arranged in a rough circle, passed the rattan ball from one to the other, using every part of the body save the hands. On this warm Saturday the scene fairly reeked of *sanuk*, that peculiarly Thai phenomenon of carefree gaiety.

Yet in the middle of all this hectic bustle, enclosed and serene, two men managed to preserve a small oasis of calm.

Both were Chinese. One was short and of undistinguished appearance; the other, flat-faced and stocky, towered over his companion to an extent that suggested guardian and ward, even though they seemed to be much the same age.

They stood beside a weeping willow on the bank of the lake, near the teahouse. The smaller man's eyes were closed and a slight frown marred the otherwise smooth surface of his youngish face, as if he were contemplating a mystical vision, but one not altogether to his liking. His companion stood a pace or two behind him and to one side, face expressionless. Slowly and deliberately, they began to work through the canon of *Taijiquan* exercises.

They began by describing a large circle in the air: *Here is the watermelon. . . .*

"Baba is dead," murmured the tall man.

The other Chinese faltered for a second, then continued the same relaxed movements of his arms. He looked an unlikely candidate for such introspective, gentle exercise: five feet eight inches tall, not more, with a downturned mouth hinting at short temper. Yet somehow he managed to perform the ritualized movements with a subtle grace that the loftier exponent lacked.

"When?"

The word scarcely carried to the first Chinese, who at once replied, "Two nights ago. Sun Shanwang is named Controller of China's Central Intelligence. It was he who sent me, Qiu Qianwei."

I cut the watermelon. . . .

"You put me in danger of death by coming here."

"No one knows me. I have never traveled outside the Middle Kingdom before."

"Speak fast. I want you—gone." The man called Qiu spoke in quick gasps.

This part of the watermelon . . . I give to you. . . .

"Already there have been many changes. The military are asserting themselves. You are ordered back to Beijing tomorrow."

"But I am to go to Singapore."

"Your orders have been changed. You must return to China. There is a major buildup under way, in which you are to play a key role."

This part . . . I give to her. . . . "Buildup?"

"The other place. Taiwan. Baba always advocated a peaceful solution. Now that he is dead, the Politburo are under pressure to repossess by force."

"What?" The word escaped in a whisper, but the taller man heard. "You are to proceed to the other place, after Beijing. Taiwan is your next assignment, Qiu Qianwei."

[4]

"How can that be?" Qiu's voice vibrated with shock, fear even. "It is like ordering me to execution!"

"Nevertheless, you are to go, and very soon."

Qiu's breathing had degenerated into an irregular series of gulps. "I cannot!"

"Those are your orders." The second man lowered his arms. "I will go now."

"No! I need more information. Tell me—"

Qiu Qianwei heard a noise behind him and wheeled around in time to see the messenger from Beijing walking up the concrete path, toward the park gates. A light breeze dried the sweat on Qiu's cheeks, making him feel suddenly cold.

He sighed and for a moment merely stood there, scowling at the happy-go-lucky people around him as if he were a head of state on a visit to Thailand who chose not to recognize the spirit of the Land of Smiles. Then he picked up his bag and stalked toward the main avenue, making for the exit. He sat down on one of the white stone steps at the foot of the King's statue and consulted his watch. He was early.

Qiu rummaged around in his bag until he found a small wooden box. The box contained two short, silvery-bright chopsticks, wrapped in crimson velvet.

The Chinese held the sticks, slender as knitting-needles, up to the light. They were made of some substance resembling niello ware: black when held at an angle, white if viewed horizontally. A smile of satisfaction crinkled his lips. One extravagance, just one. That afternoon he had gone shopping and found the child's chopsticks on a shelf at the back of a tumbledown shop in Sampong Lane, in Chinatown. As soon as he had opened the box he knew that he was going to bargain for them. That realization had surprised him, for he could not immediately think why he should want a pair of small, sharp-pointed metal chopsticks joined at one end by a fine-linked chain. Then he knew why. They would be a gift to his son, Tingchen. Something to put by, in a drawer, for when the boy was older.

For when I am dead. The words entered his brain unbidden. Qiu remembered the ominous message he had just received and, despite the oppressive heat, he shivered.

Taipei, 7:45, the same evening. A telephone on the hall table of the Ducannon Young apartment emitted a single, high-pitched squawk. When nothing happened, the instrument repeated its stri-

[5]

dent summons; and this time Mat Young knocked the receiver off its perch in his eagerness to prevent a repetition of the sound.

"*Shit!*" Mat could count the things he disliked about Taiwan on the fingers of one hand, but its telephones were high on the list. Rod Haines slung his jacket over his shoulders and gave his friend a wry grin. "Make it quick," he mouthed.

"*Wei* . . . ?" Mat greeted the caller.

"I'm at Hsinchu. I need you here."

Mat recognized the voice at once. "For Christ's sake, Lennie! This is a joke, right?" He tucked the receiver under his chin, beckoning Rod to come and listen. The Australian approached with a curious expression on his face. "Lennie's surfaced?"

Mat nodded. "Look, Lennie, you haven't been home for days, I think you're dead or God knows what, and then . . . what the fucking hell are you doing in Hsinchu at this hour?"

"Working. Mat, I have to see you. Your father's orders."

"Father's orders? Has he been on the phone?"

"No."

"Then I don't see . . ."

"Two years ago, he told me I was to phone you when . . . when something happened. And it's happened. Just now. *So help me!*"

Mat frowned. He had been friends with the young Chinese, who was also his roommate, for many years. Their childhoods, endured against vastly different backgrounds, had nevertheless overlapped. The Englishman knew instinctively that Lennie Luk was afraid. Why, he couldn't fathom. Sometimes Lennie was strange.

"Can't it wait till morning?"

"*No!*" A long pause. The line pulsated with a quiet, echoing beat. "It can't wait. Come. Just come."

Mat hesitated a moment longer, trying to delve deeper beneath the hollow connection. "I'm taking Mei-hua out to dinner." A note of longing had crept into his voice. "Is it okay if I get there afterwards?"

"Yes. I guess."

Mat slowly replaced the receiver. "What the hell was all that about?" he said to Rod.

"God knows." The Australian looked at his watch. "You really going down tonight?"

"I said I would, so yes. Maybe you'd better come with me."

"Me?"

"You're Ducannon Young's security officer. And Lennie sounded . . . in trouble. Weird."

"Well . . . look, we can talk about this later. Right now, we'd better get moving. Don't want to keep the girls waiting, you know what actresses are like."

There were four of them in the party: Rod Haines, the Australian accountant who supervised security for Ducannon Young Electronics in Taiwan, and Sonia Tuan, his current girlfriend; and Mat and his actress friend, Mo Mei-hua.

They ate at Antoine's, the Lai Lai Sheraton's fabulous French restaurant, and since they were celebrating (Mat had just made two thousand dollars by selling some Singapore Air shares short) they did it in style. Mat and Mei-hua both chose the showpiece Pear Antoine for dessert, because they enjoyed it when the waiter poured flaming brandy down the twist of fruit peel while the lights dimmed and the pianist played rippling music. Afterwards there was talk about going on somewhere, but first, Rod decided, he had to make a couple of phone calls that wouldn't wait, and then Mei-hua tugged Mat's sleeve. "C'mon, I want to show you something."

So, after they'd said goodnight to the others, she drove him to a tiny lane off Swang Cheng Road, in the heart of Taipei's entertainment district, where, not without some searching, they found the place she wanted. They entered through a dingy foyer and took the elevator up to the top floor. Mat leaned against the wall of the car; he could not stop looking at her.

She wore a one-shoulder, silk chiffon dress by Hanae Mori, handpainted with peonies and butterflies in pinks and blues. A bangle encircled each slender wrist; her glossy black hair, swept back to the side, was secured with a tortoiseshell comb; and around her neck hung a strand of freshwater pearls. Mat knew she must have worked hard to produce such a striking effect. Mei-hua was the most beautiful Chinese girl he'd ever seen, and he wanted her more than he could put into words.

She was of medium height, with well-developed hips and breasts that stayed exactly the right side of plumpness. Her cheekbones were fine, in the oriental way, but the rest of Mei-hua's facial features seemed rounded and full, giving her an air of good-humored allure. Only the eyes, which exactly mirrored the shape of her lips, gave away her mixed parentage.

At last they reached the top floor. Mei-hua delved into her handbag and fished out a set of keys. "Here," she said, handing them over. "You men, so competent."

On the other side of the landing was a door, padlocked shut. While Mat sorted out the right key, Mei-hua leaned against the frame, arms folded in front of her, and watched him from under long, curling lashes. She wants me to touch her, he thought; the point of the key missed its target, making her giggle. "Surely you can see," she murmured. "Such big eyes . . ."

"Like yours. Four big eyes between us."

"Eurasians always have large eyes."

Mat reddened. Then the door opened, and Mei-hua, who seemed to know where everything was, reached up to switch on the lights. Mat found himself on the threshold of an enormous room with stained concrete walls and bare floorboards. Dust lay everywhere in a thick layer. It all looked bleak and uninviting. He turned to the girl with a smile, his raised eyebrows soliciting an explanation.

"What do you think?" she asked.

"As an abattoir it has possibilities."

"No, be serious!" She gave his arm a playful push, then raised a hand to her mouth to cover a laugh.

"What is this place?"

She did not answer at once. Instead she clasped her handbag behind her back and began to traipse around the floor in a little hopping dance, not looking at him. She was humming a tune. After a while the hum broke into a song. Mat, recognizing its melody, strained to hear the Mandarin words. "What's that you're singing?"

" 'Clock Mountain Spring.' A love song. It is, um . . . I am sorry. My English is so bad."

"Your English is wonderful. Others speak it. You sing it."

"Uh?"

"Little intonations you give the words, sometimes. Like . . . 'don't.' You say 'do-an.' I like it when you do that. 'I do-an wa-an it.' "

"Do-an I indeed?" she teased. "We'll see. But I must tell you, my English is no better than anyone else's in the Asian film world. We all have to learn to take direction in English."

He watched her swirl around the floor, the dress floating lightly over her hips and buttocks, suggesting without defining them, and he wondered if she was high. But on what? She'd drunk a little wine with her meal and one whiskey afterwards. Yet she seemed uncomfortable, as if the material of the dress irked her. "Who owns this place?" he asked.

Mei-hua stopped and turned to face him, head cocked to one side. Her smile reminded him of a self-satisfied daughter about to tell her daddy she'd come in first in her class.

"As of this afternoon . . . I do. That is, if the bank will give me a loan."

"*You* do?"

"Mm-hm." She flung her arms wide and pirouetted. "Welcome, sir, to the Evening Fragrance Night Club." Then she walked up to him and, to his amazement, laid her hands on his shoulders. Her eyes glittered as if they were hot, and tiny beads of perspiration dotted her hairline. He was on the point of reaching up to place his own hands over Mei-hua's when she withdrew them abruptly and turned away. "I thought we would have the bar over there, raised up from the dance floor a little, and the band . . . here. What do you think?"

His heart was racing, the words wouldn't come. Mei-hua smiled coquettishly. "Don't you like it?' But the high he'd sensed earlier was fading quickly. Mat had not seen her in need of reassurance before.

"I want you to like it," she said, advancing toward him again.

"I'm flattered.'

She seemed at a loss. "Why?"

"Because my opinion matters so much, so fast."

"Oh . . . it's not *your* opinion I'm after, Mat." Her tone was arch. "I want to hear the views of Mr. Young, son of Southeast Asia's richest entrepreneur, heir to the Ducannon Young empire, general trader, manufacturer of electronics, property magnate, owner of more than a dozen banks. . . ."

Mat burst out laughing. "You're too much, y'know that? Besides, it sounds as though you want my father's opinion, not mine."

"You're wrong." Her face was serious. "Don't say that, please."

"You must admit, it's a little sudden. Rod Haines introduces us one night, I say how much I loved your last movie, and less than two weeks later . . ." He smiled, wanting her to understand, to complete the sentence for him. But instead she pouted and said, "You think I am fast. Is that it?"

Mat's smile vanished at once. "Not at all," he said quietly. "I apologize."

For a long moment she peered at him through those luminous eyes; then she slowly came up until she was almost touching him and whispered, "I would not want my English gentleman to think that. Please don't think I am fast. Please . . ."

They kissed. After a moment she laid her palms against his

chest and drew away. He tried to hold her, but only for an instant, aware that now was not the time.

When Mat finally escorted her home, he told himself he was happy, in love for the first time ever. And nothing—certainly not the faint impurity of her breath, which he must have imagined anyway—could convince him otherwise.

"Ah, Qianwei, good evening. We are late. So sorry." Qiu hastily replaced the chopsticks in their box and tried to stuff it back in the bag. But when he saw his host's hand already held out, he dithered, lost momentum, and ended up by thrusting the box into his pants pocket instead. Two men, a Thai and a Chinese, had come to stand in front of him. "Good evening, Mr. Kraisri." Then he remembered where he was, and—"Somnuk . . . Sam," he quickly corrected himself.

"This is Mr. Harry Hsiu."

Qiu was expecting Somnuk Kraisri, who had fashionably transmuted his name to the Western approximation "Sam." The Thai was under-manager of the Chinese Overseas Investment Bank's Bangkok branch, where Qiu had been working for the past fortnight. But Hsiu he had not met before. Qiu took in the newcomer: a tall, muscular Chinese, about thirty years old, dressed casually for the weekend and carrying a brightly colored paper umbrella.

"Pleased to meet you, Mr. Hsiu," he said, extending a hand.

"Mutual." Qiu's fellow Chinese tossed the umbrella from one hand to the other and shook. His grip, stiffly formal, was at once released, but not without leaving a film of sweat on Qiu's palm. Hsiu seemed nervous.

So did Kraisri. The pudgy Thai banker was far from being his usual affable self. Most of the time, Sam typified all the other smiling, grown-up children Qiu had met on his stay in Thailand, but today, for some reason, he looked put out.

"Ah . . . Harry here is a neighbor of mine, Qianwei."

"Oh yes?"

"Um-hm. He heard I was coming to meet you this evening, your last day in Bangkok, very sad, um-hm?"

"Most sad."

"So he said, 'Look, why not take Qiu Qianwei, your friend, to drink snake's blood?' and I said, 'Why not?' So here we are."

"Snake's blood?"

"Sure. Very wonderful stuff for virility." Kraisri winked, making an attempt to liven up the proceedings by appearing raffish.

The attempt failed; his dusty shoes, the circle of pale brown flesh poking between two buttons of his cream-colored shirt, everything was against him.

Qiu forced an acquiescent smile. "I'm happy to be in your hands, Mr. Kraisri—Sam."

"Good. That's fine, then. Shall we go?"

They walked a little way down Rama IV Road. Kraisri hailed a cab, dismissed it on finding that its air-conditioning unit had broken down, and tried again. Second time lucky. "Yaowaraj Street," he said to the driver as he climbed in. "Drop us by the King's Theatre."

There followed the usual spirited altercation on the subject of the fare. At last the bargaining was over and the cab set off toward Chinatown. By now it was nearly dark and the streets of the capital were blazing with a spectrum of light, from rings of white bulbs that adorned temple *chedis* like bejeweled necklaces to the flashing red neon of massage parlors, with every conceivable color represented in between.

Progress was slow. Swarms of *tuk-tuk* pedicabs weaving through the bottlenecks made better speed than any car could hope to do. The taxi's primitive air conditioner labored in vain against the smells of exhaust, stagnant water, chilis fried in freshly ground spice, the stale-vomit-and-moldy-cheese smell of durian fruit. Essence of Bangkok slithered insidiously through the car via every crack and vent in its battered bodywork.

They crossed Klong Phadung, turned left into Song Sawad Road, and almost immediately ground to a halt in what seemed like a traffic jam without beginning or end.

"I hope this thing will not go on too late," said Kraisri. "What time is your flight tomorrow, Qianwei?"

"No flight. Express Train Eleven from Bangkok to Butterworth, then on to Singapore by Magic Arrow."

Harry Hsiu was puzzled. "You like trains?"

"Oh no." Qiu blinked, slightly surprised at having to explain the obvious to a fellow countryman. "So cheap."

Kraisri guffawed. "Here we have a funny guy, um-hm? The bank sends him to Thailand, pays his first-class air fare, puts him up at the Or-en-*tel*, what does he do? He goes by train. How 'bout that?"

Qiu watched Hsiu do mental calculations and smiled when his new acquaintance's eyebrows rose in respect.

At last they reached their destination. Hsiu climbed out of the cab, swinging his umbrella. "This snake's-blood thing is amazing."

He spoke clumsy Mandarin, like a peasant come to town for the day. "You'll enjoy it."

Qiu peered through the gloom at Hsiu's face and wondered why he doubted it. All his instincts were prickling. They told him he ought to turn around, find his way to the lane's entrance, hail another cab, and go back to the Oriental Hotel.

Hsiu strode toward the small *klong* that bounded the lane at its far end. He turned into an alley illuminated only by occasional storm lanterns suspended from little spirit-houses on the walls, and there he paused, as if no longer sure of his way. He turned to left and right, chin jutting upwards; then he shot out an arm. "There."

About twenty meters ahead, Qiu could see a stall set up under an awning that stretched the width of the *soi*. As well as kerosene lanterns, there were also half a dozen of the ornamental Chinese variety containing candles. The stall—a table half-covered with a checkered cloth—was empty, but obviously the organizers expected a crowd, for dozens of chairs had been placed in a rough semicircle, blocking the alley.

Hsiu marched up to the chairs and picked out three in the front row, appropriating them by laying his paper umbrella along the seats. "All right?"

"Very nice," Qiu replied.

Mr. Kraisri mopped his face with his handkerchief, using both hands. He seemed increasingly agitated, as well as hot. His eyes flitted around, not quite liking what they saw but unable to pinpont grounds for a protest.

"Are you in banking, Mr. Hsiu?" Qiu asked as he sat down.

"No. Import-export, that's my line. You're with China Overseas Investment Bank, Sam tells me. Singapore branch manager, yes?"

"Assistant manager, overseas investment division."

"So what brings you to Thailand?"

"Surveying local conditions."

"Freebies, in other words! Good for you."

Suddenly they became aware of a commotion behind them. Qiu's nostrils flared as he heard the sibilants of Japanese spoken loudly by many voices. A rowdy party, perhaps even a little drunk, all male. Coach tour, no doubt; or one of those awful sex parties.

The Japanese invaders swarmed through the *soi* like a samurai's advance guard, shifting chairs and bumping into people. They did not at all resemble the usual busload of docile, camera-crazy Japanese tourists.

"Drunk," said Hsiu. He laughed offensively. "Must be their football team, yah?"

Mr. Kraisri pointedly turned his back on the noisy horde. *"Mai suparb,"* he muttered. Not polite.

A fat Japanese wearing white trousers several sizes too small sat down heavily next to Qiu, forcing him to pull his bag onto his lap. Hsiu lightly touched Qiu's arm. "They're starting."

Someone had placed several large rattan baskets by the side of the trestles. Now a Chinese man came forward to lift one of the baskets onto the tabletop. He was in his fifties, with only a few grizzled tufts of hair left on his pate, and his eyes glittered in the murk like reflective crystals. Qiu, looking at them, stirred uncomfortably.

The man removed the lid from one of the baskets. For a few seconds nothing happened. Then a long, dark rope oozed over the lip of the rattan, hesitated, and slowly began to make its way down onto the table.

A couple of helpers silently brought more lanterns, placing two of them at either end of the stall and suspending the rest above it. Now Qiu could see everything; his pores contracted and the back of his neck went cold. Snakes were flowing down the side of the first basket like rivulets of oil from an overfilled jar.

The master of ceremonies casually picked up one of the thinnest black ropes and let it run across his hands. Then he held it by neck and tail while he tossed back his head, holding the snake vertically above him. He began to feed the reptile into his mouth, lowering it a little, hauling it back, lowering again, until at last the whole of the creature had disappeared.

Qiu was only half-impressed. But suddenly he sat upright with a jolt—the man had let go his grip on the snake's tail and closed his mouth. For several seconds he did nothing but stand there, a tranquil, secretive smile playing about his lips, while Qiu's flesh crept. Then the man put both hands to his nostrils and, with the same playing-out gestures he had used earlier, began to feed the wirelike snake back into the basket—only this time through his nose.

There was some clapping. The Japanese football team seemed vague about it all, as if not quite sure what they'd just witnessed. The snake charmer's gaze floated thoughtfully along the front row and paused for a moment when it came to Qiu Qianwei (or was that his imagination?) before completing its survey of the audience. Then he bent down to another basket and lifted it up next to the first.

[13]

As soon as the lid of this basket came off, a long, thick shaft exploded out and up like a jack-in-the-box, making the first two rows of spectators recoil. A hissing black pole, two feet tall, with a triangular-shaped head and two eyes blazing full of hatred.

King cobra.

With a single leisurely movement the snake charmer swung the basket around through a half-circle, so that its venomous occupant was facing him, and waved his palm across the face of the snake.

Instantly the swaying shaft became absolutely still. The Chinese lifted it out of the basket by the neck, holding it up horizontally—a rigid rod. One of his assistants came forward with a tray on which stood three hourglass-shaped wooden goblets and a long knife. The snake charmer inverted the reptile and took up the serrated blade. There was a moment of suspense, during which even the rowdiest Japanese held his breath. Then the knife came down in a slow, slanting cut at the base of the cobra's neck. The head fell onto the table with a dull thud, and black liquid stained the silvery metal. Next, the snake charmer adroitly held the long body over each goblet in turn, filling it to the brim with blood.

When he had finished, he tossed the snake onto the floor and, picking up the tray, came around to the front of the table. For a few seconds he pretended to hesitate while he chose a guest of honor, but Qiu knew from the moment the performer's hypnotic eyes first made contact with his that he had been cast in the role of elect.

So it proved; the tray came to rest in front of him. Mr. Kraisri fingered his good-luck amulet, muttering under his breath. Qiu looked from the goblets to the smiling face of the snake charmer and back again. Why had be been singled out? Then again, why not? Someone had to be chosen. Besides, it would be something to tell them back at the bank, or when he next wrote to his wife, Qingqing.

Harry Hsiu whispered in his ear: "It is a great honor. Because you are Chinese, like him, and no one else here is, I think. Take it, take it!"

Qiu hesitated. Why not choose Harry, who was also Chinese? But . . . he stretched out his hand with a shrug.

Before he could take the cup, however, the fat Japanese next to him had snatched it away with a crow of triumph and drained it down, holding the empty goblet high above his head with an exultant smile of superiority at having vanquished his Chinese neighbor.

For a moment nobody moved. Qiu was too stunned by the sudden assault to take offense. But the snake charmer seemed mortally stricken. He staggered back a pace, one hand toying with his shirt collar. Qiu stared at him uncomprehendingly.

The smile on the face of the Japanese faded. He dropped the goblet and crossed both hands over his ample stomach, as if cradling a baby. For a few seconds longer he continued to stand staring into the distance, as though something puzzled him. Then, still in total silence, he fell forward, landing across the chairs with a clatter.

Qiu bent down and heaved the tourist over onto his back. He placed a finger on the man's carotid artery and laid his ear against his mouth. Dead.

The other Japanese crowded around, shouting and shoving. As Qiu stood upright, his face came opposite to that of the snake charmer and in a flash he saw the man's expression turn from shock to murderous malice. The entertainer stepped quickly back, groping for the body of the cobra. With a flick of the wrist too quick for the eye to register, he had it coiled around Qiu's neck like a lasso. Only for a second. The snake's skin was dry, it had no purchase, and Qiu unwrapped it with a single frantic gesture. But in that scintilla of time he thought he would die.

Then he was running.

As he pushed through the ring of Japanese, who by now were almost hysterical, Hsiu stepped in front of him, brandishing his umbrella like a sword. Qiu grasped that there were two assailants involved. He managed to land a heavy, sideways punch in Hsiu's stomach. The next second he was sprinting for the entrance to the alley.

Footsteps behind him. Kraisri? No, Qiu couldn't believe he was involved in this. Hsiu? Still winded, out of action. It must be the snake charmer, then—but Qiu knew better than to waste time in looking back. *Who? Why?*

At the end of the alley he darted away to the left, where he knew the *klong* was. He didn't hesitate, but plunged straight into the smelly canal. At that point it was shallow and muddy with thick sludge. Qiu splashed down the channel toward the nearest lights, ramshackle houses rising on either side of him. He caught sight of another ill-lit lane, across the *klong*, and clambered out. The sloshing sounds made by his pursuers seemed horribly close.

Qiu raced down the lane, emerged into a bright thoroughfare, and ran slap into a tout.

"Want to see something interesting, sir? Girl-show, boy-show . . ."

Qiu grabbed the tout's arm so tightly that the man howled in pain. "Yes!" snapped the Chinese. "I do!"

"Yessir, yessir, come this way . . ."

A *tuk-tuk* was parked by the curb. The tout bundled Qiu into it and started bargaining with the driver. Qiu short-circuited the process by stuffing a hundred-baht note under the nose of the astonished driver, who took one look at it and slammed his engine into gear.

Traffic was still heavy, but the pedicab dodged in and out of the worst jams, throwing Qiu and his guide from one side of the carriage to the other. Qiu managed to look back and catch a brief glimpse of someone, it might be Hsiu, climbing into a regular taxi. When he turned around again, he saw that his own driver was slowing for a red light. Qiu thumped him on the shoulder. "Go *on!*" he screamed. The driver did not speak Mandarin, but he was in no doubt as to Qiu's meaning. He accelerated.

Qiu looked over his shoulder. The taxi was held up at the light, but as he watched, it changed and the cab leaped away, gaining quickly on the little *tuk-tuk*. Just when it was mere yards behind, the pedicab's driver unexpectedly threw his passengers off balance by making a ninety-degree turn. The taxi, caught unawares, flashed past.

They had stopped in a large space along one side of a double-fronted house, constructed in the Western style. Qiu jumped down. His eyes focused on the far end of the courtyard, where there was an elaborate shrine. A number of young men were sprawled across and around it, peacefully asleep, their hands folded across their chests and their mouths open. For some reason they reminded Qiu of predators who had just finished their meal: a bevy of dormant crocodiles.

The driver sounded his horn. One of the men opened an eye and half sat up. Then, seeing that customers had arrived, he uttered a banshee wail—and the place sprang alive.

All the youths, of whom there were about a dozen, leaped up and rushed into the house through a side-door. Qiu lost no time in following. As he tripped over the threshold into a dark room, he heard the screech of a needle across a record and instantly a heavy disco beat began to pound out through the moist night air. A lantern came on behind the bar, where two of the young men were frantically getting to work. Then strobe lighting flickered into life to reveal a stage.

At the far end of the dim room Qiu could see a flight of stairs. He launched himself toward them. Before he had covered half the distance, however, he felt his arm taken in a strong grip and he turned.

"Hi," said his captor. "My name is Hans. I am Chur-r-r-man. I own this place. How. Do. You. Do."

"I'm in a hurry."

"I can see," Hans said ponderously, tightening his grip on Qiu. He was very tall, with muscles to match, and the Chinese didn't care for the way he'd had his hair shaved close to his skull. "Heff a trink."

Qiu swallowed. "Singha beer."

"Goot. Sit." Hans pushed down on Qiu's arm. One of the youths who had been supine at the shrine hastily provided a chair. Qiu sat.

"Now," said Hans, pulling up another chair beside him. "Wot you tink?" He gestured toward the stage.

Qiu took a look around. No sign of the opposition. On the stage the youths danced as if their lives depended on it, the strobes sequining their bodies with sickly yellow. Someone turned up the music.

"Which one you like?" Hans said, more affably. "Most speak English, some of them know Chinese. Prices? Well, we heff all kinds. Turd from right, now . . ."

Qiu stared at him. Then, very slowly, he directed his attention back to the stage. Most of the young men had removed their shirts. On a raised dais, two of the more forward spirits were dancing, stark naked. Qiu's mouth opened to its full extent. When his spectacles slid down his nose he forgot to push them up again. He did not understand this place at all.

"Which one you like?" Hans repeated.

Then Qiu noticed something else. The backdrop to the extraordinary scene of depravity being enacted on the stage was a black sheet, crudely painted with stars and a big moon. The moon and some of the larger stars were, he realized, nothing more than holes cut in the sheet, which had been placed against the white wall behind. Now the moon had a face. Someone was standing in the narrow space between the sheet and the wall. Someone looking straight at him . . .

Qiu was out of his chair in a second. "That one," he grated, pointing at a boy near the stairs. "How much?"

"Fif'tin hundred."

It went against all of Qiu's instincts not to bargain, but he had no time. He flung the notes at Hans, seized the boy by the forearm, and started hauling him toward the stairs. They led up to a door. As Qiu pushed through it he heard, even above the music, footsteps thudding behind him.

Beyond the door the stairs climbed up to the first floor, where a bare landing garishly lighted with blue neon tubes gave on to a number of rooms. At the far end of the nearest one was a pale square, and Qiu guessed, correctly, that this meant a window.

"Hey!" said the boy, following him inside. "Hey! What about my drink? I want, yes?" He spoke poor English; Qiu understood, but was in no mood to answer. "Hey!" said the boy. "What about my money? Tip, yes? Hey!"

Qiu pounded at the window with his fists. Shutters swung open to reveal the courtyard, Qiu's *tuk-tuk* still parked there, a dozen feet below him. Something landed against the bedroom door and the boy turned uncertainly. "Hey," he repeated. His voice trembled like a mournful lamb's.

The door burst open. Qiu dived for the window. As he cleared the sill he heard the boy say, "Hey," only this time it sounded shrill, different. Qiu landed within a foot of the *tuk-tuk*. He thought he heard confused noises behind him and looked up. A light came on in the bedroom. For an instant the boy seemed to be framed in the window as a black shadow surrounded by yellow light. Then he collapsed forward across the sill, and the shadow became that of a deformed monster; something long and thin stood out of his back. He did not move again. He did not say "Hey!"

"Right!" Qiu snapped as he climbed into the *tuk-tuk*. "We go now."

But before the driver could start the engine, another figure came flying through the first-floor window. Qiu didn't wait to identify it. He threw himself out of the pedicab and ran, tiring rapidly now. He turned a corner and found himself in a square ringed with market stalls, all doing brisk business. Qiu pushed through the crowds to a stall on the far side of the square and eased himself into the shadow of a stone archway before looking back. At first he could see nothing; then Hsiu emerged into the nearest pool of light. There was no sign of the snake charmer. Hsiu looked around, evidently undecided; he raised his eyes, for an instant looked at the arcade where Qiu was hiding, and darted forward.

Thunder rumbled overhead. One moment it was bone-dry on the streets of Bangkok, the next it was teeming with warm rain. People ran for the nearest cover. Within seconds Qiu found himself surrounded by wet, squeaking Thais. The square bloomed with brightly colored umbrellas, whirling circles of red, green, blue, every imaginable tint and hue.

Qiu slid to the end of the arcade. He was trapped, holed up. To his right stood a solid stone wall, the side of a house; to his left was the square; behind him, his pursuer.

The rain ceased as abruptly as it had begun. People were shaking umbrellas and preparing to chance their luck in the open again. They gave Qiu the cover he needed. He ran diagonally across the square. Just when he thought there was no way out, he caught sight of an alleyway leading uphill, with brighter lights at the far end—a main road. To the left was a wheeled spice stall on an island site between the lane and an open drain. He darted around to the side of it and crawled underneath, beseeching providence that the stallkeeper would not protest. But the old woman was far more interested in bemoaning the rain and the consequent loss of business than in Qiu Qianwei's invasion of her territory. An oilskin cloth covered the stall, shielding Qiu from passersby. He held his breath and waited for his heartbeat to steady.

Lightning forked directly over Bangkok, followed an instant later by a doomsday crash of thunder. Torrential storm-rain hurled itself against the square, which once again emptied as if by magic. But as everyone else converged on the arcade in search of shelter, Hsiu was left alone in the center of the open space, peering about him and apparently immune to all distraction.

While people rushed past him going the other way, the assassin slowly began to walk back toward the alley. His eyes passed over everything very slowly, rejecting possibilities, refusing to be rushed. When he was only a few steps away from the spice stall he stopped, intent on the ground. There was a lot of water in the square by now, but the stall was surrounded by a thin film of mud, rainwater mixed with blown spice; and there, cleanly represented, were human footprints leading toward the stall. Someone had left an unmistakable trail. Hsiu lifted his head and seemed to sniff the air. Then he took a step forward.

Very slowly and carefully, so as not to attract attention, he drew a blade from the sheath concealed in his waistband. His gaze seemed welded to the innocuous-looking spice stall; never once taking his eyes from it, he moved forward another stealthy step and reached out to grasp the cloth that covered its rickety counter. For a second he stood stock-still. Then he convulsed his muscles and prepared to whisk the cloth away to reveal what lay beneath.

But before this intention could be translated into action, another pair of hands, invisible to him, seized the far edge of the cloth and wrenched it violently upward. The night suddenly came alive with colors. Red, orange, ginger, green, brown—all the spices of the orient seemed to rise up in a dazzling, dancing curtain before the killer's incredulous eyes and hang there suspended for an instant before coming down on him in a dusty cloud. Pain seared his eyeballs as the lids inadvertently closed on ground black pepper and coarse-grained chili powder; he dropped the knife and vainly clenched his fists to his eyes, tears streaming down his face. Briefly he became aware of a new color coming at him out of the dusty rainbow curtain: flashes of thin, pale silver, like bodkins. One of the chopsticks sank deep into his left eye socket, blinding him with more than spice, and continued on and upward, finding the brain.

Qiu wrenched out the silver stick and fled down the alley. Behind him he could already hear incoherent shouts; someone cried *"Tamruat!"* which he knew meant "police." He doubled back through the maze of lanes and passages until all sound of pursuit had died away. Then he slowed to a walk, checked his pockets, and cautiously emerged into the nearest thoroughfare in search of a cab. Hotel first, then out. . . . Qiu gritted his teeth. He needed a plane, any plane, the first plane. The cost would be exorbitant. And after two weeks' experience of Bangkok, somehow he knew, he just knew, that he was never going to get a refund on his rail ticket to Singapore.

Fifteen minutes after Mat had dropped Mei-hua off at her apartment, he was heading out of the city through a light drizzle, on his way to the north-south freeway.

He forced himself to concentrate on the double line of amber cats' eyes that seemed to draw the car onward into the darkness like a traction cable. An all-night service station loomed up, flashed by, was gone. Only the occasional orange-and-black road sign, glowing for an instant in the car's headlights, punctuated the warm, wet night.

He flicked on the radio, tuned to FM, and found International Community Radio Taiwan, hoping that the music would help him stay awake. It didn't, so he tried one of his Chinese-language tapes instead, but he wasn't in the mood for study tonight.

The memory of Mei-hua's kiss faded very quickly. He would have liked to drink a nightcap with her, take things a stage further, but instinct told him to go slowly where she was concerned. And anyway, he'd promised Lennie.

Something about the way his friend had spoken on the phone

suggested he was under threat. A threat directed against whom—only Lennie? Ducannon Young Electronics? Or perhaps all the companies in Mat's father's diverse group? Mat switched off the cassette player and flattened the accelerator, wishing he'd insisted that Haines come with him after all.

At the one-hundred-kilometer mark, the green and white sign said HSINCHU SCIENCE-BASED INDUSTRIAL PARK. Mat took the exit ramp and turned left. As he emerged from under the bridge he passed a car, parked off the road, all its lights out. Without giving it a thought, he drove half onto the curb and stopped.

When he switched on the interior light and studied his face in the mirror he winced a little. Not good. He didn't fancy facing the Executive Yuan's security police, who guarded the park, looking like that. He reached into the dashboard pocket and took out the battery-powered razor he kept there as part of his mobile wash-and-brush-up kit.

Mat shaved quickly, reluctant as always to focus on his own face. It was broad at the forehead, tapering to a rounded chin: a strong, suntanned face. His cheeks were full; when his wide, oval mouth opened in a smile (it did that often) they folded backwards, giving him a carefree, almost jolly expression. Girls thought him handsome, but he had never been able to understand why. Perhaps it had something to do with his Eurasian features, neither one thing nor another—his father's dark brown eyes, unmistakably Western; his Chinese mother's high cheekbones—such things seemed attractive to others, but they sent Mat conflicting signals that he somehow found disquieting.

He threw the shaver onto the passenger seat and started the engine. As he drove off he glanced in the mirror again and thought he saw another vehicle's sidelights under the overpass bridge.

Moments later he turned right off the Chutung Road and drew up alongside a brown-tiled guardhouse. The policeman on duty gave his pass a perfunctory glance and raised the barrier. Mat swung his Bluebird into Industry Road East II and parked outside the two-story beige brick building that housed Ducannon Young's plant.

As he uncoiled himself from the driver's seat a wet gust seized his leather jacket, flapping it open around his shoulders like a billowing sail. Mat shivered, remembering the first lesson his boss had taught him: the weather of Taiwan is like the mood of a woman. Changeable. Unpredictable.

The ground floor of the plant was silent and dark. In the basement a single light illuminated the steel door that protected the top-secret experimental laboratory, off-limits to even the most senior of the company's Taiwanese staff. Mat laid his palm on the security membrane and the door slid open with a hiss.

"Jesus God."

He stepped over the threshold and stopped short. When he last saw this room, it had been a model of bright efficiency, with one-third of the huge floor space sealed off into a dust-free "clean area" and the remainder furnished with scientific benches, each neatly aligned with the next. Now the place was a shambles. The benches had been thrust aside, loose tools covered every available inch of space, and cannibalized keyboards and CRT units lay upended on the floor.

When he first surveyed the scene, harshly lit by overhead fluorescent tubes, he thought that vandals had kicked Ducannon Young's entire research program into chaos, and his heart thumped painfully as he wondered how he was going to break the news to his father.

"Lennie?"

No response. When Mat edged forward he found his feet entangled in a coil of coaxial cable. "Lennie?"

"Over here."

Mat's eyes shifted to the right. Lennie Luk was hurrying toward him, arms outflung. "Hi! Welcome!" To Mat's astonishment, his friend embraced him in a tight bear hug, something he'd never done before. "I thought you weren't coming."

"Hi yourself." Mat disengaged himself and shook off his jacket. "You look terrible."

"Do I?" Lennie laughed, but the sound conveyed only exhaustion. Mat scrutinized him carefully. The dirty loafers, the faded blue jeans, stained pink in places with what Mat assumed was chemical, the shirt that once had been white but now was sweat-stained . . . they were normal. When Lennie was working he often looked like that. No, it was the face that troubled Mat. Lennie Luk was twenty-five and normally he appeared healthy enough, his round Chinese face creased with laughter lines, the narrow eyes, sharply upturned at the outer corners, exuding vitality. Now, despite all the frenetic excitement he was giving off, he seemed drained. His hair looked greasy and unkempt, his wispy mustache was flecked with traces of dried food. For a second Mat wondered if the pink blotches on Lennie's denims were in fact bloodstains, only to dismiss the notion as fanciful.

"Someone black your eyes?"

Lennie took a few seconds to assimilate his meaning. "No." He giggled. "I haven't slept for a while, that's all."

Mat reached for his discarded jacket and felt in one of the pockets. "Do you want your mail?"

"No, I want to talk." But Lennie grabbed the half-dozen or so pastel-hued envelopes with an embarrassed smile and quickly stuffed them into a drawer.

"Scented paper. Very sexy."

"Yeah. Hey, listen—"

"I am listening. What's so important that you have to haul me down here in the middle of the night?" Mat's voice hardened. "And why couldn't you tell me on the phone?"

"The phone . . . that's funny." Lennie began to giggle again. It sounded like rapid hiccups, little clicks in the back of the throat delivered at breakneck speed.

"Lennie!"

The Chinese fell silent at once. "Sorry."

As Mat moved his feet, something rustled: he looked down to see a pile of empty crisp packets and cardboard tubs. He picked up one of the tubs. "You've been living on . . . chocolate-covered macadamia nuts?" Mat exhaled in disgust. "What's this all about?"

"Jesus, I thought you'd never ask! Food, mail . . . can't you just shut up! It's the future of the *world* we're talking about! Come over here." He ran toward the door. Mat followed. Ranged along the wall was a mass of electronic equipment, standing on a trestle table. Slowly his eyes broke the jumble down into its constituent parts. On the left, in the corner, a DY Starframe III-b personal computer, his father's pride and joy. But this model was different: the keyboard sat in a crude wooden frame that also held a telephone and a keypad. Cables—red, blue, green, and brown—sprouted everywhere. Mat's gaze followed them into the next component, a small disk drive, then on to a larger-than-usual screen, a printer he'd never seen before . . . and after that the whole setup was duplicated in reverse order, ending by the door through which he'd entered.

"You take that work station, there." Lennie's manner was brusque. "There's a booklet in front of you."

Mat picked up the glossy blue brochure. " 'The Future High-Tech Industrial Centre of Asia,' " he read. "Hsinchu's publicity handout. So what?"

"I've got the Chinese version over here. The translation's word for word the same, I've checked."

Mat threw down the booklet. "You dragged me—"

"Shut *up*! Now use your imagination for a moment. I'm in Taipei, right? You're anywhere—London, Hong Kong, it doesn't matter, okay?"

Mat said nothing and sat down.

"I telephone you, so . . ." Lennie picked up his telephone and punched out some numbers on the keypad. A second later, Mat's receiver purred. He stared at it for a moment before reaching out to answer.

Lennie opened his copy of the booklet and began to read aloud, using Cantonese. Mat heard him quite distinctly. Although he did not speak Cantonese very well, he recognized the dialect and was able to distinguish perhaps half the words.

He could not concentrate fully, however, because another voice, a neutral male voice, not Lennie's, was murmuring in his earpiece. His eyes strayed to the booklet in front of him. The electronic voice was reading the text of it, clearly, without pauses.

In English.

Lennie stopped reading and the voice in Mat's earpiece stopped too. Lennie began again; the English voice did likewise. If Lennie read slowly, the translation became leisured. When he speeded up again, the electronic voice exactly matched the pace of his words.

For several moments Mat stayed perfectly still. Then, "My God," he croaked.

The receiver dropped from his hands. He stared at his fingers as they curled and uncurled, possessed of an eerie life of their own.

Lennie Luk replaced his own receiver, very gently, and closed his brochure, arranging it square with the top of the table. At last he spoke, making Mat start.

"Simultaneous automatic translation, speaker-independent, programmable in any known language. All on a silver, laser-written disk, no bigger than a stereo compact disk. No more telephone operators, no need for people to do boring, mundane business tasks anymore, ever. Watch the screen."

Lennie pulled himself up to the keyboard. Seconds later, a thin white line flashed down from top to bottom of Mat's screen, dividing the display into two columns. After a brief pause, the English text of the booklet appeared in the left-hand column, quickly followed by the Chinese text in the right. Mat gasped. "You can put Chinese ideographs on a screen that fast!"

"Yes."

Mat's printer began to spew paper, to the accompaniment of the kind of noise a zipper makes.

"In Hong Kong, they've invented a machine to cope with all this," said Lennie. "At eleven hundred characters a second, it can cut through Chinese ideographs like—"

"Eleven hundred cps!"

"Yes."

"That's impossible!"

"We've done it. We can print out the Bible in less than one and a half hours."

Mat raised his hands to his cheeks and patted them half a dozen times, his mouth a round O reflected in the now-blank screen. "Lennie," he said quietly. "Have you any idea at all what this means for DY?"

"Yup." Lennie sat back. "We've done something that other people have been trying to do for decades. We've invented a machine that can respond, faultlessly, to human speech and then turn it into hard copy. And it can translate one language into another, again, faultlessly. It means your father's achieved his ambition at last. He's going to be the richest man in the world."

"Yes . . . but it means more than that!"

"Um-hm. Let's see . . . IBM, Mitsubishi, they've got about a year from now to copy and improve, or go smash. Finish. Because this is nothing less than the second industrial revolution. Why stop with industry? Agriculture, engineering, publishing—everything's going to change. Change radically. Change out of all recognition."

"That's not what I—"

"Why not? It's the natural logic of the invention. Japan said so, quite openly, in 1981. You remember the MITI conference?"

"MITI . . . ? Oh yes—the Japanese Ministry of International Trade and Industry sponsored some conference in Tokyo, all about this kind of thing."

"That's right. It covered voice-recognition systems. Robots that can duplicate themselves. And this." Lennie stroked the keyboard in front of him. "Even in those days, Nippon Electronic had a voice data input terminal that could recognize a hundred and twenty words. Toshiba was in the lead with speech-typewriters. Incidentally, of course, you realize that this thing here can be a speech-typewriter, so that soon we won't need typists anymore. Or bank clerks. Just use Apogee. That's what we call it, by the way."

Mat stood up, suddenly feeling the need to walk around. Every so often he would stop and swing his arms across his chest. "How does it work?" he said at last.

"Well . . . we've built on other people's research, naturally. But we've devised two things that are new."

[25]

"What are they?"

Lennie went across to another of the benches, where he rummaged about in a drawer. "Here's one of them," he said, holding up what looked to Mat like a small, rectangular black stone. "Catch!"

Mat held it up to his eyes. "A microchip?"

"Yes. My team's been working with Leibnitz, in Hong Kong. They had a breakthrough. They'd been concentrating on polycrystalline silicon. Leibnitz came up with this. It's composed of a thousand wafers, each no thicker than a coat of gold-leaf paint, superimposed one on top of the other. The average chip, at the moment, can carry half a million transistors, at most. The one you're holding carries twenty . . . million."

"This?" Mat held it up to the light. The chip was a little smaller than the top joint of his index finger.

"That's right. It's enabled us to create a miniprocessor that can handle two billion LIPS."

"Huh?"

"LIPS. Operations per second."

"And two billion . . . whatevers. Is that fast?"

"Let me put it this way. The Japanese are struggling to achieve a one-billion-LIPS processor sometime between five and ten years from now."

When Lennie was silent, Mat felt cheated. He made it all sound so simple. "And that's it? That's the secret?"

"No, that's half the secret. The other half's on those disks in the drives on the bench. And in my head. It's a program—or rather a whole series of programs. It's all got to do with artificial neural nets."

"Which your group invented?"

"No. Which we . . . transformed. We had a small breakthrough. Real luck. Excellent backup from your father, and a lot of peace and quiet. It's a good team."

"So if it's such a good team, why are you here all alone in the middle of the night, looking like death? Where are the others?"

"They've gone home. They're not needed now. The last bit was always down to me. Final programming."

"What makes you so special?"

"Because I seem to have the right hunches. And . . ." Lennie shrugged, then jerked his thumb toward the far wall. Mat looked up to see a huge blackboard covered with hieroglyphic calculations. "Because I can do that sort of thing. Call it a knack, if you like. I do calculations in seconds that other people can't seem to do at all."

"You've lost me. DY has any number of mainframe computer systems, yet you end up doing chalk workings on a blackboard?"

"Do you know anything about computerized chess?"

"Don't change the subject."

"I'm not. For many years now, it's theoretically been possible to program a computer to play chess perfectly. But there's one problem. Even the fastest computer would take ten-to-the-four-teenth-power million years to explore all the possible permutations before making its first move. A grand master, on the other hand, can play chess brilliantly, against the clock, with the help of only his brain, which runs on the equivalent of half a volt of electricity. See the point? I cut corners; the mainframe can't."

Mat gazed blankly at the screen. "It means we're number one in the world," he said at last, and was struck at once by the inanity of the sentiment.

"For the moment."

When Mat did not speak for a while, Lennie looked up to find himself being stared at oddly. "What's the matter?"

"I was wondering if your life's insured. And for how much?"

Lennie fidgeted uncomfortably.

"And the implications . . . you realize the military implications of this?"

"You tell me."

"Well . . . it would revolutionize war in the air, for a start. You'd cut the speed of a pilot's responses in half. You might not even *need* a pilot. Christ, think of that!"

"Don't worry—someone already has."

"And that's just the beginning. A voice-controlled weapons-guidance system might—"

Lennie was laughing. "You're a child," he said. "Do you seriously think we haven't been through it all? This *started* as a military project! What I've been doing is work on a tiny but crucial part of it. Everything else is geared up and ready for Apogee: the planes, the men. . . . They've been waiting for me to come through with my contribution for months. What you're looking at originated as a byproduct of the war machine, just like all the other great inventions throughout history."

"But I hadn't heard anything about—" Mat broke off and looked up. "Did you hear that?"

"No."

Mat shook his head, continuing to stare at the ceiling. "I thought I heard . . . footsteps."

Both men listened. Only the quiet, regular hum of the computers disturbed the silence. After a while, Mat shrugged irritably and said, "What about security?"

"Nailed down tight. Even the DY security officer doesn't know about this."

"Haines doesn't know?"

"No. No one has access to this room except me. And now you. That's why you're here: security."

Mat resumed his seat. "You'd better explain."

"Your father gave me instructions. The minute I had the product, I was to phone you, no matter what hour of the day or night it was, and bring you here. You're the son of the managing director of the whole Ducannon Young group. You're family, in other words. The only other person here he can trust."

"He hasn't trusted me much up to now. The first time I knew what you were up to, why you spent all that time away from the flat, was tonight."

"Good. That means the secret's safe. Listen, I'm to give you everything—the disks, the software, the programs, my working papers. From now on, all this"—he waved a hand around—"is your responsibility. You're to store it until he can fly a plane in to retrieve it."

"What about your copies? Are they staying here?"

Lennie averted his eyes. "Yes, of course."

"Lennie."

"What?" The Chinese looked up to find Mat's eyes upon him and he flushed.

"I've known you a long time, Lennie. As a liar, you're hopeless."

Lennie hesitated. At last he said, "Don't ask, Mat. Copies, well . . . they're a sensitive subject right now. Whatever copies exist are safe. I give you my word."

Mat thrust his hands into his pockets and sat back. He could see the sense of what Lennie was saying—or rather, not saying. Copies that no one knew about, secrets that no one could ever give away.

"You don't trust my father?"

Lennie said nothing. When the silence had gone on for a whole minute, Mat repeated the words, only this time they came out as a statement of fact. "You don't trust my father. Why?"

Lennie shook his head.

"Why, Lennie?" Wonder and irritation bickered in Mat's voice. "You've known him as long as you've known me. Your parents worked for mine, in their house, worked there before either of us was born. Simon Young saw you through university, gave you this job. He pays you well—better than me, I'm sure!"

"Oh yes." Lennie's voice was bitter. "It's all thanks to 'Mr. China'! Did you know that's what they call him? Mr. China, commercial midwife to the People's Republic, friend to the poor peasants of the Middle Kingdom—"

"That's *enough*!" The harshness in Mat's voice surprised even him. "He's been good to you. You've got no complaints."

"No?"

Mat stared at the Chinese sitting hunched on his stool, one leg kicking violently against the bench. "For God's sake, what's the matter?"

"Forget it."

"How can I? I'm Simon Young's son."

"Do you *like* being his son?"

"What's that supposed to mean?"

"I mean there was a time when your father joined in a scheme by the Red Chinese to ruin the Soviet Communal Bank. Or perhaps you've forgotten that?"

"No need to be sarcastic."

"Don't you remember those days? How they drugged you, kidnapped you, took you to a village in Sichuan, and made you shovel shit?"

"I'm hardly likely to forget."

"Maybe not. But you survived."

Mat, about to reply, suddenly saw where they were headed and remained silent.

"Yes, you survived," Lennie went on. "Your mother and father, they survived too. Mine died."

Mat took a deep breath, making himself stay cool. "They were shot," he said noncommittally. "On the orders of a man called Qiu Qianwei. My father wasn't holding the gun."

"I know that. But he loaded it."

"I don't get you."

"He used my father to witness one of the documents that ruined the bank."

Mat's mouth opened a fraction. He licked his lips, once, twice. "Say that again."

"He persuaded my father to sign his name on one of the papers, as a witness. He knew he could trust my parents. He knew

[29]

that, whatever happened, they'd never hand over the papers or tell the Red Chinese where they were kept. And that's why they were killed: because they refused to tell.''

Again, Mat forced himself to remain silent, stay cool. At last he said, "That's a neat piece of reconstruction. Do you have any evidence?'

"Yes.''

"May I see it, please?''

"It's not the kind of thing you can see. You have to hear it.''

"I don't understand.''

"Your father told me the story himself.''

When the silence at last became unbearable, Lennie said quietly, "You didn't know that?'' Seeing that shock had robbed Mat of his powers of speech, he went on, "Your father told me that he was ashamed. He could never bring them back, but he could try to make amends. So that's why I'm here, earning his conscience money, with a free hand, and no controls, and answering only to him.'' His voice was rising now. "And now your father can do what he's always planned to do, right from the beginning: hand Apogee over to the Red Chinese.''

"Like shit!'' Mat leaped from his stool and began to rage up and down the room, kicking bits of equipment out of his path. "My father would never do a thing like that! Never! He cooperates with Red China, he . . . he helps them, yes, but if you think, if you seriously for one moment think—''

"I do not have to think, I *know*! The Red Chinese paid for this, you see. Two hundred million yuan, and more. It's for their air force.''

Mat stopped in front of the trestle table and rested his arms on its surface, looking down at the keyboard with a vacant expression on his face. Suddenly he felt tired. "Why does it have to be Red China?'' he muttered thickly. "Always Red China this, Red China that, as long as I can remember. When the real China, the beautiful China, *free* China is right here, in Taiwan, when—''

He broke off. For a moment he merely stared at the screen, trying to make sense of what he saw. "Lennie . . . what's happening?''

The Chinese looked at his own screen and sighed. "Oh God.''

"It's gobbledygook. I mean, it's all got scrambled up somehow.''

"Yes. I've still got to debug it. And then I've got to improve it. All I've done at the moment is produce a prototype that more or less works. Apogee's nowhere near ready for demonstration and marketing yet."

"How long will it take you?" Mat's voice held a tremor of excitement.

"Three months."

"As little as that?"

"Yes. The hardware's been in production for a long time now. All I have to do is complete the program and have it copied. Hey, listen, please don't tell your father what I said. I had no right to . . ."

But Mat was no longer paying attention. "Three months . . . that means August at the earliest. I'm due back in Hong Kong in a few weeks. Maybe I can get him to change—"

The fluorescent lights dimmed to pale orange and instantly flashed back to full power. The two men looked at each other in silence. Then Lennie threw himself on the nearest disk drive.

"Get them out!" he screamed. "Out, out, *out*!"

But it was too late. While their fingers scrabbled to unlatch the gates, the lights died. The machines stopped humming. There was a moment of utter silence. Then Mat heard Lennie Luk say, "Oh . . . my . . . God."

"Lennie." No reply. "Are you there, Lennie?"

More silence. Then, "Sorry." The Chinese spoke in a very small voice, but he was under control.

"I can't see you."

"I'll find a match. Wait."

After a long pause, Mat saw a flame flicker on the other side of the laboratory. Lennie lit a Bunsen burner and carried it across the room, unwinding the rubber gas hose behind him.

"What about the emergency backup power?"

"That's failed too."

"But how can that happen?" They looked at each other, suddenly chilled. "Hsinchu's got its own power station, right here. Three hundred and eighty volts . . ."

"Yes."

"Then what—?"

"I don't *know*!"

Mat swallowed. "What's the damage?"

"The disks will have been erased. That's inevitable. It's one of the faults I have to iron out. This system can't tolerate any kind of power failure."

"But you said you have copies. You have backup disks. You *must* have!"

When Lennie did not reply at once, Mat repeated dully, "You must."

"Normally, yes, but I . . . I've been so tired. I said it was a sensitive subject. For the last few weeks I've been working without making any backups."

"*What!* But that's . . ." Mat struggled to find the right word. "Criminal!"

"You don't understand how these things get done. You make great inspirational leaps. It's like a graph that struggles along in a horizontal line and then suddenly shoots straight up to infinity. You don't stop to make copies. You don't stop to shit or sleep. Besides, these aren't ordinary disks. Copying them takes ages."

The burner cast a pool of yellow light in the immediate vicinity of the two men, giving their faces a sickly tinge. "How long?" Mat said urgently. "How long before you get it all back together again?"

"At least double what I said before. Six months, probably more."

The silence that followed was shattered by the sound of heavy footsteps on the floor above. The two men looked up, startled. Before they could react, the door to the laboratory shuddered under the impact of a heavy weight; the crash reverberated through the room and they instinctively moved closer together.

"Who's there?" Mat shouted. But the only answer was another bang as something landed against the door. "Who's there?" he repeated.

This time there was a response. Someone's voice, high and shrill, carried above the sound of a third crash. "Open up!"

"Who's there? What right do you have to—?"

"By order of the Executive Yuan!" The voice rose in pitch. "Taiwan Garrison Command! *Open!*"

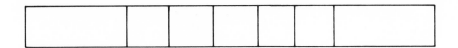

TWO

Sun Shanwang stretched, yawned, and raised his eyes to the view before him. "I had not realized the Sea of Azov was so beautiful," he remarked politely.

"In the summer it is beautiful," Oleg Kazin acknowledged.

Major General Krubykov arrived at the foot of the summer house steps in time to hear his master's words. He looked up at the veranda, shading his eyes against the sun's glare, and tried to learn something from Kazin's face.

Until lately the old man's lineaments had scarcely altered at all: bald head; rounded countenance, pink with rude good health; thin body; vigorous disposition. Only in the past few months had changes begun to manifest themselves. Now the face was not so much pink as blotchy, and the body beneath had become skeletal. Today, as Krubykov gazed on the elderly Chairman of the KGB, he felt that he was, slowly and without apparent regret, preparing to surrender his hold on life to the only power greater than his own.

Sun smiled at Krubykov. The officer's lips curled also, but there was no sincerity in his eyes. He knew that Kazin had taken a liking to this visitor and he could not understand why. Sun resembled the head of some large Japanese company, with his coarse, rectangular glasses, pinched features, and rheumy eyes; his mouth was the wrong shape for a Chinese. Krubykov had no respect for orientals, not even the head of China's secret service.

Both men had been speaking stilted English, that being the only language they had in common. Now, however, Kazin addressed Krubykov in Russian. "Join us. We had our private talk before lunch." Then, reverting to English, he addressed Sun with the glimmer of a smile: "Tell me, what are your feelings on this historic occasion? I'd like Krubykov to hear your reflections."

"I am surprised," Sun said, "to discover how little I do feel."

"Not even hope?" Krubykov put in.

"To be carefully honest with you—no. Your country and mine, General, are preparing to sign a pact that will end the differences between them and, it is said, lead to increased cooperation between the two nations. I say, one step at a time."

"Do you doubt the reality of the pact?" Kazin asked.

"No. Both politburos are discussing the small print of a document that is almost ready for signature. What I doubt is the will to make it work."

"You surprise me. The two nations' goals are identical! They always have been—the triumph of communism throughout the world."

Sun sighed. "The triumph, as you call it, of communism in the smallest of our provinces would more than satisfy me. The world, well . . ."

"All right, then, never mind the world. What about our own backyards, our frontiers?"

"Yes." Sun Shanwang's face brightened a fraction. "These past years of conflict have been fruitless. Peace between us along the frontier would be an achievement, even if nothing else followed."

Kazin resisted the desire to invite his guest not to address him like a public meeting, and said, "Much else will follow. Once we are formally at peace, Europe will be isolated. America will become 'Fortress America' again, abandoning her allies. We shall share scientific knowledge, economic resources—"

Sun held up his hands, palm outward. He was laughing. "No, no. You do not believe all that."

"I don't?"

"No."

"I wouldn't presume to quarrel with a guest." Kazin reached down to a briefcase by his side, pulled out a folder, and drew his chair up to the table with unexpected briskness. "Now. We had almost reached the end of our agenda, I think. One last item. Taiwan."

"That's our problem, not yours."

"I still think we should discuss it. We have heard rumors that Taiwan has recently assumed a greater importance in the eyes of your Politburo."

"Taiwan is never less than wholly important to Beijing."

"I shall interpret that as confirmation."

"I would not want to take issue with my host over the interpretation of dreams."

"Can we help?"

"Only by supporting us at the UN in any event. *Any* event."

"I see." Kazin's good humor evaporated. He leaned forward to rest his arms on the table. "It's as serious as that."

"I am not at liberty to discuss it."

"Then we will let the matter drop. But I can say it's a theater that interests us. You already realized that, of course." Kazin shook his head. "It's strange to be talking to you in this way. You know so much, and I know so much—we are like spouses, but spouses who tiptoe around the house leaving each other notes, not speaking, at odds with each other in public and in private also. Yet—we know."

Sun nodded appreciatively. "A good analogy. As regards Taiwan: I was aware of your interest, yes. For a long time the Soviet Union enjoyed a sound base in Southeast Asia. Moscow Narodny, Soviet Communal . . . you had a liking for banks."

"Yes. Had and have."

"And with the end of Soviet Communal's operation, you felt the gap yawn wide."

"Indeed."

"So where better to reestablish yourselves than in the newly emerging miracle economy of Taiwan, with its ten percent annual growth rate but, alas, all-too-basic financial infrastructure?"

"Quite correct."

Sun nodded gently. "We would prefer you to wait for us to issue a proper invitation."

Kazin was silent for a moment. At last he said, "Then I will recommend that we exclude the other place from our orbit, unless and until you choose to solicit our help."

[35]

"We shall not require help. Thank you."

"Perhaps you have it already, from another quarter? It has come to our notice that there is an independence movement in Taiwan."

"We have heard similar rumors about Afghanistan. Equally baseless lies, I have no doubt."

Krubykov turned his head a fraction so that Kazin would not see him smile.

"The independence movement you mention," Sun went on with sudden heat, "has no leaders. No arms. No money. And, most important—no support." He paused. "I should be sorry to think that the situation might change."

"Why should it?" Kazin shrugged. "It doesn't in Afghanistan." He pulled the folder toward him and made a pencil note in the margin of the last page. "Anyway, I must be honest with you. I've not been able to find out anything about this supposed independence movement. Now I know why: it doesn't exist."

"That is so."

Kazin flipped the folder shut and looked at his watch. "This day's gone too quickly."

"Yes." Sun rose. "Thank you for your hospitality."

"Goodbye!" Kazin shot out his right hand and Sun Shanwang took it. For a long moment they held, looking into each other's eyes, seeing there the start of a personal affinity that had nothing to do with professional regard; and so they parted.

Kazin watched until his guest had passed into the main house, out of the glare, with Krubykov at his heels. Then he shaded his eyes against the afternoon sun and breathed deeply, savoring the scent of roses and resin. For someone in his poor state of health, these surroundings were very congenial.

The summer house lay half-concealed in a birch copse. Immediately ahead of him, a tidy lawn descended gently to a privet hedge that scarcely impeded the view of the topaz sea. To the right, an expanse of grass was fringed with three terraced beds of rose standards, whereas on his left the garden had been allowed to grow wild to conceal the suburbs of nearby Primorsk. There, shrubs and mature trees combined to provide the shade that was so popular with people obliged to spend the month of May on the Crimea.

Krubykov soon returned. As he lowered himself into the vacant chair, Kazin asked, "What did you make of him?"

"Much as expected. Except for the Taiwan business. There I found the overall message obscure."

"It was clear enough, I'd have thought. 'There is no such thing as the Taiwanese independence movement.' We must have been misinformed. The man who's coming to drink tea with us this afternoon is a ghost. We must show him the door." Kazin laughed as though he were never going to stop. "Show a spirit the door . . . !" His mouth closed with a snap and he redirected his gaze to Krubykov's face. "Either Sun thinks I'm a stupid old man, or he, like his masters, is scared. Since I don't believe he regards me as stupid, he has to be afraid of these people. Whatever he may say, the brotherhood calling itself 'Our Formosa Now' does exist."

"At least we can be sure of that."

"Wu Tie-zi and his backers have aims that are quite specific: they want arms and money and support for a plan to overthrow the Kuomintang."

"As far as I'm concerned, they can forget it!"

"Why?"

"Because America would never stand for Soviet intervention in Taiwan. Nor would mainland China."

"You overstate the case. I'm not adverse to assisting OFN in its desire to overthrow the Kuomintang government of Taiwan and replace it with an administration composed of indigenous Formosans, as long as two conditions are satisfied."

"They are?"

"First, total secrecy. I take your point about the need to be circumspect."

"And the second condition?"

"That we can be sure of getting what we want in return."

"Which is what?"

"Sun knew! We want a financial and intelligence-gathering base in Southeast Asia, something to replace Soviet Communal Bank. And of course this huge commercial secret they keep hinting at; the wonderful computer that's going to transform our air force. To say nothing of our industry, our economy, our agriculture . . ."

"Apogee? I'll believe that when I see it. And even then, I'll still have trouble slotting these people into the Soviet frame. They're more rightist than the present government of Taiwan! So if they do manage to seize power, it's inconceivable that they'd deal with the Soviet Union."

"You can put that point to Wu Tie-zi, when he arrives. But don't overlook the existing arrangements, will you? The Taiwanese government has got remarkably little against the Soviet Union.

Did you know that President Chiang Ching-kuo's wife was Russian?"

"I did. But then it becomes even harder to understand why OFN should approach us."

"I'd have thought the answer was obvious: there simply isn't anyone else."

"The Americans, surely?"

"The last thing Washington can be seen to do is interfere with the affairs of Taiwan, now that the U.S. has formally recognized Beijing. They'd run a mile from Wu and his gang."

"So what are you planning?"

"I'm not sure yet. There are a lot of possibilities there, Krubykov. And Sun Shanwang knows it."

"I was just going to mention Sun. Wu Tie-zi and Our Formosa Now came on the scene *before* the Moscow-Beijing pact. Obviously, the pact changes everything. I'd assumed you were going to send this man Wu away empty-handed."

Kazin puckered up his lips and began to whistle tunelessly. After a while Krubykov tired of waiting for an answer to what he regarded as a crucially important question and he prompted, more urgently this time, "Comrade Chairman."

But Kazin merely stopped whistling for long enough to look at his watch and say: "He'll be here soon. Make yourself useful for once, Krubykov. Go up to the house and see if they managed to get that Oolung tea I ordered from Taipei."

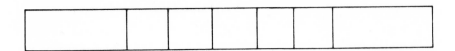

THREE

As Mat paid his cab fare outside the Ducannon Young Building's main entrance in Chung Ching South Road, it began to rain. He ran across the broad, red-tiled pavement, holding his copy of the *China Post* over his head, and paused outside the main doors long enough to give his jacket a shake.

Just outside the plate-glass doors stood a mobile stall, selling noodles and buns. It had been there since the building was first leased to tenants. At first the stall had kept its distance, but day by day it had crept a little closer to the glass doors, until after a fortnight it had attained its present location, snug and dry beneath the impressive Ducannon Young logo of dragon, bull, and phoenix.

As the son of Ducannon Young's managing director and principal shareholder, Mat Young might have been expected to disapprove of this worthless barnacle attached to the group's mighty flagship. Instead, he paused long enough to bid the owner a friendly good morning and buy a couple of sweet buns stuffed with pork before taking the elevator to the fifteenth floor. He had just finished his breakfast when the doors slid open to reveal a beige, low-ceilinged room containing several comfortable chairs and an elegant Ju Ming flying horse of burnished bronze standing on the counter that separated the receptionist from Ducannon Young's visitors. Mat nodded to the girl. "Is the Regional Director in yet?"

"No sir. Mrs. Chia rang to say he'd be a little late today."

"Thanks. I'll be in his office if anyone wants me."

"Oh, Mr. Young . . ."

"Yes."

"This envelope came for you earlier, by special messenger."

Mat ripped it open. The receptionist, hearing him gasp, looked up to see a smile appear on his face, a smile that deepened as he read the message through to the end.

Moments later he was shutting the door of the Regional Director's office behind him. He tossed his briefcase onto the nearest chair and sat down behind Chia's desk, already reaching for one of the three phones. Mat was in a hurry. This wasn't the first time he'd used the company's secure line for the purpose of contacting his father, but he was always supposed to have a good excuse, and today he did not want to be forced to produce one.

It took less than thirty seconds for Hong Kong to come on the line. "Hello? Mary? My father, please."

Mary Street was Simon Young's principal secretary and personal assistant. "I'm sorry, Mr. Young, but he's just gone into a board meeting."

"Well, please phone in, or put a piece of paper in front of him, anything you like, only get him on the line."

"Mr. Young, I really don't—"

"Tell him, 'Spring Rains.' "

"I'm sorry?"

"Just that—say 'Spring Rains.' He'll know what it means."

There was a long pause at the other end. At last Mat heard someone pick up the phone. "What's the panic, son?"

"I'm going on the scrambler, Da, okay?"

"Hang on, I'll have to get the call transferred." Another pause. At last Simon said, "All right. Ready this end. What is this?"

"Last night, two things happened. Lennie Luk brought in Apogee. It works; I saw it. And Taiwan Garrison Command busted us at Hsinchu."

A long silence followed. Mat could imagine the shock on his father's face, could all but hear the angry questions fighting their

[40]

way to his lips. But when Simon spoke, it was with his accustomed calm.

"Which happened first?"

"Lennie. He got me down there at one in the morning—your orders, he said."

Mat waited in vain for confirmation. Simon merely said, "Go on."

"I think I may have been followed to Hsinchu, by the way. Apogee works, all right. Jesus Christ, Da, you've got a world-beater there."

"Never mind that. What happened?"

"Power failure. That's the first thing. Lennie says all his disks have been wiped and he's got no recent backups."

Mat winced, awaiting the inevitable explosion from Hong Kong, but Simon said nothing. After a while Mat continued, "That's when TGC burst in."

"How can you be so sure it was TGC? In Taiwan, lots of people confuse the police with the army."

"Look, these guys were in camouflage fatigues, right? With submachine guns. Police, shit!"

"All right, calm down. How many were there?"

"About half a dozen."

"Did they break the place up?"

"No. Once we'd let them in, they cooled off." Mat paused while he marshaled his thoughts. "First thing was, they put the power back on."

"So it was the army who cut it? A deliberate attempt on their part to sabotage our research?"

"Garrison Command cut the power, yes, but I don't think they knew what effect it would have. They're not sophisticated enough to think of that."

"Oh, come on! They'd give anything to destroy Apogee."

"Why?"

"Oh . . . forget it. What happened next?"

"They said they were investigating breaches of customs regulations."

"Nonsense! Garrison Command wouldn't trouble themselves with something like that. Anyway, Hsinchu's got the loosest customs in the whole of Asia. We don't even have to pay import or export duties."

"But we do have to make returns of everything we import and export, and the Inspectorate General of Customs made waves about that once before. Anyway, next they snooped around, opening cupboards, leafing through files, that kind of thing. It was sort of aimless."

"Did they remove anything?"

"No. But they took a lot of photographs. In the end they cleared off. The captain said he'd be making a report and there could be a prosecution. That's all."

Simon said nothing for several moments. Then Mat heard him sigh. "Who else knows about this?"

"No one."

"You haven't spoken to Henry Chia?"

"No."

"Good. Don't. If you mention TGC to a Taiwanese, he's bound to panic. Tell Lennie to keep the whole thing quiet. I'll have to go very high about this, and nobody's to muddy the water until I'm through."

"All right."

"There's one other thing you can do. Get Rod Haines down to Hsinchu today and have him do an electronic sweep. I want to be absolutely sure your visitors didn't leave anything behind."

"A bug, you mean?"

"Bugs, planted evidence, anything. Impress him with the need to be thorough."

"Suppose Chia asks me why."

"I'm due to ring him later this morning and I'll deal with it then. Oh, and I must know today how long Lennie needs to reconstruct the software."

"I've asked him that already. It could be six months, maybe more."

"Well, bugger that!"

"He's upset at the moment—"

"He'll be more than upset if I have to come to Taipei and shake his brains out of his skull. Tell him he can have three months, maximum, along with whatever money and other help he needs. I've got a deadline to meet."

"Can't you extend it?"

Simon's laugh contained no humor. "The People's Republic doesn't like extensions. It likes performance."

After a few seconds of silence, Mat woke up to the fact that Lennie's story was true. "You're telling me that Red China has a stake in this?"

"Damn right. A huge stake. Now you see why I thought Garrison Command were out to sabotage the project." Simon's voice changed note. "Keep this to yourself, Mat, okay? The Reds financed our research from the beginning. They have a military application for it, though I don't know what. And suddenly it's become top priority. DY stands to make the kind of fortune that comes up once in a century, but if it doesn't meet the deadline . . . the group could be ruined. Are you *sure* that turning off the power wasn't a deliberate attempt to destroy Apogee?"

When Mat did not reply immediately, Simon said, "Hello, are you there?"

"I'm here."

"What's the matter?"

"I don't understand. You start up here in Taiwan, grab all the breaks going, five-year tax exemption, rent holiday, low-interest loans . . . and then you hand it all over to the enemy!"

"Don't be melodramatic. Beijing isn't anyone's enemy, certainly not Taiwan's. They're simply looking for reunification, and who can blame them?"

"You like communism?"

"Don't be idiotic! For one thing, the Reds haven't the first clue about business incentives and they've got no good science graduates; the Taiwanese have both, which is why our laboratories are at Hsinchu instead of Shanghai. Christ, Mat—you sit there in Taipei, surrounded by nightclubs and girly bars, good food and cheap beer, and you have the nerve to sneer at *my* ethics!" Simon's voice had turned savage. "Just get moving, will you? Brief Haines, kick Luk's arse, and then keep your mouth shut. Oh, and while I'm on the subject of Luk—tell him to keep copies next time! Now is there anything else?"

"Um . . . any news of Diana?"

"Yes. She phoned last night. She's too ill to study, so she's coming to Hong Kong to recuperate."

"Have the doctors said—?"

"That's all I know. Look, I'm very busy—"

"She's my sister, dammit!"

"She's my daughter, Mat." Simon's voice was unexpectedly mild.

"Okay," Mat mumbled. "Will you give Ma my love?"

"Of course. Jinny's so looking forward to your leave, son."

"So am I. I've bought her this bracelet. . . . Dad?"

"What?"

"I just heard this morning. I got the Far Eastern Textile contract."

As Mat waited for a reaction his mouth turned dry, something caught in his throat. He heard his father laugh, very softly, and murmur, "Did you, by God? Then I take back what I said about the girly bars."

There was no other response; the line went dead. For a few seconds Mat merely gazed at the wall in front of him, feeling inadequate. Chia's entrance came as a relief.

"Morning, Henry."

"Hello."

Chia was a lean, middle-aged Taiwanese who wore thick spectacles and kept his hair shaved to within a few millimeters of his scalp. As he watched the younger man gather up his raincoat and briefcase it occurred to him that he ought to resent the way Simon Young's son was turning a whole country into his personal fiefdom, even down to appropriating the Regional Director's office for his private business concerns; but he found it difficult to resent anyone as pleasant as Mat.

"Sorry to be taking up your space. Think you should see this, though." Mat, aware that his presence in Chia's office required justification, hurriedly handed his boss the envelope he'd picked up in reception earlier. Chia read the contents and looked up, his face expressionless. "We have been after this deal for years," he said. "How did it happen?"

Mat colored. "I worked on Roger Sung. Took him up to New Peak Falls weekends, that kind of thing."

"I see. I hope you're not out of pocket."

Mat shrugged. "It's an investment in the future." After an unfortunate dispute over expenses at the start of his career, he hardly ever claimed anything.

"Sung is the deputy finance director of Far Eastern Textiles." Chia was frowning. "He's not part of the family that owns it."

"No. But these days he's the one who counts."

"I hadn't realized that."

Once again, Mat could think of nothing to say. So he smiled politely, excused himself, and walked along the corridor to his own, much smaller office. First he skimmed through the mail. Nothing important, unless you counted the envelope bulging with banknotes—his salary. Like just about everyone else in Taiwan, high or low, Mat was paid in cash. He stuffed the money into a drawer and picked up his phone.

He let it ring a dozen times before admitting to himself that Mei-hua wasn't going to answer. Where could she be at this time? Maybe she'd gone out early. Maybe she'd not gone home the night before. . . . Mat brutally evicted the thought from his mind and dialed an in-house number. "Hi, Rod."

"How's yourself, sport?" Rod Haines chortled. He had studied in England and America, so that now you could scarcely guess his background, but every so often he would drop in a few words of heavily accented Australian, like a man registering his call sign.

"I need to talk."

"Okay. Want a coffee?"

A few moments later the door slowly swung open to admit a man walking backwards, two steaming cups in his hands. He eased himself down into a chair on the other side of the desk and pushed one cup over to Mat.

Haines was an outdoors type; he had the statuesque shoulders of a surfer. But his face, although refreshingly open, wasn't quite handsome. His nose seemed too squat, his lips too thin; and the meager, sandy eyebrows, scarcely visible beneath his forehead, made him look both older and somehow otherworldly.

Haines said "Hi!" twice before Mat acknowledged his presence. "Oh . . . sorry, Rod. Mind on other things."

"Trouble?"

"Sort of. Memories."

"Yeah?"

"When I was at school . . ."

Rod stirred his coffee and treated Mat to an encouraging smile.

"When I was at school, they picked me for the First Eleven, God knows why. Just once. I was lucky; took two wickets in six balls."

"Ye-*ow*! Call that a bum memory?"

"My father was there. Big event."

"I bet he was pleased."

Mat found himself staring directly into Haines's eyes. "I don't know," he said, very quietly. "That's just it. I don't know."

Haines studied him for a moment and decided it would be best to change the subject. "You don't look too good. Heavy night, after you left?"

"You could say that."

Haines loosened the button of his double-breasted blazer and sat back with a stretch. "She's a great girl, that Mei-hua. What a body!"

Yes, Mat thought irritably, what a body. And where was it now?

"Maybe you don't need the Haines Super-Duper R-and-R Program any more?"

Mat grinned. "Of course I need it. Who else in this town has

[45]

all the hot spots on Database III? But that's not what I wanted to talk about."

Haines put down his cup. "Shoot."

"I was talking to Dad this morning." Mat told his friend about the previous night's events. When he'd finished, Haines sat in silence for a moment.

"Aw, hell," he said at last. "I don't want to sound like a grouch, but you know, having a security officer who's only part-time isn't the most . . ."

"We're a low-budget operation. This is the first time we've had problems."

"I'm an accountant, Mat."

"Who has an impressive track record with systems security devices."

"Oh, sure, I know my way around computer software. But systems security is one thing. Physical security, locks and bars, that's quite different."

"Sorry. But no one else is available to do it. Look, Rod, straight-talking time. I don't normally tell tales, but my father once told me you came to us with some of the best references he'd ever seen."

Haines held up a hand, but Mat brushed aside the protest. "You were recommended to Dunny's by one of my father's personal friends, and since then you've proved yourself to the hilt. Dad trusts you. *I* trust you. And right now, that's what we need most—someone we can trust."

"Hadn't I better check with Henry before I go?"

"I got the impression that Dad doesn't want that."

"From the horse's mouth, eh?" Haines said, with the glimmer of a smile. "Or rather, the foal's?"

"You needn't say it: I'm only the contracts manager and you don't take your orders from me."

"Well . . . not quite yet."

Mat eyed him sharply. "Yet?"

Haines grinned back at him, quite unfazed. "Everyone knows Taiwan's yours, sport. Mat the shrewd grafter: Mat, who's got ten contacts for every one of Chia's. This'll be your country."

"I doubt it. But anyway, today I'm just a mouthpiece."

"Doesn't your father trust Henry?"

"Government agencies are involved, and Henry's Taiwanese. Father doesn't want him embarrassed."

"Then I'll be on my way." But at the door Haines turned and

said, "Just remember—*you* took those two wickets. Your father very definitely didn't. S'long."

Haines rode the lift to the ground floor. But instead of going on down to the garage, he got out and made for the street. He walked as far as the intersection of Chung Ching South Road and Han Kou Street before checking that no one was tailing him, then continued the next couple of blocks until he reached the Hilton. As the escalator bore him up to the coffee shop, he fiddled in his pocket for a one-dollar coin. The bank of pay phones, discreetly situated in the shadow of the maroon wall beside the Traders Grill, was deserted. Haines dialed. When a shrill male voice barked *"Wei?"* he said: "Nimbus. Connect me with Monsoon."

There was a pause. Then: "Yes?" The man at the other end, a different man, spoke in scarcely more than a whisper.

"Hsinchu, bull's-eye," Haines said, before replacing the receiver and walking away.

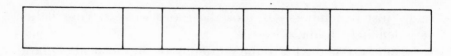

FOUR

A filament of yellow, no thicker than a knife-edge, slit the sea from the night. Dawn over the Pacific.

Wu Tie-zi met his guest as he stepped out of his car and together they went up a flight of steps, through red-paneled doors, into the courtyard of an old-style Chinese mansion. Wu Tie-zi led the way around the perimeter. As they reached the center of the second side of the square he turned right, stepping through a moon gate giving onto a terrace, and halted. Li Lu-tang had passed several steps beyond him before he saw two people standing by the balustrade. One was Chinese, the other was not; and the sight of this second person caused Li to stop in midstride.

He stood with legs wide apart, sideways to Li, who thus was shown his left profile: a brown, round face, placid in repose, orien-tal yet not Chinese—an aboriginal face. He wore a magnificent garment, a black tunic picked out with silver and gold, and a kind of kilt, or sarong, over black leggings . . . but Li scarcely had time to take in details. What brought him up short was the bow.

The man's left arm was stiff and straight by his side. It held a longbow, an arrow already fitted to the taut string. The archer's eyes were fixed on the person standing in front of him: an old man, resting on a cane, who now nodded once. With slow, measured movements the aborigine gracefully rose up on the balls of his feet and began to draw back the arrow, while at the same time swiveling his torso toward the visitor.

Li did not need a precision instrument to tell him that the barbed tip of the arrow would reach the riser of the bow in precisely the same instant as the archer completed his turn, so that then he would be looking straight along the shaft. At Li's heart.

The arrow's tip was about halfway through its journey to horizontal. Li, sensing a presence behind him, wheeled around. Wu Tie-zi had come to stand at his shoulder. He must have seen the apprehension on his guest's face, but he made no move. Li turned back to where he knew the aborigine was standing. The arrow completed the last few millimeters of its arc and became still.

Li neither moved nor spoke. He waited in silence for what seemed a long time.

"Not a very warm welcome," an aged voice piped at last, "for the man who has come to save China. You honor this house, Li Lu-tang. Ah-Huan, put down the bow; you can practice later."

The aborigine slowly relaxed the bowstring's tension and, at a sign from the elderly Chinese, withdrew. "My father," Wu Tie-zi whispered. "Wu Kuo-kan."

"If we're talking of honor," Li said quietly, "then the honor is mine. My mother taught me to equate your name with freedom, sir."

The old man laughed, dispelling Li's pretensions. His build was slight, he walked with the aid of a stick; and Li noticed that most of Wu Kuo-kan's teeth were missing, so that his cheeks were sunken, but there were few other signs of decay. His gaze was particularly bright; he wore very small spectacles with hexagonal-shaped lenses that magnified his eyes into large, well-defined circles. There was nothing watery or indistinct about those eyes.

"Then you must have had what I would call an *obscure* upbringing, Mr. Li," he said. "Again, I apologize for the nature of your welcome. Ah-Huan here is my majordomo, among other things. Have you had a chance to inspect this miserable dwelling of mine? Come over here, at least the view's not bad."

Li followed him to the balustrade. They were standing on a marble patio overlooking Taiwan's east coast, near the fishing village of Anshuo. The house was about a hundred feet above sea level, and although it had been built more than a mile inland, nothing impeded the view from its terrace down to the black sand beach below. The landscape was typical of this region: rice-paddies checkered the flat terrain near the sea, while on the lower slopes of the hills that rolled gently between coast and mountains, scrub eventually gave way to clumps of bamboo, eucalyptus, and camphor. The site was secluded: to the south and west the sheer hillside rose directly out of the stony, ash-colored bed of the Anshuo River, while on the northern and western boundaries, beyond the ornamental garden with its traditional pagoda, the land climbed sharply to a densely forested mountain range.

"Beautiful," Li breathed. "Spectacular."

"Ah! I'm only sorry that today you have to put up with our provincial poverty."

Morning had broken over southern Taiwan, its cloudless sky promising a hot June day. The old man beckoned Li. "We'll go inside, before the humidity builds up. Please forgive my slowness." He guided his visitor back through the moon gate and across the courtyard. Li's host led him through a door. At first Li could see nothing, so sharp was the contrast between the sunlight outside and the darkness within; he was conscious only of a heavy smell of incense. Then his eyes began to accustom themselves to the gloom and he realized he was in a treasure house.

The walls and floor were made of polished wood with a distinctive black grain. Against the far wall was an altar decorated with ornate *thangka* scrolls and a red lantern. On Li's right stood an old-fashioned *kang*, a raised Chinese bed, constructed of the same wood; above and around it hung somber paintings and examples of "grass script" calligraphy. The wall to his left was covered with what looked like a white sheet.

"This is my daughter-in-law, Su-liang," said the old man, pointing to a woman over by the bed. Li greeted her with a smile. Su-liang's face was narrow, oval-shaped, and hollow, as if sucked in. Her purple, high-collared blouse, fastened with buttons of polished bamboo, was free of ornament, and she had pulled her graying hair back into a tight bun secured by a metal comb. A good Confucian wife, Li thought.

"We will have some tea," the old man said. They watched Su-liang take a kettle off a charcoal brazier, pour boiling water into a glazed teapot, swirl it around, and then tip the brew into thimble-sized cups. After she had let it stand for a few seconds, she emptied pot and cups into a bowl, refilled the pot, then carried the tea tray across to where the men were sitting.

For a while the four of them sipped in appreciative silence. When Li's glance strayed to the white sheet on the opposite wall, Wu Kuo-kan, long accustomed to working in the dark, took the opportunity to study his guest's face. Li's eyes fascinated him. They were a shade too close together, almost rectangular, narrowing slightly at the point where they came closest to the bridge of his nose, and set at an angle of some fifteen degrees from the horizontal. Above them, thick black brows slashed upward, left and right; they resembled dense brushstrokes on a scroll painting. Every feature, each line, was stark. At first Wu Kuo-kan saw only ferocity in this face. Then Li Lu-tang would smile, as he did now, and suddenly become charming.

"So." Wu the Elder moistened his lips with a noisy smack. "I see you're curious about my family tree."

"Indeed."

"Seven hundred years," Wu Kuo-kan said in a matter-of-fact tone. "Give or take a decade or so. Are you interested in historical things?"

"Yes, very."

"That isn't the first version, of course. There were many earlier ones, including a draft in *li-shu* script."

"I would very much like to see that."

"Destroyed. Looted, then destroyed." The old man's chin had sunk into his chest, he was addressing only himself. Su-liang came to sit beside him, laying a hand on his arm, and the silence in the room seemed to deepen. Eventually Wu Kuo-kan roused himself with an effort. "Your message said we could be of help to you."

"Will you help?"

"If we can. I've never wavered in my determination to rid this island of the mainlanders who raped it. You're old enough to remember the Ring Riots, I think?"

"Yes. I'm fifty-five. But I was only a boy then. I recall very little."

"Then for your benefit, I'll retell the story now. There came a time when the Japanese occupiers left and their place was taken by mainlanders, under the governorship of one Chen Yi." Kuo-kan's voice was low, introspective. "On the twenty-seventh of February, 1947, his men caught two women selling American cigarettes in Taipei. This was forbidden. They executed one of the women, on the spot. The crowd reacted badly. There was rioting everywhere, for many days. In the middle of March, troops came from the mainland—to restore order, it was said. Do you know what happened, Lu-tang? I mean, of course, what happened to me? To mine?"

When Li said "No," his own voice took him by surprise, so loud it sounded.

"The soldiers came into Taipei on trains, many trains, with machine guns mounted on trucks. And when they reached the outskirts of Taipei, they began shooting. The shooting went on. And on. Until at last, in Taipei and elsewhere, they had butchered eight thousand men, women, and children."

Wu Kuo-kan tapped the cane's ferrule on the floor. His daughter-in-law rose silently and went across to fetch the kettle. She had just filled the pot when her father-in-law rapped, "They shot my wife."

The pot twitched in Su-liang's hand, spilling hot tea over her fingers.

"They took her away, along with my eldest son; they shot her and they kept my son in prison until he caught pneumonia. Then they released him. Then he died. He was the same age as you— twelve years old."

The silence in the shady room seemed very long.

"I have one particular memory of that time. We were in Taipei, all of us except Tie-zi, who was staying with an aunt, here in the south. They'd come to take my family away. I ran into the street after them. The officer in charge had roped a dozen or so people together and was preparing to lead them off. And then two United States Air Force officers came wandering down the street. Somewhat drunk. They were lieutenants, the mainland officer was a major, but he stopped his file of men and prisoners for long enough to stand at attention and salute those two young men. He stood there like one of the gods, bursting with pride, while those Americans waved at him. They didn't even return his salute. They waved. And I could see from the look in their eyes that they were puzzled. That's all."

The old man paused, then raised his cup and drained it. Li stared at the floor while the seconds ticked by. At last he said quietly, "I'm very sorry. It was an unspeakable crime."

"It was also a long time ago," Su-liang interjected. "I seem to remember that Chen Yi was executed, isn't that so?"

"Yes, executed—but not for what he did to me and mine." When Su-liang had no answer, the old man continued more gently, "On any slate, there is only room for so much history. Sometimes it becomes necessary to clear the slate and start again. Who decides? Why, the headmaster, of course."

For a moment his daughter-in-law sat in silence, mulling over the old man's words. "So long ago," she repeated mechanically, going through motions that not even she could understand.

"Is it? Is it indeed? Henry Liu, killed in San Francisco in 1984 by those gangsters, the Bamboo Union Gang—who ordered *that*, do you suppose? Ghosts?"

"All right. But we can't live in the past forever." Her voice hardened. "We've got to face realities. Martial law's been lifted. Taiwanese leaders have arisen. The Vice-President, five ministers, the Governor of the Province of Taiwan—all these people are native-born Formosans, not mainlanders."

"And what can these things matter?"

"They matter because without political leaders and without the support of the people, your independence movement can't hope to succeed. But our politicians no longer want independence, and the people are indifferent. The country's happy, full of prosperous citizens whose loyalty to central government is unquestioned."

"What you say is true. On the surface."

Su-liang spread her hands. "Then how—?"

"Because you confine yourself to the surface. The figures produced by the government, yes, they're convincing. There are no signs of discontent, of revolt, and yet you, as an educated woman, must certainly know why: because all such signs are repressed, ruthlessly, as soon as they manifest themselves."

Li focused on Su-liang. He was mentally adding to her dossier. He found the wife much more intriguing than fat, jolly, bespectacled Wu Tie-zi. She had an intelligent look, Li thought. Born in Hong Kong, where Tie-zi met her; beyond that, the Files Office in Taipei knew virtually nothing about her.

The point of Kuo-kan's cane connected with the floor in another crack that made them all jump. "Li Lu-tang, you sent a message appealing for my family's help," he snapped. "You shall have it! What do you want?"

Li sat back and for a moment merely examined the hands lying in his lap. Then he said, "We're faced with a unique opportunity. There are many of us now in positions of power. And at last we have a new ally."

"I guessed it. You wouldn't be here otherwise. The Russians. Am I right?"

"Yes," said Li. His face disclosed no surprise, but he was nevertheless astounded by the old man's acumen.

"What?"

[53]

Su-liang made no attempt to disguise the horror she felt, but her father-in-law motioned impatiently. "Of course. They're our last hope."

"Why in the name of heaven should Soviet Russia help us?" she wailed.

"Who else can help now?" Wu Kuo-kan sounded exasperated. "The Americans? They abandoned Taiwan once, and now look at them! Mending fences with the Kuomintang while they vaunt their ability to shore up the government here as a bastion against Peiping. No, the Russians are our last chance."

"It's dangerous. We could all be shot."

"Nothing's dangerous as long as it remains a secret. No one here's going to talk."

In the silence that followed this remark, Su-liang became aware of three pairs of eyes surveying her critically. Li felt sneaking sympathy for her. He could still remember looking along the shaft of the arrow into Ah-Huan's serene face. He sensed that his welcome had contained a sinister message that was only now becoming clear: visitors to this house were expected to behave with discretion when they left it.

"The Russians," Li said, "have proposed a bargain. They've offered to supply us with a lot of money and some arms."

"That's generous," said the old man. "More than we dared hope. But why now? Why, after all these years, do the Russians suddenly decide we're worth helping?"

"Because now we have something they want."

"Ah! Earlier you mentioned a bargain."

"Yes. And that's why I'm here. Your son, Tie-zi, is well placed to help. He already has helped. Because of his Western education and experience of world markets, because of the years he lived in Australia and Hong Kong, he's become a much respected, if informal, ambassador for your movement. The Russians admire him."

Su-liang could not contain herself. "You have *met* these people?" she all but spat at her husband, who nodded miserably.

"Also," said Li, conscious of a need to keep up momentum, "he enjoys vital access in the area where at present we need it most. I want to retain his services on a more long-term basis."

"Please explain."

Li turned to face Wu Tie-zi. "I think the time's come for you to tell your father about Apogee."

"Of course." Tie-zi, feeling the old man's eyes upon him, hastened to explain. "It's a computer capable of instantaneous translation—a machine that can understand Chinese in all its dialects, as well as other languages."

"Well?"

"Apogee's being developed here, in Hsinchu Scientific Industrial Park, by Ducannon Young Electronics. We have a contact in the pioneer company. He tells us that the project's close to completion."

"And this interests our new Soviet allies?"

"Oh yes," Li interposed. "The military applications of such a computer are limitless. It would revolutionize the Soviet command communications and control system."

"I don't understand all this jargon."

"We're talking about machines that respond to the human voice. Pilotless planes. Driverless tanks."

"Could our movement use such weaponry?"

"Only as a bargaining counter. If OFN can get its hands on Apogee, it'll bargain with the government for power. Bargain—or threaten. If the Soviet Union is with us . . . well, I don't think I have to spell it out. And of course, there's Ducannon Young to be considered."

"What does that mean?"

"The Russians used to run a bank in Singapore, the Soviet Communal Bank. Simon Young and the Ducannon Young group managed to ruin it. The prospect of revenge gives Moscow particular pleasure."

"I see." Wu Kuo-kan remained lost in thought for some moments. "Tell me—why do you ask *me* if you can 'retain,' as you put it, my son here? I retired many years ago; Tie-zi manages everything now."

Li's eyes flickered between father and son while he thought out a face-saving formula. "It might be of help for Tie-zi to know that you were firmly behind him," he said at last.

Wu Kuo-kan carefully mined these words for their last ounce of meaning before turning to his son with a glare. "I wouldn't like to think you lacked enthusiasm," he remarked. "You"ll give Li Lu-tang whatever help he requires."

When Tie-zi nodded, Su-liang rose to her feet. "Please excuse me, father-in-law, but I've much to do."

"Of course."

But as she opened the door, Li became aware of a silhouette outside, barring egress: the black shape of a man with a bow slung over his shoulder. Su-liang faltered, tossed her head, and pushed

[55]

past. The unseen archer continued to stand just out of vision, beyond the doorway. The three men watched until her shadow no longer stained the sunlit floor. Then, and only then, did Kuo-kan once more tap with his cane. "The timing," he whispered. "When do you begin?"

"Soon. It will take some time to distribute the arms where they can do the most good."

"I understand." The old man edged forward in his chair. "But when the time does come . . . you'll need a spark."

"We shall."

"And what is this spark to be?"

Li hesitated, suddenly aware once more of the sinister black shadow that extended from the doorway almost as far as his chair. At last he made up his mind. "We shall kill the President of Taiwan," he said, looking up with a bland smile.

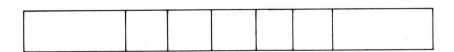

FIVE

Tingchen awoke at first light and tiptoed along the passage to his parents' room, where he wriggled his way between the two adults before settling down once more to doze. The boy's arms instinctively went around his father. Qiu moaned softly and swallowed a couple of times. Then, still barely conscious, he rolled over to give Tingchen a tight squeeze. When he opened his eyes it was to see Qingqing staring at him across the boy. She lowered her eyes at once.

"Good morning," she said.

"Morning." He gave Tingchen another hug. "Who is this big panda bear in bed with us?"

Tingchen giggled, pressing against his father. "*Not* a panda bear!"

"What time is it?" Qiu asked.

"Six. Just past."

He eased himself out of bed and went to urinate. When he came back it was to find that the bed contained only Qingqing. "I sent him to get dressed," she explained, seeing the look of inquiry on his face. "What time are you leaving?"

"Soon. The car's coming at seven-thirty."

"Then I'd better get you some breakfast."

"I'll wake the orderly."

"Don't bother. I'll do it."

A moment later Tingchen looked up from putting on his socks to find that his father had soundlessly entered his bedroom, carrying a package. The boy smiled shyly and said, "What have you got there?"

"Present. For you." Qiu squatted down beside his son. "I was going to keep it for when you're older, but, well . . . it's your ninth birthday, soon. Old enough."

"You won't be here on my birthday?" All the disappointment in the world was concentrated in those forlorn words. Qiu shook his head and looked away for a moment. "Don't think so," he mumbled.

Tingchen picked at the string that held the wrapping in place. Inside was a box. He opened it and gasped. "Chopsticks! *Silver* chopsticks."

"From Bangkok."

For a moment longer the little boy stared in wonder at the costly gift; then he put down the chopsticks and threw his arms around his father's neck, rocking him to and fro until Qiu fell over and rolled on the floor with the boy. "Pleased?" he whispered.

"They're perfect." Tingchen leaned back so that he could look at his father. "Only . . ."

"Only what?"

"I wish you were going to be here. On my birthday."

"Yes. Well." Qiu pulled the boy close, so that he could not see his father's eyes. "You . . . you're old enough now to manage without me."

"You're going away forever?" Tingchen's eyes were wide with an expression Qiu couldn't read.

"No, Tingchen—don't cry."

"You must come back! You must!"

"Of course I will! Sometimes . . . sometimes daddies have to go far away to do their work. For a long time. But it doesn't mean they don't love their families. No, don't cry, you mustn't cry."

The boy brushed away a tear with an awkward gesture, trying to be brave. "Not crying."

Qiu kissed him. His heart overflowed with messages—words

of comfort, of advice and concern—but after all, what was the point? He was leaving. That was what mattered.

"Can I write to you, Papa?"

Qiu shook his head.

"Why not?"

His father merely smiled. How to tell a child that a simple letter from home might start an investigation and end with an execution? "I'll bring you more clothes," he said. "When I come home again." For some reason the word *when* stuck in his throat. "You look nice in that outfit."

"He looks foreign."

Qiu looked round to find that Qingqing had silently come into the room. "Perhaps you could do with looking a little more foreign," he said. His voice was rough.

Qingqing flushed. "Yes. If ever you bought some clothes for me, as well as the child, perhaps I might. I came to tell you breakfast is ready."

She stood for a moment longer, looking down on the pair of them. Qiu was holding Tingchen in front of him much as he might have held a shield. Her lips formed a thin, bitter line. "Come and eat while it's hot."

"Thank you." Qiu, anxious to avoid a quarrel on this, the last day of his leave, cast around for something nice to say. "He's growing up fast. I'm very proud of my son."

"Our son," she corrected him coldly, before turning to go.

Qiu tightened his grip around Tingchen. "Mama will be lonely," he said. "Look after her while I'm away."

"I promise."

"Good boy. Will you want to travel, like Papa, do you think, when you grow up?"

"Travel to where you are?"

Qiu smiled. "Perhaps. One day."

Tingchen thought. "I'm not sure. I like it here. With Mama. And with you. Oh, I don't want you to go, please don't go."

They hugged each other tight, not daring to speak, until at last Qiu heard Qingqing call from the bottom of the stairs, "Breakfast will spoil!" He disengaged his son, gently removing the thin little arms from around his neck, and gave him a kiss on the cheek. "Come on, Tingchen," he said softly. "It's time."

At Shuitou, eighteen hundred kilometers south of Beijing, the driver turned left off the main highway to Tongan, heading for the east coast. The countryside was green and hilly, and close enough to the sea to provide a welcome respite from the sticky June heat. The car began to descend a series of hairpin curves. As they emerged onto a bluff, the driver slowed to a walking pace.

"Jinmen Island."

Qiu leaned forward to peer through the windshield. So that was Jinmen—one of the last outposts of the Taiwanese rebels. Somehow he had been expecting a more dramatic view, but the prospect before him was unexciting: a fertile, hilly island, big and solid, with a few smaller islets, much flatter, between it and the mainland's coast. The blue channel separating the two Chinas was narrower than he'd anticipated; a man in a rowboat could cross it easily.

As the driver put the car in gear again, Qiu's attention was caught by a sudden movement toward the north of the big island. A column of white water climbed some fifty feet into the air, leaned to the right in response to the wind, and slowly sank back into the sea.

Qiu felt his heartbeat quicken. He could think of only one explanation for such a phenomenon.

His guess was confirmed at the last checkpoint before the coast, where the officer in charge handed Qiu a pair of soundproof ear protectors: the mainland had resumed the shelling of Jinmen.

As the car bumped along the last few hundred meters of road, Qiu vainly tried to work out the implications. He knew that in the fifties the Communists had launched a number of forays against Jinmen and Taiwan's other remaining bastion, the island of Matsu, farther up the coast; but they had not been pushed home, and the attacks had been repulsed with heavy loss of life. There had followed the time of the "phony war," when both sides had shelled each other, but only on odd-numbered days of the month.

Then, on the first day of 1979, peace had come to the islands; and thereafter both sides contented themselves with diplomatic ventures, continuing the war by other means. Mah-jongg files were replete with accounts of agitprop experiments, some of them quite entertaining in their way. The mainland took advantage of the prevailing winds to float hot-air balloons carrying leaflets over Jinmen; while the Taiwanese, not to be outdone in terms of ingenuity, inserted messages of freedom in the guts of dead fish and bribed or bullied local mainland fishermen who strayed too close into ferrying this culinary propaganda back home. But for the most part, the inhabitants of this nook of southeast China had been left to get on with their lives.

Now the shelling had begun again. And it wasn't even an odd-numbered date.

Qiu's car drew up on a small concrete clearing between two outcrops of spiky black rock, and he got out. The coastline here was rugged. Cliffs towered above him, with only an occasional patch of tough, windblown scrub to relieve their monotony. He was standing some hundred meters above a narrow beach. Ahead of him lay the big island of Jinmen, partially obscured by one of the rocky outcrops that curled round to make a small bay of calm azure water. Qiu looked out to sea and noticed four men, clad in the bright green uniforms of the People's Liberation Army, perched on top of the outcrop, surrounded by sandbags: a forward observation post, obviously. They sat with their backs to him a few hundred yards distant, on the other side of the bay—quite close as the crow flew, but the tortuous path to their post would have deterred a mountain goat.

At the edge of the concrete apron, Qiu found an iron ladder descending to a terrace bounded by a wall of sandbags. He climbed down. From this level, some twenty feet below the place where he'd left the car, the view of Jinmen Island was even more restricted. To his right, a set of rough stairs carved out of the side of the cliff gave access to a squat concrete-block tower, its top story glazed on two sides with huge windows overlooking the sea. A command post, placed in such a way as to afford an unobstructed view of the enemy.

Qiu walked slowly along the terrace until he was almost at the steps leading up to the tower. Five men were grouped around a pair of mounted binoculars. All except one wore uniforms. It was the civilian who crouched before the glasses, staring through them out to sea. As Qiu approached, this man stood up; and the Colonel recognized Sun Shanwang.

Sun said something to the nearest officer, who promptly withdrew to the ladder down which Qiu had come, taking his colleagues with him. The Controller of Central Intelligence directed his attention back to the strait.

"How far would you say that was?" he called.

Qiu puckered his lips. "Oh . . . two thousand meters."

"Not bad. In fact, the nearest point, there, is two thousand three hundred and ten meters from the mainland. A man could swim that distance without difficulty."

"Certainly."

"Soon, men may have to do precisely that."

Qiu could not conceal the extent of his alarm. "You mean . . . we're going to repossess by force? Invade?"

Sun did not answer him. Suddenly his eyes narrowed and he pointed. "Look!"

Qiu's eyes darted to the forward observers, perched on their rocky aerie. One of the men was holding up a red flag; in the same instant Qiu saw a bright flash on the coast of Jinmen. Sun grabbed him by the arm. "We have to get down!"

For a moment Qiu did not grasp what he meant. Then it dawned on him: there were two sides to this shelling. He flung himself flat, pushing his way into the angle between the sandbags and the terrace, ear protectors held tightly in place. Almost at once he heard a high-pitched whistle, like a steam train approaching very fast; then the whistle turned into a scream, the scream became a shriek. . . .

The noise of the explosion penetrated into the dead center of Qiu's skull, where it seemed to hang and reverberate for a painfully long time before finally dissolving into stillness. He raised his head to find Sun Shanwang already up.

"Too close for comfort," Sun said as they removed their ear protectors.

"Where? I didn't see it."

"Behind us, inland. Neither side is really trying, of course."

Qiu got up, dusting off his uniform. "No?"

"This is merely warming up. They can't figure out what we're doing. Nothing's appeared in the international press yet. Taipei doesn't know whether we're playing a game or mobilizing for full-scale invasion."

"And what *are* we doing, if I may ask?"

"It's not certain. Taiwan has been relocated at the very top of the Politburo's agenda. Do you know why?"

Qiu shook his head.

"It's because at long last they think they can win. My orders now are very simple: to monitor military security in Fujian Province and tighten it wherever necessary, by whatever means. That's why you're here. I wanted to see you before you left. I couldn't meet you in Beijing, so it had to be here."

"I'm not sorry. It's interesting."

"Dangerous, also. But I, too, wanted to know how it feels when one Chinese fires on another in anger. And I must tell you—I don't like it."

"But who began this? It seems so extraordinary, after all these years. . . ."

"Who ever starts these things? You know how it is—one side says this, the other side says that."

"Please excuse my presumption, but after more than ten years of peace, somebody pushes a button and fires a high explosive shell at or from a densely populated island . . . you must know which somebody?"

Sun said nothing.

"And why did he press that button?"

"These things are beyond me. I'm not a politician. The considerations that—"

Another explosion cut him off in mid-sentence. He watched in silence until the by-now-familiar column of water had erupted into the sky and died back again. "At least you should find Taipei more peaceful than this," Sun remarked.

"I can't pretend to be very happy about going to Taipei."

"I didn't expect you to be."

"My talents have lost their cutting edge, I'm afraid."

"After what happened in Bangkok, you mean? But you seem to have dealt with the problem most capably."

"When I failed to identify Kraisri as a hostile element?"

"But he wasn't! We've checked and double-checked. The assassins blackmailed him. Did you know he was heavily in debt?"

"No."

"Of course, we had to get rid of Kraisri; no bank can afford to employ a debtor as manager. But don't bewail your failure to label him as what he was not."

"Then who were those men who tried to kill me?"

"We aren't sure. The best hypothesis is also the simplest: the Soviets wanted revenge on you and on Ducannon Young for the ruin of their bank. Ducannon Young was beyond their reach; you weren't."

"If the Soviets can identify me, even in my role as Singaporean bank manager, then so can the Taiwanese."

"But the Taiwanese have no formal links with the Soviet Union. If that weren't so, we wouldn't send you there."

"Why *are* you sending me there?"

"Because a unique opportunity has presented itself. The Nationalist government has finally granted permission for the Chinese Overseas Investment Bank to set up a branch there and commence deposit-taking. We've submitted your name as manager, and the Bank of Taiwan has approved it."

"Forgive me, but that strains credulity."

"Why? The Chinese Overseas Investment Bank is a perfectly

respectable member of the Southeast Asian banking community. No one suspects the influence we wield over its affairs. Similarly, you yourself have become a well-known banker with a considerable professional reputation. When we planted you in Singapore, two years ago, we took the utmost care to provide you with a convincing past. No one knows who you really are."

"Even accepting that, what good can I do?"

"Isn't it obvious?" Sun Shanwang was becoming impatient with what he regarded as deliberate obtuseness on the part of his subordinate. "You already have a good relationship with the man Wu Tie-zi, who banks in Singapore with COB. We know that Wu is trying to purchase arms in secret, that he has to be the way into Our Formosa Now. Whom else should we send, if not you?"

Qiu hung his head. "I'm sorry." But his voice was stubborn. Sun squeezed his shoulder. "There's something else," he said quietly. "By now you'll have been briefed on the Apogee project?"

"The so-called supercomputer?"

"Yes. I said earlier that the Politburo thinks we can win a war with Taiwan. The only reason for their confidence is Apogee. You'll be responsible for the security of the project. Remember—that computer is for mainland China. It would be a catastrophe if the Taiwanese ever got their hands on it."

"So I understand. What I can't understand at all is why, in that case, the thing's being developed on Taiwan."

"The Ducannon Young companies are an autonomous trading group, one of the most powerful in the Far East. We couldn't simply dictate to them, particularly when the managing director made what was so obviously a sound commercial decision by developing his machine in a country that offered so much in the way of incentives."

"But surely the military significance of Apogee outweighs—"

"Ah, but there you touch on the real point! How could we tell Simon Young what the military significance of Apogee *was*? It's a state secret!"

"He must guess what we want it for."

"Perhaps. Anyway, rightly or wrongly, it was decided that he should be permitted to follow his commercial instincts and have the project developed wherever he wished. The planners were apparently also impressed with the argument that the best way of allaying suspicion, of guaranteeing in the eyes of the world that this computer had nothing to do with Red China, was to allow it to be made in Taiwan."

"I still think it's daring."

"With hindsight, I agree with you." Sun's face clouded. "There've been delays."

"Delays?"

"Yes, and we're not getting satisfactory explanations for them. We've had to talk very firmly to Ducannon Young. It's been decided that we can no longer afford to be complacent while they do our top secret work under the eyes of a rebel government, in their territory. Certain situations can only be tolerated for a short time. This is one of them."

"I'm glad to hear it. How soon can Apogee be ready?"

"We suspect they've suffered some kind of major setback. That's just a guess, mind you. But they're saying we can have it by the end of the year. This would involve our granting Ducannon Young an extension of the contractual deadline. We've decided, reluctantly, that we should grant that extension."

"Noted."

"But we've imposed a condition. There must be no more delays. Any further loss of time will be punished."

"How?"

"If Apogee falls further behind schedule, we'll present Ducannon Young with a choice: repay us our investment, or put your technicians and scientists to work alongside our own."

"I'd be in favor of that course anyway. But you realize it would cost them almost as much to pull out of Taiwan as to repay the People's Republic?"

"We do. Unfortunately, we can't see any alternative. I've been left in no doubt that Apogee *must* be ready by the beginning of next year."

Sun was on the point of speaking again when a sudden movement out to sea attracted Qiu's attention. "Red flag's up," he cried.

They threw themselves into the protective angle of the sandbags. A mighty wave of pressure hammered against Qiu's ear protectors. Shards of rock pattered around him. He looked up to see the top three rows of sandbags dislodged inward; several of them had burst open, spilling fine sand everywhere.

Qiu ran across to survey the damage through the binoculars. The horizon had changed. A moment ago, his view of Jinmen had been partly blocked by the crag on which lurked the forward observation post. Now there was nothing there except a few jagged splinters of granite, looking like stalagmites that had lost confidence.

He directed his glasses toward the sea, scanning the boulders on the other side of the narrow bay. When a flash of color caught his eye, he immediately jerked the binoculars toward it. Green, something green . . .

"Qianwei . . . are you all right?" Sun had dragged himself up on his knees. "Help me, please."

Qiu relinquished the binoculars and ran over to his chief. For an instant Sun seemed to feel the earth settle a little beneath him, then he steadied. "Can you see anything?" he croaked.

"There's a leg," Qiu said matter-of-factly. "On the rocks. Severed at the top of the thigh. The uniform trousers appear to be still intact."

Sun stared at him as if at a lunatic, but the Colonel remorselessly continued his report. "Also, the boot is still attached to the foot. In the water, some ten meters from the leg, there's what might be a shoulder, naked, with part of a human head attached. Nearby, a regulation uniform cap is floating. That's all." He paused. "Do you want to look for yourself?"

"*No!* No, thank you, Colonel." Sun brushed a few flecks of granite from his shirt, as if they came from another world, nothing to do with him. "The Politburo is right," he said abruptly. "It's time this nonsense was brought to an end."

"I'm glad I saw it, before taking up my new post. It gives me a certain sense of perspective. Perhaps it will remind me of what I'm doing, and why."

Sun took a piece of tissue paper from his shirt pocket and cleaned his glasses. "You must leave within a fortnight." He surveyed Qiu cautiously, as if not sure how he would react. "You don't look pleased."

Qiu made a face. "Taiwan, well . . . and I don't like Simon Young, or his companies."

"Of course not. Your last mission nearly failed as a result of his meddling."

"He kidnapped my son!"

"He held your son hostage so that he might regain freedom for himself and his own family. You would've done exactly the same in his place."

"Perhaps I would. But he caused domestic problems that—" Qiu could have bitten his tongue out. Sun's eyes narrowed. "What?"

"Nothing. It's not important."

"Your welfare's very important."

Qiu shook his head, but the urge to confide was suddenly strong within him. "My wife's a little overprotective. That's all."

"I see." Sun continued to gaze at him for several moments

longer. At last he said, "You'll proceed from here to Fujian Military Zone Command HQ, thence to Singapore via Shanghai and Hong Kong. Travel arrangements to Taipei will be notified to you in due course. And, Colonel . . ."

"Yes?"

"I shall be interested to learn, in due course, how Simon Young reacts when he finds out that his new bank manager is also a divisional director of China's Mah-jongg Brigade."

II

DECEMBER – JANUARY

Taiwan, Inc.

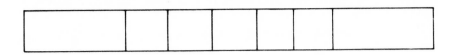

SIX

A light wind ruffled the grass on the flank of Ak Tai To Yan, Kowloon's tallest peak, but apart from the sigh of the breeze, no other sound disturbed the December night. Cloud shadows scudded across the moonlit hillside. The man lying in the scrub beside the road waited until one such black shape loomed close, then used its rippling rush up the slope as cover for his next run. It took him an hour to climb the best part of a mile in this way.

The man's employers had left nothing to chance. They had provided him with plans, aerial photographs, and a report by someone who had once worked in the target building; then they had arranged for him to walk the ground in daylight, pretending to be an ornithologist. As a result, he knew exactly where he was going and how to get there.

He was Chinese, twenty-four, thin, fit. The Crown Colony's immigration computer would have recognized him as Daniel Fen, although he had many aliases. Fen was a specialist. He estimated that his mission should last two hours. For each of those hours in the field he had spent twenty preparing.

He reached a shale-filled hollow and threw himself flat. Immediately above him, some thirty feet away, he could see the place where the mouth of the cave must be; still higher loomed the crazy house, with its protruding half-floors, terraces, and weird sandstone walls capped with gray tiles. Fen could see all these details, even though it was night, because every inch of the odd structure was illuminated by spotlights.

Time for the final assault.

Fen's skin was already coated with a mixture of coal soot and burnt cork. Now he pulled a black silk hood over his face, leaving two tiny holes for his eyes. His hands were protected by thin gloves. He wore only a dark track suit, loose around the arms and crotch but firmly elasticized at the wrists and ankles. Last, he checked his shoes, if you could call them that: yards of black bandage wrapped around his feet like a mummy's casing—warm, silent, incapable of leaving a recognizable print.

Tonight he was carrying only two items apart from the clothes he stood up in. The first was an instrument shaped like a small box, made of rubber, with two protuberant lenses at the front, which he now fitted over his head. It was a Nitefinder TH-90, a night-vision device completely self-contained in a pair of goggles that required no outside light whatsoever. It also had one other feature vital to the success of Fen's mission: an infrared light detector.

He wormed his way up the gully until he reached a pile of brushwood and stones. It did not take him long to find a small hole; air was coming through it in a steady current. Fen began to burrow. After five minutes he had made an opening big enough to admit his body. He lowered his legs through the gap, holding on to a nearby branch; then he took a deep breath and let go.

The Chinese landed on the balls of his feet and at once bounded up, hurtling to one side and spinning his body through the air like a human screw. He dropped to a crouch and listened. No sound penetrated the darkness that shrouded him.

Fen smelled stagnant water, rotting vegetation. When he adjusted his goggles he could see a square opening in front of him. As he concentrated on the monochrome image it sharpened into a surrealistic moonscape, with the gap showing up darker than the surrounding silvery gray.

Fen advanced, then squatted and studied the ground on both sides of the square hole. Nothing unusual caught his eye. He raised a hand to his goggles and turned a knurled knob in the side of the

Nitefinder. The image blacked out, telling him there was no infrared light source in the vicinity. Fen returned the knob to its original setting.

Cautiously he advanced through the square hole, the entrance to a tunnel. Before he'd gone very far, the air current died away. After progressing about two hundred meters he again turned the knob and now the image in front of him did not black out. Instead, he saw seven red horizontal bars stretching across a dark gray background. Slowly he took another few steps, until he could have reached out to touch the bars.

He rotated the wheel to restore the true image. The stone passage stretched away from him without any sign of red bars. But Fen knew they were still there; each one a beam of infrared light. If any of them were broken, an alarm would sound in the house above.

Fen sat down and rested his back against the wall, reviewing the situation.

He knew everything worth knowing about the house and its security systems. At their heart lay a computer that monitored each twitch on its giant electronic web; but the computer itself was miles away on Hong Kong Island, unassailable. More than a thousand sensors were distributed throughout the building on the hill above Fen, each linked to the computer and separately monitored by it along a single, twin-flex wire. Twenty-five sensors made up a "family," with its own control box, called a mother. Seven times a second, the computer interrogated the mothers by means of a coded signal. If a single sensor went out, the computer would know at once. It would also know why, instantly differentiating between a failed light bulb at one extreme and a major fire at the other. It was programmed to take action accordingly.

A thief gained nothing by hacking away at cables, even if he could find them; the sophistication of the multiplexing was such that any act of interference itself set off an alarm. The computer could then identify the source of the trouble as a human intruder through acoustic detectors sensitive enough to tell the difference between the breathing pattern of a man and, say, a dog. At which point it would hermetically seal the area before pumping in gas until the breathing pattern changed.

But despite all this electronic wizardry, the house was not inviolable. Not quite.

If the owners of this remarkable building wanted to enter it by the front door, they had to pass through two security fences, nine feet tall and topped with barbed wire. Sometimes it did not suit them to endure this tiresome routine. Sometimes they preferred to enter and leave undetected by their watchdog computer, taking with them material worth an industrial fortune. For this was where Ducannon Young Electronics developed the microchips that made possible the miracle of Apogee.

Hence the cave.

Fen knew that the infrared bars were not linked to the main computer. He knew that if he could only cut them, he would have access to the house above.

He stood up and twisted the knob in the rubber casing of his goggles. The bars sprang into being. Fen assessed them carefully before restoring normal vision and reaching for his second piece of specialized equipment.

This in some ways resembled a retractable steel tape measure. But the rule itself, made from a rare titanium compound, was stiff and hard to extract from its casing; when it did emerge it stuck out straight ahead, like a reinforced rod without any trace of sag. Also, rulers did not usually come in thick, insulated rubber cases. And finally, in place of the usual metal pull-tab, there was a razor-sharp serrated blade.

Fen walked back down the tunnel, letting out the peculiar metal strip until he had a rod some fifteen feet long. Then he returned as close as he dared to the red bars, using his Nitefinder to position himself in safety. He reverted to normal vision and for the first time peered through, rather than at, the bars.

About ten feet farther on, the passage turned sharp right. Set in the wall facing Fen, but half obscured by the corner of the right-hand wall, was a junction box with wires leading down from it to the floor. The Chinese backed off and picked up the rod lying at his feet, holding it at full stretch. He switched to infrared scan, then, very slowly, began to feed the rod between the fifth and sixth red bars, directing the razor's edge toward the junction box.

After eighteen inches of rod had filtered through the beams, Fen took a long, unhurried breath. He emptied his lungs and began to feed the metal forward again. Two feet. Two and a half. Three. Stop.

Another measured breath. His forehead was wet, but there was nothing he could do about that. The muscles of his left arm had started to stiffen under the strain. He brought the arm closer to his torso for support, continuing to slide the metal across his left palm.

The blade had almost reached the box when Fen heard a noise behind him.

Not a muscle moved. His left arm ached with tension; his right was trembling slightly. The rod quivered, dipped to within millimeters of the fifth beam of light, and rose again just in time. Fen turned his head away; he saw nothing but unadulterated darkness. Then he remembered: his Nitefinder was still operating on infrared frequency, and as long as he held the rod he could not change the setting.

He forced himself to remain perfectly still while he got his breathing back under control. Then he waited for the noise to repeat itself. But he waited in vain. After five minutes of anguished, total silence, a groan forced its way through Fen's lips. Behind him, nothing moved. No one spoke.

The noise he had heard must have been caused by a rat, or a distant rockfall, maybe. Nothing to worry about, anyway. Fen refocused on the box. By now the blade was almost nudging the wires beneath it. He pushed the rod forward until he encountered resistance. Then he passed the blade across the wires in a delicate horizontal sweep, careful to avoid breaking the bars of light. Nothing happened. He tried again. But his overtensed muscles were incapable of further effort. Over and over again he grazed the blade across the wires, trying to exert the necessary pressure, always without success.

Fen knew he had reached the limits of endurance. He could never hope to retract the metal rod; now it was all or nothing. With his teeth clenched in a death's-head grin, he pushed the rod forward for the last time, only to feel the scant remaining strength drain out of his arms. The rod dipped; there came a bang, a flash . . . and Fen's vision went black.

The red bars had disappeared.

He dropped the rod and collapsed against the wall, letting his exhausted body sink down until he was sitting on his haunches. Then he stretched out his legs and began to massage his arms. His breath still came and went in a series of grunts. It didn't matter, nothing mattered. The last barrier was down. The house was his.

Fen groped around on the floor for his rod and struggled upright before retracting it into the rubber case. Then he advanced cautiously down the now unprotected passage. As he passed the junction box he noted with satisfaction how the blade had cut cleanly through the thin wires. Ahead of him now was a short stretch of tunnel, bolstered with iron girders and cinder blocks, at the end of which he could see two rails set vertically in the rock. As he approached, thinner horizontal bars blended out of the darkness—but these were not bars of light, they were the rungs of a ladder.

Fen stood before the ladder and reached out to grasp its handrails.

He was very, very good at his job. Some instinct, part of whatever it was that made him great and all the rest merely competent, caused him to look down. Close to the floor it was hard to see anything, even through the Nitefinder. Fen never carried a flashlight; nothing gave a man away faster. But he felt the lack of it now. He strained to see.

At first everything looked natural; Fen, however, was thorough. He gently felt around on the ground. Almost at once he found a wire, partially concealed in rubble, trailing from the ladder into obscurity.

He crouched down to inspect this latest hazard. Nobody had said anything about wires on the ladder.

He was faced with a choice: to go forward or to retreat. Reluctantly he shook his head. Advancing was impossible until he knew whether this wire was connected to the master computer in Hong Kong. If it was, he would have to report and maybe try again later with updated information. At least one thing was certain: he wasn't going to get any farther tonight.

As Fen turned to leave, the noise that had frightened him earlier again echoed down the tunnel; only this time it sounded very close.

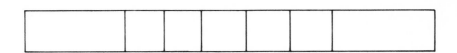

SEVEN

Kazin hauled himself into the car with a grunt. "What are you staring at?"

Krubykov hastily produced his most disarming smile. "The coat, Chairman, and the . . . the hat."

"Do you like them?"

"Very elegant."

"I've always wanted a beaver coat and hat."

Krubykov could not recall ever having heard Oleg Kazin admit to desiring some personal frippery. Snow had begun to fall again. As the general watched the windshield turn white it occurred to him that Kazin's latest whim was like another snowflake falling on rough ground. Eventually the snow was everything, the uneven surface became flat. Krubykov saw the same image in Kazin's progress toward death: ten thousand little caprices and follies, tiny balls of ice, that numbed and smoothed until the heart beneath had ceased to beat, its body covered over and forgotten.

To mask the awkward silence he turned and gazed out of the

side window. It was hard December weather, and despite the continuous efforts of fatigue-troops to keep the Kremlin's main roads clear, snow lay everywhere within Ivan's Square. The major general's car, parked outside the Senate, had its engine running with the heater turned up full blast, but Krubykov's blood was thinner than it had been this time last year. Summer spent on the Crimea did that to a man.

Summer, Primorsk . . . the general sighed. Not all his memories of that time were good. Wu Tie-zi had come to Primorsk, close on the heels of Sun Shanwang; hard to believe all that was a mere six months ago, when so much had happened since. He moved his head slightly, enough to afford a glimpse of the shriveled figure beside him. Krubykov could scarcely see his chief's face beneath the absurd fur hat, a size too large, that flopped down over his forehead, but what he saw he didn't like. Kazin had grown too old for Moscow winters.

"How was Berlin?" Kazin asked. "Is Wu talking sense?"

"By his standards, yes. Although—"

"You can tell me as we drive." Kazin picked up the telephone and buzzed the chauffeur. "Take us down Kalinin Prospect. Cross the river and find somewhere to park near the Ukraina Hotel." He smiled at Krubykov, relishing the look of puzzlement in his eyes. "I've earned a little day off."

Vykhodnoi. The idea of taking time off was foreign to Kazin's nature. Another snowflake settled somewhere inside Krubykov's consciousness and didn't melt away. The car glided silently down Kalinin Prospect, past the Council for Mutual Economic Assistance and across Kutuzov Bridge. The chauffeur drew up on the embankment opposite the bronze monument to Taras Shevchenko. For a while the two men in the backseat merely stared out of the window at the Moscow River flowing past on the other side of a single low railing. The sluggish current was coated with thick ice floes; it reminded Krubykov of an arctic landscape seen from a plane.

At last Kazin settled himself further down in the seat and wheezed, "What have *you* got?"

Krubykov unzipped his attaché case and extracted a report bound in transparent plastic. "It's much as we expected." He flicked through several pages. "They want more, always more— arms, ammunition, explosives. OFN's a greedy organization."

"Those types usually are. Any progress?"

Krubykov's eyebrows rose, he tossed his head. "They've made some impressive recruits. Contacts in the armed forces, the Executive Yuan—"

"So they claim! But is it true?"

"Yes, I think it is. Wu brought some friends to Berlin. One of them's the real thing—a man called Li Lu-tang. I've had him checked. He's about number four in the Taiwanese intelligence hierarchy, though it's hard to pin him down exactly. Very different from Wu."

"In what way different?"

"A listener, not a talker. But the few things he did say cross-checked perfectly with what we knew already."

"Did they talk about their new bank manager, by any chance?"

Krubykov's mystification must have shown on his face, for Kazin was overcome by a fit of laughter. The catarrh gargled up and down in his throat until at last he began to cough; and the general wondered uneasily if this was how it was all destined to end, with a seizure in the back of a luxury car and the collapse of a body swathed in furs to gratify an old revolutionary's fancy. But at last Kazin recovered his self-control and said: "The man who runs Wu's bank in Taipei is Qiu Qianwei."

"What? But you had him dealt with in Bangkok!"

"Botched. As usual. Wet Affairs overreached themselves and employed a Taiwanese contractor—their way of covering their tracks, throwing the blame elsewhere. It backfired."

"So what are you going to do?"

"Nothing. Yet. We've got much worse problems to worry about at this end. The GRU."

"That missing Chinese plane?"

"Yes. I can't remember how far things had gone when you left, Krubykov. Remind me."

"Oh . . . two months ago, Chinese prototype fighter, modified Shenyang F-6, code name 'Feuder,' goes down in the far south of Kazakhstan . . . pilot reported killed . . . no-go usual diplomatic channels . . . no-go usual intelligence channels . . . high-resolution spectrographic satellite photos reveal unusual night-flying patterns over western China . . . nothing confirmed when I left."

"Soviet Union denies all knowledge of missing aircraft, vows to devote resources to retrieving same . . . yes, I know. Well, it's been confirmed now! The GRU did it. So much for the Moscow-Beijing pact. What would Feuder . . . who thought up that ridiculous name?"

"I believe it is a NATO designation, Chairman."

"What would Feuder give us?"

"I imagine it would provide us with basic technology for an

aircraft that can be made to respond to oral commands transmitted either by a conventional pilot or from the ground."

"Apogee, in other words?"

"Yes—although it seems doubtful that Apogee's been perfected yet. The Chinese are upset, I suppose?"

"Spitting blood and bile."

"And the GRU?"

"On the defensive. The plane went down in flames and exploded on impact." Kazin grunted. "You'd think they'd grovel in the dirt, once they were found out, but they've some powerful friends in the Politburo now. Strategically, Apogee's very important. The United States has gotten nowhere near as far with speaker-independent, voice-responsive computers. Apogee would give us a huge edge; and in the Kremlin, that counts more than some piece of paper with signatures on it. So on the whole they're inclined to forgive the GRU for the snatch while berating them for their clumsiness."

"Why the hell couldn't they have waited?" Krubykov was angry. "The Apogee technology would have come to us through the pact."

"Apparently nobody told the GRU that."

"So we've signed a friendship treaty with the Chinese and also stolen one of their planes."

"And unless we can find a way of allaying their suspicions, we shan't get the perfected Apogee through the pact and may find ourselves buying it from OFN after all." Kazin sighed. "We have to plan for that."

"Very dangerous. The more I think about it, the less I like it. If OFN launches a full-scale rebellion, America might have to intervene, if only to preempt mainland China from doing so."

"I still can't make up my mind what America would do," Kazin said. "That's my biggest problem at the moment. But I agree about the threat from mainland China. In Beijing they'd like nothing more than a rebellion on Taiwan. 'Look,' they'd say, 'we were right! The people of Taiwan are laboring under the heel of tyranny! Let us rescue you, brothers!' How the well-worn phrases all come flooding back! The resonance! The claptrap!" Kazin guffawed.

"Then a revolt's something we ought to prevent, not support. Let's drop OFN and stay out of it."

Kazin laughed, but his heart wasn't in it. "No . . . we must go on dealing with OFN. I persuaded them of that in the end, but it was a real fight. There are three main factions now. One lot wants to go in with Red China, stage a military invasion of Taiwan, glorious Russian tanks rumbling up the beaches side by side with our yellow brothers singing. . . . Oh, it was pathetic. Pathetic! Then there are those who say we should drop China altogether—a small minority, mostly racists. And there are a few, a sensible few, Kruby- kov, who say we should give Red China such economic aid as we can afford in their underground assault on the Taiwanese econ- omy, something that's been going on for years. A course that satisfies honor on both sides, I'd have thought."

"Who won the argument?"

"For the moment, the economic warriors. I'm relieved; it gives me a chance to mend fences with Sun Shanwang."

"I see."

"We must take OFN very seriously from now on. I want to know how they managed to get so close to Apogee, who's working for them in Ducannon Young. I want the strengths, but more than that, I want the weaknesses. Got it?"

Krubykov pulled a microcassette recorder from his attaché case and muttered notes into it. "But why?" he asked, as he switched off the machine.

"Why? So that when the time comes I can blow Our Formosa Now sky-high." Kazin cackled with something of his old malevo- lence. "I want to be in a position to guarantee that Our Formosa Now can become Our Formosa *Then*, any time I fancy!"

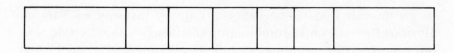

EIGHT

On the streets of Taipei the December evening struck cold and damp, but the elegant new offices of the Chinese Overseas Investment Bank afforded ample protection against the weather. Shan Lin-chun cupped her chin in her hands. From her chair by the window on the seventh floor she could, if she craned her neck, just see the rush-hour traffic starting to build up in Nan Yang Street. Five-twenty—when people were thinking of going home to dinner. When the last thing they wanted was to be bothered.

"I think I'll ring up Tony Tan," she murmured to her secretary. "Give him a fright."

Siao-ying, who shared a room with Miss Shan, rattled a sheet of paper into her electronic typewriter and chuckled. "Do you think you should?"

"Why not?" Lin-chun picked up her phone and dialed a number. "Hello? Mr. Tan, please. I'll hold. Tell him it's Miss Shan, Chinese Overseas Investment Bank. That's right—*loan* department."

There was a pause. Siao-ying stopped typing and gazed in admiration at Lin-chun, whose left hand was deftly adjusting the beads of her necklace. "Hello, Mr. Tan. Miss Shan here. You were going home? How nice! I'm so pleased to hear the boss is able to leave early, that suggests his new barbershop must be doing extremely well, I'm so glad."

Siao-ying, feeling giggles bubble inside her, raised all ten fingertips to her mouth. Lin-chun caught sight of the girl's expression and signaled frantically at her to be quiet.

"So, Mr. Tan, you won't mind me mentioning that your loan account with the bank seems to be in arrears. Or is it perhaps the bank's computer at fault? Do excuse me, please, let's be sure there is no mistake."

Now it was Lin-chun's turn to fight off laughter, as she heard poor Tony Tan writhing at the other end of the phone. "Yes, I know you have a standing order to service this loan, Mr. Tan, but at present there are no funds in the account from which we can deduct the monthly installments. I know, Mr. Tan. Yes, I *know*, Mr. Tan. You've said that, Mr. Tan. . . ."

Lin-chun's voice became ever more dulcet; she might have been coaxing a treat from a boyfriend rather than putting the screws on a client. With the forefinger of her free hand she began to describe circles in the air, until Siao-ying thought she would burst with the strain of keeping silent.

"But, Mr. Tan, if we did that, then the bank would grow poorer and poorer, and eventually it would go broke and then I'd be out of a job. I wouldn't merely be able to go home at five-thirty, Mr. Tan, like you; I'd be spending all my days at home, wondering if I'd ever work again. . . . It's kind of you to say that. Yes, it would be a worry. My mother . . . thank you, Mr. Tan. A check on the Hu Nan Commercial Bank? In the post? Oh, I don't think so; you're only just around the corner from us, so why not bring it in on your way home?"

Her eyes opened wide in mock surprise; she held one finger to her mouth. Siao-ying made a noise like "Mmmm-a-a-ah!"

"But, Mr. Tan, you told me a moment ago you were just on the point of going home. . . . *Thank* you, Mr. Tan. So kind. Tonight, then. And I am so very sorry to have troubled you, I really cannot apologize enough, excuse me. *Good* night, Mr. Tan, good night."

She replaced the receiver and dissolved into laughter. "Was I okay?" she said.

"You were splendid, Miss Shan."

At the unexpected sound of a male voice, the girls stopped laughing at once. Siao-ying stuffed her handkerchief into her bag, swept it under the desk, and began busily typing. Shan Lin-chun smiled shyly at the figure in the doorway. "Good evening, Mr. Khoo. I'm afraid I was being flippant. Sorry."

When the branch manager did not answer, she began to tidy the pens and pencils scattered across her desk, every so often darting a quick glance at him. Khoo stood in the doorway, an elbow resting against the jamb at shoulder height so that one hand could absently smooth the back of his hair while the other jangled the small change in his pants pocket. He wore no jacket, and his polyester tie, too broad to be fashionable, had come loose. As Lin-chun noticed the grime on his shirt-collar, she reflected, not for the first time, that Khoo King-hey ought to take more care of himself.

"Not flippant," the manager said at last. "You were making a forceful point, but with courtesy and good humor."

Siao-ying finished typing the letter, retrieved her bag from under the desk, and rose to depart.

"It's the kind of thing a woman executive can do extremely well," said Khoo, coming into the office to let the secretary past. "Am I being sexist?"

Lin-chun looked up at his earnest face and wanted to laugh. "No," she said seriously. "I think it's necessary to recognize that there are differences between the sexes, but that those differences are often positive."

"I find the Taiwanese attitude to female emancipation very constructive. Women seem to make better headway here than they did at my last post."

"Singapore?"

"Yes. I've been here only six months, but Singapore seems a lifetime away."

"You like it here?"

"Very much." Khoo had been standing a few inches inside the office. Now he closed the door behind him and went over to take the chair recently vacated by Siao-ying. Lin-chun sat up a bit straighter and stopped fiddling with pencils. She could not think why the boss should come to her office instead of using the phone. Her heart began to beat a little faster.

"Mo Mei-hua," Khoo said thoughtfully. "The girl who persuaded us to finance her new nightclub. This afternoon I spent a couple of hours going through the file."

Lin-chun's heartbeat quickened another couple of notches. Her biggest loan ever . . .

"A really professional piece of banking, Miss Shan," Khoo said quietly. "Sound research, constructive meetings, helping the customer."

Lin-chun was not one to dissemble. She drew a deep breath, held it a second, then puffed it out with a grin and a gasp of relief. Khoo smiled in sympathy. "You thought I was here to criticize?"

"Well . . ."

"I understand. Miss Shan, am I right in thinking that you're still only twenty-nine years of age?"

"Yes."

"Then I believe you have a great future here. I sense that this account leads to other things, other potential clients. That's why I wanted to talk it over with you. Is now convenient? Only I mustn't keep you if you've got a social engagement this evening."

"I haven't, Mr. Khoo."

"Excuse me for pressing, but an executive could say that just to impress me with her zeal, while her boyfriend was fuming outside."

"Mr. Khoo . . ." Lin-chun rolled a pencil across the desk, darted out a hand, and caught it just as it reached the edge. When her lips parted, Khoo thought it was the most disarming, the warmest smile he'd ever seen. "The fact is, I don't have that many social engagements." Her eyebrows rode up in a self-deprecating grin. "If I had a boyfriend fuming downstairs, believe me, you'd know about it!" Her teeth closed over her lower lip. "Oh. Sorry. That was forward. Please excuse me."

Khoo shook his head in amusement. "I like your frankness. In my last job, no one ever spoke up. I used to call everybody in and say, 'Today we lend off a base three-sixteenths up from yesterday,' and I'd look around, waiting for one of them to put up a hand and ask why. No one ever did."

"And here?"

"Here it's different. Everyone asks questions. They debate. But at the same time, they know their place. What's that little phrase you Taiwanese all use—'the flavor of human feeling'?"

"Yes."

"We're going to do well in Taiwan. The first set of quarterly figures is sitting on my desk. They surpass my expectations by a considerable margin."

"I'm pleased."

"Now, this Mo account. One of the things that struck me was the in-depth research that appeared in your daily case sheets. You obviously saw a lot of the lady."

"Yes. She's a little . . . excuse me, but am I permitted to be frank about a customer of the bank, within these walls?"

"You're no earthly good to me unless you are frank."

"She's a bit flighty. One day one thing, all enthusiastic, the next day quite another project, but the same enthusiasm. She's just twenty-five, of course."

"I see."

"I thought that mightn't be a very good foundation for a new nightclub, so I took care to get to know her properly. In the end I discovered she was quite tough and shrewd. But she needed guidance and she wasn't getting it from her backers."

"Your notes on the backers were very thorough. One name in particular struck me as I read them. Matthew Young."

"He's not exactly a backer."

"No. But he was present at one of the meetings you had with Miss Mo."

"Mr. Young was there." Lin-chun bit her lip and said no more.

Khoo gazed at her inquiringly. "Yes?"

"I got the impression he was rather fond of Miss Mo. And although his comments revealed a very penetrating financial mind—much more acute than hers—I felt that at times he might be allowing that fondness to override his commercial judgment."

"I see. Did he put in an appearance again?"

"Yes, once. If I may remind you, our surveyor required certain work to be done on the club. A few weeks later I went to see how things were coming along. Mr. Young was there with Miss Mo." Lin-chun paused and looked down at her lap. "They were drinking champagne."

"I hope they offered you a glass." Khoo slowly sat back in Siao-ying's chair, pushing himself away from the desk with his feet. "I don't mean to pry," he said at last, "but would I be right in assuming that you and Miss Mo have become friends?"

"I guess you could say that. I think she needs someone like me."

"Because of your employment by the bank, you mean?"

"Yes, that too, but—" Suddenly Lin-chun rose and began to walk up and down the office. Khoo watched her, taking pleasure from the sight. Her hair fell in a no-nonsense "China doll" fringe to frame a rather square, mannish face. As far as Khoo could see, she wore no makeup, but her skin radiated good health and her eyes were bright enough to do without the contrast of mascara. She wore a high-necked white cotton blouse with a vermilion ribbon at the throat, and a deep red, full skirt that stopped a little way below her knees. Her tights were plain, but then so were her legs; stubby and rather muscular, they suggested a love of outdoor sports. Now Lin-chun thrust her hands into her skirt pockets, causing her shoulders to hunch slightly as she moved. She placed one foot carefully in front of the other, like someone walking a tightrope, the gait of a thoughtful person who considers the way ahead before proceeding. Khoo's sort of person.

Lin-chun stopped pacing and turned to face him without taking her hands from the pockets of her skirt. Her stance asserted equality with the person addressed. For some reason this pleased him. "I am afraid," she said flatly, "that Miss Mo needs me to set her off."

"I don't understand."

"You know she is a film actress, a starlet in the making, or so my contacts suggest?"

"Yes."

"And now she is a nightclub singer, part-time."

"Yes. I still don't follow."

"That's all there is to it, really. She likes me. But she enjoys having a plain woman at the same table with her. It's a very old female ploy, Mr. Khoo. My business is to gasp at her and not be a threat."

"Plain? Is that how you see yourself?"

Lin-chun gave him a sharp look, wondering whether he meant to insult. "I'm no beauty, Mr. Khoo," she said, as if defying him to contradict her.

Khoo lowered his eyes and considered. "Well," he said at last, "you put me in an impossible position, Miss Shan. If I agree with you, I am both rude and a liar. But if I disagree, you will think, quite pardonably, that I'm flirting. We shall just have to leave it at that, I think." He stood up; and Lin-chun's wide, rather thick-lipped mouth smiled ruefully.

Khoo busied himself setting the chair straight and pushing it neatly under Siao-ying's desk, but all the while he was covertly studying Lin-chun. True, she was not beautiful—the nose seemed too small for her broad cheeks, and her chin stuck out in a little pink bulge—but she was attractive nevertheless. Hers was a kind, sympathetic face, one that smiled easily. That smile redeemed Lin-chun from being plain—that, and the eyes. She had wonderful, lustrous eyes, doe-shaped and shallow-set—eyes that came at you.

There was nothing pretentious about this girl. She looked a homely sort. Khoo made up his mind.

"You said you had no social engagements this evening. I wonder if you'd come with me to see Miss Mo in action, as it were. If the opportunity presents itself, I'd like you to introduce her to me."

"At the club, you mean?"

"Yes. That was the idea."

Lin-chun's smile remained intact, but Khoo's words threw her into confusion. Her brain had to analyze a thousand facts, impressions, needs, warnings, and then reach a decision, all in the space of a second. She was a junior executive, a woman struggling for a niche in a male-dominated world; the boss was asking her out; rumor said he'd never asked anyone else in the office; there'd be talk; she wasn't dressed for a nightclub; she hated nightclubs; he was so nondescript—well, not really nondescript, but a bit small; his smile was lovely, though; where could she get hold of a decent dress at this hour; pity about the body because the smile *was* sweet; she couldn't; she must; she wanted to; it was out of the question.

Suddenly a vision floated before her eyes: Tsai Zi-yang's face, calm, thoughtful. There had been a time, years in fact, when Lin-chun would have described him as her steady boyfriend. Dependable Zi-yang, the boy next door . . . what would *he* say? But Zi-yang was in the army now, a dedicated soldier. "If you won't agree to marry me, at least enjoy yourself," that's what he'd say. Besides, Zi-yang wasn't her destiny, she knew that.

"You're very kind, Mr. Khoo."

The next word had to be "but." They both knew that. In some extraordinary fashion, however, it came out as "When?"

"Shall we say nine o'clock? My experience of clubs is rather limited, I'm afraid, but I understand they don't get going until at least nine."

The next couple of hours were a frantic time, but somehow Lin-chun managed to be on the doorstep of her parents' house, making last-minute adjustments to her face with a Budlet's powder leaf, when Khoo's taxi pulled up at the curb. Finding their destination, however, wasn't easy. "It's somewhere in Lane Twenty off Swang Cheng Road," she kept insisting; but Lane Twenty contained at least that many nightclubs. "It all looks so different in the dark," she complained to Khoo as they rode up to the fifth floor in the elevator.

A hostess met them at the door and guided them through an

arbor of artificial wisteria to a table on which stood a vase containing a single flower.

"Hi!" Another Chinese girl, very tall, had quickly come over. "I'm Molly." She gestured at the bloom in its slim-necked vase and smiled. Khoo, puzzled, shook his head.

"*Mo-li,*" said Lin-chun. "Jasmine. It's a play on words. All the girls here have names of night-blooming flowers. Evening Fragrance—see?"

Lin-chun ordered a Coca-Cola; Khoo had a Taiwan beer. The tab came with the drinks. Khoo held it close to the candle burning in an orange-colored globe. "Good heavens! All that for a beer and a soft drink!"

Lin-chun stared at her Coke, wishing both it and she would disappear. Khoo seemed to wake up to her embarrassment. "Sorry, sorry," he muttered.

"I'm afraid you don't get out much. I don't either, but these prices are on the low side, I can tell you. They're still establishing themselves, so they need a reputation for reasonableness."

"Of course."

"You get between one-hundred- and one-hundred-fifty-percent markup in a place like this. Perhaps they have to pay off a bank loan." Lin-chun's voice was deadpan. Khoo snuffled in what might have been a laugh.

His eyes were becoming accustomed to the gloom. The Evening Fragrance Club was a large square room on two levels. The sunken portion occupied about two-thirds of the space, with a tiny round dance floor near the stage. The lower level contained small round cloth-covered tables, each carrying its flower in a long-stemmed vase. Beyond the dance floor Khoo could just make out the paraphernalia of a band: synthesizer, drums, guitar, microphone on an extended arm, and beside it a disco turntable. "Very striking," he said.

Lin-chun agreed with him. It was like sitting in a garden. Beyond the bar, next to the stage, stood a floor-to-ceiling plum tree, its branches thick with pink blossoms, while to balance it on the other side of the stage was a cage containing real doves. The out-of-doors ambience seemed further enhanced by the baskets of ivy that hung from bamboo rafters, wooden trellises lining the walls, and strips of coconut-fiber matting on the floors. Green and white were the predominant colors, with touches of yellow here and there to liven things up.

"How's the place doing?" Khoo asked.

"Very well, I'm told."

"You're told . . . you mean you don't believe it?"

"Yes, I do, but—well, you know as well as anyone how things work here, Mr. Khoo. There are always three sets of books: one set for the authorities, one set for the partners, and one set that tells the truth. It's necessary to interpret the figures, isn't it?"

"Yes. But on the basis of what you've been told, how is Miss Mo doing?"

"Better than projected. At this rate, she's heading for break-even in five months instead of seven."

As Khoo watched, three musicians wandered onstage and began to tune their instruments. The far end of the club was suddenly illuminated by a spotlight that flickered unsteadily before coming to rest on the guitarist, who acknowledged the smattering of applause with a wave. But while the beam was still flailing, it crossed a party of young people as they made their way to the big table next to the stage; and at the sight of them, Khoo sat up.

"Regular customer profile," he murmured, without taking his eyes off the newcomers. "Repeats—have you got anything on that yet?"

"It's too early. Management are aiming for the film crowd, of course. The idea is to have a nucleus of people whose idea of a good time is dinner at the Mei Tzu, which is *the* place if you want to see the stars, followed by drinks at the Evening Fragrance. Mei Tzu's only a short cab ride away in Linsen North Road, so it's not such a bad notion."

Lin-chun became aware that her boss wasn't listening. How rude he is, she thought despondently. But then she realized that, to him, this was business; and she resolved to stop thinking of it as an enjoyable night out.

There were five in the party at the big table: two couples and a man on his own. All the men were Westerners, both women were Chinese. "Hey, Rod, what'll you have?" The voice sounded vaguely familiar. Khoo leaned forward, straining to hear; but then the lights dimmed and Lin-chun whispered, "I believe Miss Mo is about to make her entrance."

She was right. The drummer warmed the band up into a fast-paced number, two more spots homed in on the curtains at the back of the stage, the music crescendoed into a crash of cymbals, and the curtains parted to reveal the star of the show.

A single word came into Khoo's mind—voluptuous. The singer was sheathed in a floor-length, long-sleeved dress of alternating diagonal black and white stripes, with a wildly plunging neckline that separated her expansive breasts. She stood with one foot forward, left hand on a hip jutting sideways so dramatically that Khoo felt he could have balanced his glass on it. The other hand held a microphone.

"Thank you. Thank you. Thank you all very much." Her hollow, amplified voice echoed through the club. Somebody must have been experimenting with the volume, for the word *much* was scarcely audible. "The first song of the evening, as always . . . Fragrant Flower!" She held the microphone high above her head, brought it down again with a wide sweep of the arm.

There was some more clapping. Khoo poured beer into his glass and lit a cigarette. He had a weakness for Mandarin love songs.

"Yeh lai hsiang . . ."

Fragrant flower, he hummed quietly to himself, unaware that Lin-chun was studying him from under her eyelashes. She was startled to see him so intent on the music. A trashy love song, and here was her boss, Mr. Facts-and-Figures himself, actually murmuring the words.

Khoo, for his part, couldn't take his eyes off the singer's face. This girl had sex; Khoo didn't waste time with euphemisms like "allure," or "it," or even "sex-appeal." Sex was what she had, oozing from every pore like a mixture of honey and wine. Rose-red lips, long tresses trimmed into wispy kiss-curls, flashing eyes, swaying body, exquisite cheekbones providing the framework for a face of classical Chinese beauty . . . oh yes.

She could sing, too. Each familiar phrase was accorded respect, color, tone. As the song drew to a close, the spot gradually diminished, homing in on first her face, then her mouth . . . until, as the synthesizer embellished the song's closing notes with a couple of runs, the lights all went out. There was enthusiastic applause, in which Khoo and Lin-chun joined.

Khoo smiled at his companion, taking pleasure from the knowledge that he contributed to her enjoyment, and was gratified to see her grin. He felt himself warming to this delightful girl, so refreshing after the hothouse aromas generated by Mei-hua.

"And now . . . something a little more modern, a little more . . . well, thoughtful, should I say?" Mei-hua was playing with the audience, seducing each man individually with tricks and toys. She smiled down at the big table, shaking her head lightly from side to side. "That wonderful Dire Straits ballad . . . 'Love Over Gold.' " She might have been announcing the arrival of the sacraments. "And I would like to dedicate this very beautiful song to someone here in the audience tonight." She lowered her voice to a whisper. "For . . . Matthew."

There were some cries of "Wah!" from the audience and a certain amount of back-slapping from the big table. An English voice from that quarter said, "Shh!"

Six wistful notes tinkled down into the club: the tune of a gamin who's been hurt but doesn't want to show it. Mei-hua drew a deep breath and addressed herself to the ceiling. Her low, husky voice flowed with the melody, not struggling, not fighting it. As she sang, a mist of sweet but unmistakable sadness began to drift through the smoke-blue shadows.

Khoo turned to Lin-chun. "Please excuse me," he murmured. "I'll be back in a moment."

He slipped away, toward the bar and the illuminated graphic of a black male silhouette, legs apart. To Lin-chun's surprise, he bypassed the sign to the men's room and trotted through another door between the end of the bar and the stage. She shook her head in a mixture of amusement and despair. How such a talented banker could be so hopeless in other ways was a mystery to her.

Khoo moved with great confidence, having spent most of the afternoon studying the building plans that he'd discovered in the back of the bank's file on the club. He found himself in a narrow passage lit by a single bare bulb. To his immediate left was a door; behind it, he knew, there ought to be a washroom-cum-storage space. At the end of the corridor was another door leading off to the right, behind the stage. The words of the haunting song penetrated here, only scarcely muffled by the thin partitioning.

Not much time left. She might sing a third song, she might not. Khoo covered the distance to the end of the passage in two strides and laid his head against the door. Silence. He turned the handle very gently, easing the catch back, and nudged the door open a fraction—just enough to see that the room beyond was in darkness.

He entered quickly, closed the door behind him, and reached for the light switch, all without pause. Dressing room, target! Opposite him was a second door that he knew led backstage; he darted across to it and again listened intently. He could hear voices speaking low somewhere on the other side, nearly drowned out by the singer.

The room amounted to scarcely more than a cupboard. A woman's daytime outfit was hanging on a hook behind the door through which he'd entered. A chair stood in front of a melamine shelf underneath the mirror. Toiletries and makeup were scattered all over the place. Around the mirror Mei-hua had pinned dozens of calling cards, invitations, photographs.

Photographs.

One dominated all the rest: a nine-by-twelve studio portrait of a wide-eyed Matthew Young, lips slightly apart. This photo concealed about a third of the tiny mirror. As Khoo approached, he took out his fountain pen, ready for action.

This was no ordinary pen. Khoo had found it in a shop down a Kowloon backstreet. The cap contained a micro-camera designed to be used with ultrafast film: standard equipment for a spy, but also well within the range of new executive playthings. Indeed, the shopkeeper had proudly assured Khoo that he sold dozens every week; they were designed for a mass market. Khoo had carefully kept the receipt as proof of origin.

He rapidly unscrewed the pocket clip from the cap of the pen, revealing a tiny lens aperture. He inserted the clip into the hollow inside the cap and felt around until its point engaged in a recess specially tooled to receive it. He twisted once to set the mechanism, pointed the end of the cap at the photographs on the wall, and pressed the clip home.

One. Two. Three. Khoo cocked his head and listened. Outside the door, someone had moved. To judge from the tempo of the music, Mei-hua must be coming to the end of her song. Quick, quick, quick . . . Four. Five . . .

As the door that led backstage burst open, the music instantly became very loud.

"Who the hell are you?"

Two men, one tall, very thin, say thirty-five, sunglasses dangling from a pocket of his suit; the other younger, jeans and sweater, backless leather driving gloves. Bad news, *very bad news* . . .

"I was waiting to see Miss Mo. I'm a fan of hers."

The tall man stared at Khoo as he screwed the cap back on his pen and started to put it in his pocket. "Give me that!"

Khoo backed against the door through which he'd entered. When the man in the suit reached out to grab the pen, it fell on the floor between them. "Dirty thief," said the man, as he bent down.

"Hold it!" The younger of the pair had seen Khoo's hand start to move toward the door handle behind him. Khoo stared at the knife that had suddenly materialized in the leather-gloved hand. Onstage, the music had stopped, but he couldn't hear any clapping. Mei-hua was making a meal of the last line.

Her voice died away; there followed a second of absolute silence. Then things began to happen. The audience went wild, stamping and cheering. The man in the suit undid the cap of Khoo's fountain pen and peered at the nib. The door behind Khoo opened inward a fraction, the person behind it felt resistance and pushed harder, shoving Khoo into the room so that he bumped up against the man with the pen, dislodging it from his hands.

"Why, Mr. Cheng," Khoo heard someone say behind him. "I suppose you know you're pointing that knife at Miss Mo's bank manager."

The blade disappeared like magic. The man in the suit backed up until he was alongside his companion, looking uncertainly from face to face. "You with him, Miss Shan?"

"He's my *boss*."

On the word "boss," someone wrenched open the door to the stage and shouted, "Get out of my dressing room! Oh . . . why, Lin-chun! Is it you?"

"Good evening, Jacqui."

The tiny room had never been designed to hold five people anyway. But even in all the confusion, Khoo recognized that Mo Mei-hua, or Jacqui as she now mysteriously seemed to be called, had the gift of expanding to fill any available space.

"What is this?" she said; and with cool, calm efficiency Lin-chun took charge. "This," she announced firmly, "is Mr. Khoo King-hey. He is the manager of the bank where I work. He is also your very greatest fan and he was waiting to see you when two of your employees pounced on him. And I must ask you, Jacqui, whether you knew that one of them carries a knife, because that's the kind of thing our bank has to know about."

Khoo somehow managed to fight his way around through a hundred and eighty degrees—no easy feat in such cramped circumstances—and he stared at Miss Shan with undisguised admiration.

"Knife!" The singer held a hand up to the vertical plunge in her dress, fingering its edges. Suddenly she looked pale and in need of protection. "Mat, did you hear that?" She turned her head, but reluctantly, as if afraid to take her eyes off the two bouncers; and Mat Young, standing behind her, spoke up. "Come on, you two," he said quietly in English. "Excitement's over."

The two Chinese looked at each other, calculating. They were tough but small; Mat towered over them and he effectively barred the exit.

"Knife!" Mei-hua breathed hoarsely. "My God, I have to sit

down." Her eyes flashed at the two bouncers, who started to push past Mat.

"Just a minute," he said, taking one of them by the arm. "That pen. Who does it belong to?" He spoke in careful Chinese, taking the words slowly. *"Che chi kangpi shih shui-te?"*

Sullenly the man handed it over to Mat. Mei-hua flung herself down on the chair in front of the mirror and automatically patted a stray lock of hair back into place. "I need a drink," she shouted. "We all need a drink, my God! Whiskey, *now!*"

She swiveled around and flung out an arm at Khoo's chin. "Mr. Khook. What can I say? The shame of this is going to stay with me for a long time."

"Khoo." Lin-chun rested her shoulder against the doorframe and watched the play unfold.

"They are so worried about my safety, you see." Mei-hua looked down at her lap and gnawed her lower lip. "Perhaps you can put yourself in my place for an instant, Mr. Khoo. I need my protectors. Or so my friends insist. Unfortunately, these men tend as a class to be very stupid. Oh! What am I doing? Pease excuse me. Everybody must know everybody. Mr. Matthew Young. *This* is Mr. Khoo and *this* is Shan Lin-chun, oh, dearest—" Mei-hua grabbed one of Lin-chun's hands with both of hers and addressed Mat, switching easily into English: "She's been such an angel. . . . Mat? Are you still with us? Do you two know each other?"

Mat was staring fixedly at Khoo. Mei-hua's face looked innocent, but when Lin-chun examined her more closely, she saw the eyes of an inquisitive lynx.

"I don't think we've met," said Khoo, holding out his hand. As he spoke, Mat turned his head a little to one side and frowned, like someone judging a work of art, testing it for authenticity.

"I rather thought we had. Were you ever in mainland China, Mr. Khoo?"

"Never."

"A place called Chaiyang?"

"I've never visited the mainland."

Mat looked down at Khoo's hand and, very slowly, as if afraid that any sudden movement might cause it to vanish, shook it.

"Might I please have my pen back?" said Khoo.

Mat gave it to him. Mei-hua sighed. "Mr. Khoo," she said, "I really cannot apologize enough." Hardly any trace of the nightclub performer remained; her tone was courteous, very much in the lower register.

"It's entirely my fault," said Khoo. "I had no business entering your room. Miss Shan implied I was a fan of yours, and I am, a very big one, but I'm ashamed to say I don't even have that excuse. I was looking for, eh . . . another room."

Mei-hua looked away, a smile on her face. "Of course," she said diplomatically. "It's not the first time that's happened. The . . . the facilities here are not easily located."

A hostess appeared with a bottle of whiskey and glasses. Mei-hua clapped her hands together. "I'll just put my real-life face on and then I'll come out front and join you. Please!"

Lin-chun caught Khoo's eye, looking for a lead. He nodded at her. "Yes, we'll see you in a moment, then."

"Mr. Young will, I'm sure, be kind enough to take you around the front and find you a good table."

Mat nodded and, with another of those strange looks at Khoo, ushered him and Lin-chun through the door.

Mei-hua faced the mirror and began to remove her makeup. After a moment she stopped, mesmerized by her own reflection. She felt confused. What had happened this evening? She could remember lights, excitement, the audience, power . . . and then . . . Her face, suddenly childlike, twisted itself into a wounded frown. And then came only hassle. She hated hassle. She paid people to protect her from it. She was wasting her money. Darling Mat dealt with everything so beautifully, and she didn't pay him a darned thing.

Mat. She ought to have him around more often. Mei-hua's lips moved soundlessly. He's competent, a real man . . . I need him. She felt herself slipping away. It was a very pleasant world that she entered, much nicer than her actual surroundings. When someone knocked on her door, the word *"Jin!"* exploded from her mouth in a jet of venom.

The two Chinese bodyguards entered the room sheepishly. Mei-hua let them wait for a few moments while she removed the last traces of makeup and fully restored her faltering concentration. "Danny," she said to the younger man, "is it right you let him see the knife?"

"Well, he was—"

"Yes or no?"

"Yes."

"Danny, do you know what I'm going to do if you show that knife to anyone again?" She turned away from the mirror. "Have you ever seen a Triad execution? We had to stage one on the set in Hong Kong once. Even the fake one made me feel sick, and I wasn't the only one, I can tell you. Understand?"

"I understand, Miss Mo."

"Then get lost."

But before they could open the door, Mei-hua said, "Ah-Ping."

The other man turned back. "Miss?"

"Khoo's a Hokkien name, isn't it?"

"Sounds like it."

"What's it in national speech, then?"

Ah-Ping thought for a moment. "*Qiu* would be nearest, I guess."

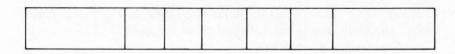

NINE

Daniel Fen studied the ladder with minute care, ensuring that he hadn't overlooked any other unforeseen dangers. But no, it all seemed the same as the first time, forty-eight hours before.

He crouched down and gently dusted the light covering of rubble away from the wires. His information was still incomplete. His employers could not say for certain whether the ladder alarm was hooked up to the main computer. The balance of opinion was against that possibility, however, because the purpose of the caves was thought to be to give access to Ducannon Young *without* tripping security devices.

Still he hesitated. Something was wrong. Two nights previously he had felt sure that other people were in the caves, watching him. No one had challenged him, but still he couldn't quite persuade himself that it was all his imagination.

Fen knew he'd wasted enough time. He cut the wires.

Nothing happened. No alarm bells went off, no lights flashed. He stood up, in a hurry now, and grasped the ladder's handrails.

He began to climb. On the sixth rung his hand met something solid. He rose another step, pushing with his neck and shoulders against the obstacle. It was heavy, but at last he managed to shove it aside. He reached up, feeling around in an attempt to judge the size of the aperture above him. It was covered with something soft, but he had been warned about that and knew it was only a loosely laid carpet.

He emerged into an area of floor that was lower than the rest, a sunken square. Yes, this was the place, all right: a large, open-plan room, slatted blinds at the windows, large French doors to the terrace over there, so the laboratories must be behind him . . .

Suddenly the room was flooded with blinding white light. Fen gasped and vaulted backward into the recess. But before he could recover from the fall, strong arms grasped him around the chest, someone had his feet pinioned, and he was helpless.

When his captors dragged him up, he saw a foreign devil crouched on the lip of the sunken square, holding a piece of plastic-covered card.

"Do you understand English writing?" the devil asked. "It gives my name, see, Peter Reade; and underneath that it says 'Assistant Commissioner of Police,' can you read that, mm?"

Siew Leng had been working in the Young household for two years now. Tonight she outdid herself; the dinner she prepared for the family was even tastier than usual. But then these were exceptional times, requiring particular care: Only Son had come back from Taiwan to visit his parents, and Only Daughter was in bed upstairs, sick. Siew Leng didn't need a fortune-teller to know the Youngs were worried. She could read it on Master's forehead as she served his food.

The old woman's standards were as high as ever. She'd known from day one what Master would expect. His appearance and manner still daunted her, just as they'd done then. Simon Young's wavy brown hair was starting to thin on top, but otherwise he appeared to have aged little. He was immensely tall, six feet four inches, with a broad frame to match. His square jaw spoke of a forceful character, but two semicircular clefts cut deep around the mouth added a redeeming touch of humor to the overall portrait. Usually his eyes were wide open, clear and steady. Tonight, however, the lids drooped half-closed, either from fatigue or out of a desire to conceal what lay behind them. Yet every so often they would rise to emit an icy flicker of light that stirred uneasy memories in Siew Leng, of days when things had not gone quite perfectly. . . . She hurried to finish serving him and withdrew, leaving the family to talk out their troubles in peace.

Simon deftly appropriated a prawn with his chopsticks. "Did you know that more than nine thousand Chinese characters describe or relate to food in some way?" he asked Jinny.

"No, I didn't, and what's more I don't believe it. And don't change the subject." She tapped her husband playfully on the wrist. "I want to know why you spirited Mat away to work when he's supposed to be on vacation."

"It was his choice to go in to the office."

Mat grinned and concentrated on his food. Every so often he glanced at his mother from under his lashes. By God, she's worn well, he thought. How many women go on taking such care of themselves when they're . . . how old? Jinny carefully guarded the secret of her age. "Most Chinese people have three birthdays a year," she used to say. "Not me. I have one birthday every three years!" As Mat watched her eat, sparing and fastidious, he thought it might be true.

Jinny's features, slightly rounded, still looked youthful enough, although the skin of her neck was beginning to show signs of slackness and her hair lacked a little of its former body. The delightful, almond-shaped eyes that all Englishmen seemed to expect from a Chinese wife still glowed with stamina, and the tiny mole at the hairline was just as attractive as ever. Apart from the neck and the hair, only a slight thickening around the waist betrayed approaching middle age.

"How's Diana?" Simon asked.

"Not good," Jinny replied. "She didn't want to come down. She looks ghastly."

"She does," Mat said grimly. "I think she ought to go into hospital, for tests. It's been months now."

"Jinny, have you spoken to the doctor?"

"Yes. He says if it's glandular fever, there's nothing he can do and what she needs is rest. But . . ."

"But what?"

Jinny shook her head. "There's more to it, I'm sure of that. I wish I knew what's really wrong with her."

"What's in your mind?"

"She's been . . . damaged." She held up a hand. "No, don't ask me, I don't know what I mean, either."

Simon ruminated. "Why don't you take her to Penang, if she's still around? You're not due to leave for a week or so yet."

"I will."

Her husband decided it was time to steer the conversation into more cheerful waters. "Something happened today you might appreciate, Mat."

"What's that?"

"Dunny's have bought Sampan Majestic."

"You're kidding!"

"No. Agreed takeover."

"And what is Sampan Majestic?"

Mat turned to his mother. "You remember, Ma; it's that outfit I invested in for the cricket club, at Winchester."

When Jinny's face remained blank, Mat turned to Simon. "You didn't tell her?" he asked incredulously.

"I did not. The letter I got from the school was so unpleasant I never showed it to anyone."

"What is all this about?" asked Jinny.

"Our son invested a chunk of his school's cricket club funds on the Hong Kong stock exchange. He'd been listening to me in the holidays, for once! Sampan Majestic was the name of the company. The shares doubled in value in a fortnight."

"Doubled? But you said the school was unpleasant about it?"

"It was. Not the kind of thing an English gentleman . . . or was it 'boy' they called him—yes, I think it was 'boy'—ought to be doing with club funds." Simon made no effort to conceal the contempt he felt.

The look of puzzlement on Jinny's face refused to budge. "Oh, the English!" she said in exasperation. "I never will understand them." Then she caught sight of her husband's expression, and at once a smile broke through. "Some of them," she said gently, reaching out to take his hand. "Others, well . . . I'm going to sit with Diana. And, darling . . ." She came around the table to cradle him briefly in her arms. "Please don't keep Mat talking long. I want to see him while he's here."

"Tell Di I'll be up in a while," Mat called after her, before turning back to his father. "Dad, I saw Hinchcliffe this afternoon. I got him to show me the Pacific Basin profile he drew up last year."

"What did you think of his figures?"

"As far as my pitch is concerned, they're far too conservative. The guy just doesn't appreciate what the Taiwanese electronics market is all about. In terms of gross expansion, we can do better than that."

"Sure?"

Mat thought it over for a few moments. "Yes," he said at last.

"Quite sure. I drink with more than a dozen Taiwanese who'd be happy to prove it to you."

"What about the wider issues? Politics."

"Oh . . . the mainland-Taiwan thing?" Mat shrugged. "That's a dead duck these days, isn't it? I mean, take Quemoy. The Reds used to shell it, we all know that—but it stopped years ago. The Kuomintang want to turn Quemoy into a holiday resort. Actually, why don't we take a share in that?"

Simon folded up his napkin and tossed it aside. "Because, for one thing, the shelling has started again."

"What did you say?"

"You heard. And the Nationalists have just begun to shoot back."

"But I haven't seen anything about this in the papers." Mat was aghast. "Taipei would scream to high heaven if that happened."

"Taipei's extremely worried. They're short of friends. The last thing they want is publicity, particularly now that they've started to retaliate. It wouldn't take much to persuade the world that the Taiwanese started it."

"But I just can't believe this has been kept secret. What about ships, aircraft? Their crews must have seen something and reported it."

"No commercial ships or aircraft are allowed within miles of Quemoy, for security reasons."

"So how come *you* know what's going on?"

"Because my sources are excellent. It won't be long before stock exchange intelligence gets hold of the story, and then we're in for a very interesting time. I'd guess that what we're faced with at the moment is the beginning of a military buildup to repossession of Taiwan by force."

"What?"

"I'm serious. After years of dithering, the decision's finally been taken."

"I'm sorry, but I don't quite follow this." Mat forced himself to speak calmly. "Are you saying they'd really be prepared to go to war? It's all dead history. Taiwan *exists*! That's been the reality for ages."

"Ah, but what about the other realities? What do you think the Reds wanted Apogee for?"

Mat was silent.

"Anyway, there's no point in getting uptight about it. These things are hardly likely to affect you."

"Affect me? I live there."

"On a somewhat fragile basis, I'd have thought. Do you have permanent residence?"

"No, but—"

"Speak Chinese?"

"Not yet."

"Have dependents there?"

The word *girlfriend* formed itself on Mat's lips and went unuttered. Not for the first time, he found himself regretting his earlier determination to take things slowly with Mei-hua. Months had passed since they'd first met, but he still wasn't quite sure where things were headed. "I'm sorry, but I don't accept that anybody's going to let them repossess Taiwan."

"Who'll stop them?" Simon sounded irritated. "And how are they to go about it?"

"I'd have thought that was obvious. America."

"No, Vietnam was enough for Washington. Besides, there's no longer a mutual defense treaty between the U.S.A. and Taiwan." Simon's voice dropped. "They're not frightened of the Taiwanese," he said quietly, almost to himself. "Suddenly they're not afraid of America or anyone else, they're bold, they're urgent." He grimaced and shook his head decisively. "They've made a friend. An alliance that will shift the balance of power away from the West, render China immune to any criticism. . . . It has to be a Moscow-Beijing pact."

"You're joking!"

"No, I'm not. The people I deal with in Beijing are confident in a way I haven't seen before. They're taking outsize risks. Look at our new bank manager in Taipei."

"Qiu? I'm still not sure it was him."

"I am. I feel it in my bones. I'm coming out there soon; then perhaps we'll know more."

Mat was silent for a moment while he digested the implications. Once the initial shock had worn off, it did not occur to him to doubt the accuracy of his father's analysis; Simon Young's access was unequaled in Southeast Asia. "I assume Mother doesn't know," he muttered.

"That's right! And she mustn't—or she'll be on at me to recall you. I take it you wouldn't want that."

"No."

"So what do you want to do?"

Mat looked up to find his father regarding him with genuine

concern and was reassured. "I don't know. Have you discussed this with Henry Chia?"

"Not yet. But soon I'm going to have to, obviously."

"Right. Can I talk to any of my contacts?"

"Be discreet."

"Of course."

"Then I'd like you to."

"Thanks." He rose. "Da, this isn't the sort of thing that can wait, is it? Mind if I make a couple of calls to Taipei?"

Simon gazed coolly up into his son's face and felt a twinge of parental satisfaction. "What about Di?"

"Why don't you go and sit with her?"

The riposte amused Simon. He was still chuckling when the telephone rang. The two men went into the hall to find Jinny there before them. She handed the receiver to Simon. He listened for a moment, then they heard him cry, "*What?* I'll be right there." He slammed down the phone, picked it up again, and dialed a number. "*Wei!* Get me George Forster . . . to hell with that, tell him it's Simon Young . . . George! Now listen . . ."

Jinny sighed. "Always business in this house."

"Di and I grew up with it," Mat murmured. "We never minded."

"You didn't, perhaps. But somehow I never got used to having my house double as an office." She eyed him intently. "Are you going down the same path?"

"Well, I think I'm a businessman by nature."

Simon replaced the receiver in time to hear his son's words. "That's good," he snapped. "Because we're going out. Make sure you've got your pass. Come on!"

"Oh, no!" said Jinny. "You give our son one week's leave in two years and then you steal him away from his mother in the middle of the night. Simon, please . . ."

"Where are we going?" Mat asked.

"The labs. Peter Reade's caught a fish. A *Taiwanese* shark."

"Oh, my God! Actually in there?"

"Actually in there." Simon turned to his wife. " 'Night, love. Don't wait up."

She sighed, then smiled dutifully, yielding up her cheek like a precious sacrifice to receive his kiss. For a moment it looked as if they were going to leave it at that; but on the threshold Simon turned and came back to take her in his arms. Mat saw their mutual expression, almost akin to pain, and wondered with a pang if he could ever hope to generate such enduring love.

Simon pushed the Rolls along the road that wound down from Repulse Bay as if he were testing it. No trace of his earlier mellow mood remained. "I thought that house was impregnable," Mat remarked. "About the only thing you didn't do was shoot the workmen when they'd finished and bury them in unmarked graves."

"Perhaps I should have done." Simon swerved to avoid a bus. "No, it's not the contractors' fault, it's mine."

"Why, in heaven's name?"

"That place was all mapped out, tunnels everywhere. When the government handed it over to us, our first instinct was to concrete them in. We did it, but we left this one cave. That one we never did hook up to the computerized security system."

"I still don't see what possessed you to—"

"Well, then, you're pretty damn stupid! If you were being funded by two bloody governments, both of 'em liking nothing better than to poke their noses into your affairs, you'd want a secret way in and out, too. How d'you think we got the new microchips to Luk without Beijing and London tramping in to bag their share?"

"As bad as that?"

"Worse! You realize, of course, that Reade has the key to our security system?"

"I certainly didn't."

"His people have a VDU the same as ours, they monitor everything."

"Looking over our shoulder, you mean?"

"That's right. There isn't one lock in there that Peter Reade can't open." Simon grunted. "Yes, there is, though. I didn't give him the key to my lavatory. Here we are. . . ." Simon sped up the last few yards of the steep drive to the Swedish-designed house on the side of Ak Tai To Yan. "By the way, be sure to remember who we're dealing with. Reade's Secret Intelligence Service as well as Royal Hong Kong Police."

They found Reade in what had been the previous owner's living room. He stood up to greet them, nodding easily at Simon and shaking hands more formally with Mat. Reade was just as Mat remembered him: hair (not much of it) carefully brushed so as to cover the bald patch; trim mustache; big belly, only half concealed by a well-cut gray suit.

"There he is," he said, gesturing toward a small lounge area on the other side of the floor recess, where Fen sat with a policeman at each shoulder. Simon stormed over to a red telephone. "Head of security, here, now!"

While they waited, Simon leaned against the wall, tapping his foot on the carpet. The door opened. Simon came off the wall like a rocket.

"Come in here, Ah Tok!" he shouted. When the guard hesitated, Simon was on to him in two strides. He grabbed the Chinese by the lapel of his jacket and heaved him bodily across the floor to Fen's chair. "Do you see that, Ah Tok?"

"I can see him, Mr. Young."

"And how do you explain his presence here?"

"He came up through the cave, sir."

"And how was the cave guarded?"

"Infrared gate, electric contacts on the ladder."

"Contacts?" Simon was taken aback. The security chief, realizing it, seized a slight advantage. "A month ago I was reviewing security. I decided infrared wasn't good enough for the cave, so I put juice on the ladder." Ah Tok gestured at Fen. "He should have triggered an alarm."

"Why the hell didn't he, then?"

"He must have cut the wires. They weren't linked to the main-frame."

"I see. I want a full report on my desk by eleven o'clock tomorrow morning—*this* morning, I should say. That's all."

Ah Tok withdrew, glad of the respite. Mat tossed his head. Simon saw it. "What's bugging you?" he snapped.

"Well . . . he monitored the defenses on his own initiative, then he improved them."

"So?"

Mat glanced warningly at Reade. "Nothing. Sorry."

Simon redirected his wrath against the Assistant Commissioner. "Who is this shyster?"

"Taiwanese penetration specialist by the name of Fen."

"Dammit, Peter, he's the third Taiwanese we've caught snooping around here in the last six months."

"They have a reputation for being good at this kind of thing. I'm going to get rid of him now, but first I need to know whether you've seen him before."

Both men said no.

"Right. Sergeant, take him down to Gloucester Road and book him."

Mat waited until the door had closed behind Fen; then he asked, "Can you find out who that guy was working for?"

"Unlikely. We're following up leads, but we won't get any-where, not with the Taiwan angle."

"Why not?"

"Britain doesn't have any diplomatic links with the Republic of China, as I'm sure you know. We can't just telex Taipei and ask them to do an investigation." Reade shook his head despondently. "In a sense, I'm not bothered about Fen at all; we stopped him. What worries me far more is that your security's been breached."

"There are limits to every budget, Peter." Simon sounded sulky. "We can't hope to plug every last nook and cranny."

"Hope to? Or want to?"

"What d'you mean?"

"I was wondering if perhaps you liked the idea of a bolt-hole, that's all. A way in and out that I couldn't monitor, because I wasn't told anything about it and your precious computer control system didn't have it on circuit."

Simon snorted. "You're crazy."

"Am I?" Reade hesitated. "I'll tell you the whole story. We caught Fen because we had an anonymous tipoff. He first came in two nights ago, with us on his tail. He was floored by Ah Tok's new gadget on the ladder. We reckoned he'd be back, so we let him run, hoping he'd lead us somewhere, but we lost him. We've been thinking about the setup in the caves ever since. And we don't like it."

"I'll see they're blocked up as soon as I can get around to it."

"Good." Reade rose to his feet. "I'd like a copy of Ah Tok's report, please."

"Good night, Peter."

When Reade had left, Simon went across to the sideboard and poured himself a whiskey. "Want one?"

"Yes, please. No ice."

Simon carried the drink across to where his son was sitting, and lowered himself down next to him with a grunt of tiredness. The red phone rang. "Oh, get that, will you?" he said. Mat obliged. "It's George Forster. He's just arrived."

Moments later the door opened to admit the Ducannon Young Group's finance director. Forster was short and tubby, in his sixties, approaching retirement. A man his age could do with-out being awakened in the middle of the night and hauled out of bed. The deep black crescent moons under his eyes made him look exhausted.

"Pour yourself a drink, George, and come over here."

Simon filled him in on the night's events. For a moment he sat in silence, then he shook his head. "I wonder if Japan isn't behind this."

"No. Everything leads back to Taipei." Simon sighed. "All we can do is wrap this project up as fast as possible and get the hell out. Mat, tell me, what's your best assessment of Lennie's progress?"

"He's nearly there."

"He has *got* to do better."

"Coming back to Fen," Mat said thoughtfully, "I suppose it's just possible he's working for Japan."

"No. This isn't *industrial* espionage at all. The Taiwanese government are behind it, after Red China's latest toy. Well, it was always a risk and we decided to take it. . . . We've got to sit on what happened here tonight; Beijing must never, never know."

"Agreed," Mat said. "We'll have to pull Apogee out of Hsinchu, though. Tonight wouldn't be too soon."

"Right."

"But that's one hell of an expensive decision to take on the strength of a hunch."

"It's more than a hunch, now. Remember how the army busted us in Hsinchu last summer? I never did find out what was behind that; everyone clammed up on me. That's why I'm going over there myself, to see what I can find out. George, do you remember Li Lu-tang?"

"That chap in the old Bureau of Information and Statistics? Would he talk to you?"

"He might. We used to be buddies, in a way. Ducannon Young provided work for a lot of Taiwanese in the early fifties, long before their economic miracle got going. Li was a young man then, but I doubt he'd forget. I couldn't trace him in the summer. He was on leave, they told me."

"Just a minute," Mat put in. "What is this bureau? The only one I know about is called simply the Bureau of Statistics. It's run by the Executive Yuan."

"Li's bureau was something else. He was a spy, you see. The genuine article."

"Good grief! Are you sure?"

"As sure as I can be. Uncle David used to sell him information about Red Chinese trade here in Hong Kong, which is how I got to meet Li in the first place."

"I don't know." Mat shook his head. "You say the Taiwan government's behind an attempt to steal the Apogee program. I think you're wrong."

Forster, seeing that Simon was about to explode, quickly intervened. "Why do you say that, Mat?"

"Because if the government really knew what was going on at Hsinchu, it would have seized everything in a blaze of publicity and put an end to the project."

"How long have you lived there, Mat? Eh?"

"Simon, I think he may have a point."

"Well, I don't. The explanation's perfectly simple, George. The Taiwanese know something, but they don't know it all, not yet. That's *why* they're spying, goddammit!"

Mat held up his hands with a smile. "Okay, okay . . . sorry. But you asked how long I've lived there, and that's just the point I'm trying to make—*I* live there. I've lived there long enough to have formed a few ideas of my own."

"What's that supposed to mean?"

Mat darted a glance in the direction of Forster, then decided what the hell. "I mean that for years you didn't exactly inspire me with confidence in my own theories. Okay, fine, I understand how youngsters can't be allowed to think they know everything. But if that's what you believed, then you shouldn't have sent me to Taipei." His voice hardened slightly. "Or was it just dynastic empire-building?"

"Of course it wasn't. But be realistic. What do you know about the Taiwanese government? What does *anybody* know—they're so secretive about everything they do."

" 'Anybody' includes you, then."

"At least I've been around Southeast Asia for longer than your lifetime."

Mat, acutely aware of George Forster's unhappy expression, drew in a hard breath and made himself count to five. "No contest," he said at last. "But let's assume your hunch is right. Why should this Li character even let you in the office, never mind talk to you?"

"I quite agree."

"Then why—?"

"Because he's our last chance, that's why! What would you do, then? You and your wide-eyed passionate devotion to the cause of so-called freedom."

Mat clenched his fists. There were so many things he wanted to say, so many irrefutable arguments siphoning up to his lips, but he couldn't find the words. Deep inside, he knew why Simon had sent him to Taipei: so that he might become his own man. But

[109]

then the first chance he had to show he'd actually learned something . . .

The telephone bell shattered the tension. Simon subjected his son to a last withering look and went to answer it. "Yes! . . . Yes, operator, I'll take it, I'm Simon Young."

In the pause that followed, he put his hand in his pants pocket and began to walk around in nervous circles. "Hello? Henry Chia . . . Henry, what can I do for you? Yes, I'm sorry, I've been unobtainable all evening. . . . No. What's that?"

George Forster put an arm along the back of his chair and turned his head so that he could look at Simon, who had suddenly stopped circling.

"Oh no. Oh no."

Mat stood up and slowly went across to stand by his father. Simon's face was taut with strain, his gaze intent on the middle distance.

"All right, I'm coming over. Get the lawyers working on it first thing tomorrow. Oh, and Henry—spend a few minutes holding Lennie Luk's hand, will you? 'Night."

He replaced the receiver. "Henry says the Bureau of Investigation have sent a written notification of referral to the procurator's office. They're going to prosecute, after all."

Mat was horrified. "That old customs thing?"

"Yes. Henry says they've got an A-one case against us. Our people have been cutting too many corners."

George Forster stood up. "Well, that's tough, but I don't think it's the end of the world. We plead guilty, pay the fine, and get on with our lives."

"No."

"Why not?"

"Because apparently there has to be a hearing in the District Court, even if we plead guilty. And there isn't court time available until late January."

"Well? I still don't see—"

Simon drew a deep breath. "They've managed to get an order out of the Executive Yuan, stopping all work at Hsinchu until after the hearing."

"*What?*"

"We have just under four weeks to produce Apogee for the Red Chinese, in full working order and ready to roll." Simon had been staring at the floor. Now he raised his eyes to Mat's. The expression on his face was murderous. "And those bastards you love so much have just closed us down!"

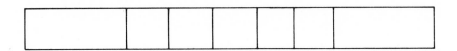

TEN

Mat and Lennie Luk shared a small flat on the fourth floor of an apartment building off Chien Kuo North Road. It was modern, with one and a half bathrooms—as the Chinese called anywhere that had a shower stall as well as a real bath—and because it faced onto a nearby overpass, it had come relatively cheap when Ducannon Young bought it in the late seventies. The flat had the additional advantage of being more or less equidistant from the office to the southwest, and most of Taipei's nightlife to the north.

This evening, however, as Mat emerged from the elevator and fumbled for his key, he felt far too exhausted to contemplate exploring the city's night spots. He'd returned from leave to find a mound of accumulated paperwork and the office in turmoil on account of the Hsinchu shutdown; all he wanted now was sleep.

He twisted the key in the lock, but the door wouldn't budge. Mat pressed the bell: one long, two shorts, and another long. At first, nothing happened. Then he heard footsteps in the apartment.

"Yes?" said a muffled voice.

"It's me—Mat."

There came the sound of bolts being drawn back. Lennie Luk slammed the door shut as soon as Mat had stepped over the threshold. "Sorry," he said sheepishly.

"Trouble?"

"Yes. Want a drink? I do."

Mat took off his overcoat and followed his friend along the corridor. It wasn't like Lennie to be the first to suggest a drink.

Lennie unscrewed the cap from a bottle of whiskey and poured two glasses. "There's a problem, a real biggie. I went across the road to Fatty Choy's for a meal."

"And?"

"I got approached. There's this guy I've seen in there before, quite a lot; I guess he must've seen me too, I don't try to hide."

"He spoke to you?"

"Yeah. He tried to get all friendly."

"Chinese?"

"Uh-huh. He was quite frank—said he worked for someone who'd pay a fortune for Apogee. Just like that."

"Christ! He actually used the name Apogee?"

"Yes. He said he worked for a business consortium here in Taipei, and did I want to talk?"

"What did you say?"

"I said I hadn't any idea what he meant, and told him to push off."

"Did he?"

"No. He started to get heavy. Do you know what he said? He said, 'You live on the fourth floor, you could fall off that balcony one day, it's happened before.'"

Mat gaped at him. "I don't believe this."

"Well, it's true. I paid and left straightaway. I thought he'd follow me, and I was all ready to grab a taxi, you know? But when I looked back, he'd disappeared. What do you think I should do?"

Mat thought hard. "We'd better tell Rod Haines. He's the security officer, he has to know. And my father, when he comes over next week. Apart from that, keep our mouths shut."

"That's what I thought, only I didn't want to talk to Haines before checking with you."

Mat treated his friend to a thoughtful survey. The Chinese was wearing his usual old, stained jeans, open-neck shirt, and a sweater. He hadn't shaved for some days. His eyes, still bright, were sunken; and this was a much slimmer scientist than the one Mat had seen that night in Hsinchu, six months ago.

"I want you to be totally honest with me," Mat said suddenly. "Is there any point to what you're doing here?"

"Point?"

"For years you were part of a team. We had a dozen people working on Apogee. Now there's only you, with a few hours of part-time help here and there. Are we kidding ourselves when we say you can bring it in on time by fiddling around in a bedroom?"

"All I'm doing now is programming, programming, programming. Ironing out the bugs. That part always came down to me. No one else has my brain circuits. And I can do my work here or anywhere." His smile was sour. "Don't you remember how I learned that, back in Hong Kong?"

"True. Even during the school holidays, all you ever wanted to do was play with that computer Dad let you have." Mat yawned, suddenly too tired to prolong the discussion. "Staying in tonight?"

"I'm going out with Selina later. Apogee's only a week from completion, and I really need a break."

"I agree. Right now, the best thing is for you to go off and enjoy yourself. Watch out for that guy who spoke to you, though."

"I will."

"Hey!"

Lennie turned back in the doorway. "What?"

"I'm really glad. About the progress, I mean. You're fantastic."

A few minutes later Mat was just taking off his shirt when the entry-phone buzzed. Selina, no doubt. From the sound of water running, he knew that Lennie must still be in the shower. "I'll get it," he called.

But it wasn't Selina. Instead, a husky voice breathed in his ear, "Hel*lo*, Mat dearest. Have you room for a little one in your delicious den of vice?"

"Mei-hua! Of course, how wonderful—come on up."

Mei-hua was holding a paper bag, from the top of which peeped a foil-covered cork. As Mat opened the door she thrust it against his chest, using it to push him inside like a truncheon-wielding policewoman. When she had him against the wall she paused, considering; then she lifted herself up on the tips of her toes and planted a gentle kiss on his right cheek.

"Thanks."

She lowered herself and tilted her head, studying him, then reached up again. "This other cheek looks jealous."

[113]

She wore a powder-blue tailored jacket that stopped just below her waist, and a pleated cream skirt with matching patent-leather shoes; no jewelry. A picture of clean, elegant simplicity. He laughed, suddenly feeling less tired. "Why champagne?"

"Christmas. It's only a few days away."

"Christmas! Here in Taiwan?"

"And why not? There are lots of Christians in Free China. Did you know our President and his wife are Christians?"

"Yes, I knew that."

"And I am, too."

When he merely laughed, taking her words as a joke, she twisted the bottle and poked him sharply in the chest with it. "I had a good convent education," she said. "And don't you dare forget it. How else do you think I learned my *wonderful* English?"

He took the bottle from her, laughing, and stripped away the bag. "Hm. Laurent Perrier, eh? Pink! Did you really go to convent school?"

"Oh yes. The Wise Heart Girls' High School. My mother was very particular."

"I'd like to meet her sometime."

Mei-hua's teasing glance faltered for a second. "Don't change the subject. What about you—didn't you have a religious education, too?"

"Yes, of a sort. They called it 'muscular' Christianity, which meant you had to take cold showers and play rugby. I loathed it. I studied Buddhism in my spare time, with the result that my friends thought I was dotty. Here, let's get the cork out."

Lennie chose that moment to emerge from the bathroom wearing nothing at all. Mei-hua looked his naked body up and down with an expression of combined shock and appraisal. Lennie acknowledged her with a vague smile. "Hi," Mei-hua murmured as he reached the bedroom door.

No reply. The door closed.

"Who *was* that?"

"That? Oh, er, that was Lennie Luk. Sorry."

"Is he all right?"

"He's fine. It's just that, well . . ."

"Yes?"

"That look on his face means he's thinking. He kind of lives in a world of his own." Faced with the impossible task of explaining Lennie to a stranger, Mat gave up.

Mei-hua wandered into the tiny living room, with Mat following. "So this is a bachelor pad," she murmured. "Where are all the women?"

"We keep them in cupboards. It's tidier that way."

Lennie, now respectably dressed in jacket and tie, put his head around the door. "All right if I take the car tonight?"

"Help yourself."

Mei-hua had been circling, hands behind her back like an inspecting officer. But now the sound of Lennie slamming the front door seemed to operate as a kind of signal. She switched off the overhead light, leaving the sitting room swathed in the soft glow from a table lamp. When Mat sat down at one end of the sofa, she moved across to take the other, but still she did not quite relax. She extended one arm along the back of the sofa and continued her survey as though she were alone.

"It's very . . . oh, I haven't got the English words for this room. Nothing matches. Do I offend you?"

"No. I like outspokenness. I suppose you're right. We just bought things when we needed them."

"I can see that. Yet you have some good ideas. White walls, white ceiling, plain and simple. Yes, fine. And the carpet is just right; cord wears well. But the furniture . . ." She tossed her head. "Mat, you can't put a purple chair in this room. And varnished pine coffee tables are a mistake anywhere. Why don't you throw me out—so rude I am."

But instead of throwing her out, he stretched a hand along the sofa until his fingers made contact with the tips of hers. For a moment she let him toy with her hand, but then she slid it away and Mat leaned back, disappointed. "You still haven't told me why you bought champagne."

"I said—Christmas."

"I don't believe you."

"Oh, you're so boring, you know that? Well, all right. Some-body's been nominated for a Golden Horse Award. Best support-ing actress."

He clapped his hands together. "Wonderful! Will you win? What are your chances?"

She shrugged. "The film world's a funny one." Her voice was sober, almost harsh. "It's everything you've ever heard about, every last little scandal you've read in a magazine and then a whole lot more." She glanced at him. "I've told you, don't be too starry-eyed about me. This"—she ran the backs of her hands down her body from shoulders to knees in a graceful gesture—"is what counts."

"I suppose so."

"I *know* so. Did I tell you how the studios always make three versions of each film—cold, warm, and hot?"

"No."

"Cold for straitlaced Malaysia and Brunei. Warm for Singapore. And wow! *Hot* . . . for everywhere else. It's no good trying to cover up anything when they're shooting the hot version."

There was a long silence. Then Mat said, "Do you think you'll ever marry? Have a home and children?"

She stood up and walked across to the windows, hands once again clasped behind her back. "I don't know," she said to her reflection in the glass. Then she turned. "I want all that. But if I marry, I intend to stay married." She was staring intently at him now. "It will take a quite exceptional man to stay with me."

"Exceptional?"

"Someone who doesn't mind if I'm away from home a lot. Who knows that I'm putting my body up for viewing, surrounded by men, being offered . . . wonderful things. Who understands the film business, and the compromises it requires. And who still loves me enough to say, 'Go on, succeed, climb, outrun everyone.' "

"You want everything, in other words."

"Yes."

"Then you are indeed talking about a very special man. Have you found him?"

She studied Mat for several moments from her position by the window; and while he waited for her answer, he felt his cheeks suffuse with blood.

"I might have," she said at long last. "But . . . he has never said anything. He is very gentle, you see. He does not . . . *push* me, in the way so many others do. He is kind. He gives. So far, he does not take. And I . . . I have been keeping him at a distance, I must confess."

Mat's heart was thumping in a patternless tattoo. "Maybe he needs to be sure of himself."

"Do you think so? Tell me, then"—she began to walk toward the sofa—"what more does this man need, to be sure?"

Before she could reach him, he had risen and taken her in his arms. At the last moment she seemed to stumble, throwing everything that went to make up Mo Mei-hua onto his shoulders. For a second he wondered if he could possibly bear such a weight of troubles. Then he kissed her mouth.

At last she cupped his cheeks in her hands and pulled away. "I'll get the wine."

He allowed himself to be pushed gently down onto the sofa, knowing he ought to be overjoyed. But he wasn't, and he couldn't fathom why perfection wasn't quite perfect. The most ravishing girl in Taipei at last was his. After so many months spent patiently waiting for a sign, of standing in line with countless other eligible men, his strategy had finally paid off. Yet there was something. . . .

Suddenly he knew. It was such a trivial thing that his mind hadn't let it intrude into the forefront of consciousness, hadn't quite made the connection that was necessary if he was to admit that in the second before their lips met, her breath had smelled rank.

She was moody, volatile. Sometimes she couldn't bear to be touched. Mat knew in his subconscious that he ought to piece these findings together and make a pattern. But he dared not.

Mei-hua brought in the bottle. She poured two glasses of champagne and lay back with her head on Mat's chest, one hand inside his shirt, picking tenderly at hairs.

"I don't know," he heard her say.

"What?"

"If this is right. For either of us."

"It's right. Real love always is."

She raised her head and rested her chin on one clenched fist, so that she could look into his eyes. "You're good for me. I've felt that since the day we met. But how can I be good for you?"

"Why not?"

She hesitated, so long that when at last she did speak, he knew she wasn't giving the real answer. "I'm Eurasian."

"So am I."

"I keep forgetting. You're half Chinese, too; only you hardly look it. Not like me." She was silent for a while. "You're a businessman. Safe. Respectable. I don't want to make trouble for you."

"But you wouldn't!"

"Sure? Your career doesn't tie in with mine. I've never talked much about my family background. . . ."

Before she could speak again, he kissed her. The taint was so slight he could almost ignore it. Now it was his turn to slip a hand beneath her blouse, feeling the firm breasts under their filmy brassiere. She gasped and chewed her lower lip; her eyes flickered, suddenly unsure. Another wild, unworthy thought slithered into Mat's mind, corrupting the moment: How many men would give their eyes to do this? And then again . . . how many already had done it? His hand became more insistent. While he pulled her mouth down on his, the free hand wandered around to her back and began to unclip the bra. As it came free, Mei-hua shuddered.

"You've done that before," she murmured.

"Would you be here if I hadn't?"

"No. Schoolboys aren't Mei-hua's taste."

"And convent girls aren't for Matthew."

How many?

He slid his hand around to the front of her body, relishing the heavy feel of her breasts as he weighed them, allowing his fingertips to brush against the nipples. Her lips parted, her breath came and went in little gasps.

Is this how it was for all of them? Don't ask; never ask. . . .

He brought his left hand from behind her neck and slipped the blouse off her shoulders. With the lamp behind her, all he could see was a series of undulating curves, tantalizing hollows. He levered himself up against the cushions and enclosed her left nipple with his lips, wondering at the force of the tremor that ran the length of her body. Her skin was warm, fabulously smooth; he had never touched such wondrous skin. He moved his mouth to the right nipple. "In case it got jealous. Like my cheeks."

"Don't stop," she hissed. "My God, *don't stop!*"

She sounded as if she were on the point of choking. Mat stood up. For an instant her eyes widened in anger; but then he bent to put one arm under her knees and the other around her shoulders, and the next second she was riding up. . . .

But no, it wasn't quite a hundred percent, not for him. Too much cerebral activity, not enough raw instinct. Would the door to his bedroom be open, or would he have to put her down? What had she been eating, to make her breath so odd? *How many other men had done this?*

Fortunately, the door was ajar. While she lay and watched, he switched on the bedside light and began to undo his shirt buttons, kicking off his shoes at the same time. His fingers seemed clumsy, as if half-paralyzed. He sat down on the edge of the bed. Mei-hua's blouse and bra had vanished, back in the living room; now he slipped off her shoes, skirt, and tights, leaving only a skimpy triangle of cotton above which a few curls of hair protruded. He bent down to kiss them while his fingers hooked themselves through the sides of the panties, and Mei-hua sat up, using her hands to stroke her pendulous breasts against the sides of his head.

When he pulled the cotton triangle gently down her thighs, Mei-hua lay back on her elbows and raised herself just enough to help him. He took off his trousers and made as if to slip into bed beside her, but she stopped him.

"No." Her voice was thick. "No you don't, you bastard." It might have been love, it might have been hate. "You've seen all there is to see of me. Now I want it, too. I want to see you."

He hesitated. Oriental girls were not like this. They were demure, shy, in constant need of reassurance, persuasion. This woman was different.

This woman was unique.

He stepped out of his underpants and stood by the side of the bed.

"Turn around," she said hoarsely. "My God." Very loud. "My God . . ." Very soft. "Where did you get . . . where does a body like that *come* from?" She fingered the curly hairs on the insides of his thighs and lifted her eyes to his. For the first time he saw doubt written there, doubt and maybe apprehension.

"You are my first Western boy ever." He could scarcely catch the words. "The very first."

Mat switched off the light.

Mei-hua was the first to wake. She pulled a chair up to the window and sat there, peering expressionlessly through the gap in the curtains at the colorless morning outside. After a while, two tears forced their way onto her cheeks and dropped suddenly into runnels as others followed, adding their weight of sorrow. She did not move. She made no sound.

She felt sick, but that was usual, first thing. Today there was more to it than the mere physical discomfort her addiction involved. Mei-hua knew the performance she had to put on, had it all worked out inside her head; but for some reason this morning she only half believed in it. She didn't want to go through with the rest of the production. And she felt so screwed up that she wanted to scream.

Mat awoke. "Mei-hua," he breathed. No reply. She continued to stare out the window, keeping her back to him. Mat came to stand over her chair. He placed his hands on her shoulders and gave them a squeeze.

"Don't!"

For the first time he became aware that she was crying. "Why, what's the matter?"

"Things . . . crawling over me, I . . ." She shuddered and fell silent. "I must go."

[119]

"Go? But you can't just . . . leave. Not after . . ."

Mei-hua picked up her skirt and started toward the door. When Mat grabbed her she stopped dead, looked at the ceiling, and sighed. "You're hurting my arm."

He relaxed his grip. "You're hurting more than my arm."

"It won't work, Mat. Best if we part now. Say goodbye."

"You're crazy!" His voice softened. "Was it so bad last night?"

She shook her head, as if the notion amused her.

"Then why?"

"Because!" she snapped. "Because . . . of that." She held up her arm so that the hand came to rest in front of Mat's astonished eyes.

"You're shaking," he said, and at once felt foolish for having stated the obvious.

"Yes." Mei-hua's voice was brisk, businesslike, and at long last Mat faced up to the fact that he already knew what she was going to say. "That's how it is, first thing in the morning. You stay awake most of the night, you wake up in a foul mood and you shake. God, how you shake! And you snivel till you think you're going to drown. And I'm still at the *fun* stage! It gets worse. And now, if you'll excuse me . . ."

He'd seen the signs, God knows he had. "Cocaine . . . wouldn't it have been easier to talk about it yesterday? Before we—"

"Yes. *Yes!* Why the *shit* do you think I'm in such a foul mood, you . . . you *idiot*!" She took a deep breath and got a grip on herself. "Listen, . . . I'm all confused. I am a very confused person, I always have been. I liked . . . like you a lot. You were different from the rest—you didn't spend the whole time trying to push me into bed, for one thing. An affair with you looked pretty good."

Mat felt his legs weaken. He sat down on the bed. "And doesn't it still?"

"An affair, yes!" She turned on him, her eyes flashing. "I wanted an affair! And you gave me . . . something different."

He stared up at her. "What did I give you. *Say it!*"

"Oh, for God's sake! You gave me love!"

"But then I didn't realize . . ." He seized her roughly. "Suppose I do love you—enough to do something about it? There are doctors who understand these things. You can be cured, if only you want to be."

As she looked down at him she was smiling, not a happy smile. "How much do you know about cocaine?"

"Not much."

"Oh, don't look so . . . so *shocked*! All right, I've been a real bitch to you. Not that I care. It does that, you know. It changes a person. Last night was a mistake. I wanted an affair and I got love; and love, to someone like me, is just a stupid dream."

She snatched up her blouse and panties. He made no attempt to stop her.

"I was seduced at nineteen. By a pusher." Her voice lacked all emotion; she might have been reading the phone book. "That was six years ago. I've had it under control for a long time, but the control doesn't last, and it's getting worse every month."

She paused at the bedroom door. "I'm going now. Don't stop me, don't call me, don't try to see me." She lowered her gaze, suddenly blinded by tears, and stumbled into the hallway. He thought that her last words to him were: "Don't forget me!" But he couldn't be sure.

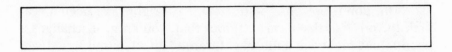

ELEVEN

Above the mantel, in a blackwood frame, was a sheet of paper bearing hurried-looking Chinese calligraphy and the smudged red imprint of the kind of carved seal known as a chop. The present occupant of the house (he would modestly have disclaimed any suggestion that he owned it) was immensely proud of this relic; he used to show it off to all his guests as one of the few surviving remnants of Mao Zedong's writing still in private hands. At first the readers stood before it in reverence, but then, as they began to decipher the ideographs, their faces would crease into frowns and the host would roar with laughter at a joke that never seemed to pall. The precious revolutionary fragment was a laundry list.

A door opened and Sun Shanwang quickly averted his eyes from the frame. As Wen Meng, the Chairman's principal secretary, prepared to usher him in, he had time to murmur, "Sorry I'm late."

"I don't think they've missed you. Bridge."

"So it's a gang of four?"

"Ha-ha!"

Sun drew a long breath through clenched teeth and marched into the room beyond.

Immediately opposite him stood a table covered with green baize. Four men sat around it. Apart from the vicinity of the table, brilliantly illuminated by an overhead lamp suspended on a pulley, the room was in near darkness. Sun found himself staring straight at what looked like a disembodied white face with two shadows where the eyes should be—a face that alternately appeared and vanished according to the movements of the man sitting opposite with his back to the door. As Sun watched, the spectral face smiled in triumph; he heard a card slapped down; groans went up.

The white apparition made noisy use of the spittoon beside his chair and spoke. "Losers pay."

More groans. "Come on, no excuses. It's time to settle!"

"I'm too old for this," Sun heard a voice grumble from out of the gloom.

"Then you're too old to command the air force, you fraud. Resign! Resign or crawl."

The white ghost's partner did not move; but the two men on either side slowly levered themselves off their chairs and knelt down.

"You go first."

"No, you."

"Aiya!"

Then, to the accompaniment of exhortations from the ghost, one of the losers proceeded to crawl under the card table until he emerged, wheezing and cursing, at the far end. His partner, less agile, followed suit. Sun looked on in fascination as the flimsy table jolted and heaved. Only when both vanquished partners were seated again did he move forward. "Sorry I'm late, Chairman."

The ghost raised a hand in greeting, lifting it high above his shoulder. "You're not late. We had to beat these fellows first. Put the light on, Shanwang."

Sun complied. When he turned back to the table, he saw that the losers were avoiding his gaze. There was some problem of face here, but not much. The five men in this room, all survivors of the Long March, had endured too much together during the bitter years to be embarrassed by just about anything in one another's presence. All of them, including the present Chairman of the People's Republic of China, had crawled under the card table at one time or another; and in the years before power descended on them like a healing salve, each had been forced to do much worse than that.

The Chairman genially indicated that it was time for two of his guests to leave. Qi Mingzong and Lin Hong, respectively commander of the air force and admiral in charge of China's fleet, made their farewells. The Chairman ushered them out, chaffing them on the result of their game.

"Come, let's make ourselves more comfortable," said the Chairman as he returned. He no longer seemed a ghost, but instead a short, slim, elderly man with twinkling eyes and a lively smile. Sun sat down beside him on a sofa. While they settled themselves, lighting cigarettes, he stole covert glances at his two companions and wondered just how much of a fight he had on his hands.

The Chairman. An enigma, always an enigma. In a country where predictability was a cardinal virtue, he had somehow managed to win by always doing the unexpected. Now in his eighties, a chain-smoker all his life, he still seemed possessed of extraordinary vitality, a zest for life to match his undimmed intelligence. Beneath thinning hair combed straight back from his forehead, he had the face of a tenacious little pug dog, or so Sun always thought: that jutting chin, those piercing eyes, one minute so warm and friendly, the next empty. His mouth was thin-lipped, potentially severe, equally good for a smile or a sentence of death. "A needle wrapped in cotton," Mao Zedong had called him.

Sun turned his attention to Wang Guoying: aged sixty-four, Marshal of the People's Revolutionary Army and successor to the legendary but decrepit Yang Dezhi as chief of staff. He was tall for a Chinese, with a face that might have been good looking were it not for the goiter that disfigured the left side of his neck, and a tendency to patchy baldness. When he opened his mouth to speak he revealed two gold teeth glittering dully among blackened stumps. Wang, Qi, and Lin together were the three "young tigers" of military might, all graduates of Guanzhou's elite Whampoa Academy, a triumvirate sharing the same interlocking network of personal connections.

The Chairman lit a Panda cigarette. "All right," he said. "I'm going to die soon. What are you men doing to recover Taiwan for me before I do, eh? It's gone on long enough, hasn't it?"

Sun nodded. "But how to put an end to it?"

The Chairman waved expansively at his chief of staff. "He knows. You've read his latest summary?"

"Yes, I have it here."

The three men opened their copies of the report. Its front page bore only a downward diagonal stroke, executed by a skilled calligrapher, in classical nomenclature called *p'ye*, "left stroke": the name of the army's plan for invasion of Taiwan. Wang cleared his throat.

"There have always been two problems, one strategic, one political. They interact.

"First, strategy. We outnumber the Taiwanese on every front. Our IRBM launchers can target all of Taiwan. They have some nuclear weapons, but we don't know how many. In any case, it's certain that neither side would use the nuclear option except as a last resort. Our army numbers some three-point-six million men; theirs . . . well, you can read the figures at leisure. We could overrun Taiwan in a week if we wanted to."

"But we don't want to," put in Sun.

"Of course not," the Chairman agreed. "That kind of all-out invasion would destroy everything."

Wang turned a page. "For a long time, it was academic anyway. Approximately one third of our forces, something like one-point-four million men, were pinned down on the borders with Russia and Vietnam, facing forty-four Soviet divisions. Now, with the Beijing-Moscow pact signed and ratified, we're free to redeploy some of those forces. The other thing to bear in mind is that Taiwan's mutual defense treaty with the United States was abrogated many years ago. Taiwan stands alone."

"So what's stopping us?" asked Sun Shanwang, who knew the answer but was anxious to hear it spoken aloud.

"Our troops have no stomach for a war with their brothers across the strait, that's one thing. But, more important, they know damn well that those brothers are better fighters!"

"Yes." The Chairman stubbed out his cigarette, directed a dribble of brown saliva into the spittoon, and immediately lit up another Panda. "So what we need is a quick kill. Give us that and we're prepared to chance it, especially with our new Soviet ally behind us."

Wang nodded heavily. "You've got it."

"And so . . ." The Chairman flipped through the folder, looking for a marked page. "Ah! Left Stroke calls first for the invasion of Jinmen Island."

"If we can take the island, that will cause severe loss of morale on Taiwan and correspondingly increased morale among our own forces. But it's at Jinmen that the Nationalists concentrate most of their best troops and equipment. Sixty thousand men, at last count."

"You say you need a rapid victory in the air, over Jinmen."

"Yes. As you know, until recently the backbone of our air force was some four thousand Mig-17s and Mig-19s. Fine planes, but long out of date. Also, they're only as good as their pilots. Many of them are now too old for active service." Wang paused, aware that he was about to tread on sensitive ground. "In the hard years, a lot of the younger pilots were purged. We've not yet replaced them."

Sun found his concentration slipping. He tried to follow Wang's arguments, but his mind kept going back to that odd statement: "*Until recently* the backbone of our air force *was* . . ."

"What does this all add up to?" the Chairman asked.

Wang shrugged. "We could expect to lose one-third of our fighter force to the enemy's F-5Es in the first three hours of fighting. After that, they could keep us at bay for between two and three weeks."

"That's no good."

"I agree."

"So what about going straight for the main island?"

"Difficult," said Wang. "We'd have to land, without heavy armor, on a well-defended coast with ground forces amounting to two armored divisions and two armored cavalry regiments equipped with light tanks. Again, we'd suffer heavy losses and be held up, probably for months rather than weeks. At the end of that time, most of industrial and agricultural Taiwan would be devastated."

"So. What's to be done?"

Wang turned another few pages. "We have to destroy Taiwanese Air Command on day one."

"And you can do that with something called . . . ah yes, here it is . . . a 'smart bomb'?"

"Yes—although that isn't the whole story. Smart bombs were pioneered by the Americans. Basically, they're missiles guided by a stabilized television camera in the nose that feeds video signals into its automatic tracking circuits. You point the thing at the enemy and a computer takes over. But that by itself, isn't enough."

"I don't see why," said Sun.

"Qi's pilots, for one thing." Wang said. "They weren't fast enough for me to be sure that they could even point the aircraft in the right direction. What we needed was something similar but faster."

Sun turned to the last page of the report. " 'A voice-responsive pilotless plane, with near-instantaneous automatic weapons system activation.' "

"Exactly. And that we now have . . . or do we?"

Sun became aware that the other two were looking at him expressionlessly. "I don't understand how it helps you," he prevaricated.

"But it's so simple!" Wang slammed shut his copy of the report. "Many of our planes are obsolete. Over the past decade we've been building better ones. All we need do is adapt the old planes, the junk, to pilotless aircraft and fit them with Apogee. We send them against the Taiwanese, directing them by immediate oral commands from the ground. We risk no men, we bring down most of the Taiwanese air force at a stroke . . . and then we send in the latest fighters to finish the task. So now, tell us—when can we expect to have Apogee?"

"I'm sorry, but I really still don't see the logic here. You have smart bombs already, so why do you need Apogee at all?"

"I said earlier, smart bombs by themselves aren't good enough."

"That's because Qi's pilots are deficient."

"That's *one* reason, I said. Smart bombs alone won't tempt the Taiwanese air force out of its lair, and the key to our success is the destruction of that air force. Smart bombs, guided missiles . . . we don't want to use them over Taiwan, because of the havoc they'll cause to the civilian population, and the Taiwanese will ignore them anyway."

"Ignore them?"

"Yes! They'll leave their planes snug in their fortified bunkers. Then, once the missiles stop coming, they'll release the planes and blast our people away. We have to tempt Air Command out and into the sky or we're going to lose. That means sending planes of our own. So stop hedging, Shanwang, and tell me the truth—when are we going to get Apogee?"

Sun Shanwang avoided the question. "How long would you need to re-equip your outdated planes?" he asked Wang. "It could take years. Apogee won't help there."

"On the contrary. The process of re-equipment is very nearly complete."

Sun kept his face expressionless, but inside he was numb. No one had told him anything about this. He tried to calculate how much the exercise must have cost, how such massive sums could have been lost from the annual budget. There was only one way. He found his eyes straying sideways to the Chairman's face. The old man was smiling.

"I'm sorry," the Chairman said gently. "But it was purely a military decision."

"Did my predecessor know?"

"Not even Baba knew."

Sun suddenly found himself sitting among strangers. The other two examined him sympathetically but could detect no trace of a reaction in his eyes.

"But . . ." Sun was floundering. "Without having Apogee itself, the actual machine, how could the technicians know what to do?"

"Very simple. Apogee began life as a military project, one in which we involved Ducannon Young at a comparatively late stage. All our people needed were the specifications from Ducannon Young, along with precise measurements and energy requirements. They didn't need to know how it worked, they need never know that."

"I understand." Sun's saliva tasted unpleasant. "Of course, that was the right decision."

"Thank you." The Chairman sighed. "Progress is slow. I'm in a hurry. Taiwan refuses to go away." His voice rose; his face grew taut with anger. "I find this situation intolerable!"

Sun fidgeted uneasily. "But what about Moscow? Can you rely on the Soviets? I don't trust them, any more than they trust us. Especially after the disappearance of our jet fighter."

"You really think the Russians stole it?"

"I'm quite sure of it." It was Sun's turn to be angry now. "Don't trust them, Chairman."

"Well, I won't have to trust them for long."

Sun sighed and spread his hands in a gesture of surrender. "Ducannon Young is facing serious difficulties in Taiwan. I had no choice but to allow them a further extension. Young assures me that Apogee will be ready by February, problems notwithstanding."

The Chairman lifted his chin at Wang in a querying gesture. The Marshal considered. "April thirtieth."

"There you are," the Chairman said softly. "You still have a little time, Shanwang. Until April thirtieth. But from now on your department is expected to play a key role."

"Mine?"

"Yes. It's vital that you prevent the Taiwanese from acquiring any knowledge of Apogee. We don't want to send up our expensively renovated planes, only to find that the rebels are jamming our radio signals. And there's something else, too. . . ." The Chairman smiled. "Something that has nothing to do with Taiwan at all. This invention, this Apogee . . . it's going to transform all of China, at every level. In the fields, the factories, banks . . . I want it kept safe. No one else is to have it. All right?"

"I understand."

"Do you? Please be very sure you know exactly where we all stand, Shanwang." The Chairman paused. "You have just heard us set the date for the full-scale military invasion and takeover of Taiwan Province."

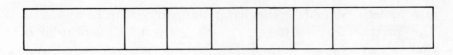

TWELVE

Father and son were signing into the hotel's health club. "I see your egalitarian principles don't get in the way of the Taipei Sheraton," Mat jibed.

"You don't make much of an effort to understand me, do you? I like comfort; I've nothing against wealth. Most of my life's been spent accumulating it."

"All from exploiting the masses?"

"You're exasperating sometimes, you know that?"

A few minutes later they stepped into the club's tiled sauna area, clad in saffron bathrobes. A heavily built Chinese wearing only a pair of shorts lumbered up and nodded to Mat. "Want a back-scrub, Mr. Young?"

"No, thanks, Ah Fan, not yet. Later, maybe. This is my father."

This time Ah Fan's nod was more of a bow. "Honor. Be back in a while, okay?"

He went out, leaving the two Englishmen with the club to themselves, or very nearly. The far end of the room was walled off by a solid sheet of glass that extended from floor to ceiling, thus creating a separate steam room. The glass ran with rivulets of condensation, and the tiny space beyond was filled with the white mist that signified a Turkish bath; but Mat could just see the color of flesh and a bright blob of pale orange where the solitary occupant had folded a towel across his genitals. He and his father made for the hottest sauna cabin, which was empty.

Simon let the sweat work out of his body for a bit, rubbing himself down with his hands. "All right," he said at last. "Start earning your keep. Lennie. What's the score?"

"He's frustrated as hell. Two reasons. First, the Red Chinese want new bolt-ons for military end-use. Lennie's tearing his hair out."

"But can he *do* it?"

"Yes. Given time. Which he hasn't got."

"I don't give a damn about that. Tell him to stay up later and get up earlier. What else is troubling him?"

Mat hesitated. "The nature of the beast," he said at last. "It's all so hellishly new. There ought to be a vast team working on this, flat out, in grade-one laboratory conditions. And instead it all comes down to Lennie Luk in the bedroom of our flat, with a few part-time helpers."

"You seem to forget the Hong Kong team."

"Programming isn't one of their strengths, and . . . do you remember what it was like when you were learning a new language?"

"Too long ago. Get to the point."

Stay cool, Mat warned himself; arguing with Dad's never worth it. "You progress so far," he said after a pause. "You've mastered the subjunctive, that kind of thing—and then, in the middle of doing something really simple, like ordering a meal, your mind freezes and you can't remember the first rule of grammar you ever learned."

"Speak for yourself."

"I am! And now Lennie's going through that phase. He's got himself all fucked up over—and I quote—'unprocessed source lines via next append to buffered text held in free memory space.' Just don't ask me what it means, that's all. Apparently it's the kind of thing you learn in whatever the equivalent of kindergarten may be in the computer world. The *old* computer world, that is. Trouble is, Lennie's inventing a new one, and apparently not all the ABCs hold good there."

Simon threw water over the hot coals and waited for the wave

[131]

of heat to break. "If we get all our equipment out of Hsinchu, fast, it's got to help."

"Yes, he says it will."

"That's why it's so important for me to see this man Li Lu-tang. He's got brilliant *guanxi*—I don't suppose you know what that means?"

"Connections. Clout."

Simon raised his eyebrows but said nothing.

"Does he know you're coming?"

"Don't be idiotic! Nobody does, except you and Chia. I flew over in the Learjet, lodged the flight plan at the last minute so I wouldn't hang around in some airline's reservations computer."

"Are you checked in under your own name?"

"Yes. There are limits. No point in provoking the police. Ouch! My shoulder's acting up. I need the masseur. I want some steam first, though."

They doused themselves in the cold pool and emerged spluttering. The glass-fronted Turkish bath still contained its single occupant. As Simon laid his hand on the handle of the plate-glass door, he turned to Mat and nodded a reminder that his son should keep his mouth shut. Then he pushed his way in. At once a soft voice said, "Good afternoon, Mr. Young."

Simon stood stock-still in the doorway, with steam billowing out around him. Mat couldn't understand why his father didn't go in. Then he heard him say, "Li Lu-tang."

When Simon took a step forward, Mat saw that the occupant of the steam room was a Chinese in his mid-fifties, tall and thin, with the skin stretched tight across his ribs.

Mat's eyes were inexorably drawn to the man's face, which comprised an assortment of striking features. The head narrowed to a sharp chin, slightly upturned. His jaw was prominent and L-shaped, its hard lines overhanging the man's slim neck. It was a long face, the mouth close to the chin, with a rounded lower lip and a straight upper one some way beneath an aquiline nose. The cheekbones were well defined, but the cheeks themselves were hollow. Not a pleasant face, Mat thought.

"Come in, come in!" Li held the towel over his groin with one hand while he extended the other to Simon. In anyone else, that gesture might have seemed ridiculous, but Li Lu-tang somehow managed to make it appear majestic.

Mat could not remember having seen his father at such a disadvantage for a long time. "But . . . this is extraordinary! I was just telling my son that no one knows I'm here. This is my son, by the way. Matthew Young, Mr. Li Lu-tang."

The Chinese smiled at Mat, but this time did not offer to shake hands. "We shall talk in English, then. Please," he said, "let us sit down." Only later did it strike Mat that the Chinese knew he could not speak Mandarin fluently.

"In fact," Li said quietly, "one or two people did know you were here. I did, for instance."

"You did?" Simon was disturbed. "Might I ask how?"

Li chuckled. "It is my business to know these things. How could I do my job if I did not know them?"

Mat longed to ask, What *is* your job? He became aware that his father was staring at him with an uncertain look on his face, and he flushed. Surely Da didn't think that he had tipped off Li? That was ridiculous, he'd never even heard of the man. . . . No, that wasn't quite true; Simon had mentioned him in Hong Kong, but for God's sake . . .

"To be honest," Li was saying, "my presence is not wholly coincidental. I was hoping to find you here."

"Why?"

"You asked the receptionist to make a reservation in the health club when you checked in, and you know how people talk."

Li's eyes showed a trace of amusement as they searched the Englishman's face for a reaction. Simon grunted. "So things haven't changed. What are you up to these days, Li Lu-tang? Still with the Bureau of Information and Statistics?"

"Oh dear me, no. That was a long time ago, Simon—may I call you Simon, as I used to?"

"You may."

"No, I have moved around a lot since then. I am attached to the Executive Yuan these days."

"But still collecting information?"

Li smiled. Mat noticed that whenever he smiled, his eyes closed for a second. "And collating statistics." His chilly gaze strayed to Mat's face, then back to Simon's. After a few moments of silence, Mat felt he could not go on ignoring the obvious message any longer. "Excuse me," he said abruptly. "This heat's too much."

He showered quickly, relishing the shock of cold water, and went out to the changing room, passing Ah Fan going the other way. To his surprise he found Rod Haines next to one of the lockers, jacket in hand.

"Hi," Mat said. "You're off early."

Haines smiled uncertainly. "Is that a complaint?"

"Sorry." Mat slung his towel around his shoulders and barked out a sigh. "Rough day, that's all." Then he remembered; no one was supposed to know of his father's visit. "Look," he said quickly, "why don't we go and have a drink? I need to talk to you."

"I've only just arrived."

"Oh, come on."

Haines looked at Mat quizzically. "All right," he said at last. "If it's that urgent."

Back in the steam room, Li Lu-tang had raised his feet and was sitting on the bench, Buddha-like, facing Simon.

"I know why you've come," he said abruptly, in Mandarin.

"Really?"

"You need to get rid of this prosecution and either open up Hsinchu again or transfer your operations elsewhere. Whichever way, you need my help. Come back to the office, we can talk more freely there. Also, there are things I want you to see."

"What things?"

"Photographs." Li twitched his chin in the direction of the door. "Your son's being a naughty boy."

Simon frowned. "In what way?"

"He's frequently in the company of a notorious actress and singer called Mo Mei-hua."

"What has the government got against her?"

"She takes drugs. Cocaine, pills."

Simon said nothing. Li allowed the message to sink in, then said: "You understand, I think, where we draw the line in the Republic of China. A little too much to drink, a little fun with an assortment of women, these things we have come to terms with. But drugs? No."

"Are you saying Mat takes drugs?"

"No, we do not accuse your son of being a drug-taker. But he is too public, much too public, in his demonstrations of affection for this girl. One Hong Kong press agency in particular is building up a portfolio of pictures of Matthew Young, did you know that? Mr. Young in the Evening Fragrance Nightclub, Mr. Young at the Trader's Grill, Mr. Young with his arm around a pretty shoulder and his head buried in an even prettier breast. . . ." Li made a moue of disgust. "This is not what we expect of foreign entrepreneurs, Simon. I don't recall you behaving like that in the old days."

"I will have a word with my son."

"Thank you."

"But this is, after all, Taipei . . . and times change. We can't go on living in the past, like dinosaurs."

"No. But neither do we have to trample down and destroy for the sake of destruction—like dinosaurs. I find this heat oppressive. Will you join me in a plunge?"

They lowered themselves into the cold pool, then quickly scrambled across the dividing wall to the warm Jacuzzi bath next to it. "You should see those photographs, I think," Li Lu-tang said. "But I want you to come back to the office for another reason. We have to talk about the Apogee computer."

For a moment Simon could not believe he had heard correctly, and was tempted to ask Li to repeat what he'd just said. "That," he grated at last, "is top secret. I will not discuss it with you, with anybody." Suddenly he felt helpless, and the sensation enraged him. "How the hell do you know about Apogee?"

"As you said earlier, times change. Try to think of me now as sitting on a mountain, one high enough to let me see all that happens in the Free Republic of China and in a great many other places as well. I will come straight to the point. My government wants a share of Apogee, which it regards as useful to it in its struggle with the Chinese bandits who presently usurp power in most of the Middle Kingdom's provinces."

"I refuse."

"I advise you not to. My department has contacts within Ducannon Young Electronics Limited. At the moment, we come to you as purchasers, checkbook in hand."

"It's the first I've heard of *that*!"

"Then your employees do not keep you fully informed. An influential Taiwanese businessman recently approached Luk, the scientist, with a proposal. Luk was exceedingly rude to him."

"I'm pleased to hear it."

"You shouldn't be. Don't overlook the possibility—pardon my directness, it is unforgivable—that we may decide to appropriate what at present we're still prepared to buy."

"Appropriate? Steal, you mean."

Li sluiced water over his head. "Appropriate," he said, without any change of tone.

Simon climbed out of the pool, reaching for his towel. "Yes," he said. "It's time we went to your office. There are some things I want to say to you, and this is hardly the place to do it."

"No. It's growing late. Soon the businessmen will be here, to drink and *deal*." Li nearly spat the word. "I don't find the atmosphere congenial, and no mistake!"

"I'll tell my son we're leaving."

While Li Lu-tang went to the changing rooms, Simon padded through to the bar. Mat and Haines, swathed in towels from neck to toe, occupied adjoining recliners, beakers of tea by their sides. Simon smiled at the Australian and bent down to whisper in his son's ear. When Mat gasped, Simon quickly laid a finger against his lips. Then he leaned across him to talk to Haines.

"Hello, Rod. How are you?"

"Very well, thanks."

"Ever see Ned Moulson these days?"

"About once a year."

"Well, give him my regards."

Haines started to unwrap his towels, but Simon laid a hand on his arm. "Listen—I need an urgent review of group security here in Taiwan, within twenty-four hours. All the weak points, all the queries over employees, anything suspicious over the past year, break-ins, you name it. Comb personnel files."

"What am I looking for?"

Simon lowered his voice still further. "Government finger-prints. Understand?"

"Not really, but I'll do my best, Mr. Young."

"Good. I want you in my suite here, tomorrow, ready to report at four o'clock."

"Yes sir."

Simon nodded and stood upright. His expression was distant, and it suddenly occurred to Haines that even the group security officer was not above suspicion.

"Your father always remembers me," he said slowly, as Simon left.

"He never forgets anyone. Is Moulson the guy who recom-mended you to Dunny's?"

"Yes."

"I see. Well, that explains why he remembers you in particu-lar: Ned's one of his oldest friends. I guess it makes you almost one of the family."

Haines laughed deprecatingly. "Hey, when did your pa show up? I don't recall hearing he was coming."

"Flying visit."

"Did you know about it?"

"Uh-huh. In fact, that's why I bushwhacked you in the chang-ing room. He was in the sauna and I thought he might not want you to know he was here." Mat laughed, without sounding amused. "Look, you'd better get going on that review. But we've time for a drink first. Steaven!" A Chinese waiter hurried over from where he had been adjusting the TV set. "Two Taiwanese beers, as quick as you can, please."

The waiter nodded and headed in the direction of the bar. Mat picked up a magazine. As the minutes ticked past and no beers appeared, he began to feel uneasy. He looked around at all the empty recliners and frowned.

"Have you ever seen this place so deserted?" Mat sat up. "Do you realize that we're the only ones here? We're the only people who've been in the club this entire afternoon."

"So?"

"It . . . it just feels kind of odd, that's all. It's so silent. Shit, how long does it take Steaven to fetch a couple of beers when he's only got two customers to look after?"

"You know, you're right at that."

Haines was about to speak again when they both heard the sound of glass shattering in the distance. For an instant the sound unsettled them still further; then the tension broke and they exchanged smiling glances.

"Whoops!" Haines said.

"I'd like to know what that was, but they'd never tell you. I'll go and chase up those beers."

"You might ask Steaven if he could—"

The shriek, not close but not far away, either, began in a lower register before hurtling up to a wail, all in less than a second. The two men froze.

Then they were running for the passage. Hotel staff converged from all sides on the door that led to the sauna area, waiters, masseurs, and manicurists forming a tight wedge of humanity around the narrow entrance. As Mat came up, someone turned away, holding both hands to his mouth, and they heard him gagging.

The whole of the sauna room was filled with white vapor. At first Mat couldn't understand why, because the partition should have contained it within the Turkish bath. He was struggling to see through the steam, now rapidly thinning out in the draft from the open door, when he heard Haines's exclamation.

"My God! There's broken glass all over the floor!"

Mat stopped and looked down. It was true. And then he understood. The shards of glass, the crash they had heard, the escaping steam—someone or something had shattered the partition wall.

"Let me," rapped Haines. "I've got sandals on."

He picked his way gingerly forward. "Oh Christ," Mat heard him mutter.

Mat could see clearly now. He could also smell something very unpleasant: excrement and urine and an altogether different odor—a hot, sour kind of stench. He turned his head to where the steam room used to be. All that remained of the partition was a jagged edge of glass, some two feet high, sticking out of the floor. Beyond it he could see the bench where he'd sat with his father and Li. Ah Fan, the back-scrubber, was lying on it, one arm casually flung down. Mat became aware of a pattern on this arm: an artistic red overlay in constant motion as sweat flowed down it to the floor.

Mat raised his eyes a fraction and unwittingly cried out, as if he'd been punched in the solar plexus.

Someone had taken a large triangular fragment of the shattered partition and used it to saw the man's neck open. His head dangled backward at a right angle to the rest of him, and his throat was one huge gash, brimming scarlet. Perhaps the killer had been interrupted; whatever the reason, he had left the glass weapon stuck, point down, in Ah Fan's stomach.

Mat was sick, violently, all over the glass-studded floor.

THIRTEEN

Banker Khoo King-hey had positioned his walnut-veneered desk in such a way that he could look across it, out of the twelfth-floor window, to the façade of the building on the other side of Taipei's Nan Yang Street. Last week some workmen had suspended a huge banner from the roof opposite, unfurling it over the two rows of office windows immediately beneath: I ENJOY MY JOB SO MUCH I FORGOT TODAY WAS MY DAY OFF!

This public avowal, made by an unknown spokesman for an impenetrable purpose, disturbed Khoo. He'd been brooding on it ever since. Today, he couldn't seem to take his eyes off the banner. There had been a time—he could remember it himself—when mainland China had been like that. The spirit, the fire . . . where had they gone?

He laid down his pen with a sigh, unable to comprehend what was happening to him. Lately, home seemed very far away and yet it preoccupied him deeply. What were Qingqing and Tingchen doing now? Was the house all right? Simple questions, missing answers.

The intercom buzzed. "There's a parcel for you in reception, Mr. Khoo. The courier needs your signature."

"Send him up."

The package was about a foot long by six inches wide and three inches deep. Khoo unwrapped the outer layer of brown paper and examined the back of it. From Mrs. M. Y. Khoo of Singapore; designation "Personal Gift," value S$25.00. He knew exactly what his secretary must be thinking: a present from home, from Mr. Khoo's mother, how kind! And if the girl could have been there to witness her boss unwrapping it, she would have seen a box done up in red foil, with a gold ribbon around it. How tasteful! Candy—how thoughtful!

Khoo carefully began to pick at the cellophane that clung to the box. It was thicker than a normal transparent protective wrapping, but no customs officer would have noticed that. He managed to peel all of it away without tearing it, then pressed the intercom button. "Hold my calls; no visitors."

Khoo went over to the table by the door where he kept his personal computer, turned it on, and patted the sheet of cellophane over the CRT screen. Soon, vague shapes began to appear as smudges on the translucent material. The shapes became steadily clearer until the entire sheet of cellophane was covered with minute Chinese ideographs.

When he'd finished reading the text, he switched off the display unit, peeled away the cellophane, and burned it in an ashtray. Then he sat back in his chair and stared out the window at the jocular inscription on the banner opposite.

The first part of this dispatch from Mah-jongg HQ concerned Bangkok. Sun Shanwang's archives chief had, with nearly total conviction, identified one of the men who'd attacked him as a free-lance Taiwanese assassin, closely connected with the KGB.

The assailant came from Taiwan.

What other "connections" did he have?

Do you want to come home?

Khoo mentally obliterated that part of the message, knowing that questions affecting his own future would have to wait. He picked up one of his phones, told his secretary he was taking calls again, and dialed an internal number. "Miss Shan . . . please come up for a moment."

Her knock aroused him from a not-altogether-pleasant reverie. "Come in," he said with a smile, and then faltered, because he did not know what to call her any more. Miss Shan? Lin-chun? On the phone, the former; but face to face the choice no longer seemed simple. That smile, those wide open eyes, they complicated matters.

"Thank you. . . ." She too faltered, and for the same reason. She had come to think of King-hey as such a distinguished name. Authoritative. *Nice.*

"I hope I'm not disturbing you?"

"Not at all. In fact, I was hoping to make an appointment to see you this afternoon. How can I help?"

"I want a rundown on one of our bigger customers. What can you tell me about Mr. Wu?"

"The Wus of Anshuo, in the south? Father or son?"

"Son. Wu Tie-zi. The unofficial version, mind! The gossip."

Lin-chun smiled, showing a set of perfect white teeth between her pink lips. Khoo noticed every tooth.

"The unofficial version, right. Let me think. Age, mid-forties. Wealthy Taiwanese businessman whose father made a fortune, source obscure. Married for the second time, with five children. His present wife's rumored to have been a mistress before he made it legal."

"A womanizer?"

"Well, he certainly knows the Taipei nightlife."

"Anything else?"

"I gather he's much in demand as a go-between. There've been one or two stories going the rounds about excessive commissions, you know what I mean?"

"Bribes."

"Exactly. Nothing can be proved, of course. He has influential friends; the government finds him very useful in its outside dealings."

"Why's that?"

"He managed to live abroad for a time, when that was difficult for us Taiwanese. As a result, he acquired Western ways and now he gets on well with everyone."

"What are his politics?"

Lin-chun lowered her voice. "He believes that Taiwan should be independent—ruled not by the Reds and not by the Kuomintang, but by the Taiwanese. At local election time he supports Taiwanese candidates, and they often win. He's not afraid to speak out on public platforms."

"Does he get a respectful hearing?"

"In Taipei he has to be very careful. Down south, where he

has his base, they tolerate him, although the Taiwanese independence movement is an extremely risky thing to be associated with, as I'm sure you know. If he weren't so close to the government, he could be in some danger, I think."

Danger.

Do you want to come home?

Khoo shook his head in an effort to clear it. The girl's words coincided with what he knew about Wu Tie-zi. "Thank you," he said softly. "We'll now proceed to something else. I've recently learned"—his mouth flashed a mirthless smile—"through the grapevine, I think you could say, that Simon Young's in Taipei."

Lin-chun's eyes widened. "Goodness! But that account has nothing to do with me, Mr. Khoo."

"Not until now, no. But you are going to be working on it closely in future. The Ducannon Young account is perhaps the most important of all those that this branch has on its books. I propose to go and visit Mr. Young tomorrow, and I want you to come with me."

Lin-chun secretly felt delighted. It meant—it could *only* mean—that she was being upgraded. "Thank you, King-hey. Oh, please forgive me. . . ."

She put her hands to her mouth and blushed scarlet. Khoo eyed her keenly. "Please think nothing of it, Lin-chun." Seeing her eyebrows rise, he went on, "In public, we shall be proper. In private, I think the rites can be forgotten. Do you agree?"

She nodded, still confused.

"And now—when you came in, you said you wanted to see me. How can I help?"

Lin-chun stammered, "I feel so presumptuous. . . . Miss Mo got in touch with me this morning and said she felt very bad about the way those men treated you on your first visit to her club. She's giving a party tonight, to celebrate her Golden Horse nomination."

"Ah! Good for Miss Mo."

"And she'd like us both to come."

Khoo drummed his fingers on the desk top. He realized that issuing this invitation must have cost the girl an effort; in the Confucian atmosphere of Taiwan, it was hardly correct behavior for a woman, however modern her outlook, to take the initiative with a man. So she must like him a lot. As much as he liked her, even.

"Yes, of course, we must go." He looked at his watch. "What time should I pick you up?"

"Say . . . nine?"

When she'd left, Khoo leaned back in his chair and gazed out the window. Darkness had come to Taipei; he could no longer read the banner opposite, but he knew it was there, silently questioning the motherland's commitment.

Do you want to come home?

With a great effort he dismissed the insidious question from his mind. Tonight, he told himself, he was going out with one of the dearest women he'd ever known. There were a few hours of sweetness, of pleasure, to look forward to. Suddenly the prospect of Mei-hua's party afforded him inexplicable joy.

He frowned. Lin-chun was right to say that the branch's biggest personal account holder enjoyed good connections. According to the recent dispatch, one photograph on Mo Mei-hua's dressing room wall was of a certain Mr. Wu Tie-zi.

At seven-thirty that evening there were few people in the Lai Lai Sheraton's second-level basement mall. The handful of shoppers congregated at the eastern end of the arcade, well away from the hotel's private banqueting rooms. Simon and Mat took the escalator and walked along to the western end of the complex. The farther they went, the quieter it became. Their feet made no sound on the deep pile of the carpet, and the lacquered wooden wall panels seemed to absorb the sound of their voices. Simon acknowledged that his son had chosen an excellent site for their assignation.

Mat looked at his watch. "He should be here."

As if in response, someone coughed. The two men turned. A slim shadow was walking toward them, out of the light, down another corridor parallel to the one they'd just traversed. Simon looked around him uneasily, aware that seclusion could also mean a trap.

The shadow emerged into the pool of dim light cast by lanterns on either side of the door to the Phoenix Suite, and Mat nodded. "There he is."

Their visitor was a tall, thin, middle-aged Chinese with tiny, colorless eyes. He kept one hand in the pocket of his shabby raincoat, while in the other he held a cigarette. When Mat greeted him, at first the Chinese hesitated; then he stuck the cigarette in his mouth and shook the Englishman's outstretched hand.

"Hello," he said in English. "How're you?"

His breathing was bad, the product of too many Long Life cigarettes; and, like many people trying to speak a foreign language, he failed to articulate the words properly, as if by mumbling one could at least cover up the mistakes. The butt between his lips scarcely helped.

"I'm very well, thank you. Inspector Hsu, this is my father, Mr. Simon Young."

" 'Lo."

Simon bowed his head slightly but did not offer to shake hands. The inspector seemed relieved.

"Father, this gentleman's daughter works for Ducannon Young Electronics as a secretary." Mat spoke slowly, giving the policeman a chance to catch up. "She and her husband became involved in an unfortunate dispute with their neighbors. Our lawyers were able to assist them. It was nothing at all; in fact, it embarrasses me to mention it, such a trifling affair."

A shy smile passed over the inspector's face. Simon, impressed in spite of himself, found his eyes straying to his son.

"However, Inspector Hsu was good enough to mention, quite unnecessarily, that if he could be of service to the company in the future he would willingly do so. And this is why I ventured to ask him to meet us here, to discuss certain matters that have arisen."

"Nobody come," put in the inspector. "Ver' quiet place here."

Mat, sensing that his father was about to speak, turned to him. "Perhaps you would permit me to ask the inspector if he can help us?"

Simon heard the note of authority in his son's voice, and nodded. Mat turned back to the policeman. "Do you know what happened here today?" he asked.

"Already there is report. I have read."

"Can you tell us what it says?"

"Ver' short. No witnesses. No one talk to us." He paused. "Staff ver' scared."

"Scared? Why?"

Hsu shrugged and took a swift drag on his cigarette. Mat frowned. "Does this report mention us—my father or me?"

"Yuh. Say, two English gen-til-men were there. They talk. Cooperate. But they don't know things."

"Is Li Lu-tang mentioned?"

Inspector Hsu looked right and left, then bent down to a nearby ashtray to stub out his smoke. When he stood upright again, he failed to meet Mat's eyes. "Is not."

"What?" Simon interjected. "Not at all?"

"Father, please . . ." Mat saw the effort Simon made to bite back his words, and was gratified. "Inspector, we both talked a little with this man, Li Lu-tang. He was there, in the steam room. There is no possibility of our having made a mistake."

Hsu's eyes danced from face to face. "Report clear. No Chinese pa . . . patrons in club this day. Not one."

"I see." Mat hesitated. "Is either of us likely to be arrested?"

Hsu shook his head.

"Or questioned again?"

"Yes. May be questioned again, soon. Please do not try to leave the Republic."

"That's what the investigating officer said. Father, have you anything you'd like to ask the inspector?"

Simon spoke in Mandarin. "Mr. Hsu, when my son telephoned you, I was in the room with him. I heard him ask you about Li Lu-tang. Did you make any inquiries about that gentleman before coming here?"

Hsu smiled. "Yes," he said, in the same language. "I made one telephone call."

"And did you learn anything as a result?"

"I learned that I shouldn't presume to make another telephone call."

"You were warned off?"

"Yes."

"By whom?"

The inspector smiled and wordlessly shook his head.

"I see." Simon thought. "Is there anything else you can tell us?"

"I don't think so. This file's going to be open for a long time, I believe."

"You don't expect to catch the killer?"

"No."

"Well. Thank you very much indeed, Inspector."

"No problem. Good to have met you, Mr. Young."

Hsu bowed politely to Simon, then awkwardly shook hands with Mat. "Sorr' I could not be more help."

"Please don't mention it. You've been very kind."

"No help this time, but you can always ask again." He thrust both hands into his coat pockets, turned on his heel, and began to walk down one of the long corridors that led back to the light. But after he had taken half a dozen steps he paused, as if in thought, and then very slowly retraced his steps. The Englishmen looked at him in surprise.

"Mr. Young," he said quietly, addressing himself in Chinese to Simon, "do you know about Ko Lau Hui?"

"The old Triad society?"

"Yes." Hsu nodded a great many times, as if weighing his next words with the utmost care. "Please be very careful," he said at last, before turning to go. This time he did not hesitate, but walked away at a brisk pace until at last he rounded a corner and disappeared.

"What was he saying?" Mat asked. "I followed the first bit, but not what he said just now."

"He implied that Ko Lau Hui are mixed up in this."

"Ko . . . what?"

"A Triad group, very powerful here on Taiwan." Simon lowered his voice and brought his mouth close to Mat's ear. "It means Elder Brothers, in Cantonese. Sun Yat-Sen used them to gather intelligence. So did Tai Li."

"Tai Li?"

"Only man allowed to wear a sword in Chiang Kai-shek's presence. The old general's head of military intelligence."

Mat gasped. "Are you saying that Taiwan Garrison Command has something to do with this murder?"

"I'm not saying anything. Neither are you." Suddenly Simon shivered. "Let's get out of here; I need a drink."

They had the elevator to themselves. On the way up, Simon said grudgingly, "I thought you handled that policeman particularly well. You've learned a lot."

"Thanks."

"It's falling into place, isn't it? The two of us are being set up. First the Hsinchu prosecution, then Ah Fan. We're witnesses to a murder, if not actual suspects. So both of us have to be available to come and answer questions whenever they crook their little fingers, and if your friend's right, this inquiry could go on for years."

"You're reading a hell of a lot into this. It happened once before, and the Taiwanese weren't behind it then. Remember how the Reds cornered you back in '85, by staging a terrorist attack at Beijing Airport in front of your eyes? Making someone a witness to a crime as a way of pinning him down is a *communist* tactic."

"Except that the People's Republic doesn't have a motive in this case. No, you're wrong—it's a *Chinese* tactic. They're tightening their grip. 'Be nice to us and we'll go on being nice to you,' that's the message."

"You think Li did it?"

"No, he was with me, the perfect alibi. But I'm starting to think

[146]

that he arranged for it to be done, yes. You remember how deserted the club was?"

"Rod Haines and I commented on it at the time."

"I believe Li had the place cleared. We—you, me, Haines—can give each other alibis, but I'm not sure how far any of us will be able to rely on the club's Chinese staff to back us up."

"Christ, I hadn't thought of that! But do you really think that Li—"

"Why else would he have given orders for the police to forget about him being present?"

As they entered Simon's suite, he made straight for the drinks table. "What time's Lennie coming?"

"Any minute. Do you want to cancel this evening?"

"No. Rule number one: The boss should never let his staff see him fazed. Besides, I've got a bone to pick with him." Simon chuckled. "I learned something the other day. Did you know that while he was still at university he wrote a paper on some aspect of chess theory? Apparently it's still the last word on the subject, or so my contact told me. He seemed amazed I hadn't heard about it at the time."

"I certainly didn't know. Lennie doesn't boast."

"He's come a long way since he used to sit in our kitchen reading Ducannon Young's computer magazines." Simon's face became serious. "I've been meaning to talk to you about a couple of things Li said, but I never got the chance."

"What?"

"First, is it true that someone tried to speak to Lennie about Apogee?"

"Yes." Mat told his father how Lennie had been approached in the noodle shop a few days previously. Simon listened with an intensifying frown on his face. "If anything like that happens again, get him to phone me at once, not three days after the event."

"We only thought—"

"Next. Li brought up the subject of a Miss Mo." Simon paused, embarrassed. "I gather you've been, er . . . pawing her in public."

Mat's fingers tightened around his glass. "We're affectionate. I wouldn't exactly call it pawing."

"Any chance of your toning it down a bit?"

"I rather resent being asked that."

"I guess I would, too, in your place." Simon couldn't quite meet his son's eyes. "But we're going through a sticky patch, and I don't want any more scandals."

"I see." Mat fought down his rising temper. "Look, there are a few things I've been meaning to say to you, too. . . ."

"I'm listening."

Mat took a deep breath and opened his mouth, but the words refused to come. "I'm proud of being your son," he managed to get out at last. "And I'm proud of the company, but whenever you're around I find it hard to keep things on an even keel."

For a moment Simon said nothing. "Can you give me an example?" he ventured at last.

"Oh . . . well, take tonight. One minute you're praising me for how I handled Hsu; the next you're criticizing my social life. It seems kind of . . ."

He spread his hands, looking to Simon for a lead, but the older man's gaze was locked onto his glass. "Isn't that a bit pompous?" he said abruptly. "All I'm asking you is to take things easy in public. You're old enough to see what's going on, you must be."

"Sorry?"

"Mat! Surely I don't have to spell it out? A lot of girls like that think of only one thing: money. Preferably marriage, but in any case money."

There was another long silence while Mat refilled his glass. "Your vanity's showing," he said quietly. "It's me she sees, not *tai-pan* Young and his riches."

"Are you so sure?"

"Oh, for Christ's sake, of course I'm sure!"

"Look. I'm trying to protect the biggest commercial secret we own. You're spending time with a tart. What am I supposed to do—just ignore it?"

"She's not a tart. And you're implying I can't be trusted, do you realize that?"

"Don't whine."

"Then don't put me down! Ever since I was a child, you've done it." Mat's face was ablaze with unaccustomed anger. "Is that how you really still see me, Father? As a child—someone who can't be trusted to do his job?"

Simon had been breathing deeply, trying to keep calm; but Mat's last words acted like a detonator. "Frankly, I don't care to see you at all when you act like this!"

"Don't, then!' Mat, likewise provoked beyond endurance, slammed his drink onto the table and stood up. "For Christ's sake, don't see anything that doesn't *suit* you, will you?"

The two men stared at each other a while longer, frightened out of their roles, unable to believe that there was nothing more to say. Then Mat turned with an impatient gesture and strode to the door. The crack of it slamming coincided exactly with Simon saying, *"Shit!"*

For five minutes Khoo and Lin-chun hovered dutifully on the outer rim of the circle of admirers who surrounded Mei-hua, before reconciling themselves to the knowledge that there was no getting near her. She was, as Khoo put it to himself, higher than Taipei's Grass Mountain—laughing and shedding tears, often at the same time, clutching arms, joking—a drama queen at the center of her enthusiastically sycophantic court.

The couple drifted to a table and sat down. "Jacqui!" shrieked a newcomer from the door.

"Why does she call herself that, I wonder?" Khoo mused.

"After the former Mrs. John F. Kennedy." Lin-chun's tone was disapproving. "She admires her style."

"Ah. But I suspect the jet-set life doesn't appeal to you."

"Doesn't it appeal to everyone?" She laughed, then lowered her eyes. "I feel muddled sometimes. There are days when I'd like to be a rich woman, and there are days when all I want is to go home."

"Home? Weren't you born in Taipei?"

"Yes. But you must know what I mean. The mainland."

"I see."

"I'd hate it, of course. All those cadres bossing one about, the shortages . . ."

"Corruption, wrongful arrest . . ."

"No decent schools or hospitals." She sighed. "Yet—I miss it. Silly, isn't it? I've never seen it, I know I'd detest it, but . . ."

The group surrounding Mei-hua had thinned out. Someone began to play a waltz on the synthesizer. Without any prior warning, loneliness descended on Khoo, rendering him immobile. For a moment he sat there, shoulders rounded, head hunched into his neck; then, abruptly, he said, "I think we should dance."

"I'm afraid I can't."

"When I was studying in America, I learned a few steps. Leave it to me. Come."

The lights were low, the music slow, and Lin-chun could no longer feel her own body. She seemed to float in some entirely personal zone marked out for her two inches above the floor. But if she no longer enjoyed an independent existence in the world, Khoo King-hey had suddenly become the epitome of reality. They danced very close. From the pit of her stomach to the tops of her breasts, Lin-chun could feel the weight and warmth of something she had never experienced before: an adult male body. It was very firm and it smelled sweet. She no longer cared that her boss sometimes looked plain. Tonight he possessed only one quality of any significance—physical presence. He was here, with her, and with no one else, because he wanted to be.

Lin-chun let herself drift forward against him, resting her head on his shoulder, until the waltz drew to a dreamy close. Her body suddenly reasserted itself. She became aware that his right hand was pressing firmly into her back, that the palm of his left was warm and dry, he was moving his head back, now why do that, why spoil it . . . ? And then he kissed her lightly on the cheek.

The girl's mouth opened in a little gasp, her eyes dilated. Her whole childhood seemed to well up inside her in a frightening billow of unquestionable rules and timeless precepts; and she wanted to run to hide her shame. But then, Lin-chun's youth drained away forever, leaving her adrift; and all this wretched castaway knew was that she desired more from Khoo than just a chaste peck on the cheek.

Khoo himself experienced a second of overwhelming tenderness: he longed to sweep her from this club, away from Taiwan, to somewhere, something better. She was so right for him! If only . . . he closed his eyes, expelling reality for a few moments longer.

As they circled one last time, Ah-Ping, Mei-hua's bodyguard, raised a camera from behind the bar and took three photographs of the couple in quick succession. Plenty of people had been snapping away; three more flashes caused no surprise.

The music stopped. Other dancers clapped, but Khoo and Lin-chun stood close together, looking into each other's eyes, unsmiling. Only when the floor began to empty did their mouths crinkle in bashful pleasure. They returned to their table, but reluctantly, as if unwilling to admit that an experience so enjoyable could either happen or end.

They were about to sit down when they heard a commotion. Mat Young was elbowing his way through the throng to the bar. "Where is she?" he cried.

"Darling!" Mei-hua held him at arm's length, then pulled him close. "How wonderful, I thought you couldn't make it."

"I'm here, aren't I?"

"Of course you are, *chingai-de*, now let's have a drink, shall we? I can see a free booth over there. . . ."

The club was packed, and people were having too good a time to bother about Mat's churlishness. Hardly anyone saw Mei-hua reach across the bar to whisper in Ah-Ping's ear, but Khoo noticed. He noticed, too, how Ah-Ping looked in his direction before answering Mei-hua; and suddenly the hairs on the nape of his neck stood on end.

Mei-hua ran after Mat, guiding him to the only free booth on the upper level. The party in the adjacent booth started to rise. At once, Khoo tapped Lin-chun's arm. "I feel like a change of scene."

He hurried on ahead, determined to seize the recently vacated seats. As Lin-chun joined him he raised a finger to his lips and leaned back, trying to ignore the new, speculative expression in her eyes. She realized that Khoo was eavesdropping, but she suspended judgment; sensing it, he suffered a momentary flicker of disappointment at her failure to condemn him. Then he gave his concentration to what was happening in the next booth.

Mat's voice was loud, unmistakable. ". . . doctor in Hong Kong. I've arranged an appointment for you next Friday. Christ, how long does it take to get a drink in this place?"

"There, there, darling, you've had a hard time."

"Your cold's bad tonight. Your nose is streaming. Oh God, you haven't . . ."

"No, I swear I . . ."

"Can you make it?"

"Make what?"

"Next Friday."

"I don't know. I'm supposed to . . ."

A waitress brought them a bottle in an ice bucket, and Mei-hua stopped talking. Khoo tried to interpret Mat's words. Why did Mei-hua need to see a doctor? What was wrong with her? Or perhaps—his eyes narrowed—there was nothing wrong with her. . . .

Suppose she was pregnant? How would it affect Simon Young, the company, Apogee?

The waitress left and Mei-hua was speaking again, but Mat interrupted her. "Don't start. Just don't start." Khoo heard wine being poured. "Jesus, I love you, you know that?"

"You know I do. I still think you're crazy."

The voices in the next booth sank to a whisper, and Khoo clenched his teeth in frustration.

"Terrific row . . . fucking Victorian. He thinks I'm a baby in short pants. I'd give anything to work somewhere else."

"So you say."

"This time I mean it."

A group of revelers had come to stand right by the booth

occupied by Khoo and Lin-chun. Khoo scowled at them, but they didn't notice.

". . . business friend I told you about, Mat?"

"What—Wu something?"

Khoo's head pressed against the partition. On the other side of it, voices rose and faded as if broadcast on a weak radio frequency.

"Wu Tie-zi . . . for years. He said . . . factory down at Tainan."

"What's he . . . ?"

"Electronic components."

"Sounds good."

Khoo removed his ear from the partition and leaned across to speak to Lin-chun. "I'm sorry," he said, meaning it. "There may be a little unpleasantness now."

She stared at him, not understanding. It had never been like this with dear Tsai Zi-yang; the one thing you could say for him was that when he was there he was *there*, with you, one hundred percent.

"I'd like you to leave. Things are going wrong next door and I have to try to put them right. I'll see you at the bank at eight-thirty tomorrow morning. My sincerest apologies."

She stood up obediently, averting her head so that he would not see the tears trickling out of her eyes, and made for the cloakroom without a word. Lugubriously he watched her go; then one of the party standing next to the booth bent down and said, "Are these seats taken?"

Khoo heaved a sigh and rose, deliberately knocking against the man. "Not at all, not at all!"

Conversation in the immediate vicinity ceased. Khoo grasped the man's arm and thrust him bodily into the seat he'd just vacated. Then he swaggered away, pausing by the next booth.

"Why, Miss Mei-hua! Fabulous party. Splendif . . . splendif . . ." He lurched against Mat, putting an arm around his shoulder. "Whassat word Westerners use?"

Mat angrily shrugged him off. "This is a private party," he snapped.

"It's not." Khoo wagged an admonitory finger at Mat. "I'm here. You're here. What's private about that?"

Ah-Ping was thrusting his way through the crowd. Khoo, aware of him, waited a second, then punched Mat on the upper arm. Mat flared up. "Hold him!" he snarled at Ah-Ping, clenching his fist.

Khoo raised his left foot high off the floor and brought it down hard on Ah-Ping's instep. The bouncer's head whiplashed back, and he loosened his grip on Khoo's arms. In the same second, Mat threw his punch. Khoo twisted sideways. Because Mat was half-standing and half-sitting in the gap between bench and table he fell awkwardly, tripping over his own feet.

Khoo jabbed his elbows backward into Ah-Ping's stomach and was free. He saw Mat directly in front of him, head bowed, struggling to extricate himself from the confines of the booth. Khoo raised his right hand and brought it down, not too hard, at the point where Mat's skull joined his spine. Mat stopped struggling and collapsed with a little "Oof!" of pain.

Khoo, having achieved his aim of shutting the Englishman's mouth, had no desire to prolong his stay. He darted toward the exit. No one made any attempt to stop him; the people standing close to the booths weren't sure whether this was a real brawl, some kind of demonstration for Mei-hua's benefit, or just a joke. Mei-hua recovered her wits first. As Ah-Ping hauled himself up by clinging onto the table, she grabbed his arm with both hands. "Twice is enough!" she hissed, and Ah-Ping understood.

While Mei-hua tended Mat, the Chinese straightened his jacket and pushed his way through the bemused crowd toward the door. In the foyer he checked the elevator's floor-indicator panel and saw that the car had almost reached street level. He turned to the hatcheck girl standing in her alcove. "The customer who just came out—did he take the elevator?"

"No. He pressed the button, then when it came he seemed to change his mind—went in, came out again. He used the stairs."

Ah-Ping nodded. His instincts were rarely wrong. He pushed through the emergency exit to the stairwell and peered over the bannisters. Nothing. Khoo hadn't had time to reach the street. Ah-Ping knew that all the emergency doors operated on an exit-only security catch, so the swine couldn't have gotten back into the building on one of the lower floors. He must have gone up.

The bouncer emerged onto the drafty landing, allowing the door to click shut behind him. Not a sound disturbed the silence. He began to climb.

A dozen stairs led up to the roof. As he pushed the bar to open the door, a gale howled through the gap, making him shiver. Taipei was cold in January, and here on the fifth floor, it was wet and windy as well. He hesitated. A man might easily fall to his death on such a night, if he wasn't familiar with the layout.

Ah-Ping felt inside his waistband and withdrew a switchblade. Then he eased his way onto the roof.

A gust of wind took the door and slammed it shut, making him flinch. He swung around and leaned against the door, but it did not yield. Only then did he remember the security catches.

Ah-Ping, shivering violently by now, pulled his jacket collar up, lowered his head, and cautiously advanced out of the shelter of the door.

In the foyer of the club, nothing happened for a few moments after he'd disappeared into the stairwell. Then the hatcheck girl murmured, "He's gone."

A close-cropped Chinese head appeared above the counter. Two beady eyes swiveled right and left before the head's owner stood upright and opened the flap.

"You were lucky," said the girl. "He's vicious, that one. I was taking a risk, you know. Even for two thousand NT, I was taking a risk. What about the other half of the money, then?"

Khoo pouted. "How much did we agree?"

"Come on, you know how much. Two thousand NT."

Khoo gnawed his lip. "It's an awful lot," he said morosely. "I suppose you wouldn't settle for twelve-fifty?"

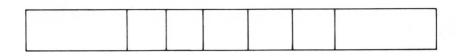

FOURTEEN

Shan Lin-chun had little to say to her boss when they met the next morning at the bank. During the short taxi ride to the Lai Lai Sheraton they stared out of their respective windows in silence. Khoo offered no apologies for his extraordinary behavior the night before; Lin-chun expected none. Why, therefore, did she feel so unhappy?

When Simon Young opened the door to the hotel suite, Lin-chun felt a little nervous. This man was something out of the ordinary. It wasn't only his exceptional height, although he did loom over her like a policeman; there was something else, a dimension that disturbed her. His taut face was pale and the eyes glittering under their straight, bushy brows made her feel as though an impersonal camera were recording her features for the file.

Khoo introduced her. "Hello, Miss Shan," Simon said. "You must meet my son. Mat!"

To Khoo's astonishment, Matthew Young emerged from the bathroom. He looked pale and his gait was awkward, as if he were in some pain, but he spoke firmly. The handshake he offered Khoo was perfunctory.

"Mr. Chia is not going to be present?"

"No. He, er . . ."

Lin-chun thought how distant Mr. Young seemed. A single lock of wavy hair strayed over his forehead, and she sensed that such untidiness was unusual in him.

". . . he's arranging to meet you next week. My son here . . . seems to have established himself as my ears in Taipei, so I've asked him to be present instead." Simon glanced at Mat in a way that confirmed Khoo's earlier suspicion: that the two Englishmen had been quarreling when their guests arrived.

Simon impatiently brushed the lock of hair away. "It's been quite a long time, Mr. . . . Khoo."

"Yes." Long enough, Khoo thought, for you to have put on weight and acquired a double chin: you have aged, Simon Young. "Incidentally, shall we speak English?"

"If you wish."

"Family well?"

"All well, thank you." Young's manner had become abrupt. Lin-chun wondered at the tension that crackled between banker and client.

"Good. Please remember me to them. How lucky you are to have a family; I'm still single."

For an instant Simon's eyes held still, but his face did not otherwise change. Then he said, "Indeed," and Lin-chun asked herself what thoughts were going through his mind at that moment.

In truth, he was finding Khoo as impossible as ever. Simon knew that his visitor's real name was Qiu and that he was married to a woman called Qingqing by whom he'd had a son; so here was one more lie to rise above, one more stratagem to master. He lifted his gaze to the smiling face of the man opposite and saw only a shifty manipulator. Which was a pity, because in his proper milieu Qiu could be a warrior worthy of respect.

For half an hour or so they discussed Ducannon Young's affairs, ranging from the group's development-capital requirements over the coming twelve months to deficiencies in the computerized payroll system. Time and again Simon would forget some detail, turn to Mat, and have it promptly supplied. Khoo realized that the young man had made himself indispensable to his father in a way that Simon Young resented. He had also acquired an intensive knowledge of how Taiwanese business worked that would have been astonishing even in a native-born Chinese. Khoo remembered last night and doodled three exclamation marks in the margin of his notebook.

It transpired that he'd forgotten to bring a vital document. He asked Lin-chun to go back to the office to fetch it, and Mat, evidently glad of an excuse to leave, offered to drive her.

After they'd gone, the banker lolled back in his armchair with a smile. "Was I too transparent?"

"How should I know? She's your employee. Why the hell are you mixed up in all this, anyway?"

"I like to work with figures. That's my discipline. I'm far more at home in this job than I was two years ago, killing traitors."

"Rubbish. You're Ducannon Young's minder, here in Taipei. Aren't you?"

"Minder?"

"You've been sent to make sure nothing happens to Apogee."

"That's part of it, yes." Khoo sat up. "And I can tell you I'm becoming increasingly frightened."

"What do you mean?"

"First, this customs prosecution. Then you appear to have got yourself mixed up in a murder. You're a sticky man, Mr. Young. All of a sudden you attract carrion."

"You can forget about the murder. I'm convinced it's just a ploy, however grisly, to put a check on my movements. And we'll weather the customs thing. Eventually." Simon stared at the floor. "Maybe I neglected this place for too long. Maybe it isn't the backwater I thought."

"I advise you not to change sides at this juncture."

"Don't be ridiculous."

"Your son seems to have divided loyalties. I hear he's deeply committed to Taiwan." The Chinese hesitated. "I'd like to talk to you as one father to another," he said slowly. "May I?"

"About Mat?"

"Yes."

Simon sighed. "Well?"

"Your son is . . . may perhaps be . . . a liability. I'm sorry." Khoo, observing that Simon was about to protest, held up his hands. "Let me finish. He's a brave young man, with many admirable qualities; I remember seeing them grow, from nowhere, in Chaiyang. But he's also headstrong and wayward."

"Headstrong, God, yes! What worthwhile young man isn't, at some point in his career?" Simon spoke bitterly, trying to convince himself along with Khoo.

"But such energy needs to be tempered with caution. When I saw your son yesterday he was not being cautious at all."

Khoo outlined the events of the previous night, playing down his own contribution to the drama. Simon kept his anger under control, but inside he was seething. "I can't tell you how upset it makes me to have to tell you these things," Khoo said. "I don't want to make trouble between father and son."

Simon waved away his sympathy with a brusque gesture. "We have problems communicating, sometimes."

"He didn't tell you about last night?"

"Not a word. I thought he looked at you oddly, but he's been acting strangely for a while and I put it down to surprise at seeing you again."

"You knew he was thinking of taking another job, presumably?"

"Oh yes, of course." It rang false. "Junior executives always go through that phase."

"Anyhow, I think no harm was done, this time."

"That doesn't matter. A fluke. I'll speak to him about it. I don't want to rush you, but if there isn't anything else . . ."

"Only the usual problem: time. When can we expect Apogee to be delivered?"

"There won't be any more holdups."

"You've said that before. We're increasingly worried about the competition's progress. You've heard of the French experimental fighter, Rafale?"

"Of course."

"Our information is that Crouzet has found a way around nearly all its teething problems."

"Except voice-recognition fragmentation at high altitude." Simon's smile was glacial. "My information is as good as yours, I think you'll find."

He looked at his watch. The dismissive gesture vexed Khoo beyond measure. "Let it wait! I've come to discuss mainland investment, the most important thing that's happened to China in a thousand years."

"You call a single aircraft—"

"Damn the aircraft! Do you think we can't see farther than our noses? Apogee's going to transform China into a different place, don't you realize that? And my job is to see that it isn't flung away in a nightclub brawl—"

"A brawl that you instigated, it might be said."

Khoo breathed in sharply and glowered at Simon through his spectacles. "I had no choice!"

"You could have spoken to him normally, one acquaintance greeting another."

"He was in no mood—"

"And I'm in no mood now to be lectured by you! I would remind you, Mr. Qiu, or Khoo, that you're a spy, operating out of uniform in enemy territory."

Qiu, dismayed, drew back his lips to the gums. "Please don't shout!"

"One phone call, that's all it would take. One phone call from this room to Garrison Command, and—"

"And Apogee would be smashed! Finished! Along with you and all your companies. Beijing would react within the hour, if anything happened to me, and you know it!"

For several moments after that, the two men remained silent, each equally appalled by the violence he had provoked in the other. "Would you like some tea?" Simon asked vacantly.

It was an unsatisfying anticlimax, but Khoo felt relieved all the same. "Yes. Thank you."

Simon brought Khoo a cup of Oolung. They sipped in silence, waiting for the aching anger to drain out of them.

"I'm sorry," Khoo said suddenly. "That's not what I intended. I meant to appeal to you as a family man. It came out wrong."

Simon stared at him. This was not like the Qiu Qianwei he remembered from the old days. "Families can cause the worst problems," he said at last. "It's possible to be dispassionate about the shortcomings of a mere employee. Sons are more difficult."

"I agree." Khoo grimaced and placed his cup on the table. "When we were arguing I kept thinking, how would I react if someone talked about Tingchen that way to me? And . . . to be frank, I think my reaction would be the same as yours."

"You've changed."

"Maybe." Khoo sighed. "Something to do with being far from home, I think."

"You miss your family?"

"Of course. How could I not?" By an association of ideas that did not strike him as odd, he checked his watch and said, "I wonder what's keeping Miss Shan? Would you mind if I telephoned the office?"

"Be my guest."

But just as Khoo reached the instrument, it rang and he

turned to Simon with a wry shrug. When the Englishman put the receiver to his ear he heard a succession of squeaks and, in the background, irregular thumps. "Who is it?"

"Mr. Young!"

"Yes . . . is that Lennie Luk?"

"Yes. Mr. Young . . . *aiya!*"

"What's the matter? Lennie? *Lennie!*"

The background noises had become louder. Lennie seemed terrified; he was having trouble breathing. "They're breaking into the flat."

"They? Who?"

"Not sure."

"I'll call the police and—"

"No! They say they *are* the police! Just listen. I copied everything that's here in the flat."

"You did *what*?"

"One copy only. Safe deposit, at the International Commercial Bank of China, in Chi-Lin Road. I've wiped all the disks here; they're clean."

"But—"

"I've already signed the reclaim ticket. It's in an envelope I gave to Mat to keep. All you—"

There was one last crash; the connection shrieked like a demented wildcat, and Simon thought he heard a voice that might have been Lennie's, shouting, "No!"

Then silence—as abrupt as if Simon had been listening to a recorded message and someone had cut the tape.

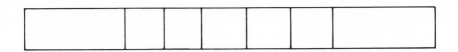

FIFTEEN

"*Please* be careful," Qingqing cried, and Tingchen nodded to show he'd heard.

She wanted to take his hand, but the boy refused to cooperate. He walked half a dozen steps in front of her, clutching a pair of skates to his chest and perusing the ground ahead of him with rapt concentration. The paths were thick with ice.

As they picked their way down toward the lake, Qingqing wondered, yet again, what on earth they were doing here, at Chengde Hill Station, in the middle of winter. True, the surrounding scenery was beautiful, and true, their quarters were more than comfortable; they were housed in the newly renovated Songhezhai Palace, once the home of the mother of the Emperor Qianlong. But—always she came back to this—why?

"Mother!" Tingchen had stopped. He pointed to his right and said, "Jinshanting."

Qingqing followed his pointing finger and, further along the shore of Saihu Lake, saw a three-story square tower artistically framed by pines, cypresses, and willows: the Golden Hill Pavilion. Its roofs were dusted with snow, making of it a tiered wedding cake. Beyond that, the hazy afternoon light washed the hills with a mixture of blues and pale mauves under an off-white sky. "Yes, that's where we're going."

She felt horribly muddled. In the first week of January, Sun Shanwang had invited her to the hill station for what he described as a seminar. It turned out to be nothing of the kind. Twenty or so women just like herself, wives of prominent Mah-jongg cadres, had been brought here to enjoy a winter vacation under the guise of attending study sessions that were never forthcoming. Qingqing disapproved. She felt that her work as the secretary of a district Party committee was more important than junketing with other grass widows; but when she voiced her disquiet, the matronly woman in charge of the dormitories said, "You should be grateful for the chance to come here. In summer the tourists have to pay, and they can't even spend one night. Have you no gratitude?" And Qingqing retired, abashed.

In China there was never an answer to the question *Why?*

But no, she was being too pessimistic. Sun Shanwang had arranged to meet her this afternoon; perhaps he would be more receptive.

About two dozen people had congregated by the side of the lake. Most of them were either skating or getting ready to do so. As mother and son approached they heard the chatter of many conversations, vibrant and shrill against the keen cold. Tingchen flopped down to put on his skates without asking permission, and Qingqing sighed. He had more independence of mind than most Chinese boys his age. That came from his father, of course. He was his father's child in so many ways, most of them irritating.

As the boy tottered down to the lakeside and hopped onto the ice, Qingqing watched him apprehensively. She began to walk up and down, trying to keep warm.

Tingchen skated with his hands behind his back. Qingqing looked on as he executed a slow circle, rounded off with a spin. He caught his mother's eye and did a pirouette, nearly losing his balance. He recovered with a nervous laugh, then moved off at a sedate pace, keeping parallel with the shore.

"Come on," Qingqing called. "We'll be late."

The view in front of her was so beautiful that she almost forgot to be cold. Crystals hung heavily on the willow branches, sagging them down to the steely blue surface of the frozen lake. Intricate cobwebs of snow and icicles hung in the pine trees like exotic New

Year decorations. Wherever Qingqing looked there was a pavilion or a palace or a pagoda peeping out of the white, wooded hillside, and every sloping roof bore its complement of icicles, as heavy and as palely translucent as the tubes of a glass xylophone. Her breath hung for an instant in the still air like a nebulous white cloud, before fragmenting into mist and then dissolving away.

"Good afternoon."

The voice came from behind her. She spun around. "Comrade Sun! I'm sorry, I didn't know you were there."

"Not at all. It's cold, isn't it? Very bracing. I enjoy this weather."

She thought enviously how fit he seemed for his age. He was wearing a short suede coat with a fur collar turned up to his ears, a wolfskin hat, and calf-length boots. He looked thoroughly Westernized. She felt embarrassed by her blue quilted jacket, so dated now and yet, to her, so reassuringly reminiscent of the past. As she smiled shyly at Sun he extended his arms and beat them to right and left, half a dozen times. "Come, shall we walk? Leave the boy, he's enjoying himself."

The party slowly approached Jinshanting, Tingchen skating while the adults walked the lakeside path. Now there were fewer people about, and Qingqing began to feel the first twinges of alarm.

High above them, on the third story of the Golden Hill Pavilion, a man was watching all that transpired. He stood alone on the western platform, smoking a cigarette, with one hand thrust into the pocket of his overcoat. Qingqing's words easily carried up as far as the platform, her singsong voice resounding in the arctic air like that of a Beijing opera singer. Sun's speech came across almost as distinctly. The man stood motionless, listening intently.

Down below, Sun spoke. "I didn't want us to keep a formal appointment in my office. People always seem to notice these things, don't they? Down here it can look like a chance meeting. Tell me, when did you last hear from your husband?"

"Oh . . . about a month ago."

"Is that normal—for a whole month to go by with no letter?"

"No . . . yes . . . nothing's happened to him, has it?" The anxiety in her tone was manifest. Sun smiled at her reassuringly and shook his head.

"No, nothing's happened to him. Not in that sense."

"In what sense, then?"

Sun began to speak, then let his pent-up breath escape in a

little sigh. "Difficult question," he said finally. "I don't know. Hence this talk with you."

"But how can I help?"

"By giving me your views." During this exchange Sun's face had been turned toward the lake; now he pointed and said, "Tell me, does Qianwei ever write to the boy?"

"Sometimes."

"Mm . . . Listen, I won't deceive you. We monitor the mail, we have to, and we've noticed a falling off. The censors report that he seems to write to Tingchen more than he does to you. And it worries us."

"It needn't, I can assure you." Qingqing found the conversation infinitely worse than she'd feared.

"You find this painful to discuss?"

"It is so . . . so personal."

"And China is not geared to the personal life. I know." Sun slapped his arms across his chest half a dozen times. "He's slipping," he said abruptly.

Qingqing, misunderstanding him, at once looked out toward the lake; but Tingchen was still on his feet.

"Your husband, he's behaving oddly. We'd like to know why." The expression on Qingqing's face was one of utter astonishment. Sun considered it for a moment and concluded that it was unfeigned. "The quality of his reports is worsening," he said gently. "But there's something else, far more serious. He's obliged to transmit messages at regular intervals, to let the Brigade know he's still operating. On two recent occasions he was late with those messages. And once he seems to have forgotten altogether. I'll have to warn him that if it happens again it'll be a major disciplinary matter."

She was shocked; it showed in her face. "I . . . I don't know what to say."

"You find it surprising that I confide your husband's shortcomings in you?"

"Yes."

"But who knows a man better than his wife? There's seemingly a loss of commitment. Can you think of any explanation?"

"No."

"Tell me . . . this is difficult, I know, but tell me . . . has Qianwei ever shown signs of wanting . . . ?"

"Another woman?" She flushed. "I really couldn't say. But he's a good man. You know that. A *good* man."

Sun said nothing.

"You don't believe me?"

"I do. But good men sometimes find themselves faced with bad situations. So I must ask you again—can you think of anything that might explain his recent behavior?"

"I? Excuse me, Comrade Sun, but I still don't understand. Surely the Brigade has better ways of checking up on its cadres than this?"

"Not in the present instance." He took a deep breath and delivered the stroke. "Your husband is working in Taiwan."

"Taiwan! *Aiya!*"

"You had no idea?"

For a moment she could not respond. "No," she faltered at last. "Singapore . . . he said Singapore, all his letters come from there." She closed her eyes, as if by doing that she could shut out the truth.

"Perhaps you understand now. Your husband is very exposed. He has no backup, no support. Direct communication with him is especially dangerous. I have to go in roundabout fashion, picking up what clues to his behavior I can. Do you see?"

Qingqing stared fixedly at Tingchen while she strove to find the words that would please Sun. They refused to come. Taiwan, her husband was in Taiwan. . . .

"Will he come back?" she said, her voice very low. When Sun did not reply immediately she repeated the question, more urgently this time.

"The situation is . . . fluid." He laid a hand on her shoulder and tugged gently, making her look him in the face. "I offered him the chance to come home. He declined."

Qingqing turned away and, through a blur of tears, saw Tingchen still executing figures on the same patch of ice. Distant voices carried through the bitterly cold air, making it reverberate with their laughter, and she became half-aware of three or four other skaters lazily cruising toward her son.

"The house is so . . . so *empty*." She sniffed, wiping her eyes on the sleeve of her coat. "Oh, you've no idea what it's like in the house without him. . . ."

The ice around her heart was cracking now; the words gushed forth.

". . . and he'd come back of an evening and the first thing he'd say was, 'What sort of day did you have?' I used to tease him about it. 'How many sorts of day are there?' I'd say. 'Monday, Tuesday . . .' "

Cracking faster and faster.

". . . and then he always gave me a kiss, always . . ."

The ice cracked.

Tingchen disappeared under the black surface of the lake with time for only one shriek; but it seemed to hover in the air long afterwards, as if petrified in ice.

For the merest fraction of a second, nothing else happened. The scene on the lake resembled a still life. Then it became an old-time movie, all black and white and superfast shaking movement.

The man on the pagoda's platform dropped his cigarette with a cry. As he ran for the stairs, the approaching skaters lowered their heads and started to sprint toward the huge, ugly hole in the ice. Sun Shanwang raced down to the water's edge and gingerly took a few steps out to where Tingchen's red peaked cap could be seen bobbing up and down.

The boy's head appeared above the surface. He had time to shriek *"Mama!"* just once before water went in his mouth and his cries were stifled. As he went down, his hands by a miracle managed to grasp the edge of the ice and for an instant he clung there, sobbing and choking, in the grip of a remorselessly fatal panic.

"Hold on!" Sun shouted. "Don't go under!"

"He can't swim!" Qingqing sped past Sun, hearing the ice creak beneath her feet, not heeding, not caring about her own safety, or Sun's. When she was within ten feet of him, the surface crumbled beneath her and she was instantly up to her neck in icy water, but she scarcely felt the cold, so intent was she on struggling toward the small body that still clung grimly to life.

She reached out to grab him; as she did so, the ice he was holding on to sheared away and he disappeared.

A groan went up from Sun, echoed by the skaters, but Qingqing did not hear them. She threw herself forward with all her strength, plunging beneath the surface and striking out blindly. She swam and swam, her heart beating faster and faster, her lungs screaming out for relief, but there was nothing except darkness.

Then she bumped against something soft. She grabbed for it, missed, grabbed again; and this time her hands got a hold. An arm. She had him. *She had him!*

She kicked upward and at once her head banged against ice. Qingqing, shocked senseless by the pain, felt the last reserves of air torn from her lungs in a despairing cry. Then everything around her seemed to shatter in a cataclysmic roar of noise. She was aware of blinding white light. A glimpse of the shore. Shivering. Darkness. Nothing.

Sun Shanwang found Qiu sitting beside Tingchen's bed, head in hands. When he touched him lightly on the shoulder, Qiu shuddered and looked up fearfully.

"No, stay there. Any news?"

Qiu shook his head. "He's still sedated, but the doctor says he's not in any danger. You're all right?"

"I am."

"I saw what you did. It was very brave. Thanks."

"I turned back quickly. I realized that it wouldn't help if we all went under." Sun peered over at the only other bed in the plainly furnished room. "Your wife?"

Qiu appeared to remember Qingqing for the first time. "Oh . . . the same. She's sleeping now. She'll be all right. If only . . ."

"If only what?"

"If only I hadn't climbed that tower. I should have been the one to save him. . . ."

"You're talking nonsense, Qianwei. It was sheer chance that you weren't in Taipei this weekend. If I hadn't recalled you, you wouldn't even have been aware the accident had happened." Sun looked at his watch. "I'm sorry to trouble you at a time like this, but it can't wait any longer. Please come with me."

He led the way down a corridor to the infirmary's entrance, where a car was waiting. Sun ushered Qiu into the backseat and climbed in beside him, closing the partition behind the driver's head.

"You have the rest of the weekend to spend with your family," Sun said as the car pulled away, "but I need to go to the airport now. The driver will bring you back afterwards."

"Thank you."

"I begin by reminding you why you *were* on the tower, not by the lake; I told you to go there because I wanted you to overhear the conversation. Since you were standing above us, I trust you heard what we said?"

"Most of it."

"Enough to know that we're concerned about you."

"And afraid I'm guilty of sexually immoral conduct."

"Qianwei, Qianwei . . . don't let things grow out of proportion. I know how hard life in Taipei must be."

"Hard?"

"The constant fear. The loneliness. Am I not right?"

"Yes." It was on the tip of his tongue to add *sometimes*.

"That, however, is no excuse for neglecting your duties. Why didn't you leave your signal at the agreed drop on the first of this month?"

Qiu Qianwei had had plenty of time to prepare for this question. "I believed it was under surveillance," he said smoothly. "The same man showed up once too often. I felt reluctant to take a chance."

To his immense relief, Sun Shanwang appeared to accept this. "Then why didn't you send a delete signal?"

"I was going to. But once you think you've been identified, it's not so easy."

"I have to accept what you say. But please try harder in future. Things are tense here."

"The invasion?"

Sun nodded. "Don't leave your escape too late. I won't be able to give you much warning. It may well be a case of 'If it's time to go, then it's too late to go.'"

"I still find it hard to believe in this invasion. With Apogee on hold—"

"You've no news for me?"

"None. You know the situation we're in. The entire project apparently hangs on Luk, and Luk's been kidnapped, I don't know who by."

"Who do you think is holding Luk?"

Qiu shrugged. "The Taiwanese authorities?"

"I don't think so. They may be renegades and bandits in the eyes of the Politburo, but they adhere to their domestic law in all cases involving foreigners. I can see them using the customs prosecution they launched over Hsinchu as a means of trying to find out more about the project, but kidnapping, no."

"Then who?"

"Simon Young himself, perhaps? To provide another excuse for delay while he covers up mistakes, or, worse, deals with other interested purchasers. . . ."

"I don't accept that."

"Nor do I—for the moment. I'll make another guess: Our Formosa Now."

"You're not serious?"

"Oh yes. We've had Wu Tie-zi followed whenever he leaves Taiwan. Last week he went to Osaka, where he took delivery, personally, of a number of crates that had come into the country under diplomatic protection. We managed to take a look inside while they were still awaiting transshipment at the docks. Do you know what those crates contained?"

Qiu raised an eyebrow. "Arms?"

"Yes. Wu took the stuff out on a tramp steamer, that same night."

"But where did these arms come from? You can't just go to some backstreet dealer. . . ."

"No. You need the kind of resources and security that only governments can provide. You remember I said the weapons came into Osaka under diplomatic protection?"

"Yes. Whose?"

"One of those piddling African countries that keeps changing its name every six months. A Soviet puppet-state, needless to say. Here we are."

The driver pulled in outside the terminal building, but Sun Shanwang made no move. "Wu met someone staying in the same hotel, ostensibly the seller's agent, traveling on a commercial attache's diplomatic passport. Our people got a glimpse, and one snapshot. The light was atrocious, but I doubt if you'll have any difficulty putting a name to the face."

Sun pulled a square photograph from an inside pocket and handed it to Qiu. The cadre peered at it, not believing his eyes. "Borisenko," he breathed. "To go to Japan . . . such a risk."

"He's a brave man. Against that, I suppose Kazin isn't going to let such a sensitive cargo travel all the way to the Far East in the care of some thick-headed private detective."

"So the Russians and OFN—"

"Are linked. I'm late." Sun got out of the car and turned back to address Qiu through the window. "I think you'd better take a look at Wu's base, if you're still in the fight."

"I am."

Sun probed Qiu's face for a long moment. "Good. All my instincts tell me that Wu's holding Luk. If he is—get him out. I don't care how you do it, but get him out."

"All right."

"And, Qiu . . ."

"Yes?"

"Don't blame your wife for what happened. It wasn't her fault."

The cadre's face darkened. "She should have watched what he was doing. She—"

"*Enough!*" Sun brought his clenched fist down on the ledge of the open car window. "Your marriage is your own affair. I'm sorry it's not working out, but you must have known that was a risk you were running when you gave up your office job, years ago. Just remember—you have a son. Who will look after him, if Qingqing isn't there to do it?"

The Controller of Intelligence read an unthinkable message in Qiu's distorted features and resolved to kill it stone dead. "Not you," Sun said shortly. "I'll see to that, and no mistake! *Not you!*"

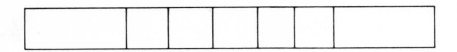

SIXTEEN

"How much farther is it?"

Mei-hua examined her mouth in the vanity mirror, sucked in her lower lip to moisten it, and began to rummage about in her totebag. "We've just gone through Meiho, so . . . say ninety kilometers."

Apart from the occasional village, the scenery had hardly changed since they left Taitung Airport. Under a milky yellow sky the color of soybean soup, they'd driven past courtyard farmhouses; feathery bamboo groves sixty feet tall; old men in pointed straw hats plowing with oxen; temples and pagodas on hillsides distantly viewed across the flat coastal plain.

"What do you think of southern Taiwan?" Mei-hua asked.

"I've always liked it."

"I didn't realize you'd been here before."

"Rod Haines showed me around, when I was first posted to Taiwan." Mat smiled and nodded toward the right-hand side of the road. "I even own a chunk of it. A few acres here and there."

"Why?"

"Because on my first visit I realized the east coast would make an ideal holiday resort. Another Hawaii—Maui, say. With the new nuclear power stations coming along and plenty of water in the mountains, facilities weren't a problem. So I bought very cheaply. And one day I'll sell it off for a fortune."

"How clever you are." Mei-hua sighed, rested her neck well back on the seat top, and stroked Mat's hair.

"It's nearly lunchtime," he said. "We ought to stop soon."

"There are some caves in the hills up ahead. The guidebook says they've got 'atmosphere.' "

The caves turned out to be half-concealed in cliffs that towered high above the spectacular east coast. The climb to the highest one, sometimes up a rickety wooden stairway, more often on steps gouged out of the soil and pounded hard, left them breathless and uncomfortably wet.

"My God!" Mei-hua gasped. "Worth it, huh?"

From this perch they could just see a black-sand beach washed by breakers. Smoke from rice straw being burned in the distant paddies and the scent of camphor trees sat heavily in their nostrils.

"Ugh . . ."

Mat ran over to find Mei-hua transfixed by an enormous spider, lying in its self-made hammock spun between two branches. "Don't touch it!"

"You think I'm crazy?"

He wiped the sweat off his forehead. Slowly, almost imperceptibly, he felt his senses yielding to a peculiarly potent atmosphere—an experience not unlike mild anesthesia. It dawned on him that here the air did not move *at all*.

"I don't like this place," Mei-hua pouted.

"I do. It's got . . . I don't know, spiritual power. There's an altar at the back of this cave; did you see it? I think the statue's of the Goddess of Mercy."

"You're wonderful." It's true, she thought; I've never known anyone half as good as you.

Confusion invaded her brain. What was she doing here? Of course—she had a job to do. She felt nauseous. Withdrawal symptoms. Say something.

"I'm jealous. Of you. Good-looking bastard."

"You've no cause."

"Oh, I'm always jealous. I'm even jealous of people who aren't."

"Aren't what?"

"Jealous. D'you want a sandwich?"

She watched him eat, unable to face food herself. His eyes went everywhere, just as they sometimes did when there were other women around, making her writhe. "You're planning to go a long way, aren't you?"

Mat smiled. "Yes."

"So why are you fiddling about here, on Taiwan? With Daddy?"

"There wasn't much else on offer. I don't have a degree."

"Why not?"

"Because I didn't want one. I've seen too many graduates out of work. Here in the Far East, degrees don't match up to practical experience. University's just a putting-off of life's battles."

"Sure you didn't just fail the entrance exam?"

He grinned. "I won a scholarship to Emmanuel, if you must know. I turned it down. Dad hated me for that."

"I'll bet. So you ended up as a humble contracts manager."

"That's right."

"Not very ambitious-sounding."

"Maybe I'm frightened of failure." He became serious. "It's a good start for someone who's going to inherit an empire."

"Why?"

"Because if everyone works, and is seen to work, with no favoritism and no one having a right to the soft jobs, people are happier all around."

"You learned that at school, I'll bet."

"No. A village called Chaiyang, actually." He raised his voice, suddenly anxious to avoid being questioned. "If you want to take over something from a strongman father, you need to start at the bottom. For my sister, it's different. She'll go her own way."

"Oh yes, Diana. Is she better?"

"A bit, thanks."

"I went my own way, too."

"Yes, but you're different. Diana's studying the history of Korean art. She'll be an academic all her life—not like you."

She gave his cheek a playful slap. "You think I'm so dumb. Let me tell you—"

But he had pushed her over, and for the next few minutes her mouth was too occupied to tell him anything, except that she loved him beyond salvation.

They reached the house below Anshuo in the late afternoon, when the sun was well down behind the high backbone of Taiwan's central mountain range. Mat got out and looked around in awe. "What a place!"

"I'm glad you like it," said a man's voice, in English, behind him. "Mr. Matthew Young, yes? I'm Wu Tie-zi."

"Hello."

"And this is my wife, Su-liang."

The two women at once began to chatter in Taiwanese, an Amoy dialect that Mat had heard many times but never tried to master. Wu put a friendly arm around his shoulders and began to lead him up the steps to the front door. "Remind me to tell you what my Chinese friends call me," he said quietly. "Make you laugh. *Tie*, in *guo-yu*, means 'iron.' According to my pals, I have all kinds of iron features . . . appendages is the word, I think." He guffawed. "Iron balls! Come, I want you to see the garden while it's still light."

His host escorted him along the terrace to where a double flight of stairs led down to the pool area, with its changing rooms and bar. Mat paused on the steps for a moment, enjoying the view.

"It's beautiful."

"Thank you. Everything planted here has a meaning, you know. There you see bamboo, pine, and prunus, planted together—the 'three friends,' we call them. Pomegranate for fertility. You must ask my wife about it all."

The garden had evidently been modeled on a classical northern Chinese pleasure park. Mat could see a moon gate, a pavilion in a copse beside a waterfall, and an ornamental pool full of carp. There was every conceivable kind of plant, shrub, and tree, including cherry and plum. Bright poinsettia bloomed early this far south, adding color to the scene. To the right, a hundred yards away on the side of a little hill in one corner of the property, stood a pagoda five stories high, octagonal, its white walls decorated with red paint under a sloping gold roof.

Wu Tie-zi went behind the bar and poured a couple of beers. "What was the weather like in Taipei when you left?" he asked.

"Cold and wet."

"Were you surprised to find such a change in the south?"

"It was a stark contrast, I must admit. This is spring weather." Mat made a face. "No doubt I'll be getting used to it."

"Why?"

"Because I'm being transferred to Dunny's Kaohsiung office next month. Less interesting work."

"Whose idea was that?"

"My father's, I think, although he denied it when I asked him.

The trouble is, he's rushing around trying to deal with so many problems at the moment that his mind isn't really on me at all."

Wu hooted with laughter. "You don't have to tell me! The Chinese like their businesses to be family concerns, but it isn't always easy." He put down his beer and swiveled in his chair so that he could look at Mat. "Cards on the table. Shall we talk before the ladies come along?"

"I'm listening."

"Mei-hua and I have been friends since God knows when. She's told me a lot about you. You didn't really want to work for your father in the first place, did you?"

"Not really. But there weren't that many opportunities, and I was lazy. . . ."

"I understand. When I was young I lived in Melbourne for a while, then Hong Kong. I bummed around, enjoying myself, and I don't regret any of it. But now you want to branch out on your own, and I like that. You have a lot of potential. Let me be frank— you also have a good family name, here in Southeast Asia. A lucky name."

"That's fair."

"The question I have to ask myself is, Who can this bright young man bring with him?"

"And the answer?"

"The answer I'm looking for is Luk and Haines. A good scientist, a good money man. Computer software, that's your future. Luk to do the technical side, Haines to supervise the accounts, you to provide the ideas and the drive."

"And you?"

"Me to provide the cash, in exchange for fifty percent of the equity. There'd be a lot of detail to discuss, but what do you say about it in principle?" Wu picked up his beer glass and drained it, as if unconcerned with Mat's response.

"I'm tempted."

"Yes, go on. I hear a 'but' somewhere."

Mat smiled. "All sorts of buts. It's a big thing to raid your own father's firm and take two of his best men. And I'm still young, you know."

Wu shrugged. "The very fact that you say that means you're not as young as you think. What else?"

"It's a bad time. Lennie Luk's still missing. It hardly makes sense to set up a new company when one leg of the tripod's vanished into thin air."

"Of course, I take that point."

"Then there are family considerations. It's not just my father I have to think about. There's Mother as well."

"Ah. Now that I respect. It's a fine sentiment."

"Is it? I feel it may be just my way of making excuses for not breaking out. Like I ducked it before, when I joined Ducannon Young. How much time do I have to think this over?"

"Oh, there's no hurry."

Mat hesitated. "You've been very kind to me," he said at last. "I wouldn't want to hold back on you. I'm going to say something now that you may find hard to understand."

"Try me."

"Well, the thing is . . . I feel, very strongly, I want to give my father another chance. I still respect him and . . . well, I've seen the power of 'family' at work. I don't have to tell you that 'family' can achieve one hell of a lot."

Wu lowered his eyes and sighed. "How can I quarrel with that? It is exactly what I would expect a Chinese son to say." He glanced at his guest with respect. "You're like your father, you know: oriental in outlook. Did he ever tell you about dragons, how they're made?"

"No."

"Many people think that dragons and snakes are the same in some way, but that isn't so. Dragons evolve from fish, not snakes. The story goes that if a carp can leap over the Long An watergate on Yellow River, he'll become a dragon. That's why the dragon has become a symbol of hope." Wu nodded decisively. "You're a fine, healthy young carp. Going to be a dragon, no mistake. But—going to do it in the correct way, and that I admire."

"I'm still not sure it isn't all to do with guilt. Ah! Here are the ladies."

Su-liang and Mei-hua came down the stairs. Wu's wife was wearing a dark green patterned pantsuit; Mei-hua had changed into a cheongsam the colour of cinnabar, with a lace yoke. Mat looked at them approaching and thought how classically Chinese they seemed, each in her own distinctive way representing a generation.

The two men stood up to greet them. By now the dusk had begun to gather and a servant brought stylish modern glass oil lamps to light the terrace. "What about drinks?" said Su-liang.

"I'll make us some cocktails."

Mat had once more been surveying the garden. "I'm dying to take a look at that pagoda of yours. Is it possible to climb it?"

"I'd rather you didn't," Wu said apologetically. "It looks very attractive, but in fact it's an ornament to cover up our drainage system."

"Of course."

"But if you want something to do . . . I know! Ah-Huan!" Wu raised his voice. "Ah-Huan, come here!"

They heard light footsteps on the garden path, and the next moment an aborigine appeared; first his head, then his body, and finally his long, sturdy legs hove into view. He strode majestically with head held high, as if conscious of how to make an effective entrance. Mat stole a sideways glance at Mei-hua to find that her lips were moist and slightly parted, with the very tip of her tongue just visible between them.

"Ah-Huan is head of our household staff. He's a member of the Lukai tribe. They live in a village called Wutain and are famous for two things, marathon running and archery." Wu turned to his retainer. "Ah-Huan, our guests would like to see you shoot."

The aborigine pattered back along the path without a word, only to reappear a moment later with his longbow and a quiver full of arrows.

Ah-Huan strung the yew bow. His muscles flexed beneath the glistening skin in a movement of perfect smoothness, without any hint of strain. That done, he selected an arrow some three feet long, fletched with black goose feathers.

Wu picked up a pomegranate from the bar and handed it to his wife. "By the carp pool," he said, "if you'd be so kind?"

She nodded and set off down the garden path. Wu smiled at his guests. "Please remember not to eat the fruit afterwards—the arrows are used for hunting, so they're tipped with poison."

When Su-liang reached the pool, about a hundred meters away from where the others were standing, she stopped and held up the pomegranate.

"The bow has very high draw-weight," Wu commented. "The arrow flies at approximately one hundred and twenty feet per second."

"She's going to throw the pomegranate up and he's going to split it," Mei-hua said excitedly. "How *fabulous*!"

"Not quite," murmured Wu Tie-zi. "But you're close."

Su-liang did not throw the fruit. Instead, she stood holding it between thumb and forefinger, her hand extended at right angles to her body. The light was fading and Su-liang stood deep in the shadows of the garden. Mat gasped. "He's surely not going to—"

Ah-Huan raised his bow. For a moment the barbed tip of the arrow traversed the strip of royal blue sky above the mountain range; then it was coming down through bands of yellow and gold, across the face of the hillside, down, down, down. . . .

A twang, a hiss, a streak of silver.

Mat's heart bucked and he cried out. Mei-hua was jumping up and down beside him, clapping her hands in excitement. "He did it, he did it!"

Su-liang bent down to pick up the two halves of the pomegranate; she held them aloft for a moment, a calm smile on her face, before making her way back up the path. Mat took a deep breath and expelled it. He looked at the spot where Ah-Huan had been standing a moment before, but of the aborigine there was no sign.

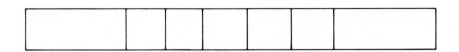

SEVENTEEN

From his vantage point in a dense pine grove to the west of the house, Qiu Qianwei had an uninterrupted view, across a deep gulley and the ornamental garden, of the terrace and pool. To his left stood the pagoda. This structure intrigued Qiu. Its unglazed windows were about three feet high by two feet wide, but the building was unlit and he could see nothing of the interior. He knew, however, that the pagoda was occupied, for, shortly after taking up position in the pine grove, he'd observed a man carrying a tray of food down from the house to the tower. This man used two keys to unlock the door before going inside, only to emerge a moment later without the tray.

Qiu watched Mat and Mei-hua leave early on Sunday morning. When another guest arrived, he knew he'd been right to take up Sun Shanwang's suggestion and visit Wu's headquarters.

The new guest's arrival, at four o'clock, had been unostentatious. Under Qiu's inquisitive scrutiny a black Yue Loong sedan circled the house and came to a halt beside the main entrance. It was an odd car to find in such a wealthy household. The rear window on the driver's side had been broken, and instead of repairing it with a black-tinted pane to match the others, the garage had inserted a sheet of plain glass, giving the vehicle an air of seediness. Qiu noted that its license plate was beige, which in Taiwan meant that this car was classified for commercial use.

Then one of the rear doors opened to reveal Major General Krubykov of the KGB.

The Russian disappeared inside, and for about two hours nothing else happened. A few minutes ago the Wus and Krubykov had come onto the terrace, and now Wu Tie-zi was shaking cocktails behind the poolside bar. Qiu rummaged in his satchel. He brought out a compact rectangular instrument resembling a Sony Walkman, with what looked like a telescopic aerial painted camouflage green. It was a miniaturized directional microphone. He pointed the aerial toward the house, put on the earphone, and began to adjust the frequency.

". . . part of Our Formosa Now. It's a sworn brotherhood: *siek-sai*."

"What?"

"Oh . . . acquainted, familiar. One of us."

"Like the Mafia, Cosa Nostra, that sort of thing?"

"In a way, except that most provincial businesses also depend on legitimate *siek-sai* to get along. Everyone does favors for everyone else."

"It sounds like the KGB to me."

Su-liang chuckled. Tie-zi brought the drinks and she explained the joke to him. Qiu made a fine adjustment to the microphone.

"So." Krubykov raised his glass. "To the liberation of Formosa."

"To the sworn brotherhood between the KGB and OFN!"

"Siek-sai!"

The three people on the terrace laughed. Qiu knew this was not the time to digest or analyze what he had just heard. But he must remember. He must remember all of it.

"And now," said Krubykov, "Apogee."

It was Wu who responded. "Our man is making quiet progress. There's no doubt he'll succeed in penetrating the Ducannon Young research team here, in Taiwan, within the next few months. Hong Kong may take rather longer. But now we have a shortcut."

"What kind of shortcut?"

"We have Luk. Luk's the key to Apogee, the technical whiz-kid, isn't that the expression? And we're holding him there"—he raised an arm and pointed—"in the pagoda. It has a cellar, it's quite secure."

"Isn't that risky?"

"Risky? When we have such excellent connections in Taiwan Garrison Command?"

Qiu turned up the volume control to "max." His mouth was dry.

"And even if Luk can't be persuaded to talk, there's always Matthew Young."

"He's no technician."

"Ah, but he's the son of the owner of the Ducannon Young group."

Krubykov frowned. "There's no sophistication about this project," he said. "You're behaving like a bunch of thugs. If Young makes a big enough stink, not even the Taiwan government is going to risk losing all its foreign investment. Don't push that man too far."

Qiu smiled.

"I think our guest has an excellent point," said Su-liang. "It might be said . . ."

The conversation was turning acrimonious. Qiu decided he could achieve only so much by listening to what was said on the terrace. He packed up his microphone and stowed his knapsack in a hole beneath a large pine that he'd excavated earlier, carefully marking the bark beforehand. What to take? A flashlight, that should do.

Qiu hugged every scrap of cover he could find, worming his way through the undergrowth like a lizard. At last he encountered a rusty mesh fence. He was on his feet and over the obstacle in a trice.

As he reached the pagoda, he stole a glance up at the terrace. The three people sitting there were still deep in conversation.

Qiu, keeping the pagoda between himself and the house, subjected the nearest window to critical examination. There was no glass to worry about, but were the gaps protected electronically? No. This place wasn't designed to be used as a permanent prison.

The lower edge of the window was some three feet above his head. Qiu reached for the sill, hauled himself up, and peered in. Nothing was visible. He dithered a second longer before slipping inside. He landed safely, his rubber-soled shoes making little noise on the concrete floor.

Qiu fingered his flashlight. Should he risk using it? Better not, he decided. Instead, he began to feel his way around the structure's perimeter. After a moment he came to the door and, nearby, the first step of a circular stairway leading upward.

Qiu closed his eyes and strained to listen. He could hear nothing, but for the past few minutes he had been aware of an increasingly uneasy conviction that someone was listening to him. Someone immobile. Someone *silent*.

Qiu moistened his lips. He'd come this far, there was nothing to do but go on.

He began to inch across the floor. Before he had gone very far his hands made contact with a solid obstacle raised a few inches off the concrete. He ran his fingers over it. Wood. Qiu leaned forward, testing the extent of the obstruction. A panel, some four feet square, set into a frame not quite flush with the floor, with a beam resting on it. Qiu quietly slid the beam through its fastenings. On the side of the panel farthest from him was a ring. He padded around and lifted the trapdoor.

Qiu cocked his head, listening. You are alone, he told himself firmly. There's no one here.

He lay flat on the cold floor and put his head through the opening. "Luk."

"Who's there?" The voice rose out of the pitch-black recess as if from a grave.

"Qiu Qianwei. Can you move?"

"No. I'm tied." Lennie sounded weak.

"I'll come down."

"Where are you?" Qiu said as he reached the bottom step. "Keep talking."

Lennie began to count aloud. Qiu groped his way forward, keeping his head turned in the direction of the spectral voice. As Lennie felt Qiu's touch, he recoiled with a whimper.

"Are you all right? Have they injured you?"

"No. But I was drugged. And there's a rope around my wrists. Can you loosen it?"

The knots were tight but unprofessional; it took Qiu only a minute to untie them. "Ai . . . my God!" wailed the captive.

"What's the matter?"

"My wrists . . . the blood . . . pounding."

"Rub them hard. Listen—we're going out. What sort of shape are you in?"

"Okay, I think. My legs are all right; I kept walking up and down."

"Here, take my hand. Hurry."

[182]

Before long, they had resurfaced on the floor of the pagoda. "What are you doing here?" Lennie's voice cracked with suspicion. "Are you working for them?"

"Who's 'them'?"

"I don't know, for Christ's sake! Why did those men take me?"

"For Apogee, of course. But if I was with them, would I be taking you out now? Listen. There's a long trek ahead of us, through the hills. Are you up to it?"

"I have to be, don't I?"

"Yes!" Qiu hauled himself up to the nearest window. It was almost dark outside; as far as he could see, the garden was deserted. He dropped back to the floor. "Follow me at all times. If we're separated, don't waste time looking for me. Run. Keep going west. We're only about forty kilometers from the coast."

"Why go west? I don't understand."

"This is Wu Tie-zi's country. His fief. Once you're missed, he'll have people out hunting for us. They'll assume we've taken the east coast highway; nobody'll think of looking for us in the hills. Now come on."

Qiu pushed Lennie up onto the sill of the window farthest from the house. As soon as he heard him drop to the ground he followed. For a moment the two of them stood listening to the evening breeze; then Qiu grasped Lennie's forearm and began to climb the hill to the west, making for the cover of the nearest gulley.

"Stop!" snarled a voice.

Qiu sorted through impressions. A man, perhaps more than one, was standing in front of them, some twenty paces distant, shining a powerful beam into their eyes. Behind them, farther away, others were climbing the hill. He was on the point of shouting "Run!" to Lennie when his sight started to clear and he discerned a shadowy figure (there was a second man, then) standing close to the source of the light, holding something at arm's length. A drawn longbow, leveled at them.

"What's this?" Wu Tie-zi sounded uncertain. Krubykov pushed him aside. "Shine that light up!" He stared at Qiu in astonishment. "You!"

Qiu glanced sideways at Lennie. There were no signs of panic. As the light flickered here and there, Qiu began to count faces. The archer, barring the path. The lamp-bearer. Two Chinese, one man, one woman. Krubykov. The Chinese couple stood ten feet away, to one side; Krubykov much nearer. No exit.

But no guns, either.

Krubykov turned to Wu Tie-zi. "I've met this man before, in Hong Kong. He's a Red agent. Do you know what he's doing here?"

Wu shook his head. "He can tell us himself," Krubykov said. "At the house."

Qiu felt his options halving. He knew that once they were on their way, hemmed in on every side, they were finished. He cast a desperate look at Lennie, willing him to read his expression, then opened his mouth and stuck his fingers inside. Everyone heard a distinct snapping sound. A second later Qiu fell to the ground, keening in agony.

"Stop him!" Krubykov shouted. "Suicide pill!"

He pounced on Qiu, stabbing at the cadre's clenched lips with the points of his fingers. Wu and his wife stepped back. The man holding the light ran up, seeking to focus the beam on Qiu's face. After a second's hesitation the archer lowered his bow and laid it on the ground.

Qiu saw Krubykov kneeling over him; his ruse had worked! He jolted the side of his hand into the Russian's Adam's apple and poked the fingers of his other hand at the eyes directly above his own. Qiu screamed, "Lennie! Run!" He catapulted upright, heaving the Russian to one side, and wheeled around in time to see the archer dart for his longbow. Qiu threw himself on to the aborigine, fighting for the weapon.

Within a second he knew he had miscalculated. The aborigine was as hard as stone and immeasurably stronger than any opponent Qiu had ever fought. The instant his body hit the ground he rolled over, Qiu still attached to his back, and pinned him to the ground by sheer weight. Qiu gasped. He had less than a second to reverse the odds. The aborigine began to sit up. Qiu's hand flailed between his opponent's legs, seeking the sensitive skin at the top of the inner thighs. But Ah-Huan had the advantage now.

Qiu felt himself blacking out. His hand wrenched uselessly, his feeble movements making no impression on the mountain of a man above him. A fold of skin was all he needed, just one little fold. . . .

Ah-Huan's sarong had ridden up almost to his waist in the violence of Qiu's attack. Suddenly Qiu's hand made contact with something more vulnerable than the skin of the upper thigh, and his fingers convulsed around the aborigine's scrotum. He wrenched with all his might.

He was free, he was up, he was running.

Qiu heard someone being sick behind him; the noise gave him

satisfaction. As he ran the light flickered, sometimes capturing him in its beam, but there seemed to be no one capable of directing it. "Lennie!" he cried.

"Here!"

Qiu groaned. Lennie's voice came from the wrong direction. He must have run downhill, toward the riverbed. Qiu made off through the trees, stumbling over roots and boulders but somehow managing to keep upright. "Lennie!" he shouted again.

Then he heard footsteps ahead of him. Qiu began to sprint. Before very long he had caught up with Lennie. "Keep to the *right*! We need the cover of the hills."

They were nearly his last words. First Qiu heard a kind of rushing noise as the air beside his head seemed to dissolve in an evil shiver; all his nerves contracted; a loud, deep twang reverberated a few feet away—and in that instant he realized that the bowman could judge a man's position from the sound of his voice, from the noise his feet made on stones.

The arrow had passed within six inches of Qiu's head and embedded itself in the bole of a tree. Where? It was too dark to see, but the noise of the impact had been very close. "Down!" he whispered in Lennie's ear. "Lie flat!"

He started to blunder toward where he thought the arrow had landed, hoping he'd remembered right. He wanted that arrow, wanted it desperately. His feet scrunched on the stones and a little gasp of fear escaped his lips. Noise. Ah-Huan could shoot by ear; he had no need of light.

As if in recognition of Qiu's fears he heard the first ripple of sound behind him, precursor of the vicious arrowhead closing inexorably on its target. Then the air at the back of his neck seemed to vibrate, all his hair stood on end. . . . Qiu Qianwei had time to shriek just once, very loudly, before he fell.

The drive from the airport to Mei-hua's apartment took them past the Executive Yuan, a sprawling complex set back from one corner of the city's largest intersection, between Chung Hsiao East and Chungshan roads. There seemed to be a lot of troops milling around, but Mat had time for no more than a glance before Mei-hua cried, "Lin-chun! Oh, darling, do stop."

He pulled up to the curb, braving the wrath of the MP on guard at the gate.

Lin-chun stood just inside, watching a lone soldier march away; but when Mei-hua called out, she hurried over to join them.

From what Mat could see of her in the rearview mirror, he gathered she was distressed. "Is everything all right?"

"Yes. Fine. That is . . . Jacqui, do you remember me ever mentioning Tsai Zi-yang?"

"Who, dearest? Oh—your old MP flame?"

"Mm-hm." Lin-chun blushed. "I hadn't heard from him for months. Then suddenly he . . ." She fell silent and looked down at her handbag.

"Yes?"

"He asked me to come out to meet him. I said I would. He sounded strange. Worried."

"Is something wrong?"

"He wanted to say goodbye to me."

"Why? Where's he going?"

"He wasn't sure; he's only a captain and whatever's going on is top secret. But . . . oh dear, I shouldn't be telling you this. He thinks he's being sent to Quemoy, along with a lot of other units. And he suggested that if I could get my parents away, for a holiday or something, I should. And I should go, too."

"Why, for goodness' sake?"

"I don't know. He was worried that someone might overhear us. They don't tell him much, and of course he wasn't supposed to confide in me."

"I expect it's all a false alarm. There's been nothing in the papers. Everything's normal."

"I know." Lin-chun smiled uncertainly out of the window, as if seeking confirmation of her friend's opinion in the bustling Sunday shoppers who clogged the streets of Taipei. As Mei-hua began to prattle about the Cloud Gate Ensemble's latest choreographer, only Mat noticed that Lin-chun wiped away a solitary tear.

The cold was their worst enemy. Hunger was unimportant, fatigue could be fought, but the weather was a more insidious foe. At first Qiu was scarcely aware of the chill; then he'd grasp a bush to help him climb and his numb hands would slip.

They'd never stopped moving since they left the riverbed behind them, climbing up through the undergrowth in search of higher ground. Qiu hadn't even stopped to remove the arrow that dangled from the sleeve of his camouflage jacket, pinning two folds of the thick material together within a centimeter of his elbow. At last the trees and scrub had thinned out, boulders had become more frequent, and they stopped to rest. Lennie was exhausted, his body still weak from drugs and shock. After Qiu had

[186]

dragged him for the best part of a mile he knew they could not go on.

But the archer could. He was lean and fit and full of warm, nourishing food. . . .

Drizzle hung in the night air like a chemical suspension. A chill wind rose and fell. Somewhere close by was a waterfall, its incessant sough reminding Qiu of a crowd of people murmuring in the distance. Apart from the occasional pine tree and clump of bamboo, there was no cover at this level.

When he moved his arm, the shaft of the arrow knocked against the ground. Qiu began to work away at the barb, easing it through the cloth until at last it came free. He weighed it in his hands, assessing its potential as a weapon in the absence of a bow. Useless. But somehow he could not bring himself to discard it.

He turned onto his side and placed his lips against his companion's ear. "We have to move on."

"Can't we rest a bit longer?"

"No. He's there. He's followed us."

"How can you be sure? Won't they wait for daylight?"

"Killing's best done in darkness." Qiu put as much viciousness as he could summon into his whisper; Lennie badly needed a jolt, like a car with a dead battery.

"What's the plan?"

"We have to stay ahead of him all the time, keep silent, move fast." As he spoke the words, Qiu's eyes alighted on the arrow. Something about the arrow told him to wait, think, not be so hasty.

"Get up very quietly. Take my hand."

As Qiu rose to his feet like a black shade, somewhere down the slope a heavy object crunched on stones. Qiu sniffed the wind, head darting that way and this; then he grabbed Lennie's arm and hissed, *"Run!"*

Upward, ever upward, and all the while Qiu was terrified they might come to a dead end. He navigated on instinct, taking the easiest option at every turn, hoping that the way ahead did not culminate in a gulley, a waterfall, the edge of a cliff.

Then suddenly, and without any forewarning, they emerged on the top of a ridge. Qiu stopped.

"What is it?"

"Not so *loud*! I'm trying to remember the map. We want to go southwest, to hit Road Nine. There's a village called Tsao-pu. . . ."

The arrow thudded into the ground mere feet away from where Qiu stood, sending up a shower of granite chips. He shoved

Lennie over the skyline that had nearly been their undoing and swooped for the missile. By sheer luck Qiu landed on top of it and without a pause rolled over, only to realize, too late, that the slope on the other side of the ridge was sheer. Twigs and leaves seared his face, drawing blood. A rock jutted into his stomach and he grunted as if he'd been stabbed. Still he rolled, one hand scrabbling to get a hold.

He careened down thirty feet and rolled into a boulder. For a second he lay winded. Then, as his senses began to return, he became aware of the two arrows he was still clutching to his chest.

He dragged himself up onto his knees and listened. Somewhere not far away Lennie was crashing through the undergrowth, mindless of how much noise he made. The sound of his passage grew fainter by the second.

The hunter had pursued them. He knew exactly where they were. Qiu fought to stifle his desperate breathing. How could it be possible? To shoot blind in that way, so unerringly, so close? Shut up, he told himself; shut up, shut up. He missed, didn't he? He's not infallible. His hands must be as cold as yours, that's why he missed; this isn't hunting weather; he hasn't got a night-sight, he's relying on his ears.

On his ears . . .

As Qiu started off down the slope again he found himself struggling to pursue the idea, but always it eluded him. The aborigine couldn't see them, but he could hear. He had to *listen*.

Qiu didn't know how small the gap between hunter and quarry had become. Lennie was in front, running wild. Qiu felt stirrings of despair. What could he do? *Nothing!*

His feet fell automatically into a loping, downhill stride. He zigzagged crazily, heedless of the risk to himself, anxious only to put yards, miles between him and the unseen archer. Even if they found the road, what then? Wu had had plenty of time to organize his forces.

Shut up, shut up, shut up . . .

Qiu glanced at the sky. Was it his imagination, or was the light turning gray? No, he hadn't imagined anything. How many arrows did the archer have left? Had he stopped to collect the ones he'd already shot? Did he wonder why two were missing?

Qiu resumed his downward trot while his brain seized on this new dimension. Three things were jumbling about inside his head, meeting, colliding, bursting apart, like plastic balls imprisoned by a jet of compressed air in an amusement-arcade game: first, the archer was accustomed to shooting by ear; second, Qiu now had two spent arrows; third, *did the archer know that?*

Down and down Qiu ran, his stride lengthening as light came into the sky to shorten the odds against him. Streaks and streamers of filmy moisture entwined themselves around the largest boulders like the silken pennons of a slow-motion ribbon dance. He was descending quickly now, there was even a path of sorts; it wound gently down the hillside in a hairpin pattern. Sometimes Qiu followed it, but more often he cut across it, only to meet the increasingly well-trodden trail a moment later.

Where was Lennie? There was no trace of him. Where was the road?

Dodge right, dodge left, never run in a straight line. . . .

The path leveled out for a few hundred yards between thick clumps of bamboo interspersed with eucalyptus and longan trees. Qiu slowed his pace, glad to find himself under cover at last. Suddenly he missed his footing and fell, twisting his ankle under him. He sat up panting. No break, no sprain, thank goodness. He was about to rise when the incipient light showed him a curious mark in the sandy brown soil of the path. He bent down to look at it. Was it a print of some kind? Qiu moved very slowly back on all fours. Yes! Here was another. . . .

Footprints. Lennie must have found the path, and followed it. But then Qiu's face clouded. Who was to say that others might not have used this path, over the weekend? He had no means of knowing when the prints were made. But maybe . . . *maybe.*

He began to run again. His feet kept up a steady rhythm: Hopeless. Hope-less. Hope-less.

The path climbed, then leveled out. Suddenly his feet felt stones; he realized that he had landed on the edge of a partly dried-out riverbed. Qiu splashed into the middle of the stream and fell to his knees, throwing water over his face and shoulders. The shock brought his mind sharply back into focus. On the far side of the broad riverbed, shingle gave way to rising ground dotted with trees and a melon bed, the first sign of cultivation. Qiu remembered the map and knew an instant's hope: a road lay on the other side of the hill.

Ahead of him, in the direction of the river's flow, two rounded outcrops converged to make a gateway through which the water fell to a lower level. Cover—not much, but better than nothing. With a grunt of relief he tumbled through the watergate and realized he had emerged into a pool, its surface lightly touched with early-morning mist.

The first bar of sunlight illuminated the brow of the hill down which he'd come. Qiu looked about him. The pool was clear to the bottom. At his feet he could see every size and shape of multicolored pebble, their surfaces worn smooth by the river. Bubbles dotted the surface in a gentle pattern, dangerously hypnotic and soothing to the eye. Twenty feet away, at the far end of the pool, a silvery thread of waterfall fanned out to form a screen, like a sheet of ribbed glass.

Deep orange sunbeams suffused the first moments of the new day, throwing the hollows and crevices of the rock pool into contrasting light and shadow. Qiu stared up to see the waterfall disappear into the mists many hundreds of feet above his head; his eyes followed its progress as it descended like a closely woven string of silvery pearls, now one stream, now parting. His gaze finally came to rest on the liquid curtain where it melted into the pool, and he gasped. Someone was standing behind it.

He looked over his shoulder. The space between the outcrops that guarded this peaceful place was still empty, as was the hillside. "Lennie?"

No answer.

He strained his eyes to pierce the curtain, but what with the shadows, the distorting effect of the water itself, and the deep sunlight, as yet imperfect, it was impossible to see anything clearly. Qiu splashed across the pool and launched himself through the falls.

He found himself in a large gloomy cavern of black stone, covered with algae and smelling of rot. Countless eons had concertinaed the walls into razor-sharp ridges, their sawtooth tips very close together. Lennie Luk stood spread-eagled against the farthest wall, eyes closed, his head thrust around to the left as far as it would go. Qiu was momentarily startled; the young man was about two feet away from the place he'd anticipated. Then he remembered how water refracts light, and understood.

When Qiu touched Lennie, he shrieked. The cadre was about to plaster his hand across Lennie's mouth when the three bouncing balls inside his head finally coalesced.

"S-s-sorry I screamed," Lennie said.

Qiu looked back across the placid pool, to where the two outcrops stemmed the river. And there on one of them he saw a figure that rippled in the morning sunlight when seen through the cascade, but that still was unmistakably human: a figure with its legs apart, one arm held out straight, a bow uplifted. . . .

When Qiu turned back to face Lennie he was smiling. "Scream now," he said.

They made love twice, dozed, awoke, made love again.

"So beautiful," Mat said when she was once more quiet by his side. "Your body. Your name. . . ."

"What about it?"

"Mei . . . it's the national flower of Taiwan, isn't it?"

"Mm-hm. My mother was very patriotic."

"Why don't you ever talk about your father?"

"I've told you, he died." She pushed him away, suddenly feeling awkward. "Can I put on the light? I want to look at you."

He laughed. "Such a greedy child you are." As the light clicked on he picked up his watch from the bedside table. "Three o'clock. Hungry?"

"Not very."

"You ought to be." When she did not reply he rolled over so that he could look down on her. "No appetite?" he said lightly.

She shrugged and pouted. "I haven't. Honestly I haven't."

"Haven't what?"

"You know." She held her open palm up to her nostrils and sniffed.

"I *know*. Silly." He smoothed the ball of his thumb across her cheek a few times, ever so gently.

"I never thought I could kick it. Never. Till I met you. The stuff that Hong Kong doctor gives me is marvelous. I'm starting to feel human again."

"I'm glad. Even if nothing else comes of it."

She brought her other hand up from beneath the bedclothes and held it at arm's length. "I think something else will come of it, now. Don't you?"

The ring looked good on her third finger. They had bought it that afternoon, after leaving Lin-chun at her house, on a sudden impulse borne of irrepressible optimism. He had wanted to keep the price secret, thinking she might feel bound to protest, but Mei-hua had smilingly shaken her head. "Now it's an investment in both of us; if anything should go wrong, it'll be an investment for you. I'll keep it until you ask for it back." And because he was touched, he'd let her see the Amex slip for three hundred thousand NT.

She slipped out of bed, drawing a silk robe around her shoulders, and glided over to the dressing table. "Music," she said.

Mat propped himself up on a pile of three pillows while Mei-hua sorted through her cassettes. If you were going to spend Sunday evening in bed with a glorious woman, this was the place to do it. A master switch beside him controlled the lighting, at present little more than a subdued glow. Everywhere was mauve, lavender, a touch of purple lace, with satiny sheets, stuffed toys, and a vast, tented canopy above the circular bed to crown it all.

"Mandarin love songs," Mei-hua said as she slithered back between the sheets. "My heroine."

He picked up the cassette case. "Pai Kwang?"

"Yes. She was the idol of the forties and fifties. Rhumbas, sambas, offbeat cha-chas—what a star! I still think of Pai Kwang when I go onstage."

"You're such a mixture." He pointed to a row of shelves next to her dressing table. "How many girls are there like you who keep, oh, fifty or so books in their bedroom?"

"When I was a child, I read everything I could. It was a good time for Taiwanese literature. A whole generation suddenly knew where it was going."

"And that was new?"

"God, yes! We'd had the revolution, the withdrawal, twenty years of Nationalist rule. We'd lived—well, all right, my mother's generation had lived—in a state of siege. Then the sun started to come out. Those books there"—she pointed—"we used to swap them among ourselves, at school. The teachers would have killed us if they'd known; that was part of the attraction. Huang Ch'un-ming, Lin Huai-min. Every word they wrote, we gobbled up. Because we recognized ourselves."

"You did?"

"Yes. Those writers didn't concern themselves with lords and ladies and bandits and monks. They wrote about ordinary people—on the breadline, a lot of them. And we were fascinated by that." She shook her head sadly. "Where else were we to get our view of reality?"

The bedside telephone rang. Mat's hand closed over hers. "Don't answer it."

She sighed. "I must, my love. It might be work."

"Work? At three o'clock in the morning!"

"Of course. At any time. My friends know I don't sleep much. The movie crowd's all the same. . . ."

Mei-hua listened for a few seconds, then broke into a torrent of Mandarin that Mat didn't even try to follow. After a few moments of conversation she tossed the receiver back onto its rest and lay back with a melodramatic laugh. "Producers!"

"Problem?"

"No, not really. Some cowboy thinks I'd be flattered to work for him for nothing, that's all."

Her eyes did not quite meet his. Irrational jealousy flooded through him. When he came to force a smile, the muscles of his upper lip ached with strain. She patted his chest and said, "I broke one habit for you, my darling, but one is enough. I need a drink."

"Mix one for me, too. Scotch." His voice was rough; suddenly he felt like a spoiled boy, disposed to be difficult.

"Coming up."

As soon as Mei-hua entered the kitchen she threw herself on the spice rack, scrabbling for a tiny, unmarked pot tucked away at the back. Straw, paper, razor blade . . . the dose took longer to work these days, but at last the familiar warm serenity flowed through her tense body, making her feel as if all her nerves were unfolding within her. She closed her eyes and breathed deeply before sweeping the paraphernalia of addiction into a drawer.

She knew she couldn't go on like this much longer. Mat wasn't entirely stupid. He suspected. Mei-hua ran a hand over her forehead. He was a dear boy. She didn't like doing this to him. But it was necessary, necessary. . . . Why was she in the kitchen? Oh yes . . .

Mat heard her clinking ice and glasses in the room next door and let himself slip into an uneasy reverie. When they were married, he decided, they wouldn't have a phone by the side of the bed. . . .

The faint noise sounded like the click of Mei-hua's front door. But when she came back a moment later with a glass in each hand he forgot all about it, overwhelmed yet again by her beauty.

"Here." She handed him a cut-crystal tumbler. Mat felt very comfortable lying in Mei-hua's bed, looking up at the inside of the paladin's tent.

"Thanks," he murmured.

The material of the tent was gathered into a point above his head. The folds seemed to rush upward into that one focal spot, taking his eyes with it, sucking them in. Slowly he dragged them away from the tent and gazed at her. What enormous eyes she had, what wonderful, shining eyes. . . . Mat felt exhausted. Perhaps he had a virus. Mei-hua seemed spineless all of a sudden; she was rippling up and down like a TV picture in need of attention. So was the man beside her.

The man beside her. Now that was interesting. Mat didn't remember asking another man into this bedroom. A tall, thin man, with his face in shadow. The stranger approached until he was standing beside Mei-hua. He lowered a hand onto her shoulder and murmured a few words. She nodded. Mat recognized the newcomer. He knew perfectly well who it was; only the name escaped him. He knew, too, that he ought to be doing something about this, that action on his part was mandatory; but it seemed a long time since his body had obeyed his brain's commands.

Mei-hua reached out and, using only the tips of two fingers, gently closed his right eyelid. It stayed shut. Then she did the same with the left.

Ah-Huan held the same position for long minutes, watching. Something troubled him. But he did not know what.

He'd heard the scream behind the waterfall and instantly an arrow sprang into his hand. Before his eye could blink again the shaft was on its way, to be followed a second later by a deep grunt, the noise a man makes when he starts to vomit. As the sound died the second arrow left the bow. This time there was no cry.

Both arrows had sung true, piercing the opaque wall of water within seconds of each other. But five minutes later he was still sitting on his haunches, watchful and alert, with his eyes riveted to the fall of crystalline water that was now silvered by the rising sun.

At last he slung his bow across his shoulders and jumped from the rock, careful to keep the string dry. He knew he must look behind the waterfall. Wu Tie-zi would demand evidence that his secrets were safe. Besides, Ah-Huan's balls still occasionally radiated lightning-forks of pain, and he wanted to touch the corpse of the man who had caused that.

As he approached he could see dim shapes lying in the recess behind the shower. Drops of water landed on his skin. He paused. Water was the bow's enemy. Reluctantly he turned to one side, unslung the weapon, and laid it on a rock high above the pool, alongside his quiver.

When he was three feet away from the waterfall he stopped again. Something tugged at his gaze: an open hand, palm upward, lying on a rock in such a way as to part the cascading water. Several drops had already landed on the skin, diluting the red blotch at the fingers' ends.

Ah-Huan stared at the bloody hand for a long time. At last he made up his mind. In a movement that contrasted strongly with his earlier caution, he dived through the water.

One of the two men, the one they had caught on the hillside, lay with his back to the archer, a hand clutching his stomach. Ah-Huan could just see the goose feathers. The second man lay almost under the waterfall. The arrow had penetrated deep into his chest; only half of it was visible. One hand clutched the shaft at the spot where it had entered above his sternum; the other, which Ah-Huan had already seen, was flung outward.

The aborigine relaxed at last. There was one task still to be performed. These unusual weapons with their poisoned barbs might be traced back to him. It was necessary to retrieve them.

He went first to the man lying on his back. Ah-Huan knelt beside him, clasped the shaft of the arrow, and pulled.

It came away without effort. There was no wound. He was holding only half of an arrow. The archer reacted instantly, but before he could rise the other "corpse" was on him. Ah-Huan thrust himself into a backward somersault through the wall of water and swam with all his might for the rock where he had left his bow.

He surfaced, spluttering, and shook the water from his eyes. One of the two men was wading toward him with an arrow raised high, like a dagger. Behind him the aborigine could see the second of his quarries emerge through the water-screen, only now he too had a barbed arrow, the other half of the broken one. The aborigine fell backward, threshing wildly with both feet in an attempt to blind his pursuers.

Ah-Huan was a powerful swimmer. Three more strokes would take him to the rock. He gulped down a lungful of air and dove. When he felt someone grab his ankle he pulled it away before kicking forward again. His foot made contact with flesh, and Ah-Huan, encouraged, made one last dive toward the rock on which he'd left his bow.

He hauled himself out of the water and onto dry land in a single agile vault, rotating his body as he did so. He caught a glimpse of Qiu still floundering in the water. As the cadre came up for air, spluttering and cursing, it was to see Ah-Huan crouching on the rock, bowstring already taut.

Qiu dived straight down, turned over in the water, and surfaced beside the rock with his back to it. Ah-Huan, thrown off his aim, was forced to rise to point the arrow downward almost vertically. The jerky movement caused his right foot to slip on the wet rock. Ah-Huan lost his balance. He felt himself falling backward;

the next second he landed on his coccyx with a jarring pain that made him squeal.

Qiu turned to see both of Ah-Huan's feet sticking straight out beside his own head, and without thinking, he slashed down hard into the legs with the point of the arrow. The aborigine yelled. Qiu stabbed a second time. He was about to drive the arrow down yet again when he realized that the bowman wasn't moving. Ah-Huan sat on the rock, unable to take his eyes off the savage wounds that lacerated his legs. His face assumed a sickly blue color; his eyes turned up until only the whites were showing; and then, like a stone statue being torn down by the mob, Ah-Huan toppled sideways.

For a moment longer Qiu watched his body bob up and down in the current. "Lennie!" he shouted. "Grab him!"

Together they managed to haul the aborigine behind the waterfall, but it was no easy task and Lennie Luk was sobbing by the time they'd finished. Qiu shook him hard. When that had no effect he sluiced water over him.

"Now *listen,*" he shouted. "We're *alive!*"

The sun was now well up over the ridge. The two men stripped and laid their clothes out on a rock to dry. Qiu went through his remaining belongings. Money—intact, if damp. Flashlight—useless. Cigarettes, no; food, no; sunglasses, no. He squinted up at the sun. It was getting late, perhaps nine o'clock. Wu's men would be on the alert, waiting for the archer to return. How long before they began to search the countryside? What sort of power did OFN wield in these parts? If Wu was a really powerful local boss, he might be able to influence the police.

"Why did he die?" Lennie asked.

"The barbs must have been poisoned." Qiu was brusque. "It's time we got dressed."

"Your cut's still bleeding."

Qiu raised his hand to his forehead. It came away red and shiny. "A clean wound."

"That was clever, gashing your forehead against the stone like that."

Qiu shrugged. "I wanted him to see blood, it's the first thing he'd look for. Let me tell you something—I nearly used the point of the arrow to cut myself."

"Suppose he hadn't missed?"

"Then we'd both be dead."

"But how did you know he'd miss?"

"I didn't *know.* But I hoped the waterfall would fool him, just as it did me. And it worked; we weren't standing where he expected us to be."

"He might have allowed for that."

"He might. But he didn't. Ready?"

They walked into the village of Tsaopu, about halfway between Taiwan's east and west coasts. Qiu's cotton shirt and trousers had dried out a little in the early-morning warmth, but Lennie's denims were still sopping wet, and both of them were heavily scarred. Fortunately, the villagers were an incurious lot; few people bothered to glance at them as they entered the tiny shop that served as general store and post office.

Qiu shut himself up with the cracked Bakelite telephone in the rear of the shop, surrounded by coarse brown sacks of rice and jerry cans of cooking oil, and asked the operator to connect him to a Taipei number. He was phoning his "red flare" contact to leave a one-word message that meant "cover blown, all up, abort." At last he heard the ringing, but no one answered. Qiu became increasingly anxious. Then he remembered, and his heart contracted. He was supposed to call in at regular intervals; Sun Shanwang had warned him of the consequences of failing to do so.

"Lennie."

The scientist looked up with a start to find that Qiu had noiselessly lowered himself into a chair opposite him. "What's happening?"

"We have a problem. My people will be coming after me now."

"Your people? You mean—"

"Don't say anything." Qiu spoke quietly. "Just listen. I was supposed to call in at a certain time last night. I couldn't. So the lifeline's been cut. And my own side will want to dispose of me. Because I didn't make contact when I should, they've written me off." He surveyed the anxious young face opposite him, wondering whether to spell out the message: If they find me they'll kill me; if they kill me and you're there, they'll kill you too. Better not, he decided.

"I have to make another call." Qiu looked at his watch. "The storekeeper says there's a bus in a few minutes' time. Go outside and keep watch for it."

"Where are we going?"

"Kaohsiung, first. Then Taipei. But we mustn't miss that bus."

"Okay."

"And be careful. Wu must have organized his people by now.

He'll have told everyone I work for the mainland. He can mobilize a lot of people by saying that." Qiu hesitated. "As soon as the bus comes, board it. Don't worry about me."

"But where will you be?"

"I'll be all right. If we separate, make for the office in Taipei. Tell them to get you out of Taiwan."

Lennie nodded and stood up. Qiu watched him leave the shop, then returned to the telephone.

Lennie glanced back to see Qiu gesticulating while he chattered into the phone. From far away down the road there came the sound of an ancient engine laboring against the incline. Lennie stood on tiptoe and shaded his eyes. Another glance over his shoulder. Qiu's lips were still, but he kept the telephone to his ear. Lennie turned back to the road. Yes! There it was! An old green and white bus, all its windows open, bicycles and boxes and tin cans roped to its roof, hove into view. Lennie heard a car hoot, and a black Yue Loong sedan overtook the bus. It sped into town and ground to a halt on the other side of the road, opposite the store.

"Hey!" Lennie yelled, diving back inside. "The bus!"

Qiu looked up. Through the window of the shop he saw the Yue Loong. One pane of glass was a different color from the rest; he knew that its license plate would be beige. He slammed down the phone and hurled Lennie into the shadows. "Out the back. Quick!"

They raced through a small kitchen into an alley running parallel with the street, and sprinted to the end of the block. Qiu flattened Lennie against the wall before risking a quick look around it.

The bus was parked outside a building that looked to Qiu like a police station. One passenger had his foot on the step and was talking to the driver; Qiu sensed that as soon as their conversation was over, the bus would start off.

His eyes switched to the Yue Loong, parked on the same side of the street as the bus, some thirty yards behind it. Two men had gotten out of the car. One of them chopped the edge of his hand into his other palm, making some point that his companion evidently didn't like.

Qiu breathed deeply. The bus passenger had lowered his foot from the step and now was standing on the sidewalk, hands on hips. The engine revved a couple of times. Qiu knew that in another second he'd hear the gears engage. He had to do something *now*.

He surveyed the bus, looking for a way in. His eyes fastened on the metal ladder that gave access to the roof, still piled high with a precarious heap of junk.

Then the man from the Yue Loong who had been pounding his hand turned away from his companion and marched into the police station. Qiu's fears were realized; Wu was important enough to be able to call on the local militia for help. The cadre grabbed Lennie's arm. "Keep in close to the wall. Go down the street, this side of it, until you're opposite the bus. *Move!*"

Lennie found himself automatically responding to the steel in Qiu's voice. He walked as silently as he could, but his gaze was fixed on the second man from the car, who still stood indecisively in the road.

The bus began to pull away. Lennie looked around in desperation, to see Qiu streak toward the Yue Loong and stick his head in through the driver's window. A second later he was running for the back of the departing bus, with a frantic wave to Lennie. The bus was traveling at about five miles an hour. Qiu threw himself onto the ladder, got a hold, wrapped one arm through the rungs, and reached back with his free hand to grab his companion. For a sickening second Lennie felt himself being dragged along the road; then fright lent power to his hands once more and he managed to swing up onto the lowest step.

As the exhausted young man flung himself down on the roof, Qiu raised his head and saw that the Yue Loong was still parked outside the police station.

"Keys," gasped Qiu, holding them aloft. "That should hold them off for a while."

"Thank God," Lennie sobbed. "Thank God, thank God."

But Qiu Qianwei merely eyed him grimly. "For *what?*"

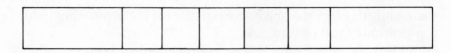

EIGHTEEN

"This weather," Jinny said with grim determination, "is foul."

She had hoped to provoke a response from Diana. But her daughter remained slumped in a cane chair, fingering one of the Rasa Sayang Hotel's grass-green tablecloths and staring out to sea.

"I'd be better off in London," Diana said suddenly.

"I'm not having you recuperate from glandular fever in some ghastly flat in Regent's Park."

"Swiss Cottage. It's not ghastly."

Jinny said nothing. Instead, she drank her last cup of breakfast coffee, frowning at what little she could see of the beach and its fringe of soggy palm trees.

Penang was like a swamp. It had rained, more or less solidly, for a week. They were sitting in the open part of the restaurant, but the monsoon blinds had been unrolled on the day of their arrival and had stayed down ever since, so that on the enclosed terrace it felt like a not-very-clean sauna bath. Outside, torrential rain flooded down in a dense gray bead-curtain, shutting out the view, shutting out the sun, shutting out hope that anything might change, ever. Somewhere beyond the blinds and the rain, the Malacca Strait seethed and heaved in a bad-tempered sulk.

"You should try and eat something."

"Can't."

Diana's face, normally rosy, had a honed-down look, chiseled to a point at the chin as if she were a weasel. Her eyes were sunken. Of all the girl's usual healthy, vital features, only the dark red-tinted hair remained the same.

"The kissing disease," Jinny said darkly. "That's what Mrs. Goh called it when I told her."

Diana's lips, pale green in the light reflected off the tablecloth, twisted contemptuously. "So?"

Silence. Jinny thought of ordering another coffee and decided not to. She was about to rise when Diana said unexpectedly, "I'm sorry. It's just that putting two words together is a bit of an effort, right now."

"Because of the illness? There's nothing else troubling you?'

Diana grimaced "I don't get what—"

"Glandular fever isn't all you can catch from kissing a man, especially when you're still only nineteen." Jinny began to count off her fingers. "There's sadness, joy, suicidal mania, heartache, heartburn, heartbreak. . . . Do you want me to go on?"

"Honestly!" Diana rested her chin on a clenched fist. "Say heartburn. Maybe."

"Is it over?"

"Yes." Diana sighed, putting her soul into it. "Over like the Ming Dynasty's over."

"I'm sorry. Do you want to talk about it?"

"Oh, for Christ's sake, Mother, do I look as if I want to talk about it?"

Fortunately at that moment a boy came over. "Your taxi's arrived, madam."

Jinny looked at her daughter. "I suppose you're too tired to come."

Diana considered. "No. I'd like to."

"Wonderful! Thank you, darling."

The drive from Batu Ferringhi to Georgetown took less than half an hour. By the time their cab pulled up outside the house the rain had ceased, but the sky remained sullen. Diana got out, stretched, and crossed Northam Road to get a better perspective. She quite liked this place, she decided. All those beautiful Angsana trees . . .

"Awfully big," she said at last. "For you and Father, I mean. You weren't planning it as a family home, were you? Because quite honestly I don't think I want to spend the rest of my life in Malaysia."

"I never thought you did. Mat might like to spend some time here, though."

"Don't bank on it. He likes Taiwan, out of Da's way. Less competition." Diana gave the house another thoughtful look. "What's *that* monstrosity?"

"The fence? Security."

Another taxi cruised up to the house, to disgorge a portly Indian gentleman carrying an attaché case. "Is he the agent?" Diana asked.

"That's Mr. Raj, yes."

"Christ. What a charlatan *he* looks."

Mr. Raj trundled toward the two women, undecided whether to concentrate on waving expansively or trying to prevent his attaché case from slipping to the ground. In the end he attempted and failed at both.

"Ah, ladies . . . this must be Miss Diana, I think?"

"How do you do?" said a prim Diana.

"Charmed. Delighted."

"My daughter was just commenting on the fence, Mr. Raj. It's a little stark, isn't it?"

Mr. Raj spread his arms wide. "The geese," he explained portentously.

"The what?"

"Geese, Miss Diana, geese." He waggled his outstretched arms haplessly, as if in imitation of a bird flying. Diana frowned at him. Mr. Raj wheezed gently but seemed incapable of contributing further.

Jinny came to his rescue. "It's a double fence, darling. The present owners used to run geese between the two sides, to scare burglars away."

"Oh." Diana's face had unexpectedly assumed a tinge of healthy pink. Jinny concluded that Mr. Raj was doing her good, and started off across the road. The agent trotted after her, Diana by his side.

"You know Penang, Miss Diana?"

"No. First visit."

"You know what they call Northam Road?" Diana did, and was about to say so, when Mr. Raj forestalled her. "Millionaire's Row! Come and I will show you."

The property, set in an acre of neglected grounds, overlooked its own private beach. There was a swimming pool full of water, with leaves covering the surface; a garage for four cars; servants' quarters; a tennis court, somewhat cracked; a barbecue and outdoor bar. The house itself was square with semihexagonal wings, long verandas on both floors, and scalloped yellow awnings above all the windows.

Diana's footsteps echoed through the high, empty rooms, each with its ceiling fans that did not rotate when Mr. Raj hopefully pressed the switch. "Why's the house in such a mess?" she asked him.

"Ah, Miss Diana!" This time Mr. Raj remembered to plant his case on the floor before spreading his arms. "Lack of Vitamin M, isn't it?"

"I'm sorry?"

"Vitamin M." Once again, the agent's powers of explanation sank to the occasion, and Jinny was obliged to interpret. "No money."

"I thought only wealthy people lived here," Diana said.

"Tin," Mr. Raj said gloomily, rubbing his upper lip. "Not a good market. Not at all, no."

"The price is still extremely high."

"Of tin, Mrs. Young?" Mr. Raj frowned, torn between conflicting desires to show off his superior knowledge of the Malaysian economy and agree with a potential client.

"Of the house."

"But Mrs. Young, this is Penang, this is Northam Road. Here the houses are not for giving away, no, not by any means."

"We'll see." Jinny stood on the front step, looking bored, while Mr. Raj padlocked the door and then started to walk down the drive. Diana, hearing voices from the garden to the north, sauntered across to see who was there. She found a place where the hibiscus hedge had half collapsed to reveal the goose-fence. As she approached, a little boy ran up to it on his side and put his fingers through the outer mesh.

"Hello."

"Hello." He was Chinese, about six years old, running a little to chubbiness, dressed in smart red shorts and a T-shirt. "What's your name?" he said.

"Diana. What's yours?"

Before he could answer a woman called, "Ah-Boy!"

The child's mother came up behind him, very quietly. Then she grabbed Ah-Boy around the chest, tickling his ribs. He dissolved into giggles and shrank up, feet raised off the ground, like a wood louse closing.

"Are we going to be neighbors?" the woman asked.

Diana liked the look of her. She wore a crisp white blouse over cotton culottes and sandals and spoke English with hardly a trace of accent.

"It's a bit early to say, to be honest."

"Ah!" She let go the child and laid a hand on his head. "I think you like children."

A lead weight comprising an assortment of recent memories seemed to attach itself to Diana's heart. "Yes," she mumbled.

"Are you a student?"

"Yes. In England. Oriental studies."

The woman smiled. "I don't know what that is," she confided.

"It means I learn Korean art and a bit of history, philosophy, politics, that kind of thing."

"Education is so demanding these days. Oh—I think that lady is waiting for you."

Diana turned and raised a hand to Jinny. "My mother," she explained. "I have to go now. Glad to have met you, Mrs.—?"

"Fifi Foo."

"I'm Diana. Diana Young. Goodbye, Ah-Boy."

"By-eeeee!"

"What a nice lady," Diana said as she got back in the taxi.

"Good." Jinny's voice was hard, warning Diana that she was not to say anything that might be construed as approval of the house. "Now, Mr. Raj . . ."

"Madame?"

"I will talk to my husband and maybe come back to you."

"Can't we talk now?" The agent sounded forlorn. "What about some cup-of-teas?"

"No, thank you."

As the car pulled away, Diana looked out the rear window to see Mr. Raj standing in the middle of the road, staring after them, as if by sheer force of will he could induce Jinny to come back and make him an offer.

"Well," said Jinny. "What do you think?"

"Hm. Very old, very run down. But lots of potential. That long room, on the ground floor . . ."

"The one with the sea view?"

"That's it. If you expanded the windows, say, and gave it a conservatory sort of feel . . ."

"Plenty of orchids and wicker."

"Yes, and perhaps a Langkawi marble floor."

Jinny eyed her daughter. "I'm glad you came. You're looking better."

"Am I?" Diana consulted her wristwatch. "Ma?"

"Goodness, it's so long since you called me that."

"Do you think the hotel could do me a satay at this hour? I'm suddenly *starving.*"

"They'll provide you with satay," Jinny said fiercely, "if I have to slaughter the animals myself."

It was still only ten o'clock when they arrived back at the Rasa Sayang, but there was no difficulty over the satay. Diana was just dispatching the last one when the headwaiter hurried over to their table. "Excuse me, madam, but the call you booked to Taipei . . ."

"Give my love to Father," Diana called after her mother.

Jinny fled to her room and snatched up the receiver. "Hello, my dear, how are you?" she heard his husky, well-loved voice say.

"Missing you. Missing you dreadfully. Otherwise I'm all right. And you, darling?"

"Tired. Angry. Apart from that, I'm in reasonable shape. Although . . ." His voice softened. "I miss you, too. Very much."

"Any news?"

"Not much. They say I can leave Taiwan whenever I want, but there doesn't seem to be any point. Now I can't get hold of Mat. Has he rung you, by any chance?"

"No."

"Listen, how's Diana?"

"She seems to have bucked up this morning. It was viewing the house that did it, I think. Darling, is there the slightest chance of your coming down to see it? Now that you're free to leave, I mean."

"None. Sorry. I'm glad about Diana."

"Oh, Simon . . ."

"If Mat rings you, please tell him to get his act together as well. I'm fed up—"

There was silence, but the connection had not been severed. Long experience told Jinny what was happening. Her husband had placed a hand over the mouthpiece and was talking to someone else.

"Hello?" he said at last. "Are you still there?"

"I'm here, darling."

"Sorry. It's great to hear your voice again, but—"

"I know. Oh well, I mustn't speak up your bill."

"Love you."

"I love you, too." The line went dead.

Simon replaced his receiver with a sigh and pulled a sheaf of telexes toward him. "No more calls," he muttered to the secretary temporarily assigned him by Taiwan head office. And of course, at that moment, the phone rang.

"Damn! Hello?"

"I have a Mr. Qiu for you, sir. He says it is very urgent."

"Put him on."

"Hello . . . Simon Young?"

"Yes. What can I—?"

"There's no time. I'm in the south. I've got Luk."

"What?"

"We're in great danger." Qiu's rapid voice vibrated with tension. "So are you."

"I can't—"

"You must immediately remove your entire research team and anything of Apogee that remains. Get out of Taipei. Wait for us; we'll be with you later today. You *must* prepare a diversion, to cover our retreat. You'll be under surveillance, so take care."

Simon was scribbling notes. "Go on!"

"If we haven't made it by six o'clock, *flee!*"

"I understand."

"I'll need protection. I . . . I rely on you, please. Can you find a way to take me out?"

"Who's after you?"

"The Taiwanese. The Mah-jongg Brigade. Everyone. And there's one more thing."

"What?"

"Your son. You must—"

Someone shouted at Qiu; Simon heard it, indistinct though it was. "Hello! *Hello!*" Then there came the confused sound of a scuffle and the connection died.

"*Hello!*" Simon jiggled the bracket up and down. "God give me strength . . . !"

The hotel's switchboard was helpful, but the call had definitely been terminated. No, there wasn't any record of place of origin; no, regretfully, they had no means of finding out.

Simon went across to the window and stared over the roofs of Taipei. The research team, that's what Qiu had said. There were two assistants working on the project with Lennie, part-time. It wouldn't cost much to send them on vacation for a few days.

Did he trust Qiu?

Simon hesitated a second longer, then wheeled around and spoke to the secretary. "We need two seats on a plane to Hong Kong, soonest." He reeled off the names. "Track them down and see they make it to the airport."

While she was talking to China Airlines he picked up the other phone and got hold of Henry Chia, to explain what he was doing. "Has my son shown up yet?" he asked.

"Sorry, no."

"Well, when he does, get him round here fast."

As he replaced the receiver his face was tense. Qiu Qianwei had been on the point of saying something about Mat when the line went dead. What had Mat suddenly got to do with it? Where *was* he?

A diversion. Qiu had spoken of the need for a diversion, something to cover a retreat. "How long would it take to arrange a full-scale press conference?" he asked the girl.

"I really don't know, sir. Shall I find out?"

"Please." Simon looked at his watch. "I'm going over to my son's flat for a while. See if we can get space here in the Lai Lai for a large conference, this evening. Say . . . oh, say five o'clock. When you've done that, I want you to ring the labs in Hong Kong and give the director this message." He jotted it on a pad.

"You want a . . . a crate of dates and raisins delivered by courier to the Lai Lai Sheraton, Taipei, this afternoon. Dates and raisins?"

"They'll know what it means. I'll speak to the director myself, within the hour, confirming his instructions, but I want him to start the packing now."

"Yes sir."

"And phone my pilot. Tell him to file a flight plan for Hong Kong, but to do it at the last possible moment for a seven o'clock departure. I'm off now."

Simon was halfway out the door when yet another idea struck him and he paused. For a second he stood still; then he came back and picked up a phone. "I want to place a personal call to Penang. . . ." While he waited for his wife to come on the line he had a few minutes in which to work through his instinctive decision, testing it for flaws. He couldn't see a down side.

"Hello . . . darling?"

"Simon? How lovely! What—?"

"This house, the one you saw this morning. Have you checked it out thoroughly?"

"Why, yes."

"Have you got your company power of attorney?"

"Yes, you know I always carry it. Simon, why are you asking all these—"

He took a deep breath. "Because I want you to buy the house, using the company's name." He paused. "I want you to buy it today."

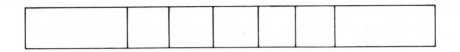

NINETEEN

Qiu and Lennie got off the train from Kaohsiung to find themselves caught up in a melee. The schools were out and Taipei's commuter rush hour was just beginning. It took them nearly ten minutes to file past the platform barrier, and after that they could scarcely move at all. Qiu stood on tiptoe but he wasn't able to see anything except bobbing heads and the occasional raised fist. The mood of the crowd was unhappy. Then word filtered back: the police had set up a security check at the main entrance. Nobody could go in or out of Taipei station without being searched.

Qiu grabbed Lennie's arm and began to maneuver them both, crabwise, to the wall where the phones were.

"What's going on?"

"I don't know. They wouldn't make all this fuss just because one bank manager didn't show up for work today. An alert . . ." Qiu shook his head. "Wu's behind this."

By the time they'd fought their way into a vacant phone booth,

Qiu had his plan worked out. He punched a coin into the slot. "Hello . . . Miss Shan, please." A few minutes later, Qiu replaced the receiver and emerged from the phone booth to rejoin Lennie. "Help's coming. But we have to move."

By now several more trains had arrived to disgorge their passengers. Qiu and Lennie could scarcely force their way along the wall, so thick was the press around them. "See the sign?" Qiu grated, pointing. "Toilet. That's where we're going."

The crowd was like an ocean. It had levels, depths; but above all, it had currents. Two broad streams of humanity heaved and weaved in opposite directions. A baby began to cry, and suddenly there were babies everywhere. Three schoolgirls, their blue uniforms crumpled like their faces, simultaneously began to snivel. "Hysteria," Qiu muttered to Lennie. *"Move!"*

When the loudspeakers vented an unintelligible announcement, the ocean divided: some fell silent while others shouted, "Hush!" Those who had kept quiet turned on the shouters. The temperature rose several degrees. People pushed against Qiu's back, compressing him into a deadly sandwich. Then, just as he knew he couldn't draw another breath, something gave and he pitched forward, with Lennie still miraculously at his side, into the relatively torpid bay that was the men's room.

At four-fifty, an armored van pulled up at the side of the station, next to the parcels office, and two uniformed bank guards got out. As they stood on the forecourt, adjusting the straps of their yellow helmets, Lin-chun's taxi drew into the curb. "You've got the case?"

"Here, Miss Shan." The senior guard patted a steel-lined briefcase. This was a sensitive job, it seemed. Special delivery, those were Miss Shan's words.

"Hey!" Two policemen were on duty outside the parcels office, checking anyone who tried to go in or come out. "You can't park there. Emergency regulations."

"Why?"

"None of your damned business."

"We have to collect a special delivery, for the bank. It's urgent." The guard turned beseechingly to Lin-chun, who nodded. "Priority One delivery from Kaohsiung, the Municipality's office." She flashed a sheet of yellow paper under the policeman's eyes. He looked down and saw an official-looking form, authenticated by a red seal.

"Well . . ."

"It'll only take a second. And if this doesn't get to my chairman by five, it means my job." She fixed him with a beady stare. "Mine may not be the only one."

"Hurry up, then. You've got two minutes. *Two!*"

No sooner had they entered the parcels office than Lin-chun had to put out a hand to steady herself against the wall. She was breathing very fast. "Are you all right, miss?" asked the second security guard.

"I'll be okay."

But she wasn't. As the senior guard put his case down on the counter, Lin-chun uttered an alarming croak and sank to her knees. The room was stuffy and full of people. Nobody was manning the office. There was a bell, but when one of the guards hammered on it, all he provoked was a bad-tempered shout of "Wait, can't you?" from behind a partition.

"Water," whispered Lin-chun. She couldn't seem to raise her head. Passengers crowded around, each with a different remedy. The younger guard looked up and, through the door leading to the concourse, saw the men's-room sign. He ran off, pushing his way through the crowd.

When nothing had happened after a minute, Lin-chun groaned and fell backwards in a faint. The remaining guard swore and pounded on the bell again. His two minutes were long since up, the police would be coming to investigate any second now . . .

A man emerged from the back of the office, wiping his hands on a filthy towel. "What?" he growled.

"She's fainted. Help me get her up."

The custodian of the parcels office grudgingly raised the hinged flap and came out. "Here," said the guard. "You hold her head. I'm going to see where my mate's got to." He jumped up and began to shoulder his way through the crowd on the concourse. Seconds ticked by. Suddenly Lin-chun heard a voice cry, "I said *two* minutes. You've had five."

She moaned softly, but the policeman was unmoved. "If you're ill, you shouldn't be here. Where are those two you had with you?"

Before Lin-chun could answer, one of the uniformed security guards marched into the office and mumbled, "Ready?" He was so busy adjusting his chin strap that Lin-chun couldn't see his face, but it didn't matter because he was through the door and into the passenger seat of the van before she could think of a response. Evidently, however, the sight of him had done her good, because she was able to stand up and snatch the briefcase from the counter. Then the second guard came up behind her, and he must have caught a cold in the toilet, because he blew his nose in a large handkerchief all the way to the driver's seat.

The policemen looked on in puzzlement. One minute there was no sign of the guards, and their lady colleague was lying on the floor; then suddenly the van was zipping off the forecourt like an armour-plated sports car. So stunned were they by this performance that they continued to stare until someone came up, tapped one of them on the shoulder, and said, "Do you know there's a couple of drunks in the toilet? Out cold, they are."

The press conference was scheduled to start at five, but the guests took much longer to arrive than anticipated. Simon stood at the back of the Lai Lai's main conference suite with Henry Chia, watching the room fill up.

"How many are we expecting?"

"About eighty."

Two lines of tables had been arranged down the room, each place equipped with paper and pencil. At the far end was a raised platform. To the right of it stood another table, with a microphone; to the left was a row of trestles bearing the Apogee project, with long blue cables snaking away behind a curtain. Directly in front, a TV crew was busily setting up lights and foil umbrellas. Rod Haines, frowning, watched closely from the aisle.

"Simon, I really shouldn't say this, but—"

"I know what I'm doing, Henry."

"But our *hsin-yung* is on the line. You do know that, don't you?"

Hsin-yung. Commercial credit, the goodwill any venture needed to stay alive in Taiwan. Simon thought of it and shuddered inwardly. "Where the hell's Mat?"

"No news, I'm afraid. I'm sorry. Maybe I give him his head too much."

"And he takes liberties?" Simon shook his head. "You shouldn't do that, Henry. But no, it's not your fault he's gone missing. And what's holding up the guests? Roadblocks, police everywhere—what's going on?"

Chia shrugged helplessly. "There's scare talk. Did you read the papers this morning?"

"No, I hadn't time."

"The police have reported a huge upswing in the violent crime rate. You know what that means? They've decided to have a crackdown on all known dissidents. It's their stock excuse. But why now?"

Simon tossed his head in irritation. "Luk's late, too. He said on the phone he'd be here in ten minutes, and that was a quarter of an hour ago."

"They're nearly all here now." Chia eyed his boss doubtfully. "I hope we've got a show for them."

There was a commotion at the door. Simon wheeled around, took one look, and barked a short laugh. "Is that the best you could do?"

Qiu was wearing a loud checked jacket, at least a size too large for him, over the security guard's trousers. Lennie at least had on a suit, but he couldn't have buttoned it up to save his life. "By God, I'm glad to see you," Simon said. He looked at Lennie. "You okay?"

"Yes, thank you, sir."

"Because there's work to be done. I found the deposit ticket in Mat's bureau. He's missing—can either of you think where he might be?"

They shook their heads.

"I went to the bank and retrieved the disks and stuff." Simon pointed down the room. "It's all there, along with the hardware I had shipped from Hong Kong this afternoon. All you've got to do, Lennie, is make it work. What are the chances?"

"Is it all linked up?"

"Yes. The Hong Kong technician did that. It hums."

"Are the disks booted? Sorry—have they been loaded into the machine?"

"No. We thought we'd wait for you." He turned to Qiu. "You're group banker, you've given massive support—without you, no project. Got it?"

"Yes."

"You'll be leaving any second in a rented car. We'll meet at the airport, I'll try to bluff you through in my party." Simon lowered his voice so that only Qiu could hear. "You'll need a passport."

"Someone's getting it from my apartment."

"In the name of Khoo?"

"Unfortunately, yes."

"Too bad. You go out that door; the driver's waiting." Simon reverted to his normal tone. "Henry . . . let's go!"

Simon strode down the central aisle. There was some polite applause as he stepped onto the dais and raised his hands. "Ladies and gentlemen . . . thank you for coming at such short notice. . . ."

He ran through the introductory patter while Lennie pored

over his machines, checking out connections. Two phones, black box of tricks, keyboards, screens, printers—it all seemed okay, but he couldn't throw off his nervousness. Audiences weren't his style.

He slipped the silver disks into their slots and loaded the programs. Almost to his surprise, Apogee came on line. Simon finished his remarks and directed an inquiring glance at Lennie, who nodded unhappily.

"Ladies and gentlemen, my chief scientist and technician, Mr. Lennie Luk." More applause, with greater enthusiasm now that Apogee had been introduced. Lennie felt a curious mixture of skepticism mixed with awe, and knew for the first time in his life what it was like to be faced with people who desired your failure.

"Mr. Luk needs a volunteer from the audience. Somebody who's not hitherto been acquainted with this magnificent achievement . . ."

On the last word his voice dropped. Lennie, startled, looked up from the screen he'd been working on to see Simon's gaze fixed on the back of the hall, where a Chinese was standing just inside the doorway. The newcomer began to walk along the aisle. When he reached the dais he sat down beside one of the telephones. It was as if he knew what to do without being asked.

The silence was beginning to crackle. Lennie stared imploringly at Simon, but the Englishman's eyes were cemented to the stranger's thin, fierce face. "Ladies and gentlemen . . ." Simon swallowed. "I think we have our volunteer. A representative of the department which, perhaps more than any other, has contributed with encouragement and funds and other assistance to the success of Apogee—the Executive Yuan." He paused. "Please welcome . . . Mr. Li Lu-tang."

At first Mat was conscious only of the light behind his eyelids: deep dark red shot through with crimson forks. Slowly the coloring changed until at last it became a brilliant, blinding white; and with that he awoke.

He found himself staring at a cracked and grimy ceiling, with cobwebs in the corners. A single bulb generated the intense light that had awakened him. Wearily he turned his head away.

He could turn his head, then. That was good. He could feel his toes, too, and when his brain ordered them to wiggle, they did. Nausea . . . and a headache that pounded inside his skull as if determined to drive a wedge between brain and cranium.

A light. What else? Four walls that he suspected had once been green but now were of no discernible hue beneath their veneer of grease and dust. Concrete floor. No doubt about it—this was a jail.

The light in the cell was extinguished without warning.

Mat screwed his eyes tightly shut and gently massaged the lids. Why had they done that? He raised his head, anxious to find out more about his environment.

He was lying on a metal-framed bed, its springs covered only with a wafer-thin pallet mattress. There was no sheet, blanket, or pillow. In one corner of the cell stood a galvanized bucket with a cloth thrown across it. Nearby, but not directly over the bucket, was a tap. Water dripped from it in a slow, maddening trickle. He longed to muster up enough energy to go and move the pail under the tap, but exhaustion held him pinned to the lumpy mattress. His eyes continued to explore this tiny world.

A window set into one wall admitted an evening twilight that stained rather than illuminated the air inside the cell; it was as though his jailers had imported a machine that could manufacture grayness. The door was made of wood and looked like any ordinary door, except for a metal grille that had been hung on hinges in front of it.

Mat next turned his head sideways. He obviously wasn't the first person to lie on this bed; the plaster beside him was covered with Chinese characters, some scrawled in color but for the most part in pencil. The heart with a crude arrow through it, an engorged phallus—some things were universal. There was even a sentence written partly in English: "Pete"—then an ideograph—"here twice"—and then a finger pointed to an oval stain on the plaster. Mat struggled to decipher the character. "Hand," that was easy. *Yin* . . . "Obscenity?" "Dirt?" Hand-obscenity. His lips parted in a weak smile.

It was growing darker outside. Why, then, had they switched off the light?

He clenched his fists by his sides, took a deep breath, and sat up. For a split second nothing happened; then a vast, evil wave—a mixture of vomit, headache, muscular pain, shivers—ran up and down his torso and exploded into his head. Mat fainted.

He was out for only a moment. Electricity crackled behind his eyelids and he came back to consciousness with a rush to find that the cell looked exactly the same. For a moment he lay still, forcing down the contents of his stomach; then he rolled to one side and propped himself up. The vile wave retreated. He levered himself fully upright and carefully swung his legs off the bed, sitting with his head in his hands while he waited for the nausea to die away.

Mat tried to speak. "One . . . two . . ." His voice sounded unnatural, as if echoing through a decompression chamber.

He lowered himself onto his knees and crawled across the floor toward the bucket. As he pulled away the cloth his nose was at once assailed by the fetid, vinegary fumes left by other men's urine. Mat groped upward with his right hand and tried to turn on the tap. The handle was stiff but after a while it shifted, and a mean trickle of water came out. It was neither cold nor warm and did nothing to refresh, not even when he crawled underneath the tap to let the stream run over his head, down his neck, and into his shirt.

His throat felt like sandpaper, but something warned him not to drink the water that came from the tap. Liver disease had been endemic in Taiwan before they'd embarked on a purification program; and even nowadays by no means all water was potable.

How had he come here?

He wormed his way back to the bed, still not daring to stand up lest nausea overwhelm him. He lay down with a moan and folded his forearms across his eyes. How had he come to be here— wherever "here" might be?

He had been lying in bed with Mei-hua. Had they eaten? Had they drunk anything? Drink. Water. Cold water, with ice cubes bobbing while frost formed on the—*Leave it!*

Whiskey. They'd drunk whiskey: the aftertaste still lingered in the fur on the back of his tongue. Mat rolled his head from side to side, vainly trying to recapture what had happened next. *She* had drunk with him. Hadn't she? If so, her drink must have been drugged as well. Then—what had they done with Mei-hua?

The door. Someone at the door of the flat. That's right, and then, and then . . .

He flung his arms wide in despair. He couldn't remember. But he couldn't just go on lying here, either. He had to do something. He had to get out.

Mat lurched over to the metal grille. He raised his fist to pound on the door and paused, realizing that it would be counterproductive, for the grille was made of steel and if he beat on it he'd only succeed in damaging himself. But when he hit the wall instead, he produced only a dull thud.

Suddenly the desperation that had been hovering on the fringes of Mat's conscious mind flattened all the protective barriers he'd tried to erect against it. He went berserk.

He climbed onto the grille's steel frame. He shook it until it rattled, screaming at the top of his voice. After what might have been ten seconds or ten minutes of this, the door on the far side was wrenched open.

Mat's primeval hollering died in his throat.

The Chinese face inches away from his own was wrinkled, fat, unshaven. Mat dropped to the floor and hastily backed away. His jailer's lips were parted in a grimace, to reveal misshapen teeth stained with nicotine. His breath stank.

Mat retreated farther into the cell, suddenly glad of the grille that separated them.

"What you want?"

The words were barely recognizable as English. Mat hesitated only a second. "I want a lawyer, I want a drink, I want a shower. In that order. *Now!*"

The giant laughed. Then he made as if to slam the outer door. Mat cried, "Wait! Please wait."

"What you want?"

"Please . . . just don't go away." Mat heard tears siphoning up inside him and struggled to preserve a semblance of self-control. "Please tell me, where am I?"

"Where you are?"

"Yes."

"Prison. Taoyuan."

Taoyuan was Taipei's main prison, Mat knew. "Why am I here?"

For a moment the jailer made no reply. Then he moved. For the first time Mat noticed that he was carrying a truncheon, about three feet long, tapered like a baseball bat. He tucked it under his arm while he fiddled with a bunch of keys at his belt. The steel grille swung open and the Chinese swaggered into the cell. He approached until he was standing within a few inches of the prisoner, never taking his eyes from Mat's own. "You are here . . . why?" he said.

"Yes. Please tell me. Please. Would you do that?"

"Because . . . you are kill-person."

"Kill-person?"

"Yes. That is so. You kill hotel man."

"Hotel man . . . They think I killed Ah Fan?"

The jailer's mouth wrinkled in a smile. "You very damn right. They *know* you kill-person."

"Know? How can they know?"

"Prosecutor say so. Court say so. You guilty."

Mat began to articulate some protest, but the words wouldn't come. The jailer swung his truncheon up to waist height and, in a gesture surprisingly delicate for such an uncouth man, placed its rounded head against Mat's navel. Then he shoved forward with all his might.

Mat went flying against the far wall. The floor of the cell rose up at an angle to deliver a neck-jarring blow. Agony flowed into every crevice of his body. Bile filled his mouth, the cell seemed to revolve.

By the time he'd recovered, the jailer was already outside, locking the grille. "They shoot you now," he observed casually. "Yes, I think so." He slammed the door, leaving Mat once more in a silence broken only by the dripping of the tap.

Simon Young knew things were going well about five minutes into Lennie's presentation. From his seat behind the table on the dais he observed several people begin to leave in purposeful fashion. They were not reporters; indeed, the press steadily moved to the front of the auditorium, somehow still managing to keep their pencils racing over the paper. No, the defectors were on their way to telephone their stockbrokers with the biggest "buy" orders they could handle.

Simon redirected his attention to Li Lu-tang. The man was an enigma. He sat with a smile on his face, obediently following each of Lennie's instructions. Could we try Japanese? Li asked politely. Yes, of course. Lennie reprogrammed Apogee with five brisk keystrokes. The translations worked perfectly, but Simon still couldn't relax.

At the front of the hall, where the professionals sat, pencils were already raised for questions; but the exodus at the back was starting to become a flood. Simon lowered his wrist below the level of the table and looked at his watch. Suddenly a flash of light distracted him. One of the two screens had blinked.

The flash could mean only one thing: danger. Simon stood up and raised his hands for silence. "The future of Apogee . . ." He was drowned out by reporters who, sensing that the demonstration had come to an end, were clamoring for information; one or two already had their feet on the dais. "The future of Apogee," he repeated, more loudly, "is not in doubt."

That phrase was a prearranged signal. Two helpers rushed from behind the curtain, already trailing disconnected cables. A third man, with a suitcase, neatly swept up the black box and disks and went out by a side door before the press could grasp his presence. Lennie was after him in a second, while Simon covered his retreat.

"Brief questions . . ." Lennie heard him say as he ran for the nearest escalator. ". . . limited time available, I'd be more than happy . . ."

A Mercedes was waiting by the Lai Lai's side entrance in Chen Chiang Street, its engine already running. As the car roared away, Lennie snatched the suitcase from the man in the front seat and checked his invention. Everything was there.

"Problems," the driver said laconically. He raised one forefinger off the wheel in the direction of a convoy of jeeps going west along Chung Hsiao Road. A policeman at the intersection held up his hand. The driver ignored him, cutting across with a screech of tires, heading for the main north-south artery that led to Chiang Kai-shek International Airport. The shrill of the policeman's whistle seemed to go on for a long time.

"This may get rough," said the driver. "Hold on."

Back at the hotel, Simon was making a less dignified exit. A barrier of executives and secretaries extended across the corridor, moving slowly backward under the onslaught of overexcited reporters, while Simon and Chia retreated smoothly toward the escalators. Mimeographed fact sheets were handed out as fast as possible, but when the press corps realized that Simon really meant to abandon them, an angry cry went up and within seconds they'd smashed through the protective human barrier. Simon made it to the car with a second to spare.

As the Jaguar zoomed away from the curb he looked out the rear window to see Chia, hands upraised, surrounded by a horde of people. Suddenly the hands weren't visible anymore and Simon's heart gave a thump.

By now it was nearly dark. The streets seemed less crowded than usual, although the buildup of police vehicles was still ominously noticeable. Simon's driver opted for a secondary route, turning north just short of Sung Chiang Road and making for Chungshan through the maze of backstreets. The gamble paid off. Minutes later the Jaguar swung onto the freeway and headed across the Keelung River. "I have the Mercedes's license plate in my headlights," the chauffeur said.

"Are we being followed?"

The driver glanced in his mirror. "No."

"Keep your speed down. I don't want us pulled in."

"Remember, the toll station's coming up. There'll be police there. Oh-oh!"

"What?"

"More lights coming up fast. Shall I run for it?"

Simon looked back to see a pair of bright orange headlights filling most of the rear window. "Police?"

"I don't think so. Unmarked."

The pursuing car pulled out to overtake them. Simon followed its progress. "They're waving at us. Press!"

"You want me to throw them off?"

"No. They're our safe-conduct. Let them cut in, but make sure you keep the Mercedes in view."

The three cars proceeded in convoy across the broad Tan Shui River, racing through San Chung. At the toll station the Ducannon Young drivers took different lanes in a well-executed maneuver, slowing just enough to drop money into the expert hands waiting to receive it. They were through and away while the press car was stalled at the gate, its occupants stuck for change.

Simon picked up the car-phone and got through to Flight Dispatch. "Dan Carroll, please. . . . Hello . . . Dan?"

"Speaking."

"How's it going?"

"Okay here. They've given us the usual route to Hong Kong. It means we have to fly south along the coast as far as Tainan."

"Can't you change it? I want us out to sea, *fast*!"

"No chance. Not if you want to leave on time."

"What's the weather like?"

"So-so. There's a monsoon moving southeast of Tokyo; reports of wind shear and turbulence. The sky's six-eighths cloud, and rain's expected within the next hour. We can be away through all that, no problem."

"Good. We're about ten minutes from you now. I want to be airborne soonest, okay?"

"Got it."

The driver spoke. "More lights coming up. Not the last lot."

"Hell! Talk to you later, Dan." Simon slammed down the receiver and turned around. This time the headlights were brilliant white. But the car to which they belonged pulled out a quarter of a mile behind the Jaguar and raced straight past, its indicator winking. The light was still flashing a minute later as it turned onto the airport spur.

Where was Mat? Simon knew he was going to have to take some hard decisions about his son—decisions he'd been ducking for too long. Even so, he was worried. God alone knew when he'd be able to come back to Taiwan now; but Mat was being left there to represent the family. So where the devil was he?

As the Jaguar pulled in, Qiu came forward to open the door

and Simon felt relieved to see he'd made it. The press car screeched to a halt moments later. Simon, Lennie, and Qiu posed for pictures, arms around one another's shoulders. Then, amid much breezy talk of urgent meetings to attend with merchant bankers in Hong Kong that same night, they entered the terminal.

At the barrier a pretty girl came up to Qiu and handed him an envelope, from which he extracted a passport. Simon looked closely and to his surprise recognized Miss Shan, who'd obviously been crying. Qiu took the girl by the arm and led her to one side. A moment later he was coming through while Miss Shan turned away, her hands held up to her eyes.

The passport officer showed no interest in Qiu. Customs were the next hurdle. While they waited for the inspector to reach them, Qiu whispered to Simon, "I have bad feelings about this."

"Why?"

"They're near, I can tell. If they've got the contacts I think they have, we won't get out."

"They'd have stopped us back there if they were going to. Who are 'they'?"

"Our Formosa Now. The independence movement."

"They're the last people to turn you in to the government, aren't they?"

"You don't understand. I believe they're *in* the government."

Simon stared at him, aghast. But before he could speak, the customs inspector beckoned.

Lennie was still clutching the suitcase to his chest. This time there had been no shortcuts with the documentation; everything was neatly typed out in quadruplicate, and the contents of the case corresponded precisely to their description on the forms.

The Lear 35 awaited them on the tarmac, engines already started. Even as Simon pounded up the steps, Dan Carroll was requesting permission to taxi. Simon slipped into the right-hand seat and grabbed his headphones. "Get us up," he rasped.

Seconds later the tower came through with permission and soon Dan was heading for the main runway. But then a new voice crackled over the radio, ordering them to stop. For an instant Simon refused to admit the evidence of his own ears. It was Li Lu-tang.

"Look to your right, Mr. Young."

At first Simon could see nothing but the two rows of violet lights that defined the taxiway. Then he zeroed in on a China Airlines Boeing 727, parked a hundred yards distant under strong floodlights. As Simon watched, a man climbed rapidly to the top of the Boeing's stairs, followed by another who kept his hands clasped behind his back.

When the second person was halfway up, he too stopped and turned around, not moving his hands, and Simon guessed he'd been manacled. He was Caucasian, very tall, wearing a white shirt open at the neck. Simon stared at him for several moments before he realized that he was looking at his own son.

The headphones hissed with silence. "What do you want to do?" asked Carroll.

Simon said nothing. He was waiting for Li to speak again. Then it occurred to him that there was really no need for Li to say anything. The message struck him as perfectly plain: We have your son. You can leave Taipei, we will not prevent that, but we have your son.

Simon removed his phones, slung them around his neck, and brushed his palms across his hair. He felt sick. The tableau on the steps of the 727 had not changed.

In the back of the Learjet sat Lennie Luk, holding the key to China's future. The contents of his suitcase must be delivered to Beijing. If not . . .

Under the floodlights, Mat looked pale and exhausted. Where was the 727 going, Simon wondered. To what unimaginable hell was it routed?

"Boss," Carroll said gently, "our flight plan expires in less than a minute."

Simon replaced the phones. No voice intruded upon the quiet hissing in his ears. His own son, against the whole future of Ducannon Young.

"Boss . . ."

Then Simon had an inspiration. "Anyone got a camera?" he yelled.

Dan shook his head. Simon threw off his headphones and leaped for the rear cabin. "Lennie—camera?"

"No."

"*Shit!* Never mind—look out of that window, there! See it? See Mat? You're *witnesses*! I need you to be able to tell the outside world, so *look!*"

"My God," Lennie cried. "What . . . why are they—"

Simon retreated to the flight deck. Carroll saw the indecision on his face and took a deep breath. He had known Simon Young for years; now was the moment to discover if that was time enough. "Captain's orders," he snapped. "You can't help him, Simon. We taxi and be damned! Now *sit down.*"

Seconds later the Boeing 727 had vanished into the darkness behind them. Simon concentrated on the final eleven checks, making himself think of nothing else.

"Probe heat . . . flaps selected . . . yaw damper . . ."

"Goodbye, Mr. Young," said a quiet voice. Simon had been expecting more—threats, blackmail—but nothing came. Instead, the voice of the air-traffic controller came back on the air and murmured, "Cleared for takeoff, Delta Foxtrot six-zero-nine-two."

As they flashed down the runway Simon Young saw the 727 out of the corner of his eye and deliberately looked to starboard where only darkness showed. The thousand-feet-to-go boards were looming up, the runway center lights had dissolved into a continuous blur. V-1, V-R. Dan eased back the stick. V-2. Blackness everywhere. Some buffeting, quickly stilled. Climb-out.

Simon removed his headphones and distractedly smoothed his hair back into place. He craned his neck. "Qianwei—come up here, will you?"

The cadre unstrapped himself and hauled his way along the aisle, fighting the angle of climb, until he was sitting in the chair nearest the flight deck. "I'm sorry," he said quietly. "That was not a decision I'd like to take. Thank you."

"To be honest, I wasn't really thinking of you." Simon managed a smile. "I'm not even sure it was my decision. Anyway, you made it, though God knows how. It all seems too easy, doesn't it?"

"I don't know . . . maybe you're underestimating yourself. You have great imagination. Guile. Resource. You should have become a Mah-jongg."

"I may yet have to. Plenty of people could be out of a job quite soon, me among them. How did you and Lennie escape?"

Qiu told him. When he had finished, Simon was silent for a moment. "What will happen to the girl?"

"To Lin-chun?"

"Yes."

"She'll be all right, I think. At the airport I countersigned the requisition she used. Under bank regulations, when I didn't show up for work my authority was terminated at noon, so I had no right to do that. But if she keeps her head, she can say that she didn't know I was missing, she was merely following my instructions." He shook his head sadly. "I worry about her. I wish she could have come with us."

Simon stared at him. "You surprise me."

"You think I don't have emotions?"

Dan tapped Simon's arm. "That man who spoke to us earlier, he's come on again. Wants to talk to you."

"What! Dan, can we tape this?"

"Sorry. No facilities."

Simon replaced his headset. "Li Lu-tang?"

"Yes," whispered a faraway voice.

"What is it?"

"I have your son."

"I know that. Well?"

"He has been formally accused of the murder of the hotel's employee."

"He didn't do it."

"I think otherwise. But that's a relatively small matter. There's business to do. Are you listening?"

"Go on."

"The government of the Republic of China wants the Apogee project for itself. For itself and no one else. Do you understand?" When Simon said nothing, Li went on, "I'm sure you realize what the consequences will be if you fail to deliver."

"You won't kill an innocent boy to blackmail secrets out of me." Simon's voice was dry. "You'd lose more than your seat at the United Nations if you tried that."

"No need to talk of killing, not yet. Your son will no doubt be telling us about Apogee in due course."

"He knows nothing about it. Nothing." But Simon's face was moist. How much had Lennie told Mat about Apogee?

"Are you still there?"

"I'm here."

"Good. I find it hard to credit that your own son, who seems to run your Taiwanese operation, knows 'nothing.' However. This afternoon a military court-martial tried your son and found him guilty of murder. He will be shot. But not quite yet. We propose to hold him, alive, for the next thirty days. At the end of that period, he might be pardoned and released. But one of two things must happen first."

"Well?"

"Either he'll tell us the Apogee secret of his own accord, or you will deliver it to us. I must add that if, during those thirty days, Apogee should find its way into the hands of the Reds, your son will be executed within the hour. Tell Mr. Qiu that; I know he's with you. Oh, you might also congratulate him for me. I'm still trying to find out how he escaped from my cordon at the station."

"You'll never kill Mat, I'm sure of that."

"And why?"

"Because as soon as I land in Hong Kong, I'm going to contact your Minister for Internal Security. And I'll make sure he understands just what the international consequences of blackmail, theft, and murder by underlings will undoubtedly be."

Again the soft laugh. "Yes, we anticipated something of the kind. While your pilot was filing his flight plan this evening, one of my colleagues took the opportunity of visiting your aircraft. Have you inspected your map case recently?"

Simon grabbed the case from the flap in the back of Carroll's seat and ripped it open. Several charts fell out, along with a glossy black and white photograph. The photo showed Mat slumped in a chair, facing the camera. He looked unconscious. Behind him stood two officers in dress uniform. Between them was a bespectacled Chinese civilian wearing a suit; and with a sinking heart Simon recognized Taiwan's Minister for Internal Security, holding up a newspaper in such a way as to make the date clearly visible. Today's date.

"You should be most careful whom you talk to." Li's voice had taken on a hard edge. "This government is serious. Any high-level protest, or even undue publicity, could result in your son's body being discovered in, say, a brothel? Just another Westerner come to grief in shamefully squalid circumstances—and where would your fine protests have got you then?"

"You're bluffing. You . . . are . . . bluffing."

"That's your decision."

"No, not entirely. You see, I watched my son being taken aboard a China Airlines Boeing. Or have you forgotten that? I'd be surprised if you had; after all, it was you who arranged it."

"And who'll take your word? A wretched father, inventing accusations to numb his pain."

"My pilot and my two passengers also saw him." Simon hesitated, took the plunge. "And we had a camera on board. You know that cameras don't lie. You've just proved it. We're taping this conversation, too."

For the first time, Li had no ready reply. When at last he spoke again his voice sounded almost conciliatory. "I'm sure that within the next month you'll be able to provide a solution to this impasse." There was a click. That was all.

"You shouldn't have done that, Simon. The camera and so on."

"Why?"

Carroll shook his head. "Just a feeling I have. It wasn't necessary."

"To hell with it. I stopped him, didn't I?"

"I'm not sure you did."

Simon shrugged. "Tell me when we're over Tainan." He turned back to Qiu. "You heard?"

"Only your side of it."

Simon filled him in. "Any ideas?"

Qiu shook his head with a sigh. "I know how difficult it is to think in situations like this."

For an instant Simon was puzzled. "Know . . . oh yes, of course. Your own son was . . . kidnapped."

"By you. And held hostage."

"Rough justice," Simon murmured.

"That's past. We must forget. I'll do all in my power to help you."

"I'm grateful. But it's an empty offer, isn't it?" Simon pounded the arm of his seat. "Jinny! What am I going to tell her?"

Dan Carroll interrupted. "Tainan coming up. I'm getting ready to turn. Only we have a problem."

"What?"

"Look to port."

Simon stared across Carroll. "My God," he whispered. "They're close."

"Yes. Military. Two F-5Es. Now I know why I felt bad when you told Li you had photos and tapes. They're trying to raise me on the radio. Shall I answer?" When his employer said nothing, Carroll prompted him. "I really do need to know."

"No. Call Hong Kong. Make a formal complaint. Get onto every damn ATC within range, say we're being fired on, do a Mayday. Dammit, make us the most visible speck on every radar screen between here and New York!"

Before Carroll could reply, one F-5E pulled steadily ahead of them and dipped its wings in the standard signal meaning "Follow me and prepare to land," while the other dropped away behind. Dan turned to Simon. "You do it. I've got a plane to fly. And for Christ's sake, make it convincing!"

He need not have worried about that. As Simon clicked the switch on the side of his microphone the first tracers sizzled past the windshield and dropped away to be lost in the Straits of Formosa, twenty thousand feet below.

III

JANUARY-APRIL

"Do not forget
when you were last in Ju."

TWENTY

The road veered to the left beneath a vast granite outcrop, on which was inscribed this legend:

Do not forget when you were last in Ju.

"What does that mean?" Mat asked in halting Chinese.

"All children have to learn it in nursery school. The words were written by an emperor who had been forced into exile and would not allow his followers to forget their birthplace." Captain Tsai Zi-yang spoke hesitantly, eager to explain a vital episode in Taiwan's history, but unsure how far he was allowed to go with this prisoner. "You'll return, that's the meaning of the inscription. One day you'll go back to where you came from."

"Do you believe that?"

"Do you?"

Mat stiffened but made no reply.

Zi-yang glanced at the prisoner in the jeep beside him. He seemed very young to be a threat to internal security, but only political prisoners were sent to Quemoy. He wore a suit, scant protection against the January cold, and his shirt was open at the collar. No wonder he looked pale. "Where are you from?" Zi-yang asked.

"Taipei."

"No. I mean—your country."

"England. Can you tell me, where is this place?"

"You'll be told."

"Why am I here?"

"I don't know."

"I'm sorry. I don't want to get you into trouble. If you don't want to talk . . ."

Zi-yang merely smiled. He had no complaints about this prisoner; if only they all behaved so well! A chill, early morning drizzle seeped through his fatigues, causing a shiver. It was the lack of color that depressed him most—that, and the cold damp which seemed to imbue Quemoy even on the sunniest of days.

The captain saw his charge staring at the view with a frown, and shook his head in mute empathy. The countryside was quickly reverting to the way it had looked in the fifties and sixties: slit-trenches, barbed wire laced through huge wooden crosses, and shell-holes everywhere. This is a scarred place, Zi-yang reflected sadly. He had known it in a time of prosperity, when market gardens flourished between fields of rice and millet, cabbages and sugar cane. The farmers continued their toil as usual, but warily, no longer sure of their commitment's worth.

Outside the tiny village of Nanshan the jeep turned left, ran alongside a beach where children played in the lee of rusty barbed wire, and began to wind its way up a steep cliff road. Zi-yang pointed out some ruined houses by the water's edge. "The Reds invaded there, in 1949."

"I see." Mat's throat was dry. "This is Quemoy."

Captain Tsai shrugged.

The jeep passed a pom-pom gun, well camouflaged by painted netting, and stopped before a huge oblong opening in the side of the granite cliff. A pole barred the way. Sentry boxes painted in yellow and black zigzags stood on either side of the road where it vanished into darkness.

Zi-yang disliked having to visit Post Q-4. It was under the direct control of Taiwan Garrison Command, the only place on the island not even formally subject to local army regulation. Quemoy District HQ supplied protective artillery in the nearby hills; but that was all.

An MP inspected Zi-yang's papers. Then a sentry raised the

pole and the jeep entered an echoing tunnel, brilliantly lit by neon. After about five minutes this tunnel broadened out and came to a dead end, where several other vehicles were already parked. Zi-yang led his charge up to a steel door that slid open at their approach.

Zi-yang crossed the threshold and found himself in a reception area containing a desk, several chairs, and telephones; somewhere close he could hear the clacking of a typewriter. On the far wall hung a photograph of Dr. Sun Yat-sen, *Guo-fu*, father of the country.

A woman sitting behind the desk laid down her pen. "The Director wishes to see you, Captain. Report to room five." She pointed down a corridor. "It's that way."

"The prisoner?"

"He'll be dealt with."

Zi-yang nodded at Mat and went in search of room five. He knocked and went in. At first he thought the office was empty; then someone closed a filing cabinet and he turned to see a man standing in one corner, his eyes glued to a file of papers.

"Come in, Captain Tsai," the man said softly, not raising his eyes from the file. "Sit down."

Zi-yang obeyed. When nothing happened for several minutes the captain felt himself becoming nervous. What was the man doing? Why didn't he speak?

A split second before Zi-yang could nerve himself to swing around in an attempt to find out the answers, the mysterious officer broke the silence. "Did he give you any trouble?"

"No sir."

"He spoke to you." It was not framed as a question, but Zi-yang nevertheless knew that comment from him was required. "Yes."

"What did he say?"

As Zi-yang told him, he was uncomfortably aware of the other person standing at his shoulder. For some reason, the captain still could not bring himself to look around. When he had finished, there was a long silence. Then, at last, the officer did come into view. He walked behind the desk and sat down, resting his elbows on the blotter before cradling his chin in his hands.

On the whole he approved of Tsai, he decided. The captain was impeccably dressed and the squarish, suntanned face beneath the regulation razor-cut hair wore a suitably serious expression. The man behind the desk sensed that here was someone who rarely smiled.

Zi-yang, on the other hand, did not care for the face opposite.

[231]

It was too cold, too cruel, to inspire anything other than blind obedience. Then he noticed the uniform.

It had gone out of fashion many years before. The tunic, made of thick khaki cloth, had four large button-down pockets and a wide collar in the shape of an upside-down **V**. The epaulets were bare of insignia. The man wore a Sam Browne belt with a square metal buckle; the leather, though obviously polished and well cared for, was old and cracked. Zi-yang realized where he'd seen the uniform before: in photographs of Chiang Kai-shek.

At last the anonymous officer spoke. "My name is Li Lu-tang. I'm in charge here. You've not hitherto been acquainted with Q-4?"

"No sir."

"I've arranged to have you seconded to me. From now on you'll work here, under my supervision."

Zi-yang knew it was important to pay attention, but somehow this enclosed room stifled concentration. "I hadn't heard about this," he ventured at last.

"No. Your transfer papers are here. General Lo signed them this morning, while you were at the airstrip. From now on you'll live here, in Q-4."

Zi-yang's lips tightened. Li saw it and smiled again. "Life underground, is that what troubles you? You'll get used to it. We all do. And you'll be in the fresh air a lot, I promise you."

"Sir." Zi-yang hesitated. He urgently needed some bearings. "Excuse me, sir, but the controller's rank is what?"

"Think of me just as the director of this post."

"Sir."

"I'm pleased you spoke to the prisoner and that he spoke to you. It's a start. I've been following your career with interest, Captain. It's because I believed you'd speak to him when others might not that I arranged for you to meet the plane." Li lowered his hands to the desk. "Let me begin your education. About Q-4. And . . . other things."

Mat understood immediately what the room signified: disorientation. It was square, perfectly silent, and white; even the floor had been painted brilliant white. The only minute contrast came from two large panels covered with closed slatted blinds, through which filtered a cold artificial light. If he stared at them for too long they seemed to turn into huge TV screens, their blank pictures vastly magnified into numberless rippling lines. So he tried to avoid gazing at them, but always they drew him back, until his eyes burned.

He sat on one of the two white wooden chairs that were the only items of furniture, wondering who would come to occupy the second one. They had taken away his watch, so he had no idea how much time had passed. It seemed very long, but he knew that the glare was dulling his perceptions. Perhaps only minutes passed before the door opened to admit a newcomer.

A woman—pale, with two black marbles for eyes, hair cropped short, wearing a smock. As the door slammed she leaned against it, trembling. When Mat ran toward her she turned in the door, as if trying to dissolve her way through it.

"Mei-hua!" But she avoided his outstretched arms, running into the far corner of the cell, where she slid to the floor and hid her head in her hands. Mat stood over her, uncertain what to do. At last the trembling gave way to intermittent shivers. When he gently turned her head she did not resist.

He helped her up into one of the chairs and sat beside her, caressing the hands that lay listlessly in her lap. After a while she tore them away. She was sniveling again, but her face seemed less distraught.

"They took my stuff," she whimpered. "No coke. Christ . . . awful . . . *don't touch me!*" Sometimes it was nice when he stroked her. Sometimes it was as if thousands of volts pulsed through her nervous system.

"You told me you kicked it. You saw the doctor, he gave you medicine—"

She laughed. It made her sound insane. "Easy . . . f-fool. You . . . kid, Mat. Fucking . . . kid."

"Fool?"

"Ugh!" She crossed her forearms across her breasts, trying to stifle the creatures that were crawling out of them. Then, on the instant, her mood changed. She reached out a hand to touch his. Her palm was wet and cold. "Fool," she repeated.

"I don't know what you're talking about. You're saying you don't love me, is that it?"

"Yes. *No!* Didn't love you at first." She waved one hand across her face in a despairing gesture and broke down. He let her sob herself dry, continuing to stroke her other hand, but absently, his mind a blank. At last she wiped her face on a sleeve of the smock. "Such fun. It looked. Ducannon Young millions, Christ almighty, what girl wouldn't? Then . . . s-screw it all up. Started to *like* you." She laughed again, only this time the sound was sad, rather than cruel. " 'Cause half-and-half. Like me. Yellow-white, bread and rice. Eurasian."

"Is that how you saw me?"

"Hell, *yes*! You . . . nothing to call your own . . . father, company, you seemed ready to sell the lot the second I dangled Wu Tie-zi in front of you. And I liked that. Even if no millions. Joke . . . fucking joke." Her voice rose to a shriek. "Love!"

"You were wrong. I told Wu it wasn't the right time. . . ." Mat shook his head. What was the point? He'd been unbelievably naïve; well, that was no crime, not in love, anyway. She'd fooled him about the drugs. He'd genuinely believed her claims to have beaten the addiction, when all the time . . .

No! These puerile thoughts could wait. Right now there were more important things to worry about.

"Mei-hua, listen to me. Who brought you here?"

"They did."

"Who's 'they,' for God's sake?"

She shrugged. "Intelligence. Taiwan Garrison Command. Peace Preservation Corps, maybe." Her voice, suddenly monotonous, chanted the names like a litany. "National Security Bureau. Files Office. Goes on. And on. And *on*!"

"I see. Did they tell you why I'm here?"

" 'Cause they want something. Have to tell you. Message. Apogee. Need it. But your daddy wouldn't play. Left Taiwan yesterday. Took Apogee with him."

"So they told you about Apogee. . . ." Mat withdrew his hands from between hers. "Dad left, you say. . . ." He stood up and began to walk around the room. When he stopped, Mei-hua saw that he was smiling his gentle smile, the one that seemed to glide inside her stomach like a warm drink, soothing and stimulating at the same time. "They told you my father left yesterday?"

"Yes. He's abandoned you."

"No. I don't think so. It's like he's saying . . . I've got to make my own decisions for a while." Mat chuckled, without humor. "Problems."

"You don't say."

"It's just that I've sometimes thought the Taiwanese ought to have Apogee, anyway. And if Dad's leaving me to make the decisions . . ."

"What is this Apogee?"

"Doesn't matter." He pulled his chair up next to hers and reversed it so that he could rest his arms across the back. "The problem I'm facing is that I know a little about Apogee. And I'm a coward. Long before they pull out the first fingernail, I'll talk."

"Crap! You're no coward."

"No? Well, how about this, then? The trouble is . . . I'm not against them. I'm not against anybody who works to save this country."

"You'd give away secrets? To them? You're crazy."

"Am I? I don't think you ever really knew how much I love Taiwan." He paused, seeking the right words to convince her. "You said I was Eurasian, neither one thing nor the other—"

"It's true!"

"Oh yes. But I've always believed there was more Chinese blood in my veins than English. When I came to Taiwan, something funny happened. I fell in love with the place. Then I fell in love with you, too." His smile faded. "So now you see the problem."

"I don't see anything."

"Apogee's a commercial secret. It belongs to my father. But I wouldn't have the . . . the *will* to keep it to myself if I thought it'd save Taiwan. That's why I need to know who's holding us, what sort of people they are."

"Because Taiwan . . . it's . . . it's your country?"

"Right."

"But your father—"

"Knows the position I'm in. He doesn't want my death on his conscience. He's fulfilled his side of the bargain he made with mainland China. If giving away Apogee is the only way to save my life, then I'm expected to give it away. Or at least"—his voice cracked—"that's what I have to believe."

For a long moment she held his gaze, searching for guile and finding none. "You don't seem afraid."

"Don't I? Good." In truth, he was terrified. Whichever way things went, the future looked hopeless. If the mainland invaded, Red troops would destroy Quemoy within the first hour. Mat knew that his captors couldn't afford to let him go, not ever, because as a witness he was too dangerous. He dreaded the thought of being tortured. He did not know a great deal about Apogee, certainly not enough to reconstruct it for the Taiwanese.

"Listen," he said, "I still don't understand why you're here. They could have given me the message themselves. They don't need you."

Mei-hua had begun to shake again. "Arrested . . . last night. They sh-shouted at m-me. Said I had to persuade you to co . . . cooperate." She turned her ravaged face away, unable to come to terms with the hurt in his eyes, then ran into a corner. When she heard Mat approach she knew he was going to put his arms around her again and she cried to the wall, "Don't! Please . . . just . . .

don't!" They were still standing thus when the bolts were drawn back and Li Lu-tang entered the room.

He stood in the center of the floor, staring expressionlessly at Mat. "Sit down."

Mat lowered Mei-hua gently into one of the chairs before taking the other. Li rested his back against the wall. He seemed in no hurry. "Tell me, Young," he said at last. "Does the name Tai Li mean anything to you?"

"Chiang Kai-shek's chief of intelligence." Mat remembered the conversation with his father in the Lai Lai's shopping arcade, the night they'd met inspector Hsu. "The only man . . ."

"Yes?"

"The only man allowed to wear a sword in the Generalissimo's presence."

"Very good." Li patted the sheath by his side. "This is the sword." He tapped his tunic. "This uniform belonged to him. I wear it now." He smiled, and for a moment was silent. "Have you any complaints about your treatment so far?"

"You're damn right I have! I've been drugged, imprisoned without trial, threatened with execution—"

"You were tried. And found guilty. And sentenced to death." Li allowed the words to sink in. "Whether the sentence is carried out depends on you. But don't delude yourself. You *were* tried."

"Then it was a travesty, and no doubt my father's taking steps to ensure that the government will regret that abuse."

"The government? Of Taiwan?"

"Of course."

Li laughed—an insolent sound. "That rabble in the presidential office hardly constitutes a government. The Kuomintang— self-appointed arbiters of the three principles of the people. You know that glorious phrase? *San min chu-i*. Nationalism, democracy, livelihood. A recipe for disaster."

He advanced toward Mat, stopping inches away from his chair. "Do you know when these islands were last ruled properly? In 1945. The last true government of the Republic of China was not Chinese at all. It was Japanese! They knew how to impose their will, and they did!" His voice sank to a whisper. "They killed my father."

Mei-hua's chair scraped on the floor. As usual she felt confused, but she understood enough to realize that things were going wrong. This wasn't the way to deal with Mat. Li's gaze darted to her face and read there the beginnings of a message, but by now he was too far gone to stop. "We need that kind of government again! Do you know anything about the Formosan independence

[236]

movement, Young? It's been alive ever since the black days after the war, when the Kuomintang stole our lands."

"Really?" Mat was surprised to hear how calm he sounded. "I heard they stamped out some of the worst abuses in Southeast Asia and paid compensation."

"Did we ask for money? Did our fathers work that land for a thousand years so that those swine from the mainland could come and steal it?" Li's voice rose, he brought his face down to within an inch of Mat's own. "How *dare* you, pig?" And he spat. The spittle landed on Mat's right cheek. When Mat twisted his head around, trying to wipe the sputum away on the cloth of his suit, Li's hand lanced out: one blow to the right cheek, one to the left. He stepped back, dabbing with a tissue at the palm of his hand, which had collected some of his own saliva.

"Now . . . contrary to what you said earlier, vast changes are about to take place, here in China. We Formosans have been consolidating our position for years. We've infiltrated the armed forces, local politics, commerce, banking, even Taiwan Garrison Command itself. Your friends, the so-called government, only know what *I* want them to know. For example, they don't know anything at all about Apogee, because I've taken great care to conceal its existence from them."

Mat saw he was dealing with a genuine fanatic; with that perception came the knowledge that he was lost.

"We're about to assert ourselves, we intend once again to take charge of our own affairs. The mainland will shortly invade Taiwan. As soon as Apogee has been incorporated into their armory, they'll come." Li's voice dropped. "They will come. And that will be the signal for the ending of the Chiang dynasty."

"Ending? You'd . . . *kill* the President?"

"Oh yes. That is the first of our many tasks—there is none greater than the removal of the figurehead. And then the bandits in Taipei will find themselves without a leader. Defenseless. Unless . . . someone hands them the weapon the Reds themselves are using."

"Meaning you?"

"Meaning me. In exchange for the abdication of the Kuomintang, I will save China. And this country will once more find itself governed along appropriate lines."

"You intend to sell Apogee in exchange for power, is that it?"

"Yes. So now you understand your role: either you have the secrets of Apogee or your father will give them to us to save your life. He has thirty days in which to deliver. But just in case he doesn't, we won't neglect you. I believe your father trusts you and that you therefore know all about Apogee. So now—will you tell us, or do we have to extract the information from you like a diseased tooth?" Li's smile was demonic.

Mat regarded him fixedly. At last he said, "Am I allowed to ask a question?"

Li slowly withdrew to the wall and rested his back against it. "What?"

"Suppose I tell you what you want to know, or that my father cooperates with you."

"Well?"

"Suppose you go to the government in Taipei and offer to make your deal. And they refuse. What then?"

Li frowned at him, like a man convinced he was missing something obvious. "It won't happen."

"Suppose it did."

"Then it might be necessary for us to negotiate with other . . . interested parties."

"Who?"

Li ignored the question. "Perhaps we'd just do nothing. Let the Reds invade. They'd certainly win." He shrugged. "One evil will be replaced by another. The Formosan people will be no worse off than before."

"I see. Thank you."

"That was your question?"

"Yes."

"So—what's your response to *my* question?"

Mat's gaze drifted away from Li's face. His breathing had become very fast. When first he tried to speak, the words were garbled. On his second attempt he fared better. "My answer is . . . you should stick Tai Li's sword up your ass. Where I'm sure it will be very much at home."

For a moment Li held himself perfectly still, like a bas-relief carved from the wall against which he stood. Then he shot forward as if propelled by some gigantic spring. One boot snagged itself under the bar of Mat's chair and pulled backwards, hard. Mat went over, cracking his skull against the white floor with a smack that made Mei-hua cry out. Li picked up the empty chair, raised it over his head, and brought it down into the Englishman's stomach. Mat's agony went far beyond a scream.

Li Lu-tang straightened his uniform, retrieved his cap from the floor, and put it on, feeling with his hands to make sure it was correctly aligned. "Thirty days," he said, as soon as he had recovered his breath, "can seem a long time, under certain circumstances. We shall begin now, I think."

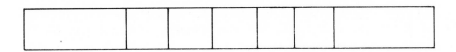

TWENTY-ONE

It was eight o'clock on a February morning, and Penang was already hot. Diana lounged in a wicker armchair with her hands in her lap, staring at the sea.

Qiu approached silently and placed a hand on her shoulder, making her cringe. "Lennie Luk came in from China last night. I hope he didn't disturb you."

"Lennie? What's he doing here?"

"Hiding, like me. Your father must be starting to find this place very useful."

"But Lennie doesn't need to hide."

"Yes, he does. He's been showing my people how Apogee works. Now Simon must put him where the Taiwanese can't get at him."

"You mean they might try to kill him again?"

"No, no. They wouldn't pull such a stupid trick twice." He grunted. "If your father hadn't had the sense to transmit that Mayday message—"

"He's good at brain waves like that. I saw in the papers that the Executive Yuan went berserk. Denied all knowledge of the incident. So did the air force."

"Beijing went berserk, too. They didn't think much of your father holding a public demonstration in a Taiwanese hotel. Simon's upsetting everyone lately."

"Well, you can't have everything. At least Apogee worked." Diana stood up. "Want some coffee?"

"Please."

She quickly returned, carrying a tray. "Lennie's awake. I took him some—"

Qiu was standing at the window. "There goes Ah-Boy," he interrupted her. "He's wearing those armbands again. So fat! He looks like the man they use to advertise the tires, you know?"

"Michelin Man." Diana went to stand by the tall windows. From this vantage point she had a view of the lawn edged with frangipani trees and the beach beyond, where Ah-Boy was waddling along the tideline with a shrimp net somewhat taller than himself. Qiu filled a cup and came over to her. She stole a glance at him. "You like children, don't you?"

"I love my son. Yes, I suppose you could say I like children."

"When do you think you'll see Tingchen again?"

"Never."

As Diana heard the despondent reply, her womb rippled with pain. That still happened, sometimes. The nurses had predicted the spasms, but they never ceased to overwhelm her with a feeling of violation, of outrage.

"I once made myself sick on a particular brand of chocolate," she said. "Afterwards, I could eat chocolate again, as long as it wasn't that brand."

Qiu looked at her as if she'd gone mad. "What are you talking about?"

"Forget it. I've been sick lately, that's all."

He stared at her, trying to fathom what lay behind her patent wish to confide. But she walked away, keeping her arms folded and her head down, until she reached the far wall of the room and could go no farther.

"What's wrong with you?" he asked.

"Glandular fever."

Qiu snorted. "Now the truth!"

"I often wonder why Ma didn't come right out with it, like you just did."

"Tell me. It won't go any further."

"I *want* to tell someone. It might as well be you."

"Thanks!"

"Don't be like that. It's not so easy. The last time I saw you, you were pointing a gun at me."

Qiu turned his head away.

"But that was five years ago," Diana went on. "You've softened since then. Oh well . . ." She traipsed back to the window and allowed her forehead to rest on the glass. "There's my sickly brand of chocolate . . . Master Michelin Man."

Qiu, still puzzled, followed her gaze. All he could see was Ah-Boy as he shuffled along the shore, lugging his net after him. And then Qiu did understand.

"You had a child," he muttered. "You lost a child."

"No. I had an abortion."

"I'm sorry."

"I don't know why I told you that. No one else knows. Not even Ma. Especially Ma."

Qiu's next act was so out of character that Diana, surprised, let him do it without finding the strength to protest or resist. He lifted her hands to his lips and kissed them before leading her to the wicker chair and lowering her gently into it. Diana knew that to him, at that moment, she was precious. She cried.

"Why did you do that?" she asked, wiping her eyes.

"Don't know." He sat down on the floor, arms resting across his knees. "What happened?"

"Nothing much." Diana twisted her sodden handkerchief. "We . . . the man and I . . . talked it over, very sensibly. And he . . . we agreed. An abortion was the right thing. That's all."

"I know how you must be feeling."

"You don't."

"But I do! I'm losing my own child. I can't go back, the Mah-jonggs would execute me. If I'd gone home straightaway, perhaps not. But now I've forfeited their trust. I stayed out for too long."

"How terrible for you." Diana shuddered and again hid her face in her handkerchief. "I suppose you do understand, then, in a way," she said at last. "They say I can have another child one day. You could make a new life for yourself, perhaps marry again—"

"You're wrong. The Mah-jonggs could always find me. A newcomer in a Chinese community stands out even among his own people."

"Then go back to Taiwan. Defect."

"You think I haven't thought of that?" He shook his head with a smile. "It sounds easy. Hardly anything still links me to China. My marriage, I believe, is over. Both my parents are dead long since. And because you confided in me I'll tell you something that will perhaps shock you. In Taiwan, I fell in love."

For an instant Diana wanted to laugh. The idea of Qiu being in love was somehow too outlandish to be true. But then she saw the sincerity in his face and the temptation to ridicule faded.

"She's younger than me, very pretty, very nice."

Diana wanted more—the words of ecstatic poetry in which she herself would have chosen to declare true love. None came. Young, pretty, nice—after all, she realized, what more was there to say?

"Yes," Qiu ruminated, "I could go to Taiwan. I'd stand out, as I said earlier, but at least I'd be in a society used to harboring and protecting defectors from the mainland. I could settle down with Lin-chun, maybe even have children."

"And then you'd be happy. So go to Taiwan."

"Ah, but there's another problem." Qiu leaned back, placing his palms on the floor. "The People's Republic is on the point of retaking Taiwan," he said matter-of-factly. "By armed force."

"That can't be true! I mean . . . someone, the Americans, they'd stop it."

"The United States may well intervene, but as long as we strike fast and hard enough, we can't lose. So, as I say, that's another problem." Qiu stood up. "It's hot in here. Let's go on the veranda."

She followed Qiu outside to find him staring down the lawn. "Your brother . . ." He swung around and rested his hands on the balustrade. "Something's got to be done."

Diana flopped down into the sofa-swing and looked away. "Nothing can be done."

"Don't you care what happens to your brother?"

"Passionately. I adore him, I always have. The thought of anything bad happening to him scares me to death. But none of that alters the fact that just at the moment no one can help him. Why won't you see that?"

"Perhaps it has something to do with duty, with gratitude! To your father, who saved my life."

"Aren't you being just a little bit quixotic?"

"No! You Westerners are so draped in self-pity, you can't see anything above your own petty problems."

"Petty! You really think I'm being *petty*? It's my *brother* we're talking about!"

They glared at each other for a few seconds longer; then Diana swept into the house, not looking back. Qiu slammed his hand against the swing and swore.

"Hello. Who are *you*?"

He turned around to find that Ah-Boy had crept up behind him unheard. "I didn't think there were any men here. Can you help me with my net, Uncle? It's caught."

Qiu gnawed his lip. "All right, if I must," he grumbled. "Where is it?"

"Down by the pier." Ah-Boy looked up at him shyly. "I told the man there weren't any other people here. I didn't know about you."

"What man?" Qiu lowered himself to a kneeling position, until he was eye-to-eye with Ah-Boy, and somehow managed to drum up a smile.

"The man on the beach yesterday. He was in-spec-ting your house, Uncle. That's what he said when I asked him. In-spec-ting. He wanted to know who lived here."

"And what did you tell him?"

"Auntie Diana," the boy said promptly. "I didn't know about Uncle, then."

"Good. Did he seem interested in this house?"

Ah-Boy nodded his head slowly and deliberately, half a dozen times.

"Uncle's leaving very soon," Qiu said softly. "If the man comes back, best not to say anything about Uncle. Uncle doesn't live here, you see. He's just on a quick visit."

"O . . . kay."

"Now," said Qiu as he stood up, looking at his watch. "Let's see about Nephew's net. Hurry, please. Uncle has a plane to catch."

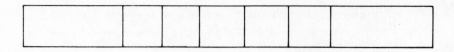

TWENTY-TWO

Mat awoke. He counted to five and forced his eyelids open. Lights exploded, obscuring the cell with flashes of purple. He clapped his hands to his forehead, waiting for the amoebalike blobs to disappear.

Mat didn't know how long he had been in the cell. For him there was no yesterday or today; instead, there were periods—before periods, current periods, and future periods, each separated from the adjacent segment of time by sleep. He had no means of measuring these segments.

The room he slept in was fifteen feet long by twelve feet wide. It was white, like its contents. Light came from two recessed globes in the ceiling and another of those panels covered by slatted blinds, set in one of the longer walls. A door led to a tiny washroom containing a squat-down toilet and a basin with a cold-water tap. The door to the washroom was on an electronic locking system; sometimes it wouldn't open. Then, without warning, the door would be freed. Since the lock worked soundlessly, Mat had to guess when he could use the washroom. So far he hadn't soiled himself, although he'd come close.

His bed stood against the other long wall, with the door to the outside at its foot. The white metal frame was covered with white sheets and a white blanket. There was one white pillow. Nothing else.

Mat extended a hand in front of his face. His brain played a nasty trick. For a moment it would not let him remember how many fingers he was supposed to have. Was it indeed five—four fingers and a . . . a . . . the short, stumpy one. He heard a low moan in the cell. Had that noise come from him?

Thumb, you fool!

He swung his legs off the bed. Suddenly his ears were buzzing; that meant they had turned on the noise machine. Even the noise here was white.

Mat spoke aloud. "My captors are seeking to destroy me through a process of programmed disorientation. But it won't work." His voice rose. "My name is Matthew Young. I am twenty-two years old, British, I was born in the year of the monkey. My birth-sign is Gemini. And twelve twelves are one hundred forty-four. . . ."

His vocal chords hurt so much that he had to stop. He peeled off the white nightshirt they'd given him and examined his flesh. The muscles were losing their tone. He lowered himself to the floor and tried a few push-ups, wincing at the pain in the region of his stomach where Li had beaten him. After thirteen he had to stop. In the last waking period he'd managed fifteen. Decline.

Mat struggled up, sat on the edge of the bed, and stared down at the hands clasped between his knees.

Where was Mei-hua? What was Li doing to her? This was bad enough for a healthy person to endure, but she wasn't healthy. Don't think about it. Block it out.

How long have you been here? He could remember seven periods, four waking, three sleeping. He thought it was seven. There had been meals, always the same meal, served with white rice. Fish soup, steamed vegetable, bean curd. The food was neither hot nor cold; it tasted of nothing. Mat longed for a bottle of soy sauce, a huge brown bottle with a yellow label and red letters on it. . . .

Seven periods, not counting the day when Li's man had brought him here. There had been a sleep period. And a waking period. Another sleep period. And after that . . .

Since he woke up the lighting had undergone a subtle change, he was sure of it. No, he thought it probable. Mat squinted at the slatted blinds. Bars of light alternated with bars of shadow. The dark lines seemed marginally thicker than usual. No, not seemed, they *were*. Hold on to that! No doubt about it, *the lines were thicker than before.*

Mat began to speak again. "I was roused from sleep. People grabbed my shoulders. Their hands tugged my body upright in bed. My heart was beating so fast I was sure I'd have a coronary." He faltered. "I have never, never been so frightened as when I was awoken in that way. . . ."

Yes. *Good!* Get it out in the open, face it, admit the things you don't want to remember.

"My eyes opened. But before I could see anything, they placed a . . . a bucket over my head. A metal bucket. I struggled, but someone was sitting on my ankles by that time and I couldn't move my arms at all. Then . . ."

He fell silent. A vein throbbed in his forehead. He could feel the vein. It hurt.

"They began to hit the bucket with iron bars, very quickly, one on each side of me. I screamed. I screamed so hard and so long that when I woke up in the next period, I couldn't speak. My throat had swollen up. It was like being at the center of all noise. Like a factory coupled with the loudest rock concert connected to a train going through a tunnel while a supersonic plane broke the sound barrier overhead in the middle of a thunderstorm. That's what the noise was like. I can find the words to describe the noise. That's not so difficult. But the pain . . ."

He stroked his palms up and down his thighs, enjoying the feel of callused skin on smooth. He rubbed harder. Mei-hua used to do that. Yes, but don't think about her, not on any account; above all, don't think of her being made to endure the same torture. *Don't!*

"The pain began like a fireball explosion at the dead center of my skull. My brain was frying. The bones around it seemed to shatter and crack. Then the hurt became a throb. Soon it spread all over my body. It was like when you touch the oven accidentally, only it went on and on and it was *inside* me.

"I wanted to faint. My body wouldn't let me. Then they wrenched the bucket off my head and left. I fell over. I couldn't get up. I was completely deaf and I could not open my eyes to see without being sick. I could not think. I fell asleep. When I awoke, I was lying in bed. Someone had cleared the vomit off the floor. That was the fourth period. As much of it as I can remember."

The door to the outside opened. Mat sprang off the bed and

hurled himself against the slatted blinds, hands to the wall. "No!" he croaked. "Please no . . ."

A soft voice said, in hesitant English, "Mr. Young. We have met once before. Do you remember?"

Mat opened his eyes and for a moment stared at the blind, mere millimeters from his face. "Not the bucket . . . don't use the bucket."

"Bucket?"

Mat turned to stare at the newcomer. A soldier, dressed in short-sleeved shirt and green trousers. The uniform seemed so bright it hurt. He tried not to focus on the rectangular name badge above the soldier's left breast pocket, because that alone was white. He saw that the man's coarse webbed belt was brown, with three holes in vertical rows at regular intervals around the waist. The holes were protected by metal eyelets a darker shade of brown than the belt. Each collar-point sported a small gold bar with dumbbell ends. Mat could not take his eyes off this plethora of colors.

"Mr. Young, I am here to take you for exercise. Get dressed and come with me, please."

"Dressed?" Mat came to himself with a start. The stranger moved his hands and for the first time Mat noticed that he was carrying a bundle of clothes, which he now tossed onto the bed.

"I will wait outside."

Mat, suddenly conscious of being naked, folded his hands across his genitals and looked away. There was no dignity left in his world.

Dressing, an unfamiliar process, took time. As he emerged into the corridor the soldier handed him a pair of sunglasses. "You will need these, I should think so."

"Thank you." Mat's glance lighted on the soldier's breast badge. "Tsai . . . Zi-yang. Is that your name?"

"It is. I am a captain in the military police. Come with me, please."

Mat followed him in a daze. This man said "please" and "I should think so"; he brought clothes and discreetly waited outside while his prisoner put them on. What was happening?

At the end of the corridor was an elevator. It traveled so smoothly that Mat had no idea how far they went or in which direction. At last they came out into another corridor that led to the reception area he remembered from his first day on Quemoy. Zi-yang's jeep was waiting outside, minus its driver. The captain took the wheel. Moments later they drove out onto the cliff road; Mat felt a breeze on his face.

Without dark glasses he would have been terrified. Even as it was, the world seemed full of monstrously lurid, somehow threatening colors. By the time they'd driven through the village, however, his vision had settled down.

The sun shone in a sky of dark blue, crisscrossed with wispy clouds. A wind blew from Fujian Province, three thousand yards away, flicking the tops off the green waves. Zi-yang drove for a while, then turned right down a track and parked on top of a sand dune overlooking the narrow beach. He killed the engine and got out. Mat followed. "What am I supposed to do now?"

"I'm really not too sure." Zi-yang smiled. "Maybe you should run about. It is much too cold to swim at this time of year, although"—he glanced at the sky—"for February the weather is unusually good."

"It's not cold. It's wonderful!" Mat raced down to the water's edge, slowed, began to jog. When he reached the black rocks at the far end of the deserted bay he circled back, alternately sprinting and walking, until at last he arrived at the jeep. Zi-yang applauded. "Did you enjoy that?"

"Very much. Thank you."

Mat looked up at the officer, who continued to stand beside his jeep on the sand dune. Zi-yang did not appear particularly strong. "What would you do," Mat said slowly, "if I ran into the sea and started swimming toward the mainland?"

"Well, I would stop you, of course."

"How?"

"I suppose I would have to shoot you. Please do not make me do that. It would spoil my day off."

Mat frowned. "If it's your day off, what are you doing with me?"

"I volunteered."

"Why?"

"I want to practice my English. Why not?"

Mat threw himself down on the sand and thought about that. This amiable man was hiding something; but he seemed to enjoy the prospect of a talk. "What'll happen to me?"

"I do not know."

"Why am I here?"

"Why? So that Director Li can find out if there are any more copies of Apogee left in Taiwan, I suppose."

Mat laughed. "If that's what he really wants to know, I shan't be here much longer."

"Why?"

"Because there was only one backup copy, in the bank, and my father took it with him when he left."

"I see. Would you like something to eat?"

"Yes, please!"

Zi-yang carried two large brown paper bags from the jeep to the beach. Mat snatched a pork bun from him and sank his teeth into it.

"Not good," said Zi-yang. "You will get cramps in your stomach. Please be careful. Drink some tea."

"Where did you learn to speak such good English?"

"Ni bie gei wo kai-wan-hsiao."

Mat stopped in mid-chew and looked at him sharply. "I'm not making fun of you. Truly. How did you learn?"

"I was taught English at school."

"But school's some time ago. How old are you?"

"Thirty and one little bit."

"Did you study abroad?"

"No. But in Taiwan there are six good secondary schools and I was lucky to attend one of them. Afterwards, I continued to learn in my spare time. Because English is important."

"If you speak it with an American accent it is, I suppose."

"No. The Americans are not acceptable people to me."

"Why ever not? Oh—because of the Taiwan Relations Act? President Carter and so on."

"Say rather because the U.S. betrayed and abandoned China, the real China. Those words are shorter and easy to understand. Also, they are true."

"I see. But not all Taiwanese would agree with you. My girlfriend, for instance. She likes Americans."

"You have a Taiwanese girlfriend?"

"Yes. Mo Mei-hua."

"There is a singer of that name, an actress, but you can't mean—"

"That's her."

"Jacqui Mo is your girlfriend?" Zi-yang made no secret of his disbelief.

"Yes. She's here. On Quemoy."

"Then I know you are lying! What would a girl like that be doing in the middle of the war zone?"

"She's been arrested too."

Zi-yang laughed out loud. But he recovered almost at once and said, "That was rude. Excuse me." He slapped his knee. "Mo Mei-hua, here . . ." He became serious. "You really know her?"

"Yes. On my word of honor."

"I have a friend who knows her also. Shan Lin-chun."

"I've met her!"

Zi-yang had been squatting on his heels, but now he jumped up, eyeing Mat in amazement. "It cannot possibly be the same."

"She works for a bank, Chinese Overseas Investment."

"Yes! How do you know her?"

"I met her at Mei-hua's nightclub; and then again with my father, on business."

"How strange!" The look on his face slowly gave way to a shy smile. "Did you like Lin-chun?"

"I hardly knew her, but yes, a sweet girl."

"She is, she is." Zi-yang's lips puckered. "Ah . . . we should drink to absent friends." But when Mat held out his plastic tumbler for more tea, the officer shook his head and went up to the jeep, where he collected a raffia-covered bottle. "You like this stuff?" he asked, squatting down beside Mat again.

"What is it?"

"Kaoliang. They make it here. Try it."

Mat took one suspicious sip. "Ugh!"

"Never mind. We will drink to absent friends anyway. To Shan Lin-chun!"

They drank. "You're close friends?" Mat asked.

Zi-yang rubbed his tumbler between his palms. "Close . . . once." He grunted softly. "Lost opportunities."

"Don't you have a girl here?"

"No time. We all must work very hard."

"There isn't much to amuse you here, I suppose?"

"Not much. I feel sorry for the local people. At least we get leave in Taipei; they haven't any entertainment here."

"What will happen to them, when the Chicoms come?"

Zi-yang looked toward the mainland and was silent for a moment. Then he said quietly, "They will die, most of them. In a morning, I should think so, yes."

Mat stared down into the clear plastic tumbler that contained his ration of spirit. The pale fluid danced and sparkled in the sunlight; and as the glint pricked his eyeballs, his reviving memory took a tremendous leap across time and space.

He was sitting up in bed. Mei-hua went to answer the door. He took a drink of whiskey. He was drifting off, under the influence of a drug. And then Mei-hua was sitting on the bed with the stranger.

But it wasn't a stranger. It was . . .

Mat raised his eyes from the tumbler and looked across the strait, beyond Little Quemoy, to where the cliffs of mainland China swept down to the sea. "I've been there," he said abruptly.

"You have?"

"Yes. A place called Chaiyang." Mat held a forearm up to his brow. He felt confused and hot. Li Lu-tang had been at Mei-hua's shoulder that night! No, it couldn't be, it wasn't possible. "Why aren't they shelling?"

"We do not know. It's been quiet for three days now."

Li Lu-tang had drugged him. Or Mei-hua had done it, on Li's orders. Yet she had said nothing of that in the cell. Nor had she shown any sign of having met Li before.

"Tell me—how were things on the mainland?" Zi-yang asked.

It was Li Lu-tang in Mei-hua's apartment, *it was*! And suddenly Mat understood why he was sitting on a sunlit beach with this friendly military policeman. "No," he said quietly. "I don't think I'll tell you anything at all, Captain Tsai."

He felt sick. Casually, without noticing, he'd confirmed to Tsai what perhaps he hadn't known before—that there was at least one backup copy of Apogee and that it had been kept in a bank.

First a metal bucket over the head, now the picnic. Cruelty followed by kindness. These people were professionals, they knew all the tricks.

And Mei-hua was one of them.

He lifted his head to find the captain's somber gaze upon him. "There is *one* thing I'd like to tell you. You know what hippies are?"

Zi-yang frowned. "In the West it means a dropout, I know. But here, it can mean other things as well."

"Yes. In Taiwan, one meaning is: someone who's above the law. Isn't that right?"

Zi-yang nodded.

"Then Li Lu-tang's a hippie."

The officer's expression did not change, but Mat saw how his eyes moved and knew an instant's hope. "In fact," he went on rapidly, "he works for Our Formosa Now—the Taiwan independence movement. Do you understand? Your superior officer is a traitor. He told me so himself—boasted of it."

Zi-yang's eyes were questing over the Englishman's face. "You are a crazy man, you know that? Crazy. Better be careful what you say here."

"He told me so himself," Mat repeated firmly. "When the invasion comes, he plans to assassinate your President, as the first step toward power. And I wasn't the only one to hear him. Mo Mei-hua was there."

Zi-yang rose. "We must return to the post."

Mat got up more slowly. "Thank you for lunch."

"Listen. Before I take you back, there is something I must say. I should not do so, but . . . you know Lin-chun, so I will take my chance. Be careful. If you offend the Director . . ." He drew a forefinger across his throat with a grimace and started up the sand dunes.

"Does that matter to somebody in my position?"

Zi-yang stared at him. "I do not understand."

"I've been sentenced to death. For murder. You didn't know that?"

"I knew about it. I do not understand you at all."

"Why?"

"Because you are so calm. About to die, and yet so . . . so very calm. It is unnatural."

"You think I don't feel it, too?" Mat shrugged. "I'm not the panicking kind."

Zi-yang chewed his lower lip, as if weighing things. Then he said in a low voice, "They have told you that you have been sentenced to death. But it is not so. It is something Director Li wishes you to believe, that is all." He winced. "I have spoken too much. Forget what I said."

"No, I won't forget. I'm grateful. I just hope you're not lying, that's all. And you mustn't forget what I've told you: your Director Li is a traitor. You should get a message to Taipei, Captain, before he can kill the President; maybe you'll even earn yourself a medal."

Zi-yang examined Mat's face for a long time, his eyes darting up and down, left and right. "Like I say—you are crazy," he said at last. "Tell the Director what he wants to know; then maybe he will let you go before the killing starts."

"I don't—"

"You do not understand? Then let me explain it in words that you *will* understand! Our intelligence reports all say the same thing. There is only a little time left, days maybe, before the invasion comes. And then"—Tsai Zi-yang laid a hand on Mat's shoulder—"no one will leave this place, ever again. You know, I know— not one person will get away from Quemoy alive."

Li Lu-tang saw Mei-hua emerge from the terminal building and reached across to open the car door for her. "Fuck Quemoy!" she

[252]

stormed, throwing her bag on the backseat. "It's about as exciting as a chow-chow's cock."

"You look a mess. What happened?"

"Nothing. Have you got the stuff?" The question came out too eagerly; she could have bitten her tongue off.

"Oh yes, I've got your cocaine."

Li drove quickly onto the main road and headed north, toward Nanshan. "What's the matter with you?"

"Oh . . . I had a row with Mother, that syphilitic old tart. Know what? She's sold my best painting. A genuine Cheng Tsai-tung. *Tea Drinking.* It was priceless—and all she got for it was a few thousand NT!"

"No need to shout. I gave you orders to be seen, let people know you were still around. What were you doing at your mother's in Peitou when I wanted you in Taipei?"

"I've got to see the bitch once in a while."

"Don't do it again. I need you calm and steady for this job. As calm as that white powder allows."

Mei-hua glowered out the window. "God, how I hate this place. All those frigging trees . . ."

"They protect the roads from aerial reconnaissance."

"So dull, trees. I hate them." They passed a complex of slit-trenches before rounding a corner under the barrels of a heavy-artillery battery. "And guns," Mei-hua added. "I read somewhere that this is one of the most heavily defended places on earth. Is it true?"

"Yes."

"Why bother to defend such a dungheap?"

Li drove on in silence until he sensed that the fight had gone out of her. "Young's displaying great powers of resistance," he said eventually.

"You amaze me."

"You expected that?"

"Of course. He's tough. He's fit . . . *very* fit. Mmmm . . ." Mei-hua made an effort to pull herself together. A memory of her last conversation with Mat came into her mind and she chuckled. "Have you tried pulling out his fingernails yet?"

"No. Do you think that might—"

"Oh, forget it! Look, Lu-tang . . ." She put on her best wheedling voice. "You know how grateful I am. You gave me a purpose in life, a cause, an ideal. But let's face it—this really isn't my kind of work."

Li was about to reply when two jets flew low overhead. He

jammed on the brakes and they both ducked. "You were saying?" he asked, as they resumed their journey.

"Never mind."

"Something about causes and ideals, as I recall. Nice words to hear in the mouth of the daughter of a whore and a Yankee sailor on the town, yes?"

Mei-hua lowered her head. "Yes."

"Then of course there were the roles, weren't there? And the Golden Horses? And the coke, let's not forget that."

"I've said I'm grateful."

"Then show it!"

"How?"

"By getting inside Young's head."

"Do I have to?"

"Certainly you do!" Li paused. "You're fond of him, aren't you? *Aren't you?*"

"Yes, if you want the truth."

"More than fond?"

"Sometimes."

"That's definitely your problem, not mine. And I'll be watching you. Clear?"

"Clear." Mei-hua sighed. "How long have I got?"

"Not long. It's nearly the end of February now. Say three weeks at most."

"Jee-zus! I'm not sure I can take three more weeks on Quemoy."

"Oh, you will. You'll find the days passing all too quickly." Li downshifted with a vicious wrench on the lever. "Tomorrow I'm going to show Young the gates."

Mei-hua clasped her hands behind her neck and massaged gently with the tips of her fingers. "Do you have to? The gates are terrible."

"Yes, they're terrible, but nothing compared to what's being prepared over there." Li nodded at the mainland. "Their troop mobilization is well under way by now. I can guess why. They know we're holding the Young boy, and they're afraid of losing their secrets."

"How long will our own people need to adapt Apogee for use against the Chicoms?"

"Too late for that! Even if we got Apogee tomorrow, there still wouldn't be enough time. No, we'll have to sell it to the Americans as the price of their intervention—but only *after* we get power. And it's all taking too long. Simon Young won't be idle."

"What can he do?"

"I don't know. He was bluffing when he told me he'd got photographs and tapes on his plane, I'm sure of that now. Otherwise he'd have published them already. But he's a fighter; he won't be sitting quietly in Hong Kong, doing nothing."

"Then why haven't you worked Mat over before this?"

"Because if I rush it I stand to risk losing everything!"

"So where do I come in?"

"Where you always did—with the boy. Tomorrow I'll send him through the gates. After that, you can comfort him. As I say, there's been no formal interrogation as yet, but it's clear he knows something."

"And he'd have told you what he knows, too, if you hadn't opened your mouth so wide that first day. He likes Taiwan, I can't think why."

"A small miscalculation," Li said smoothly, "and one easily corrected."

"Oh yes?"

"Yes. Tsai Zi-yang worked on him today. He's good. It's that friendliness of his—Young picked up on Tsai's connection with Shan Lin-chun, by the way. Something else I've got you to thank for. And it worked, to an extent. Young's a talker. It's all inside him, ready to spew out. He came close to it this morning—talked about a backup copy."

"A copy? Still in Taiwan?"

"It's possible."

"That would solve all your problems."

"It would. Trouble is, Young told Tsai that the only copies have already been taken away."

"Sounds as if Zi-yang's doing a great job. Why not let him get on with it and leave me out?"

"Tsai hasn't got the hold over him that you have." Li smiled. "Young assured our good captain that I'm a traitor and a member of the Formosan independence movement. He's not above taking a few risks."

"Damn right," Mei-hua said admiringly. "How did Tsai react?"

"He told Young he thought he was mad and reported it to me as soon as he got back. Now listen—I want you to tell Young you've been devising an escape plan."

"You seriously think he'd believe that?"

"He'd better!"

"But anyone would know that escape from here's impossible."

"Nothing's impossible when it's packaged right. That's your job—presentation. Soothe him into believing he'll soon be free." Li's face tightened. "He may be free for real, anyway. If he doesn't know as much as I think he does, or if there really aren't any backup copies of Apogee left in Taiwan, I'm going to have to consider doing a trade."

"Trade?"

"Yes. An exchange. With—aiyee! Look!"

They were driving out of Nanshan village. Over on the mainland there came a sudden flash, followed by a belch of smoke. Li pumped his foot down on the accelerator. "Shelling! They've started again."

A whistle-scream pounded its way into Mei-hua's ears. She had time for one shriek of terror before the car hurtled past the sentry boxes, reinforced steel doors clanged shut behind them, and they were safe inside Q-4.

As Li drove on, Mei-hua experienced an uncomfortable sensation: her panties were wet. Fear had done that: fear of dying on this terrible place, dreary and threatening beyond belief; fear of being blown into hundreds of raw, red pieces.

The familiar amalgam of confused and wayward thoughts bubbled up inside her, shifting her loyalties first one way, then the other.

"This escape plan," she said thoughtfully. "It sounds like a good ploy to me. Tell me how you think I might make it sound convincing to Young. He's not a fool all the time."

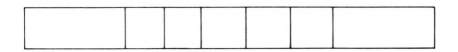

TWENTY-THREE

"You sure that's the place you want, miss?" The taxi driver sounded doubtful. Lin-chun followed his pointing finger and saw why.

Two dragons sitting on top of square gate-pillars guarded the entrance to an old mansion. The concrete drive was potholed. In one corner of the front lawn, next to a fountain where no water ran, stood an open-sided gazebo, its columns and roof eaten away by rust.

Lin-chun peered through the misty windshield at the house's green and white façade. It was a large, two-story edifice with many rooms. The veranda that extended the whole length was bounded by a low wall, bearing balsam plants in red flowerpots. One whole wing had largely disappeared beneath a tangle of traveler's palms and bougainvillea, its stucco-work peeling. The place had a sad, rundown look.

The cab stopped beneath an arched shelter above which a room had been built out from the frontage. As Lin-chun got out she saw a crack running up one wall for two-thirds of its height, near where a banyan tree tilted at a perilous angle, and she felt sorry for this wonderful house.

"Roots," the driver said, pointing at the crack. "Very sad. Happens a lot here in Singapore."

Lin-chun paid him off and waited until the taxi had driven away before pressing the bell. No one came. After a while she peered in a half-open window. "Hello," she called. "Anyone there?"

The house echoed with her voice. Lin-chun could smell stale cooking, with just a hint of durian fruit to tickle the nerves at the back of the throat where vomiting began. She looked at the slip of paper on which she'd written the address. Yes, this was the place. So where was Mr. Khoo?

She began to circle the house. Cempedak trees overhung the boundary fences on every side, their leaves brushing the sodden lawn of coarse lalang grass. A metal swing-chair sat lopsidedly in one corner of the back garden, half covered by a pile of dead branches. There was a swimming pool, kept filled and overflowing by the rain. As Lin-chun reached the shelter of the kitchen porch, waves swept over the sides of the pool. She realized they must be caused by someone swimming. Then she saw Khoo.

He had been resting with his back to the wall of the pool nearest the house when first she appeared. Evidently he had not heard her approach, for now he launched himself forward with a powerful kick and began to crawl up the pool, forging through the leaves that bobbed everywhere on the surface. As Lin-chun saw the powerful shoulder-muscles propel him effortlessly onward through the water, certain things that had been troubling her resolved themselves.

He made the turn, raised his head, and saw her. For a second he hesitated, tossing his head to clear the water from his eyes; then he began to speed back down the pool as if all the sharks in the South China Sea were snapping at his heels. He placed both hands on the side and pushed himself out.

They stood and looked at each other, oblivious of the knitting needles of rain that separated them. Lin-chun found she could not help glancing at his body, nearly bare. It was so unexpected. Those calf muscles, those pectorals padding out his chest, flat stomach, rounded rump . . . a swimmer's body.

"I wasn't expecting you so soon," he said.

"The flight was early."

"Ah." Rain poured down Khoo's face, neatly sweeping his black hair, grown longer now, into a straight fringe. "Please, would you pass me my towel?"

He entered the kitchen and began to dry the water from his body, while Lin-chun covertly studied him. He had seemed insignificant in a business suit. But he was wiry; he had sinews and muscles. When he put a foot on the chair to wipe between his toes, she saw how his back curved, how the elastic skin molded itself around his trim body without sag, and she thought, Oh yes. Yes.

He caught sight of her expression, knowing it matched his own. For him, too, things suddenly became simple, and this surprised him, for he had not previously thought of love as being easy. "You're looking good."

Lin-chun ran a hand down her full green skirt and smiled at him. "Nothing special. Just my traveling outfit."

Khoo tossed the towel away and, before Lin-chun could decide what was happening, reached out to pull her close. He stood with his legs apart, planted firmly on the floor, and for a moment just let her feel him through her cotton blouse while he rested his forehead against hers. His chest, still damp, was tight against her breasts: she could see how the dark brown nipples peaked with pleasure under the soft friction. His torso was like steel, and below that . . .

Lin-chun felt all kinds of bittersweet things rise up in her throat and she choked a little, pushing him back, but halfheartedly, as if in a dream. He was letting her feel the hardness just at the place where the tops of his legs met. She could not see the masculine swelling but she knew it was there. It struck her as a little scary and teasingly erotic but, above all, potent; the magic dispensed by the wand between his legs was real.

She had been brought up to believe in the power of the mind. Firsthand experience of the body's sway generated cracks in her like the crack in the wall outside, and for the same reason—a root was forcing its insistent way through every obstruction.

"Miss me a bit?"

"I . . . I missed you a lot," she confessed. He lifted her chin with two fingertips, surveyed her face tenderly, and kissed Lin-chun full on the lips. She thought, I can't stand this, I really can't, it's like taking drugs. I'm lost, she thought. Sweetness began to radiate inward from her lips. Then something cool and assertive probed between them, unsealing her mouth, and she shuddered, aghast, but . . . Go on, go *on*! Don't stop!

He began to stroke his hands up and down her back, massaging the ridges on either side of her spine. With every stroke his hands sank a little lower. Lin-chun jolted against him and moaned, but the sound was lost inside his mouth.

She found that her hands had moved, all by themselves, without orders. They were on his upper arms—no, they weren't, not any longer, they were doing to him what his were doing to her.

He was a doctor, administering pre-medication; another second and she'd go under. But it didn't matter, because at any moment she could say the word and he would stop and things would be all right. She could go home to her parents, look them in the eye, and . . .

His tongue became more urgent. Lin-chun pressed herself against him and in that moment knew exactly what she was doing. She wanted to dissolve into him. Separate existence had ceased to matter. Goodbye, she thought. Goodbye, goodbye.

Her fingers slipped inside the band of his swimsuit. He moaned, pulled her harder against him, and began to thrust his pelvis against hers. And at that Lin-chun woke up. Her eyes opened wide, she hastily pushed him away and covered her face with her hands.

"What's the matter?" His voice was gentle with concern, but Lin-chun couldn't bear the sound of it. Soiled, disgraced . . . "Give me a minute," she muttered.

After a while she felt her body return to normal. The tingling stopped, so did the pleasurable nausea. Life was once more mundane. But her gaze couldn't help straying to his swimming trunks, where it lighted on a still-large manifestation of that terrible potency she'd just experienced, and for an absurd moment she wanted to ask him if it hurt. But instead she said, "Get dressed, please." When he started to say something, she put her hands to her ears. *"Please!"*

He left the kitchen and soon came back wearing an open-necked white shirt over black slacks. She felt her treacherous eyes seek out the topmost point of the **V** between his legs, but now there was nothing to see.

"I don't like this house,' he said. "Let's talk outside."

"It's still pouring."

"We can sit in the summer house out front. I spend a lot of time there." He walked to the door and plucked an oil-paper umbrella from the rack. She followed him unwillingly, reluctant to be too close to him but knowing she'd either have to brush against his body or forgo protection from the downpour. Somehow she made it without becoming either violated or excessively wet.

Two stone chairs occupied the center of the gazebo. Lin-chun took one, Khoo the other. "We have lots to talk about," he said. "Thank you for coming."

"You said it was urgent. I had some leave due." She laughed nervously and spread her hands. "So here I am."

"Did you tell anyone where you were going?"

"My mother, that's all. No one at the bank."

"In the circumstances, it was good of you to trust me by coming here."

Lin-chun said nothing. In truth, she had no clear idea why she'd come.

"Lin-chun, I've many things to tell you. I've been hiding, first in Penang, now here. I was seen in Penang. Here's even less safe. I'll have to leave soon."

"What *is* this place?"

"It belongs to a man called Ng. I introduced him to Simon Young, many years ago, and they became business associates. Friends too, I think."

"I see."

"I work for Young, now. Ng owes Young a favor; he's agreed to keep me here, safe, for a time. But it's still dangerous for me."

"Why? Because of the police—"

"The police have no interest in me. Whatever the bank's directors may think, I'm no thief. The real danger's different. Mr. Ng maintains close unofficial links with mainland China, and they're my biggest threat right now."

"The Reds are after you?"

"Yes. And this makes life difficult for Mr. Ng, because his friends in Beijing wouldn't like it if they thought he was protecting me."

"But where else could you go? Where's safe?"

"Nowhere's safe. Listen—I've many difficult things to tell you. The story of my life, really."

The deluge was easing off, but huge drops continued to beat upon the iron roof high above their heads, sounding as if a double bass were playing a tuneless cacophony of the lowest notes in its register. At last the rain stopped completely; and Khoo began to speak.

An elderly gentleman stood motionless at an upper-floor window, behind the shutters, watching them, wondering what had brought this oddly matched couple to his house. After a while Khoo began to gesticulate, and the watcher could see from the way his lips moved that he was speaking rapidly. Then the girl began to protest. She interrupted him. She stood up, sat down, stood up again. The old man observed this pantomime with keen curiosity.

The conversation in the garden lasted about twenty minutes. It ended with Lin-chun running out of the gazebo, down the drive, and onto the main road.

She ran for a long time before the tropical heat obliged her to slow to a walk. For a while she had only the vaguest idea of her surroundings. There was a park, with a steep hill in the middle. She climbed all the way up to the top, and then somehow she must have come down again, for she found herself sitting in a bus shelter opposite an orange-colored shopping complex, watching the traffic flow by.

She thought and felt so many things: relief that she'd stopped him from making love to her; grief that he was a mainlander and a spy and a married mainlander spy; self-contempt, for having been so stupid and weak; self-pity, because she loved Qianwei, she now realized, and it was impossible that she should ever see him again. Or that she would ever meet anyone one-tenth as attractive. Or a hundredth part as good. She'd waited so long, keeping herself for this one man, and now look where it had gotten her.

She cried. She detested herself for doing it, but there was no stopping the tears that coursed down her cheeks; so she hid her face in a handkerchief and pretended she had grit in her eye.

After a while she dried up and just sat, rocking gently backward and forward, hugging herself tightly for comfort; only that was no good, because it just brought back memories of how *he* had held her.

She sat for an hour or more, working her way silently through the past in an attempt to discover what it was that had brought her there. She had been swimming aimlessly around in an ocean called Life, and now she was on a raft. This bus shelter was a breathing space, a retreat where she could take stock. But any minute now she would have to dive back in the ocean. She would have to choose a direction and follow it, as far as the horizon and then over the edge of the known world.

She hailed a cab and told the driver to take her to Changi Airport. He was elderly and must have been somewhat deaf, for he turned around to stare at her and said, "Airport?"

Lin-chun took a deep breath and for a moment forgot to let it go: only when she started to feel dizzy did she realize what she'd done. "No." The single word came out as a short, dramatic sigh. She searched her handbag for the scrap of paper with the address of the mansion written on it.

The journey was a short one. Lin-chun looked over the cab's hood at the gazebo, where Qiu Qianwei sat with his legs wide apart, hands lying loosely clasped between his thighs; she took note of the rounded shoulders, saw how his head lolled to one side, his lips curved downward, his brow wrinkled in despair. . . . Lin-chun jumped off her raft and started swimming mightily for the shore.

"I've come back," she announced redundantly, lowering herself into the second chair. She sat on its edge with her back quite straight, a hand on each knee, for she did not intend to stay there long. Qiu bounded out of his seat and retreated a step, his hands awkwardly finding their way into his hip pockets. There was a long silence while he nerved himself to ask the vital question. "Why?"

She lowered her eyes and for a moment examined her hands. Then she said, "You shouldn't start what you can't finish."

She expected him to understand the allusion; then he would lean down to take her hands and she could drift. But he did nothing except stare at her as if she were an insect, maybe dangerous, possibly not. So in the end Lin-chun was left with no alternative but to follow through. She stood up and grasped one of his wrists. "I resent the way you make me do all the work, Qianwei."

She gave his wrist a tug. Qiu, caught off balance, lurched forward a step. Then he took another. Lin-chun seemed to know instinctively where to go.

Much later, as they went out into the tropical darkness, Qiu noticed a solitary light burning in one wing of the mansion, and an alarm went off in his mind. He stopped. "Funny . . . The house is supposed to be empty. No one lives here anymore. See that light?"

"Yes."

"It's where Ng keeps his office. He must be working late, I guess."

Lin-chun slipped a hand through the crook of his arm. "You worry too much," she said.

"Perhaps."

The gate clicked shut behind them, leaving only a chorus of cicadas to disturb the peace of the garden.

Inside the office, the same elderly gentleman who had watched them earlier lay dozing on a leather sofa. At about the moment Qiu and Lin-chun slipped away, the machine on the floor beside him emitted a loud click and its twin spools stopped turning. Mr. Ng woke up with a start. He removed the full reel of tape, dropped it onto the cushion next to him, and picked up the phone. When the operator answered he requested a personal call to Beijing before once more lying back, folding his arms across his chest, and contentedly closing his eyes.

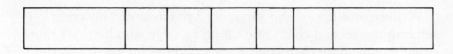

TWENTY-FOUR

The atmosphere felt moist and smelled rank, as if no fresh air could penetrate this far down. Mat tried to see what was in the void on the left of the rough concrete stairway, but the darkness there remained impenetrable.

The stairs began to circle, round and round in an ever-descending broad spiral. The only light was shed by flambeaux fastened to the raw granite at irregular intervals, their dull flames smelling of oil and soot. Mat was starting to feel cold.

When the stairs finally ran out, he found himself in a broad tunnel, hewn from the bedrock of Quemoy. At the far end was a square of white light, framing the figure of a man.

As they advanced toward the source of the light, Mat became increasingly sure he knew who the silent figure was. The peaked cap, sword, and pinched tunic could belong to no one else.

"Good morning, Mr. Young," said Li Lu-tang, when they were still some yards away. "Welcome."

Mat shivered. A pair of torches threw Li's face into intermittent shadow, working his features now this way, now that, but never disclosing his entire countenance.

"Come." The Chinese took Mat's arm, as if he were an honored guest. "There is something I want you to see. Something unique."

This passage also was illuminated by flambeaux, but these were electric, mounted in cast-iron brackets and protected by translucent globes. As Li and Mat progressed the air grew steadily warmer and purer. Eventually they came out into a circular domed chamber from which two galleries led off at an angle of sixty degrees to each other. Li came to stand in front of Mat.

"I am going to show you an exhibition. A very old display, but one that is constantly updated. It's been here for a long time, although its purpose, its true function, has always been the same. It is arranged in a circle." Li pointed. "That opening, there, is the start. We shall walk around, until at last we arrive back here."

When Mat plucked up the courage to speak, Li heard him out with a pleasant smile. "What is this . . . exhibition?"

"It might perhaps be entitled 'Persuasion Through the Ages.' Something like that."

"Why show it to me?" Mat's voice sounded metallic in his own ears, and at once he knew he was afraid. Everyone knew it.

"Mr. Young." Li's voice was thoughtful; he seemed to be preparing to deliver a set speech. "It should hardly be necessary for me to spell out the position we have reached. Your father's company has developed a weapon for the Red Chinese. We need to find out all we can about it. We think you know a lot. Therefore, we must take steps to compel you to disclose what you know."

He looked at Mat inquiringly, as if to see whether any further explanation was needed. By now it was so warm in the enclosed room that Mat could feel himself sweating. "There is nothing I can tell you. You've got the wrong man. I just . . . don't . . . know."

Li shook his head. "There are many ways of extracting information," he said politely. "Some are scientific, some are crude. The scientific methods—drugs—are powerful but dangerous. I say that for two reasons: first, because the chemical effect, once set in motion, cannot be stopped and may destroy the mind of the subject before he can communicate what he knows; and second, because it is possible for a person of average strength and intelligence to resist drugs for a long time, either putting out false information or talking nonsense."

Mat's mouth tasted unpleasant. However hard he tried, he could not summon up enough saliva to rinse the acidic flavor away.

[265]

"Then, of course, there are rough-and-ready methods that have been resorted to over the centuries. Irons that tear, flames that consume, knives that cut. And here, in China, clever tortures, using only the tips of the fingers, that can drive a man mad. These pressures are physical. But do you understand the psychology of successful *mental* pressure?"

Mat said nothing. His breathing had quickened and he found it hard to contain his heartbeat.

"The strangest thing of all, to me, has always been that it is not torture that produces results, but the *fear* of being tortured. You see, a man in extreme pain may say anything in order to make the agony stop; indeed, he may not even be able to control what he says. But one who fears, truly *dreads* being hurt . . . he will tell the truth, because he is still rational and he knows that this is the only way he can save himself." Li became more animated, like a lecturer approaching his pet subject. "I am going to show you what we Chinese have learned about persuasion over the past two thousand years. So come, Mr. Young"—again he laid a hand on Mat's elbow and made as if to begin the tour—"let us go. But first I draw your attention to the name of the door you are about to pass through. Look there."

Above the first doorway Mat saw some Chinese characters carved into the rock.

"Can you read them? They're not too difficult, I think."

Mat willed himself to think. He must not give way to panic, to despair. If only he kept calm, he would come out of this. Captain Tsai had said so. No doubt about it; he would. *He would!*

"*Li . . . ching . . . men.*"

"Yes! Very good! Now what do those words mean?" When Mat said nothing, Li affected disappointment. "Oh, surely now! *Men*, what about *men*? That is an easy one. It is a picture, is it not?"

"Door. Gate."

"Gate, yes. In this case, gate. And *li*, what of that?"

"Beautiful?" The word cost Mat an effort, but he got it out.

Li pursed his lips and shook his head. "Well, perhaps. Something a bit stronger?"

Mat could think of nothing to say. Part of him wanted to laugh, but he felt sure that once he started he would never be able to stop. Hysteria gathered somewhere in the dome above his head, like an invisible cloud of gas.

"All right, leave that for a moment. Can you tell me what *ching* means?"

Mat strove to concentrate his entire attention on the linguistic problem. Because that way he could not think about anything else. That way, maybe he could conquer fear. "*Ching* means . . . clear. I think."

"Almost. Not bad." Li waved his arm across the inscription and said, "Mr. Young, I welcome you through the gates of exquisite view. Those words were carved above the entrance to the torture chamber of Lai Chun-ch'en, executioner to the seventh-century Empress Wu Chao. Do you know what is to be found beyond them?"

Mat shook his head.

"The most frightening thing in the whole world. Knowledge. *Self* knowledge. Please come with me."

They walked through the darkened doorway. Beyond it was a dimly lit passage just wide enough to allow two men to walk side by side. On the right was the wall; on the left . . .

Li Lu-tang stopped, turned, and laid a hand on Mat's shoulder. "We start at the beginning," he said, "in a time of myths and legends. This, what you're looking at now, is hell, the Chinese hell."

Mat stared and stared, unable to assimilate what he saw.

It was a tableau, that much was obvious even at first glance: a recess some twenty feet long by ten feet deep, containing the depiction of a scene. The lighting was for the most part dim, except where a single spot picked out a square board on the back wall bearing Chinese ideographs, evidently an explanation of what was going on below.

Three wax figures occupied the recess. Two of them were devils: they wore terrifying, multicolored face-masks with huge teeth, pointed ears, and forked tongues. The third was recognizably human—just. He lay strapped to a bed of metal spikes. His head was raised so that he could see what the devils were doing to his torso. The expression on the man's face was one of extreme pain and terror; the demons were sawing him in half at the waist. Two or three ribs were visible beyond the jagged-tooth saw. Pools and streams of blood, as dark as burgundy wine, spattered the scene.

Mat wanted to laugh.

The last quarter of an hour had wound him up into a state of tantalizing uncertainty. Li, meaning to create fear, had succeeded admirably. Now this—a crude travesty of a waxworks chamber of horrors, a joke.

Li slapped his shoulder. "Does it remind you of anything?" he asked affably. "Tiger Balm Gardens, don't you think?" He laughed and Mat, unable to control himself any longer, burst into giggles. At first the sense of relief was profound. Only when he had been chortling to himself for the best part of a minute did he realize that no one else was laughing and that Li had his gaze fixed on him with one eyebrow raised.

"Yes," said Li. "In Singapore and Hong Kong you can see these displays, can't you? How the children squeal."

He led Mat a few paces deeper along the gallery. Mat noticed how gently it curved and understood that if Li was right, and they were going round in a circle, the tour would be a long one.

The next recess was much the same, except that the square board at the back bore a series of dates and the scene it contained was not dim, but brilliantly lit. Mat stared up, shading his eyes against the glare, and saw three mobile spots mounted on a metal track. This time the hapless victim lay strapped to a table. Another man, dressed in dusty ceremonial robes and a mandarin's hat, was in the act of placing what looked like an upturned metal bowl on the victim's stomach. A second official carried a small wicker cage, while a brazier glowed with artificial red light in one corner.

"Do not struggle with the Chinese inscription," Li said. "I will explain it to you. The cage contains a hungry rat. They will slip the animal under the bowl, which is then strapped to the man's stomach. They pile hot coals on the bowl. The rat at first becomes restless. Then it resolves to escape. It cannot gnaw its way through the bowl. After a while, it discovers that there is an easier way. . . ."

And suddenly the waxworks display seemed a shade less funny. A thin sweat coated Mat's forehead; he brushed it away with a quick, almost angry gesture.

"Now, moving forward slightly in time, we go on to the celebrated 'death of a thousand cuts.' You will observe how a skilled executioner could keep his victim alive in that cage for hours, days, even weeks. Notice the knife. Its edge is serrated. . . ."

The displays went on and on, tableau succeeding tableau, until Mat could no longer distinguish reality from the foul world depicted in the recesses before him.

Every kind of physical torture was represented behind the gates of exquisite view. Men were impaled on hooks, children cut up before the eyes of their agonized parents, limbs were burned, hot sulfur poured into suppurating wounds, women strung up by their wrists tied behind their backs. Noses were rubbed in buckets of excrement, genitals electrocuted, skin flailed with whips of razor blades, thumbs dislocated. And everywhere that same deep, dark, rich wine, blood-red.

"The *tago*—an astonishing device, popular in parts of South America. The darts you see there are connected by that wire to an electric generator; the subject is paralyzed until the current is switched off. Useful for crowd control in confined spaces; an off-shoot, that, of course. . . . *Bastinado* you will be familiar with already . . . kneeling on broken glass, something they borrowed for their distasteful cultural revolution, over the strait. . . ." Li's refined voice droned on, explaining every detail, its owner anxious that nothing should be left unclear. "Grinding a man between the village millstones—very old, that one, but you see it in this section because the Chicom cadres became fond of it under Mao. Nothing passes away forever, mm?"

White wall to the right, electric flambeaux, stone floor, recesses on the left—there seemed to be no end to this sickening progression. The air was growing ever hotter; even Li Lu-tang sweated a little, with tiny droplets of water appearing under his eyes. Just at the point when Mat thought he couldn't bear any more horrors, any more heat, Li stopped in front of a recess that was different from all the others. "Here we are, nearly at the end," he said. "After this, there is one more thing to see and then we can have lunch."

At the lip of this recess were three shallow steps, leading downward. No wax figures stood there; indeed, the heat was such that they would probably have melted. Mat screwed up his eyes, not comprehending the vista before him. The far wall of the sunken alcove was painted black, except for a representation of what looked like the interior of a steam locomotive's cab in the center. The ceiling was low, enhancing an impression of stuffiness—it was easy to imagine the fireman laboring to shovel coal, fighting shortness of breath. . . .

Yes, every detail looked right. Under the powerful spotlights mounted in their metal track, Mat could see the sides of the cab built out toward the front of the recess, the regulator, brake, dials, even a whistle-chain. But he did not understand the significance of what he saw.

"On your first day we talked of Tai Li, my predecessor." Li Lu-tang patted his sword scabbard and was silent for a moment, as if remembering events long since past. "He was greatly feared. People called him 'the Bogeyman.' He devised a method of dealing with traitors and suspected traitors that became widely known. His men were, in consequence, fanatically loyal, even though he forbade them to marry." Li raised a hand and pointed. "He used to throw traitors into the firebox of a locomotive. Alive. And to stifle their screams—which were terrible, Mr. Young—he would . . ." Li reached for the chain. A high-pitched whistle erupted into the cramped chamber. Mat clutched his hands over his ears, but to no avail; because the screech continued to slice its way through his brain without diminution.

Li released the chain and stood back. "Amplified," he said. "Quadrophonic sound. But authentic, oh yes, completely. Have you climbed Ali-shan? There are several coal-burners at the mountaintop depot. The whistle you just heard was recorded there."

He saw the look on Mat's face and smiled his faint smile. "Look!" He lifted an iron from the side of the cab and unlocked the fire-gate. There was a roar, and flame rolled outward in a melange of reds and oranges and bright yellows, as if hungry for flesh to consume. The grate was about three feet square, just big enough to take a human body. Mat squeezed his eyes tightly shut, trying to dismiss the images of burning hair and skin that insisted on forcing their way into his mind; but always the flames drew him back.

Li slammed the door, and the noise of the fury within was silenced. "We burn a mixture of coal and wood," he murmured. "It contributes to the hot-water system and in winter, of course, it provides us with heat." He mounted the shallow steps, once more taking Mat's arm. "The final representation is always personal—a thing we invent especially for each visitor."

In some strange way Mat divined what he would see even before they came to the alcove. There was no descriptive board, but here the lighting seemed doubly intense. A plain white room. Seated on a chair, hands tied to its arms, a young Englishman, the representation perfect, eyes wide, lips parted in horror. Himself. His clothes, his shoes, his facial expression. Mat gazed at this other, waxen self, feeling sick: it was too lifelike. Then his attention shifted to the other side of the tableau.

A wax soldier stood behind another chair, holding a cutthroat razor in each hand. Between the blades was the head of another figure, also fastened to the chair in which it sat, but the features of this third person were entirely concealed by a flimsy-looking white cloth extending down almost as far as the breasts. Nevertheless, Mat knew who this was intended to be, beyond any doubt. He knew, because the seated dummy was clad in a one-shoulder, silk chiffon dress handpainted with peonies and butterflies in pinks and blues; a bangle encircled each thin wrist; and just below the cloth he could discern a single strand of pearls.

It was the outfit worn by Mei-hua on the night she'd first shown him what was to become the Evening Fragrance Club.

The heat here was scarcely less than in the previous alcove. Mat felt faint; the next second he was on his knees, hands pressed to the cold stone floor, panting like a stag at bay. His stomach ached with the need to be sick, but nothing came. "The razors," said a smooth, familiar voice above him, "cut downward with considerable force, severing the ears from the head. There is much loss of blood; the pain is indescribable, the disfigurement permanent. Mr. Young, we want to know about Apogee. In particular, if there are copies and where they are hidden. This afternoon, you can tell us. But just in case you should forget the lessons you have learned this morning, allow me to conduct you on a refresher course."

They again embarked upon the tour. This time, things were very different.

In hell, there were no demons. Instead, there was a modern operating table, covered with green sheets, behind which stood two men—live men—wearing green surgical gowns and masks that obscured the lower part of their faces. Executioners covered up their features, but then so did surgeons. These men stood in the "at ease" position adopted throughout Taiwan's armed forces: legs apart, clenched fists resting on the thighs, elbows slightly protruding; and Mat was reminded of how menacing the posture looked.

In front of the table stood a chrome trolley, laden with scalpels, pliers, bone saws, and a Chinese chopper like the one chefs use to dismember chickens.

"Come."

A soldier, real enough this time, but dressed in the mandarin's dust-caked robes, was opening the cage to reveal a live rat. The brazier, piled high with coals, glowed red-hot. Another soldier held the bowl upturned above the table . . . the empty table.

"Come."

The metal cage stood ready for its victim. Nearby stood a soldier holding a knife, its serrated edge winking coldly in the bright lights, as if ready for a thousand cuts and more.

"Come . . . Come . . . Come . . ."

All the tableaux were the same: real people had replaced the waxen torturers; there was no blood to be seen anywhere; always the central character, the victim, was missing. By the time they came to the final scene, Li was having to support Mat and literally drag him along the stone corridor.

"No, no, no." The words came out in a continuous stream, a tired whimper. "Not her, not her, no, no, no . . ."

The figure of the Englishman had gone, its chair was empty. But the soldier who stood behind Mei-hua was alive; the tips of the razors wavered a little as he stared across them at Mat. The girl-dummy looked the same, except that the fingers were moving gently and the face-cloth wrinkled in front of where her mouth would be. She was panting: quick, gasping breaths that sucked and blew the cloth.

Li was silent for a long time, allowing Mat to digest every detail of the scene before him. Then he raised his chin and nodded once. The soldier jabbed downward, slicing the blades through the cloth. Mei-hua's scream echoed through the stone chamber, screech upon screech; redness erupted against the white cloth, oozing through it from her severed ears; her hands writhed; and all the while Li Lu-tang laughed and laughed, like a delighted child who goes to the fair for the first time and sees the marvels there.

Mat had buried his head in his hands and was shivering uncontrollably. He staggered back until he was resting against the wall of the passage; then he sank down, curling himself up into a foetal ball. Li signed to the soldier, who drew away the remains of the cloth.

"Look, Mr. Young." When Mat did not respond, Li grabbed a handful of his hair and raised his head. *"Look!"*

Mat turned his eyes away. Li's hold was inexorable, however; after a moment he had no option but to view the torturer's handi-work.

The head of the figure in the chair had virtually no features—eyes, mouth, and ears were all missing—but a tube led up from the neck of the dress to where the nostrils would be, and he understood how, when air was pumped through, it gave the impression of a person breathing. Two other tubes still oozed red paint, or ink, in a desultory stream of bubbles. The hands had moved, though. . . . Of course. Clockwork. He took it all in. He remembered what Li Lu-tang had said to him, that here was the most frightening thing in the world, self-knowledge; and in that second he understood the choice Li would soon present. Then he passed out.

He came to in his cell, with the real Mei-hua leaning over him. She was wiping his face with a warm scented towel. "You're all right," he croaked. "You're alive!"

Mei-hua nodded somberly. "Li told me what he did."

Mat eased his legs off the bed. His head spun and he moaned. "You must eat," Mei-hua said. "And there's tea."

Again the memories stirred inside Mat's head, just as they had done on the beach with Zi-yang. A flat in Taipei. Drinks. Doorbell. Slipping into unconsciousness.

"Is it drugged?" he asked.

"Don't be silly. I made it myself."

But he pushed the glass away. "You drugged me. I wasn't quite under when Li came into your apartment that night. I saw him."

"Yes. It's true. I *did* work for him, once."

Mat stared at her. He'd been expecting protestations of innocence, tears, the big scene.

"There's a well-known plot." Her voice was firm, slightly self-mocking. "It concerns the casting-couch girl who makes good, gets the starring role, comes to God. Perhaps you've even seen me play it on the screen?"

"What are you saying? I don't—"

"And at some point in this plot, the leading man, who's been fooled, is given the chance to have his revenge. But he doesn't take it. Not in the movies."

"You think I'm enjoying this." Mat looked down at the floor. "You're not painting a very attractive picture of me."

"On the contrary. The picture of you I carry inside my head is wonderful."

"But you *have* been working for Li ever since I've known you?"

"He said I was to trap you, and I said yes, because, hell, why not?"

"I see." Mat was remembering the row he'd had with his father in the Lai Lai Sheraton. What was it Simon had called her? A tart. But she wasn't behaving like a tart. Still no tears, no scene. Her composure gave her dignity. It also lent a certain credibility to what she was saying.

"Would you like to hit me?" she asked calmly.

"Yes, I'd like to hit you." He examined her for a long time. "But I'm not going to."

"Why?"

He shook his head. "Tell me something. How did you get involved with Li?"

"He gave me a reason for living. He told me I was nobody,

but he had a use for nobodies. Every nation, however great, consisted of lots of nobodies, that's what he said."

"And you believed him?"

"It was true! He *made* me. My first film contract was provided by Li Lu-tang." Mei-hua saw the look on his face and smiled faintly. "It's not what you think. He's stricter than the strictest Buddhist."

"Really?" Mat's tone was sarcastic. "Then what did he think of the cocaine, eh? Or didn't he find out?"

"Of course he knew about it; it's not the kind of thing you can go on hiding forever. In the end, he even supplied it." Her voice was charged with sad self-awareness. "He knew I was slipping away from him, and by then I'd become too useful for him to let me go."

"Slipping away?"

"Yes. Whatever you believe now, I genuinely fell in love with you. And others saw that, very clearly. Well. It doesn't matter, does it? Too late."

"I've been stupid, haven't I?" He sounded bitter.

"I'm a good actress. I've fooled a lot of people over the years."

Her cold words made more of an impression on him than any avowal of innocence would have done. Mei-hua busied herself with a tray that someone had left on the floor of the cell. "If you eat, you might feel better."

But Mat ignored the food. "Why are you telling me this?"

"Because there came a point when my ideas changed. I stopped working for Li—in my heart, I mean."

"Why?"

"You weren't a fantasy anymore. You'd become a man instead."

"I wasn't aware . . . when did I do that?"

"It's hard to pinpoint. It began the day you bought me an engagement ring. But I think it was after I saw you in the cell, here, for the first time. You weren't your father's son, you weren't the Ducannon Young heir, you were just yourself. I wasn't in a fit state to register, then, but later I understood."

"You're trying to make things sound so easy." Mat rose and began to pace about. "But you've been working for Li; you just told me so yourself."

"And now I've stopped. Do you love me?"

Mat wheeled around. "Why do you ask that?"

"Because I want to be sure you understand what's going to happen this afternoon. Li won't torture you. It's *me* he'll work on."

"Yes. I know that."

Mei-hua looked at him, searching his face for signs, but he

kept it closed against her. "You don't trust me," she said quietly. "But at least you realize what he's capable of. This afternoon we're going to do it all again, only this time . . ." Her voice cracked. "It might just be for real. Li's unbalanced. He's using me, he says he's still got plans for me in the future, but . . . would *you* trust him? I don't want to die, I . . ." She looked away, trying to hide her tears. "It's the . . . the pain!" The words seemed wrung out of her across a barrier of sobs. "It won't be quick. I'll . . . I'll f-feel it."

Mat looked at her, trying to fathom the truth, but he only succeeded in stirring up more mud from the murky depths of his brain. "Would you trust me, if our positions were reversed?"

"I can't think of a single reason why you should believe a word I say."

'Mei-hua!' He squeezed her chin, forcing her to raise her eyes to his. "Forget about the past. Forget about this afternoon. Just concentrate on now. Do you really love me?"

"Yes." She looked into herself and had no doubts. But Mat, struggling to fit himself inside her mind, her heart, was beset by nothing else. He was watching for that telltale twitch of the eyebrow, the flicker of light beneath the curling lashes that would tell him she was lying.

"My desires became so simple in the end. Do you know what they were?" She looked him full in the face, her eyes reflective and lit with the glimmer of a smile. "A wonderful white wedding, in Hong Kong. At the Regent Hotel, with every producer and mogul, and a trillion-dollar wedding present from your dad . . . there, I've said it. I don't care anymore. I'd have overspent like mad, of course I would. But I'd also have been a good wife to you. There'd have been children—not at first, but later, when I felt myself on the threshold of age."

She kept her gaze on his face, not flinching, although she knew he was still probing for flaws. "The cocaine helped, of course. Helps, I should say—I had a fix before coming in here. It does its job. Its job is to keep reality where it belongs—on the outside."

Suddenly Mat knew she wasn't acting any longer; she was brave. He wanted to touch her, but dared not. "Listen to me." His voice was no more than a whisper. "Suppose I tell them something, this afternoon? Tell them a little—enough to keep them busy."

She raised her head. "What?"

"I'll trust you, because I've got no other choice. I'm going to escape. Will you help me?"

Mei-hua gaped at him. It was like being asleep and getting

your dreams all mixed up. Li had told her to devise an escape plan. It was Li, wasn't it? "What did you say?"

"I've got to think up a plan of escape."

"But that's . . . I . . ." Mei-hua tried to pull herself together. "There might be a way. I'm not really kept prisoner here on Quemoy, not all the time. Sometimes they let me go back to Taipei. Boats run in and out of Quemoy. I've got a friend who could sail in here. I'm friendly with the guards, I think I can fix them. They all recognize me, they feel sorry for me, only they're scared. It might work."

"That's very neat." At once he was suspicious again. "You thought all that up in one hell of a hurry."

"I've been thinking about it for a long time."

"Did Li put you up to this?"

Mei-hua hesitated only a second; at some point in the recent past she had made her decision and it was irrevocable now. "Li suggested the idea of an escape plan, yes. He thinks it'll disorientate you even more. What he doesn't know is that I've seen a way of making it work."

Mat was astonished. "Why take such a gamble?"

"I've worked it out for myself: Li can't afford to let you go now. *He has to kill you.* And I don't want that."

Mat remembered Tsai Zi-yang's words of comfort and was silent for a while. "Li can't risk killing me as long as I keep my mouth shut," he said at last.

"Even if that means hurting me?"

In the silence that followed, the rattle of a key in the lock sounded abnormally loud.

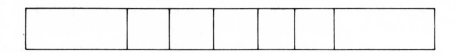

TWENTY-FIVE

The Chairman of the People's Republic of China traveled through the night to Yinchuan, on his way to the borders of the central northern province of Gansu. A fleet of helicopters ferried him and his staff across the Helan range to the edge of the desert. By that time the sun had risen to herald a cloudless March morning, but it was still very cold. An evil wind blew down on the plain from the mountains to the east, bringing with it flurries of dust and grit that danced across the expanse of reddish sand, whipping up fresh dervishes wherever it went; but the forecasters predicted calmer weather by nine o'clock, and Marshal Wang Guoying pronounced himself satisfied that flying conditions would soon be perfect.

Next to Gansu B-10's antiquated control tower stood a prefabricated, two-floor building, bristling with antennae and a pair of radar dishes. Marshal Wang led the way up a staircase to a door on the second story.

The Chairman, Wang, and Controller Sun found themselves inside a hangar about the size of a football field, looking down at rows of empty desks laid out on the floor below. Wang placed his hands on the gantry-rail. "This is a mockup, you understand. It's just to give us an idea of how things will look in Fujian Zero Nine on the day."

"Each of those desks represents one aircraft?"

"Yes, Chairman. It's necessary, because each plane will be operating on its own separate radio frequency. Fujian Center will be several times larger, of course."

"Those desks look like computer consoles."

"Basically, that's what they are. Each controller has a screen on which is projected the view through the nose of his aircraft. In addition, he has an instrument readout mirroring the one in the cockpit. He must use his keyboard to input certain commands at the start of the mission, when the various takeoffs have to be coordinated; but after that, it's voice control."

Wang stepped back and gestured with his hand. "Up here, where we're standing now, the mission directors will have larger screens to give them an overall picture of how the attack is developing."

"I can't understand all this modern flimflam. What's the controller supposed to do—mumble 'left, right, left,' that kind of thing?"

Wang laughed. "Not quite. There are only so many ploys in air combat. The various maneuvers have all been assigned numbers. For example, 'fourteen' might cause the plane to roll left, dive rapidly, and come up. Come on, let's see if it works."

At the far end of the gantry an officer sat before a live screen. At their approach he rose and stood to attention. "Yao Xuanling, Major, Seventh Division, Lanzhou Military Region, Yinchuan Military District."

"This is the big day, then?"

"Sir!"

"Sit." The Chairman put his head close to Yao's. "Relax," he whispered. "You'll do better that way."

"So where's the plane?" asked Sun Shanwang.

"Here it is." Wang was standing by a small window overlooking the field. He pointed. A fighter, devoid of insignia, stood at the runway's end, its engines idling. "Yao, take her up. And tell us what you're doing."

"Sir!" Yao flourished a sheet of paper. "This is the weather report, coupled with instructions for rate of climb and initial course. The information on it must be input—so!" The officer began to tap on the keyboard. After a moment the sound of the idling engines rose swiftly until it was uncomfortably loud inside the hangar. Yao entered three digits and a carriage-return. The jet-scream peaked and suddenly diminished. When the Chairman looked out the window the airstrip runway was empty. He craned his head. A plane was lifting off into the sky, one tongue of flame visible from each engine exhaust.

Wang turned to the base commander. "Do we have a tracking camera on it?"

"Yes, Marshal. Down there." The commander pointed to the lower floor, where, at the far end, a huge, wall-mounted monitor had flickered into life. The Chairman looked and saw a clear representation of a fighter plane climbing steeply. "That's the plane we just saw out there?"

"That's it," Wang confirmed. "Come on, Major Yao, show us a few tricks."

Yao entered four nines and a double carriage-return. He pulled a microphone toward him and barked, "Zero-eight."

The large monitor showed the plane leveling off. "Seventeen," said Yao; the plane circled to the left. Wang inspected Yao's small screen. "Look—while it's banking you can see the ground!"

"So you can! Before, it might have been anything."

"That's because there are no landmarks in the sky, Chairman. Nothing to get your bearings on. But remember that at the time the sky will be full of planes. There'll be plenty to shoot at, lots to see."

"What about the early stages, before the enemy's sighted? How do you know where to point the thing?"

"As I say, Yao's got an instrument panel that mirrors the one in the cockpit. He knows everything about the plane's performance that an in-flight pilot would know, including his bearings."

Yao embarked on a series of numbers, each of which was translated into an aerial maneuver reflected on the screen below. The Chairman shook his head. "It's clever. But can it win a war? I thought that the outcome of all air combat was determined by the skill of the pilot, the speed of his response. No machine's going to beat that."

"Perhaps not. But it doesn't have to."

"Explain, please," said Sun.

"It's important to remember why we needed Apogee in the first place. Guided missiles aren't enough for what we intend."

"Because they won't tempt the enemy's air force out of their hangars?"

"That's right, Chairman; and it's their air force we have to beat."

"Go on."

"In effect, we're going to lure the Taiwanese into the sky by giving them our obsolete machines, fitted with Apogee, as target practice. Many, perhaps most, of our planes will be shot down. But before that happens, they'll each have discharged four computer-directed missiles."

"How accurate are those missiles?"

"One hundred percent. Every one of them's going to represent an enemy loss. And so, slowly, the Taiwanese will exhaust their men and their machines."

"Then we put up the cream of our fighter pilots, who will really fly their planes, unaided, and they'll shoot down what's left?"

"Yes, Chairman—but our weapons systems will be voice-controlled from the cockpit. And from that moment on, we really can't lose."

"Really?" Sun Shanwang's tone was skeptical. Wang smiled. "If you don't believe me, watch. Major, test the weapons system."

Yao rapped out some numbers. As the Chairman watched the big screen, he saw the plane go into a shallow dive. When Yao spoke again the rate of descent increased.

At first the screen displayed only the ground rushing up to meet the plane, spinning like a top beneath its nose. Then a white speck appeared and the Chairman leaned forward. "What's that?"

"Target," Wang replied. "A small decoy plane."

The speck now had wings, a tail, all the substance of a real aircraft. "Weapons twenty-one," snapped Yao.

"That's the order to the missile system, to arm and lock on," Wang murmured in the Chairman's ear. "Any minute now . . ."

The target filled a third of the screen; and suddenly a row of figures danced across the top, recording distances, airspeeds, and time. "Weapons ten," cried Yao. At once, two white plumes of smoke forged out and up. One second, there was the other plane; then there was nothing except a ball of black smoke, showering debris. The Chairman exhaled. Wang slapped his thigh and laughed aloud. "You see! You see!"

"What happens now?"

"He's going to land it."

They all trooped down the stairs and onto the field. Just this side of the western horizon they could see a plane skimming toward them, only a few hundred feet above the desert. By the time it crossed the airfield perimeter it was traveling at less than two hundred miles an hour.

"One of the few that ever *will* land," Wang commented as the aircraft came to a halt.

"What do you mean?"

The Marshal shrugged. "Chairman, most of our planes are destined to be shot down by the Taiwanese. Those that escape will simply cruise on until they're over Taiwan's main island, at which point they can be brought down on selected military targets, just like the flying bombs of World War Two."

"Very well. Is there anything else to see?"

"No."

"Then we'll get back to Beijing. Oh, tell that young man Yao he's a good fellow. Make him a lieutenant colonel or something, yes?"

"Certainly, Chairman. Do you need me anymore?"

"No, Marshal, you're released. But I want daily reports from now on as to our state of readiness."

"Got it." Wang saluted and withdrew to join the base commander.

Sun looked after him through jaundiced eyes. "That thing's radio-controlled, you realize?"

"Of course. So?"

"So radios can be jammed."

"But not if the enemy doesn't realize what's going on. They have to know radio's involved before they can do anything about it. Which is why you're so important to all this, Controller. Security must be *tight*."

"Don't worry, I've taken precautions. The whole of the Ducannon Young Apogee team, anyone connected with it, is now subject to saturation surveillance."

"Good. Never forget, all this"—the Chairman gestured around the airfield—"is of very little significance to me, when compared to what follows."

"Please explain."

"I mean that Apogee is going to bring the Middle Kingdom to life. For the first time. All this military gadgetry, it's fine, but it's only the start. If we fail to reunite with Taiwan, that'll be a tragedy, but at least we'll still have our future. So I say again, Shanwang—there must be *no leaks*!"

"Understood."

"Come on, then. I'm freezing into an icicle, standing here."

Before long the airfield was just a blob on the edge of the

desert, with only a thin razor-slash in the rocky red ground to indicate a runway where aviation history had been made.

"You know what they say about this area?" Sun asked his companion. "You'd have to walk a hundred leagues to hang yourself!"

"It's a dump, I grant you that. Useful, though. People are hardly likely to go looking for our latest weaponry here."

"On the contrary. Our tracking station at Lop Nor reports a sudden change in the Soviets' satellite-surveillance pattern over Gansu Province, and a Russian flotilla was sighted off Tsushima yesterday morning, sailing southwest. It could be going anywhere, but I say those ships are heading for Taiwan."

"Coincidence."

"Chairman, please face facts. First, our missing plane: we haven't found it and I'm certain our so-called 'allies' have stolen it. Then there's the satellite, the flotilla, and to cap it all this man Krubykov. He's involved with the Formosan independence movement. We weren't told about that, although it's precisely the kind of thing the Moscow-Beijing pact was designed to cover. The Russians can't be trusted."

"As long as the Americans don't intervene, we—"

"But they're starting to get suspicious, too! Look. For years the Taiwanese have been increasing their foreign exchange deposits in the United States. Those reserves now amount to several billion dollars. If Taiwan called for the money overnight, it would cause really serious trouble for a number of important U.S. banks. We've heard rumors that Taipei's set up just such a run, as a way of exerting pressure."

"That'll take some time to organize."

"I suppose so. I just don't know." Sun grunted. "The best banking expert we've got is on the run!"

"Oh yes . . . what was his name—Chen, was it?"

"Qiu Qianwei. We've been tracking him. He's heading back to Taiwan, according to our source in Singapore. It may seem ridiculous, but it looks as though he's going to try to rescue Matthew Young."

"With what prospect of success?"

"In my estimation, none. Nevertheless, I see no point in trying to prevent him. It's common knowledge that Young ought to be either rescued or neutralized, just in case he knows something. Chief of Staff Wang has been talking of a diversionary tactic, something to distract them from our plans. A rescue operation for the Young boy—"

"But we don't know where Matthew Young is."

"Oh, but we soon will!"

"How's that?"

"Because Qiu's on the point of finding out."

"Suppose he does—why should he tell us? He's to be treated as a defector, isn't that what you said?"

"Yes. But don't worry about that. Colonel Qiu can be found, brought back, and milked of his information any time we want."

The Chairman's eyes widened. "How?"

And while the helicopter forged a way through the passes of the Helan mountain range, Sun Shanwang told him.

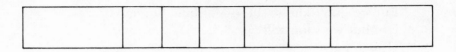

TWENTY-SIX

George Forster brought Qiu to the Ducannon Young boardroom a little after eleven o'clock at night. Simon Young was seated at a long table with papers spread out in front of him. "Welcome," he said. "There's the drinks tray; help yourself."

Qiu and Forster sat at either end of a sofa, while Simon came over to take a leather armchair. He removed a pouch from his pocket and self-consciously donned a pair of bifocals. "I can't manage these," he growled.

"I didn't know you wore them."

"I didn't, until recently. Growing old." Simon tapped a folder that was lying on the coffee table in front of him. "This is remarkable stuff," he said. "What's it going to cost me?"

Qiu's smile was bleak. "Make me an offer."

"All right. In future I want you to work for me full-time. Basically, I'm buying your skill and experience as a senior member of China's intelligence service."

"That's blunt."

"Honest, call it. The salary's negotiable, but you can expect to find yourself in the top upper decile."

"I don't know what that means, but I'm sure it's generous."

"In addition, you'll get protection. A new identity if you want, although I think that's a bad idea. Much better if you leave me to do a deal over your future with Sun Shanwang."

"Do you think you can?"

Simon hesitated before answering. "Sun's bound to be against you," he admitted. "But I think I can persuade him to treat you leniently."

"All right. I'll accept your offer."

Simon studied him for a moment, trying to fathom his thought processes. "Sure?"

"Yes. I'll tell you how I see it. From my brush with the Wus at Anshuo, I know the Russians are involved in a plot with the Formosan independence movement to overthrow the present government of Taiwan. I don't mind contemplating the end of the Kuomintang regime—I'd welcome it, in fact—but not if it means going in with the Soviets. That would only destroy what is, after all, a province of the People's Republic of China."

"But I don't see why—"

"Let me finish, please. I have commitments in Taipei now. Someone I care about very much—my source, Miss Shan. And then, finally, there's you."

"I don't understand," said George Forster. "How does Simon enter into this?"

"Because he saved my life. There's an obligation. And because of my detailed knowledge about his son"—Qiu pointed at the folder lying on the table—"whom I'm uniquely placed to help."

Forster still looked beset by doubt. "You certainly seem to have extraordinary access. I think you'd better tell us the history behind that report of yours."

"Very well. This person I mentioned earlier, the one in Taipei . . ."

"Shan Lin-chun," said Simon.

"Yes." Qiu colored. "I . . . love her. That's how she enters into this. She'd become friendly with Mo Mei-hua."

"Who turns out to be involved in this. Guesswork on your part?"

"Not exactly. We had one lucky break, when Mo phoned Miss Shan in a terrible state. Apparently her mother had sold a priceless painting for peanuts, and Mei-hua wanted a shoulder to cry on; it's not the sort of thing she'd tell the movie crowd."

"Go on."

"She went around and saw Mei-hua immediately. The girl was in a bad way. Drugs. She didn't know what she was saying. And slowly the story started to come out. She was terrified of being killed."

"Or pretending to be terrified?"

"No, Miss Shan was quite adamant: Mei-hua genuinely believed she wasn't going to get off Quemoy alive."

"Hm!" Simon opened the folder, seeking a particular paragraph on the first page. "Of all the godawful places, it had to be Quemoy. Why does Mo keep going back to Quemoy, if she's so frightened?"

"Miss Shan says it's because Mo's genuinely in love with Mat. And she certainly has some reason to care for him: it was only when your son broke a little and started to reveal some details about Apogee that Li released Mei-hua from the island."

"I see." Simon pushed his hair back from his forehead. "So Mat's talking to the Kuomintang, then."

"I don't think you want to worry too much about that. The important thing, as I see it, is that Miss Mo eventually cracked."

"Because of the attempt on her life?"

"No, not entirely. At first she was very suspicious. But Miss Shan played her cleverly. She steered the conversation around to the disappearance of your son and said that her bank was anxious to help a valued customer in any way it could."

"And Mo fell for that?"

"Not as easily as you suggest, perhaps. Miss Shan let her believe that she was, er, not uninterested in Matthew herself . . . but that she was determined not to stand in Miss Mo's light, if you see what I mean." For a second his serious face dissolved into a smile. "Most artful! Apparently, Miss Mo was so overcome by gratitude that she cried."

"Tell me, Qianwei—just how much of this frightful jumble do you believe?"

"Mo's account of the torture chamber, you mean?"

"Yes, and this business with the friendly soldier. He's a decoy, presumably?"

"I'm sure of it. He's been put there for the same reason as Mo Mei-hua: to win Matthew's trust and render him open to suggestion."

"Why the girl *and* the soldier?"

"Who can say? But my guess would be that Mat's shown signs

[286]

of seeing through Miss Mo. So his interrogators need another ally."

Forster broke the ensuing silence. "Your report mentions an escape plan. . . . How much mileage is there in that?"

"None," said Qiu. "But as a lever to be used on your son, Mr. Young, it makes a lot of sense when seen from Li's point of view."

"Why?"

"It's designed to raise his spirits. I think that this attempt will look like it's succeeding, and his hopes will run high. Then—disaster! Detection, recapture. At that point, if Li's skillful, he should be able to extract from Mat whatever he knows."

Simon looked at George Forster, who shook his head. "I still don't get it."

"It sounds good to me, George. You're desperate; you see the light at the end of the tunnel; you get careless." Simon flapped the folder up and down on the table a couple of times and flicked it away from him. "Right," he said. "Let me bring you up to date. When I received your report, Qianwei, I studied it carefully, as you can imagine. Particularly the description of the place where Mat's being held. I've made certain arrangements."

Qiu's eyebrows rose. "What?"

"According to your report, this so-called escape, the pantomime put together by Li, is due to take place tomorrow night."

"Yes."

"It's been carefully planned. We've a lot of information about Mat's prison. Mei-hua even supplied a sketch-map, apparently, although we haven't seen that. She also gave away the timetable."

"So?"

"If what the girl Mo told your contact is right, Mat's to be allowed to get as far as the sea, where he'll find a boat waiting. The boat sails away—"

"And is intercepted. Right."

"Wrong," said Simon. "When your report arrived, three days ago, I contacted your friend, Miss Shan, and asked her whether she trusted Miss Mo; she said she did. So I persuaded her to get in touch with Mo and give her some new instructions." Simon looked at his watch. "A fast boat left Keelung four hours ago, heading for Quemoy. Its captain is an old friend of mine, someone who owes me many favors. If I know him, his boat will *not* be intercepted at sea. And Mat doesn't come off Quemoy tomorrow. He comes off tonight!"

Shan Lin-chun sat in the back of the cab, holding a pink plastic briefcase upright on her knees. The case was heavy but she could not bring herself to lay it down on the seat, for it contained fifty thousand United States dollars and she was obsessed by the fear of losing so much money.

Although she'd lived in Taipei all her life, and the two cities were only a few miles apart, she had never visited Keelung before. She knew next to nothing about it, except that it was the rainiest port in the world. How strange, then, that this afternoon it should be sunny.

Keelung was frenetic, grimy, very much as she'd expected it. The streets were full of bicyclists returning home after the day's work, and the air tingled with their shrill warning bells. Every kind of small business seemed to have found a niche in this hilly place beside the sullen northern sea. Restaurants and barbershops predominated, the welcoming lights of the former dimmed by ageless accretions of dirt, and the doorways of the latter thronged with neatly dressed, smiling hostesses. But there was nothing grand about these establishments, as there sometimes was in the case of their Taipei counterparts. The houses they occupied were crammed into tiny pockets of space carved out of the surrounding nondescript grayness. All of the town's electricity seemed to be carried in overhead lines that crisscrossed the narrow streets and alleyways, parceling up the sky into irregular chunks of pale white light.

The driver let her out at the busy junction of Ai Three and Ren Two roads: a place where, in the Chinese language, love and kindness met. Lin-chun thought this singularly inappropriate as a cold wind siphoned off the nearby harbor, bringing with it tufts of paper, cotton waste, assorted trash.

She felt exposed. The briefcase in her hand seemed to flash a message of opulence to the denizens of backstreet Keelung, just as the lighthouse in the bay beyond emitted its regular signal of danger. After she had been standing on the same spot for five minutes, she noticed that an onlooker had plucked up enough courage to cross the road.

Lin-chun quickly turned her back. There was no sign of a policeman; Keelung did not strike her as the kind of place where the law was omnipresent. When someone tapped her shoulder she jumped.

"You are Miss Shan?"

The person she'd observed crossing the road proved on closer inspection to be reassuringly elderly. His face was wrinkled and the skin had the texture of putty; there were two deep depressions in his cheeks, as if the sculptor had gouged them with his thumbs. He wore a canvas panama hat with a hole punched in its side. Anyone's neighbor. Not a threat.

"You're expecting me, Uncle?"

"Yes. Why, you seem surprised?"

He spoke *guo-yu*, but his accent was atrocious and the girl had difficulty following him. "I didn't know who was going to meet me," she said. "They said to carry a pink briefcase and be here at six. That's all."

He raised his hand and beckoned. A black Yue Loong accelerated away from the intersection behind them and stopped next to Lin-chun. "Come, then." She hesitated a second before getting into the backseat with the old man. She caught a glimpse of the driver's face in the mirror and made herself be calm. For he was young, unkempt, and he chewed gum incessantly—her idea of what the Taiwanese styled a *loma*, a gangster.

They were emerging from town now, running along the dockside, past the modern round lighthouse on the shore opposite. Lin-chun caught sight of a street sign, Chungcheng Road, and a few moments later a signpost to Hoping Tao district, but these names meant nothing to her. On her right, warehouses, humble shops, a lumberyard; on her left, the black and ochre hulls of cargo ships; and everywhere above her, that endless, jumbled pattern of high-tension cable.

The car turned off the main road and descended a ramp to a wooden pier. The old man opened the door and got out, followed by Lin-chun. Immediately in front of her was a small strip of weedy sand covered with plastic containers, bottles, all the detritus of a port. Beyond that, row after row of small fishing boats bobbed at anchor, many of them covered with tarpaulins. Three children— two boys and an older girl—were playing catch on the strip of sand, using a punctured plastic buoy for a ball. Lin-chun could smell salt fish drying nearby.

"Uncle" plucked Lin-chun's sleeve and pointed to the pier. It was about fifty feet long, with several of the fishing boats moored to its left side. Lin-chun expected to be taken to one of these, so it wasn't until she'd gone about halfway down the pier that she looked to her right. And looked again.

There, floating in a sea of ink, lay a long, menacing streak of steel. At first she thought it must belong to the Taiwanese navy, but a second glance disclosed the lack of any armaments or military numbering and she realized the craft was civilian. She'd never seen anything like it: shallow draft, swept-back lines, high in the bow with a lip that jutted forward aggressively, like a falcon's beak, and a cutaway superstructure behind the bridge. There was enough light left to show that the ship had recently been painted; and the chrome rails glittered dully through the gloom as though someone had polished them that day. She took in the revolving radar scanner, innumerable aerials, gold-on-blue pennant at the stern. . . . The overall picture was of an extremely fast and expensive motorized craft.

Lin-chun read the name painted on the prow: *Kum Ying*, meaning *Golden Eagle*.

The old man guided her along the gangplank and pointed out a steel ladder. As Lin-chun climbed it she noticed that all the ship's portholes were covered with sheets of steel. At the top of the ladder she turned to her right and stepped over a high threshold onto the bridge. It was empty. The old man slid the door shut, leaving her alone.

She looked around. Two chairs were set before a sloping console overlooking the prow, one for the helmsman, one for the engineer. An impressive array of gadgetry was on display. That tall white column with a screen, now what was it? She peered at the manufacturer's plate on the front. Thomson CSF: Diodan (TSM 2314) Sonar. And this round screen must be the radar: Selenia RAN 10S. It all seemed so exotic, so much a rich man's toy. But she couldn't think of any wealthy Taiwanese who chose to indulge himself on this scale.

Behind her, a new voice babbled in a dialect she didn't understand and she wheeled around, one hand to her throat while the other nervously convulsed on the handle of her briefcase. A short, fat Chinese was standing in the passage, surveying her grimly. His gaze disturbed Lin-chun. She stared into his eyes and saw there only two tiny rings of silvery light, menacing and sharp. At first she thought he might be blind, but then he said, in bad Mandarin, "See you're inspecting my ship."

"Yes. It's . . ." A hard ball compressed her throat; she forced it down. "It's very nice."

"Thanks. Come."

She followed the newcomer into a dayroom. He sat behind a table, one forearm resting on its surface, the other stretched out along the top of a padded banquette. At a gesture from him the girl took a stool opposite and the old man guarded the door. Lin-chun felt cold.

"You don't speak Cantonese," said the fat man.

"Only a few words."

"National speech, then. You're expecting Cheong To? I'm him. You've got the money?"

She placed the pink briefcase on the table. His forearm angled across the surface to rotate it; he checked inside, nodded, and pushed the case back. "Okay. Give it to the old one to count."

She did so, and Uncle disappeared. As Lin-chun turned back to the ship's owner she could not help staring at his peculiar eyes. He saw the reason for her unease and laughed softly. "You like them? Mirrored contact lenses. Latest thing. Can't stand bright light. Glad you like the ship. Know what it is?"

Lin-chun shook her head.

"Converted 'Brave.' Made by Vospers. Know Vospers? Used to be England Royal Navy; now excess . . . sorry, surplus to requirements. Fast attack craft. Fine ship. Speed fifty knots over, maximum. Smoke?"

"This is a . . . a naval ship?"

"Not any more. Converted. Smoke?"

"No, thank you."

"I will." Cheong reached inside the top pocket of his shirt and extracted a thin cigar. "You met this Mo Mei-hua person?" he asked, lighting up.

"Yes. She's a friend."

"Yah? Lucky you." His eyes narrowed as he studied her through wreaths of smoke. "Wonderful actress. Great movies. Saw her do cabaret, once. Great voice."

"Yes."

"How'd she get into this?"

Lin-chun stared down at her hands and said nothing. After a while Cheong said, "O-kay. Never mind."

"I have to go now, Mr. Cheong."

A hum suddenly reverberated through the dayroom, followed by a roar that swiftly softened to a whisper beneath Lin-chun's feet. Cheong smiled. "Guess that means the money's right. Wouldn't give the order to start otherwise."

"I don't want to hold you up," she said quickly.

"Perhaps you don't quite understand, miss. Security on this operation's tight. Mr. Young doesn't want loose talk in Taipei."

For a moment she failed to grasp his words' import; when she did she sprang up and tried to wrench open the door. It was locked. She spun around. "Did Mr. Young—"

"Nah! Nothing to do with him. But I'm a nervous guy, miss. And when we meet that fishing boat, I want someone with me who can identify the parties. Get me? My contract says, 'Pick up the *real* Miss Mo Mei-hua and the *real* Mr. Matthew Young.' No substitutes, no look-alikes. And if this is a trap . . ." He trailed off, smiling.

"It's not a trap!"

"No?"

"Let me off this boat. I demand to be let off this boat!"

"Sure?"

"Don't be stupid, of course I'm sure." She was starting to panic. "Let me *go*!"

"Well. If you're sure . . ." Cheong stood up. Lin-chun sidled along the wall as far as she could go, keeping her face to him. He removed a key from his pants pocket and opened the door. It wasn't until Lin-chun emerged into the passage that she realized they were moving. The shore already seemed dismally far away.

"Come take a look," Cheong called from the bridge. "You'll enjoy this."

Lin-chun, dazed, let him guide her into the main cabin, where the bright neon lighting had been replaced by a velvety green glow. The steel shutters had disappeared, giving way to a panoramic view of the open sea. She saw they were passing the bar and whimpered softly. "Where are you taking me?"

"Quemoy's what my deal says; that's where I go."

Cheong slotted himself into the engineer's high swivel chair, next to the old man. "Stand behind me, that's right."

Lin-chun looked around the cramped cabin, trying to make sense of the instrument panels with their lights flashing green, red, and amber, but it was all chaos to her. Then she noticed a gun clamped to the rear bulkhead. "What's that for?" she asked.

"What? Oh, that! Yankee FC-180. In case, y'know."

"In case of what?"

But he merely grinned, and reverted to concentrating on the bank of dials in front of him. He jabbered a few words of Cantonese at the old man, who eased the throttles back until the *Golden Eagle* was barely moving. "You're going to like this," Cheong said. "But you must hold on. Grip the straps on our chairs, grip hard . . . *that's* right! You ready?"

"For what?"

He laughed, stretched out a hand, and killed the green cabin glow. For a few seconds Lin-chun could hear nothing but the sound of the waves against the side, the whisper of the breeze in the nest of aerials above her head. Then Cheong's hand dropped to the twin throttles; he flipped open a safety-shield covering the slots, and palmed the levers forward as far as they could go.

For about ten seconds the ship accelerated smoothly and then, without any warning, there was a stab of power that nearly knocked Lin-chun off her feet. Her stomach was left behind, as if she were riding on a roller coaster. To grip the straps was difficult because her hands were slippery with sweat. Then they were hurtling through the water in a shower of liquid, phosphorescent sparks, a tearing race against the sea, now no longer choppy, but flat and motionless beneath the *Golden Eagle*'s hull.

The ship left the surface. It rode through the air to land with a splash some twenty yards forward. Lin-chun stared as though hypnotized at the green glowing eye of a dial set midway between the two chairs. The luminous red needle swam up through forty, forty-five, forty-seven . . . forty-nine . . . fifty! Fifty knots!

She raised her eyes from the dial and was conscious only of an endless boiling passage over the mysterious face of the sea. For a while she remained half aware of Taiwan to her left; then that sank away into darkness, leaving only the night.

"Fun?"

Lin-chun couldn't answer at once. The excitement of the last few moments had left her drained. "Fifty knots—how fast is that?"

"Sixty mile an hour."

"How long will it take us?"

"To get to Quemoy? Depends. On weather, on winds, on what other ships we meet. Five hours, maybe; perhaps less. " 'Bout one hundred seventy nautical miles."

"But surely you can't keep this speed up forever?"

"For a long time. We've extra fuel stowed on deck."

After a while Cheong took her back to the dayroom and made tea, lacing it with whiskey, but discreetly, so that she would not see. The girl turned out to be a good sailor, and the hot drink revived her spirits to the point where a tiny part of her even began to enjoy the experience. At last the helmsman gave the *Golden Eagle* twenty degrees to port and brought her down to fifteen knots. Lin-chun realized they must be nearing their destination.

Cheong hurried them back onto the bridge and slid into his seat. The glow rising from the bank of dials in front of him revealed his profile, alert but not tense, as he scanned the surrounding void. He slid open the nearest window and stuck his head out for a few seconds. "Land," he muttered. "Can smell it. We're early."

"But aren't there patrols?" Lin-chun's voice was hushed, as if she feared they might hear her.

" 'Course. Coastal radar, too, though we're out of range of that. Mostly the patrols stay on the other side of the island. Mainland side. And our radar's good enough to detect them long before they get close. I'll check our position."

Cheong cut the power. He consulted the sonar and went to

fetch a chart, every so often looking up to study the pattern on the radar screen. Suddenly he whistled softly. "Cargo's coming."

She looked down at the rotating beam, trying to make sense of what she saw. "Those dots . . . there." Cheong pointed.

"What are they?"

"Night fishing fleet, out of Quemoy. See that one? It's peeling off."

"How can you tell they're boats?"

"Because they're small, they're moving, and nothing else is! Ssh!" He raised his head and listened. "No beat of engines," he said. "Small craft . . . that's them!" He frowned. "They're off course. I'm going to cut this short; we take her in."

He fired the engines and the *Golden Eagle* began to slice through the water at a steady fifteen knots. The old man steered while Cheong, bent to the radar, murmured adjustments to their course.

Lin-chun stared through the windows. Was there really anything out there? She felt her eyes growing heavy. The harder she tried to penetrate the black veil in front of her, the less she saw.

A tiny pinpoint of light flashed somewhere forward and to port. Lin-chun blinked. Her imagination . . . no, there it was again. "I can see a light," she breathed. At once Cheong was beside her, holding a pair of powerful night-glasses. "Where?"

She pointed. Cheong leaned against the bulkhead and scanned the open sea. For what seemed like a long time he held his position without speaking; and Lin-chun's heart gradually sank. She had imagined it, after all.

"You're right. Ten degrees to port, half a mile ahead. We'll close." He snapped orders at Uncle, who increased power. Now there was no mistaking the light: a steady dot-dot-dot, followed by a long pause, then dot-dot-dot once more. "That's them," Cheong said decisively. "Come on, miss, I need help outside."

In order to leave the bridge he had to pass close to the radar screen. Something about it evidently disturbed him, for he paused with one foot on the threshold.

"What is it?"

"Look there. See how the rest of the fleet's all bunched up?"

"Yes."

"Some of those dots . . ." He brought his face down to within a couple of inches of the glass. "I can't make out . . . bunching, or is that one big ship?"

She tried to decipher the cause of his concern, but the cluster of tiny lights beneath the sweep meant nothing to her at all. "Shit!"

Cheong muttered. "I smell something. And this time it surely isn't land!"

"Feeling better?"

"A bit."

As Mei-hua crawled back from the side of the boat, Mat lifted the sacking that covered most of his body and pulled her close to him. She resisted a little. "My breath's horrible. Sick."

"Don't be silly."

It was cold on the deck of the fishing bark. Mat arranged more sacks over them both and stroked her head against his chest until she stopped shivering. "I'm scared," she whispered. "How come you're not?"

"Because it's going all right. Thanks to you."

"I thought we were lost in the caves, once. I'm sorry I—"

"Forget it."

"Oh, Mat . . . how much longer?"

"I haven't got a watch." All around he could sense the presence of other boats; sometimes he could even hear the creak of wood; but there were no lights anywhere. "Soon," he said. "Very soon now, darling."

"Don't call me that." Her voice was husky with sadness.

"I'll always call you darling. It's—"

The helmsman called softly above their heads and received a quiet reply from the darkness at the prow. Mat was silent for a while, in case they repeated the exchange. "It's the way I see love," he said at last. "Everyone sees it in a different way."

"What's so special about your way?"

"Nothing, really. If you love somebody, you have to . . . *distinguish* her."

"What?"

"I used to fuck around in Taipei. Then you came along and I had a choice. I could go on fucking around, in which case I'd be relegating you to second class, one of the crowd. . . ."

"Or?"

"Or I could distinguish you from the rest. I could ... well, mark you out. Put you in the number-one spot. Which meant going with you and no one else."

"Number-one concubine."

"Don't put yourself down. Or me. What I'm saying's very important to me. Love means lots of things: caring, being considerate, all that stuff . . . but I've got to isolate the person I love. Not isolate, bad word. Make her unique."

Mei-hua squeezed him tightly. Life seemed so much easier since she'd given herself up to Mat. No more confusions or conflicts . . . "You do make me feel unique," she confessed. "You always have."

"Good. That's why I think you'll always be 'darling' to me. Once you've made someone unique, it's kind of hard to go back. It doesn't seem to matter what they do; you stay committed, at least until you know there's no more hope. I think . . . I feel love means giving the other person more than just a second chance." He laughed quietly. "God, doesn't it sound trashy? Maybe you can get me a part in your next movie."

"Oh, I'll never understand you! What makes you the way you are?"

"Makes me?" He was silent for a long while. "There was a time . . ."

"Yes? Go on."

"It was a difficult time. We, the whole family . . . got taken to Red China. We lived in a peasant village. Chaiyang. We worked there as—"

This time the soft call came from the stem of the boat, to be answered instantly by the steersman. At first Mat thought the wind had changed, but then he realized they'd altered course. "Something's happening."

"No!" Mei-hua tugged his chin, making him face her."Tell me!"

"It . . . it was the first time I really had to work. Christ, how I did! Manuring, harvesting. We all worked."

"You said '*had* to work.' "

"Yes. It's too complicated to explain. The thing is, we survived because we were *together*. I saw how much love I had for my father, even though we quarreled a lot. I learned how to make allowances, be tolerant, forgive. And above all . . ."

"Yes? Don't stop!"

"Above all . . . I came away from that place really wanting Ducannon Young."

"Wanting . . . I don't understand you."

"The companies." His voice rasped fiercely. "I hadn't given a damn about them before; but suddenly they were my inheritance, they were *mine*!"

"You didn't feel that way in Taipei."

"It wasn't always clear. But now I know that's how it always was." He paused. Mei-hua had been expecting him to talk more about Chaiyang. When he said, "I can hear engines," her stomach gave a nasty lurch.

Mat pulled Mei-hua to her feet. "Get ready. They're close now."

Cheong raised his head and sang out to the old man, obviously commanding an increase in speed. He turned to Lin-chun. "Come on, miss. We're in a hurry now."

She followed him out. The steel ladder ended on a deck that was frighteningly narrow. She clung to the rail for support, wondering what would happen if she fell in. She could see nothing. Where was the fishing boat? Had Cheong misread the radar? Oh please, she murmured to herself, come on, come on! Please hurry!

But the sea and the night yawned before her aching eyes, empty.

A lick of spray splashed up, showering her with cold mist. Her lips tasted salty. She was shivering, but she would rather be on deck than confined to the bridge. Somehow there seemed to be more of a chance here.

"Look!" Cheong's arm lanced out. Lin-chun stared in the same direction, willing herself to see whatever it was that had caught his attention. Then she heard a clunk of wood on wood . . . and there it was! An embryonic lump of darkness, thicker than the rest, suddenly transformed itself into a boat, its square sail flapping in the breeze. "Ahoy!" Cheong called. "Be quick!"

The fishing bark came alongside the *Golden Eagle*. Cheong unhooked a rope ladder from the bridge's superstructure and tossed one end of it overboard. Unseen hands grabbed the ladder, pulling it taut; and a second later it began to sway under the weight of some moving burden. Lin-chun's blood tingled with excitement. "Mei-hua," she called softly. "Mei-hua, are you there?"

"Yes!" Another female voice, rippling with tension, rose out of the bowels of the fishing boat. "Lin-chun, is it really you?"

"Yes."

"Mat's coming up. Help him."

"I will, I will. Oh my dear, you've done it, you've *done* it!"

But as she reached down into the gloom, ready to help Mat over the side, Cheong raised his head sharply like a frightened bird. At the same moment Lin-chun heard it, too: the unmistakable shushing sound of high-powered craft off the starboard beam. Then came its echo, on the port side, farther away but not a mere reflection of the other—there were two ships. Two ships converging on the *Golden Eagle*.

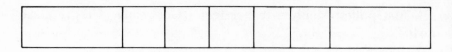

TWENTY-SEVEN

Cheong's response to the crisis was immediate. He tugged Lin-chun away from the rail and pushed her against the steel ladder that led to the bridge. "Up! *Up*!"

"But Mei-hua—"

He lifted the girl bodily and swung her around, forcing her face against the rungs. "Up!"

Lin-chun squealed, her feet probed for something solid to rest on. As she reached the top of the ladder with Cheong at her heels he gave her a shove, elbowing his way past her on to the bridge.

Lin-chun regained her balance. She looked back in time to see two searchlights slash out toward her, locking the *Golden Eagle* in their crossed beams. With an oath, Cheong flicked the wheel right, then left, and opened his throttles wide. As they roared away, Lin-chun heard the woodpecker rattle of a machine gun shredding the night, and she cried out in fear.

Uncle was frantically working the *Golden Eagle*'s own light in an attempt to blind the gunner. Its erratic beam suddenly threw up the shape of the starboard pursuer, half a mile off and closing fast. The Taiwanese were firing tracers to mark each other's position. White chains spattered the blackness over the sea, like sparks from a blast furnace.

The noise was appalling: three sets of powerful engines, two machine guns, and now the sound of a bullhorn. Lin-chun clapped her hands over her ears. Another few seconds and the nearest patrol would ram. Cheong swung the wheel hard to starboard, whisking the *Golden Eagle* under the very prow of the other ship, and screamed to Uncle, "Take the wheel!" The old man wrestled with the rudder while Cheong dived for the gun. Uncle spun the wheel too far, overcompensated, and then, guided more by instinct than judgment, landed the craft on a course midway between its reconverging enemies.

The bullhorn had fallen silent, but the machine guns kept up their relentless chatter. One burst sprayed just above the *Golden Eagle*'s waterline; the succession of pings told Lin-chun they'd been hit. Uncle weaved left, then hard right, almost putting the ship on her beam ends; suddenly one of the windows shivered into flakes of glass, leaving him miraculously untouched but turning the bridge into a howling wind tunnel.

Lin-chun lurched forward, tripped, and fell. She clutched at Cheong as he was in the act of lifting the 180 from its clip. In the same instant the *Golden Eagle* began a tight circle to port, into the path of the nearest Taiwanese vessel, an Auk-class corvette. The violence of the course-change hurled Cheong and Lin-chun into the passage. Then they were plummeting through the air to land on the exposed deck, six feet below. Cheong's body helped to break the girl's fall. As she raised herself on one knee, gasping for breath, the *Golden Eagle* made another lurch sideways. Lin-chun teetered, fell backward, and slithered over the side.

As she toppled, her flailing hands touched something solid. A rope ladder! She had become entangled in it. She was being dragged just above the surface of the sea at sixty miles an hour while her arms were wrenched from their sockets and the coarse hemp inexorably scissored the palms of her hands to pieces. Somewhere close by she heard diesel engines. She saw a vast hulk looming over her, its dark face spattered with light; a wave left her choking and vomiting; the last threads of strength in her hands were severed. The next lurch, one more wave, and that would be the finish.

A half-memory exploded behind her eyelids: two people cradling each other on a bed in a Singaporean mansion. . . .

Lin-chun screamed. Everything inside her seemed to spew out with the sound. Then hands grasped her hair and forearm. First her torso bumped over the rail; next her knees were skinned raw and she was lying on the deck in a pool of sea water and vomit.

After what seemed like hours of staring at the unresponsive deck, her mind began to function again. A trickle of water oozed out of one ear to admit only the sound of the rushing sea and the wind of their passage. The firing had ceased. Every bit of her ached, and some of her bled. She crawled upright with the aid of the rail and looked astern.

"One of them's still after us," Cheong shouted. "Maybe they'll start up heavy guns soon. We've got to refuel some time. You all right?"

"Yes. Thank you. You saved my—"

"*Tew neh lo mo.*"

"What are we going to *do?*"

Cheong was already climbing the ladder. "Try to outrun them," he said over his shoulder. "We're out of their territorial water now. Hot pursuit's what they call it. Figure we can make it. Come on up."

Only when she reached the top of the ladder again did she remember Mat. "The English boy! Where is he? And Mei-hua?"

Cheong shook his head. "Miss Mo, can't say. The round-eye . . ." He examined her critically, wondering if she could take it. "Sorry. Round-eye went into the sea."

The *Golden Eagle*'s initial surge of power had communicated itself directly into Mat's shoulders and back, making him lose his grip on the rope ladder that would shortly save Lin-chun's life. As he fell he jarred his head against the side of the fishing boat and for an instant was stunned; then the shock of the icy sea brought him thrashing to the surface. He came up terrified by the thought of being ground between the two hulls, but by the time he broke water, Cheong was already in full flight. Mat drew a deep breath and swallowed what felt like most of the *Golden Eagle*'s wake. He gagged, panic clawing at his guts. "Help!" he cried. "Help me, someone!" But a swift glance showed the fishing boat already a dozen yards or more away from him, apparently drifting. "Mei-hua!" he shouted.

One of the corvettes had already abandoned its pursuit of the *Golden Eagle*. It came around in a wide arc to cut Mat off from Quemoy. He took another deep breath, jackknifed, and swam—but in the wrong direction. When he surfaced, it was to find himself farther away from the fishing boat than ever. It wouldn't take long for the Auk, a mere fifty yards distant, to trace him. With a cold feeling in the pit of his stomach he watched the silent beam dart ever closer, always toward him. Then suddenly—contact! Mat trod water in the center of a white circle while the muffled cries of the gunners indicated they had their target. A dozen feet away a column of water shot up and simultaneously he heard the machine gun's clatter. He swallowed another gulp of sea and sank back into the deep.

A shock wave sent him turning over and over, deaf and doubled up with pain. Depth charges! His lungs were bursting, his mouth full of water . . . but the moment he surfaced, those lethal, liquid pillars spurted all around him. The ranging was perfect. Another few seconds and the marksmen would finish him off.

The gun started up again, the light hit Mat full in the eyes, he heard another vessel behind him, traveling slowly. Suddenly he was yanked out of the water by brutal hands, and his face was rammed hard up against a hull. As he lost consciousness the last sounds he heard were steady, distant gunfire and a Chinese voice saying, "He's alive."

He was under for only a few minutes. The deck rose and fell, engines throbbed quietly, but otherwise the night had become peaceful. Then a bucket of water was thrown over him and he sat up in time to meet a second pailful across the face. Marines dragged him to his feet. Mat had a vague impression of steel decks, life rafts, aerials, armed men. The marines pushed him through a hatch and up a narrow stairway, knocking his head against pipes, and on to the captain's dayroom. Mei-hua was already there. She lay on the floor, trussed hand and foot, with a gag covering most of her face.

Li Lu-tang sat in a canvas chair, holding his sword in his right hand, its tip resting in the notch formed by his crossed ankles. As the escort hustled Mat inside, Li raised the sword and delicately placed its point on the girl's neck. "For treason," he said quietly, "there is but one punishment."

He laid his sword aside and stood up, straightening his uniform. Mat stared at him. "Don't touch the girl," he managed to blurt out. "She's been a fool, leave it at that. . . ."

He swayed, making a mighty effort to clear his head. His eyes lighted on the sword recently laid aside by Li, but his reactions were hopelessly slow: long before he lunged his guards had sensed what was coming and redoubled their grips. For a moment the human pyramid tottered, with four Chinese hanging on to Mat like oriental Lilliputians clinging to a present-day Gulliver, but within seconds they'd forced him to his knees. One of the marines slotted Mat's head between his legs, using his weight to pin the prisoner's neck to the floor; and with that the brief struggle ended.

Li spoke a few words of *guo-yu*. Something hard smashed down on Mat's skull. A vast chasm filled with dancing sparks opened up in front of him. Agony swamped his brain, obliterating thought, and with a groan he fell forward into the abyss.

Mat fought the return of consciousness with all his might. For what seemed like a long while he floated near the surface, putting off the pain, but it was no good. He felt as though someone had taken a hot poker and run its point all the way down the back of his head to the nape, from which focal point the burn radiated out over his shoulders. At last his eyes opened. A wave of intense light rendered him temporarily blind; and when at last his sight did steady, it was to reveal only a black floor.

"You had better drink this, Mr. Young."

Tsai Zi-yang stood over him, holding a beaker. The captain knelt down and supported his head while he drank. The beaker contained cold water, blissfully refreshing; but the moment it reached his stomach it rose up again in a bilious fountain. Mat gasped for breath. "What happened?"

When Zi-yang did not reply immediately, Mat looked around him. He recognized this place. It was the stone chamber before the gates of exquisite view. He eased himself backward until he could rest against the wall.

Zi-yang's normally tranquil face distorted into a frown. "I'm sorry," he said quietly. "You must prepare yourself now."

"Prepare? For what?"

Zi-yang said nothing. Mat tried again. "I'm to be killed—is that it?"

"No. I've told you before: Li won't kill you. Not . . . you."

Knowledge penetrated Mat's skull with the sudden awful force of a bullet. "Mei-hua."

"You must stand up now."

"No!"

"You must. It will soon be over. This is very terrible for me; I have . . . I have not seen such a thing done, ever. Don't make me use force upon you as well."

"Why must I go? It's . . . it's barbaric!"

"She needs you," Zi-yang said quietly. "She has no one but you. If even you desert her . . ."

Mat wiped a hand across his mouth. "I'll come."

Zi-Yang assisted Mat to his feet. They went through the opening at the end of the exhibition and proceeded quickly to the last display but one. The locomotive cab.

At first it seemed to Mat's muddled brain that here was another wax display. The space was crowded with human figures, all perfectly still. Center foreground stood Li Lu-tang, hands clasped behind his back, one leg straight, the other bent at the knee with its foot turned slightly outward. To his right were two marines, holding Mei-hua. Her hands had been tied in front of her, there was a hobble-rope around her ankles. She still wore the tight blue jeans and plain white blouse he'd last seen her in, but her feet were bare. A cut disfigured her lower lip.

The heat in the chamber was overpowering. Mat took a step forward, but Zi-yang held his arm, gently restraining him. "You can't do this," Mat said.

At the sound of his calm, rational voice Mei-hua raised her chin slightly and looked around for the first time. She was panting in short, clipped gasps. Every ten breaths or so she would stop, draw down one long, deep gulp of air, and resume panting.

Torchlight rippled across Li's features, illuminating generations of atavistic cruelty. The knowledge of what was about to happen washed through Mat with crippling power. A thought, unbidden and resented, rushed into his mind—he imagined himself horizontal, a prisoner, being thrown into the flames, through the fire-door, imagined what the first shock would feel like, seemed to smell and hear his own hair sizzling, his skin blistering, his eyeballs melting. . . .

But it was not going to happen to him. It was going to happen instead to the woman he loved.

Li reached up to adjust one of the spots, sliding it along its metal track until the light was concentrated on the fire-door behind which the furnace was raging. "Better, I think," he murmured.

Tsai Zi-yang, not understanding Li's intentions, unbuttoned his holster and drew out a pistol. "Controller?" His voice sounded tremulous.

"She will pay the price laid down by Tai Li, and go into the flames alive." Li's voice was icy, the only cold thing in this terrible, burning room. He unhooked the iron from the wall and used it to wrench open the fire-door. Flames billowed out in a black cloud of smoke, forcing the soldiers to retreat with their prisoner. Li dropped the iron on the floor and turned to give the order.

Mei-hua screamed and screamed. On and on it went, until eventually the ghastly wail deteriorated into a series of hiccupping moans. She threw herself from side to side; the soldiers had to work hard to restrain her. Mat wanted this scene to stop, stop now, even if it meant . . . no, not that, *how could you think that?*

Zi-yang had taken a pace forward and was addressing Li in respectful tones. At first Li merely listened with a disdainful smile on his face, but then he started interrupting. Mat couldn't follow their rapid Chinese. Li began soberly enough, a mentor explaining some lesson to his gifted but difficult pupil. Zi-yang flapped his arms around. Li became steely and slashed sideways with the blade of his hand, dismissing Tsai's arguments. When the captain politely stood his ground, Li's voice rose; so did the junior officer's.

Mat took a step forward. No one noticed. The guards were still struggling to cope with Mei-hua, their eyes locked on the protagonists in front of the flames, and the girl herself was past seeing anything. At last Mat managed to edge around to where Li had dropped the fire-iron. He stood over it, legs apart, and quietly spoke her name.

The discussion between Li and Tsai Zi-yang had become an altercation. Their high, Chinese voices flickered to and fro like an electrical storm. Zi-Yang looked frightened, he was stammering, but still he would not yield. Li, for his part, seemed unwilling to believe that a subordinate could dare address him in this way.

"Mei-hua . . . look at me."

Mat's words must have reached her across the awful gulf of horror over which she swayed, for she raised her gaze to his. Her eyes were staring, empty. "Do you remember the songs?" he murmured. And to the guards' astonishment, in a quavering voice he began to sing an old Mandarin love song.

His saliva dried up. *You cannot do this thing! Cannot, cannot, cannot!* He had to do it. There simply wasn't a choice.

The argument behind him was reaching its climax. Both guards were transfixed by the sight of their controller apparently being called to account by a mere captain. Mat smiled at Mei-hua, infusing his expression with every ounce of love he could manage. But he wasn't even sure if she knew him. Her eyes were crazed. She had reverted to the simplicity of babyhood, her mind no longer capable of appreciating the ravages of the adult world.

Mat struggled to remember some more words, another song, any song.

If you do it, you'll have to live with the horror for the rest of your life. Memories—have you thought what they'll be like?

Li struck Tsai Zi-yang across the face. The captain gasped. He stepped back, holding a palm to his cheek. The guards exchanged frightened glances, but the girl's eyes remained glued to her lover's. He was managing to make contact. Her mouth writhed; she was trying to imitate the words as he sang them. Then Zi-yang spat what must have been a particularly dire imprecation, for one of the guards released Mei-hua's arm and indignantly stepped forward, as if to apprehend this insolent captain. There was no time left. Mat gently flexed his muscles, testing first his right leg, then his left. . . .

He dropped to the floor, snatched up the fire-iron, and leaped from a crouching position, aiming for the forehead. *You cannot do this thing.* For a second he hesitated; then he thought only of achieving maximum speed before she could realize what he intended to do. He brought the iron down with all the force at his command. Blood spurted. The second guard, who had kept hold of her throughout, now relinquished his grip and lashed out at him. Too late. Mo Mei-hua sank limply to the floor without a sound.

The quarrel stopped in mid-sentence. Mat dropped the iron and staggered back against the wall, sweat bursting from his skin. Without warning he was sick again. Then he lost his balance and fell over.

Li surveyed the scene for a moment. At last he said, "You astonish me, Young. Did you *seriously* think I was going to kill her?" He shook his head, a man perplexed. "Frighten her, yes, she needed that . . . but she was far too valuable ever to throw away."

He waited for the horror to dawn in Mat's eyes before turning to Tsai. "I'll deal with you later, Captain." With that, he gestured to the guards.

They rolled Mei-hua over on her stomach, lifted her by the arms and thighs, and carried the body toward the eager flames. They began to swing it like a battering ram. "One . . . two . . . three . . ."

They must have been too close to the furnace, for on the count of "three" her hair caught fire and went up like dry gorse. The stench permeated the chamber within seconds, but by then the momentum of their swing was so great it didn't matter. Her body sailed through the air, for a moment it glowed dark in the firebox, as when the sun is eclipsed, and the smell of charred flesh was added to that of burned human hair.

Li Lu-tang picked up the iron that Mat had dropped and used it to slam the firebox shut.

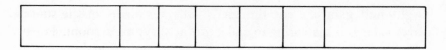

TWENTY-EIGHT

In the end they chose Tokyo's Narita Airport as the venue. Japan, conveniently close for all parties, was neutral territory; and there were certain features of layout that made the transit area particularly suitable for what Simon Young and Li Lu-tang had in mind.

Fong Mun Wah was first to arrive. Fong, a physics graduate of Shatin University, had been employed by Ducannon Young International in Seoul for the past three years. His name was one of those thrown up when Simon ran a computer search for Chinese male employees in their early twenties whose stature and facial appearance corresponded roughly to Lennie Luk's. In the end Simon chose Fong because, like Lennie, he had a long, wispy mustache.

He checked in for China Airlines' evening flight to Taipei, then went through immigration and followed the signs until at last he came out in the round, glass-walled lounge, where he spent a few minutes just getting his bearings. Fong nodded sagely. Exactly as Mr. Young had described it in his letter.

He picked up a smart new cabin-bag and made for the stairs to the toilets. There was no one else in the men's room. Fong darted into the cubicle nearest the wall and bolted it shut.

He unfastened the cabin-bag and swiftly changed into a second set of clothes, very different from the ones he'd had on previously. Now he was wearing cream-colored slacks, a double-breasted chocolate blazer ornamented with two rows of shiny brass buttons, and a knit tie. Fong Mun Wah strapped a new Cartier Tank to his left wrist in place of the usual Swatch and pulled a wide-brimmed felt hat from the bottom of his bag. It had gotten a little crumpled; he rubbed his hand over the felt until it looked less battered. And that was it.

Jinny Young lay back in the first-class cabin of Northwest Orient's Jumbo on flight 9 from Honolulu to Tokyo, with an eyeshade over her brow. She had a headache, she felt a little sick, and having flown across the international dateline twice in the past forty-eight hours, she no longer knew what day it was.

A hand plucked at her arm. "Mrs. Young," Lennie said softly. "Sorry to wake you, but we're nearly there."

"Where's Simon?" she asked, pressing the button to raise her seat upright.

"At the back. He's trying to spot the tails."

"Oh, not again!" Jinny massaged her temples. "It must be worse for you. At least I got off in Hawaii on the way out. If Simon had made me go with you all the way to Los Angeles, I don't think I could have coped."

"We had to do it in order to make it look like a real business trip. Transiting in Tokyo makes no sense, otherwise." He hesitated. "Mrs. Young?"

"Yes?"

"There's something I want to tell you. You've been so kind to me always. But I don't want Mr. Young to know yet."

She looked at him, sensing what was on his mind. "Go on."

"I've been thinking about my future."

"And?"

"I . . . don't see myself staying with DY much longer."

Jinny sighed. "Nor do I."

"You mustn't misunderstand me, I want to do this thing for Mat, I really do!"

"I never doubted it." She reached out for his hand. "It's very brave of you."

"No. He's my best friend, that's all. And I don't care about giving Apogee to the Taiwanese. I think that's only just, don't you?"

"I honestly don't know."

"Both sides should have it. Things are more even that way."

"Perhaps. But isn't that what they call a balance of terror?" When he said nothing, Jinny went on, "Is that why you're leaving us? Because you don't like your discoveries being monopolized by my husband?"

"Partly. Apogee's so much more than a weapon. Because of it, nothing we do in business is ever going to be the same again, and Mr. Young doesn't seem to realize that. Apogee's going to replace people on a scale we've never known before and—"

"Not everyone agrees that's a good idea. Those people it replaces—what's to become of them?"

He peered at her in anguish, his features all screwed up. "Do you want me to stop doing the only thing I'm good at—my reason for existing?"

"No. Of course not. But if that's why you're leaving, perhaps my husband would—"

"There's something else. I've had an offer, from America. There wouldn't be any difficulty over a green card, I could apply for citizenship. Do you mind me telling you this?"

"No."

"Is it a good idea?"

Jinny thought. "Yes, in my view. Since your parents . . ." She broke off with a thin smile, mirrored on the face of the young man beside her. "What I mean is, there's nothing to hold you in Hong Kong now. And with 1997 coming closer . . ."

"That's what I think. I feel Mother and Father would have approved."

"They would. All they ever wanted for you was the education they never got for themselves on the mainland. You remember how hard they made you work?"

Lennie felt mixed up. He knew Jinny was deliberately making the memories come as a way of helping him to face them; but the pain still refused to go away. "I remember. No play until I'd done the school's homework, and then—"

"Then the books they made you read as well . . ."

"Even though they couldn't read them."

"*Because* they couldn't read them. But it was worth it." Jinny nodded her head emphatically. "I'm sure it's what they'd have wanted."

"I'm definitely going, then. Just as soon as this is all over. Only you won't say anything—"

Simon slipped into the seat behind Jinny. "No, don't stop, Lennie. You were saying?"

But Lennie kept quiet. Simon saw two hostile black eyes studying him through the gap between the seats, and looked away.

"Did you trace them?" Jinny asked.

"Yup. *Him,* not *them.* Middle-aged Chinese in business class. Watch out for him when we land; he's about forty-five, wearing a pale blue suit. Silver-rimmed glasses, pigskin briefcase with brass fittings."

"I think I've seen him before," Jinny muttered.

"When?"

"Last week. A man followed me down Nathan Road. Oh, Simon, I do wish Peter Reade would leave us alone!"

"What makes you so sure it's Peter's mob?"

The No Smoking sign came on; Jinny glanced out the window to see a red-and-white-striped mast glide across her field of vision and knew they were almost on the ground. "Because in Hong Kong he seems to be behind everything. You yourself said he's always on about the need to maximize security."

"I don't think it's Peter." The plane touched down. "Okay, here we are. No rehearsals, no false starts; this is the take."

As they filed through the door, Jinny looked into the rear section of the plane. The Chinese that Simon had described was stuffing a newspaper into his briefcase. She caught her husband's eye and nodded.

They exited through gate 45 and stood for a few moments, trying to establish the best place to sit. "Remember," Simon whispered, "we have just under three hours on the ground. Flight Seventeen to Hong Kong leaves at ten to five. Everything, *everything* has to be slotted into that time." He paused. "Lennie, are you sure you want to go through with this?"

"Yes. Perfectly sure."

"Only we have no right to ask it of you. You don't owe me any favors; it's the other way around."

"Because of what happened to my parents, you mean? Leaving Mat to rot isn't going to bring them back."

"No, Lennie, but . . . you realize what these people are capable of?"

"He's right," Jinny said; but her voice quavered, lacking all conviction. She must have been aware of it, for she went on, "You know what makes me most angry about all this? It's that I ought to forbid you outright to have anything to do with this madness . . . but it's Mat who's out there somewhere. And . . . and I can't."

"Mrs. Young, I wouldn't be here if I wasn't absolutely sure. I'll go, I'll do my job, and then they'll let me come back home. That's what I believe."

"Okay," Simon grunted. "Let's try to relax a bit."

They made for the nearest set of seats. Simon leaned back and took a long look at the young man beside him. He saw a Chinese in his early twenties, serious-faced, mustached, intent, wearing cream-colored slacks, and a double-breasted chocolate jacket with brass buttons, and carrying a soft felt hat. "You do know that I'll never be able to repay you for this? Not as long as I live."

"I don't want payment." Lennie's tone was cold. "I want Mat freed."

"Thank you." Simon smiled. "I suppose you don't regard Apogee as any great loss."

Lennie stayed silent.

"I see. Well, then. Over your left shoulder—no, don't look around—on your left, behind you is the Chinese I saw earlier. What I'd like you to do is get up and walk in such a way as to make him see you, however hard he tries to appear not to. All right?"

"Yes." Lennie rose to his feet. "Think I'll get a sandwich." "Mrs. Young," he said more loudly. "Would you like anything?"

"Oh . . . coffee, please."

As Lennie sauntered off, Jinny changed seats to be next to her husband. "All right?"

"Mm? Oh yes. Why?"

"You must be tired."

His skin was moist and pale, making him look as though he hadn't shaved in a while. Purple crescent moons bulged under his eyes. Simon twisted his head, as if to ease the tension that had built up in his neck muscles. "Long flight, that's all. Darling . . ."

"Yes?"

"Thanks for coming. I don't know how I'd have managed without you."

"That's all right. I couldn't just . . ." Jinny felt tears in her eyes. "Simon," she murmured eventually.

"Mm?"

"Is it . . . ruin?"

"I think so, yes," he said calmly. "If this goes through, I'll have sold out to the Taiwanese. Beijing won't forgive."

"We won't starve."

"No. But there are other ways of dying. They might want to make an example of us."

Jinny's face crumpled. "Oh my dear . . . are you sure you want to go through with this?"

"What choice do we have?" He subjected her to a long, brooding look. "It's our son's life at stake."

"Simon." Her voice was very quiet. "When you say, 'what choice do we have,' you make it sound as if you mean what choice do *you* have—what choice does Jinny have?"

"You're wrong. We decided on this together."

"Not the other boy," Jinny said quickly. "I don't approve of involving Fong."

"You didn't mind getting Lennie to—"

"He's different. He volunteered and he's Mat's friend. But to use an ordinary employee like this . . ." Jinny shook her head. "It could be dangerous for him. Doesn't that worry you *at all?*"

"It's convenient."

Jinny looked at him and wondered if he had the faintest perception of how mechanical he'd become. It was the perfect Chinese phrase to meet this situation—polite, positive in tone, and meaningless. He'd reached the point where he didn't even bother to think anymore when dealing with orientals, even his own wife; he merely punched the right button and out came the appropriate platitude.

Simon saw her expression and suddenly felt helpless. He had been through so much with the woman beside him, yet now, at crisis-point, he could not find words to express the love he felt for her. And it frustrated him to the point of rage. So, instead of making an effort that might only make things worse, he stood up, severing connections. "Where's your coffee? I fancy one myself, now."

The tension affected them in different ways. For the most part, Jinny just stared into space. Sometimes Lennie came to sit beside her, not saying much but conscious of her need to have him nearby. Simon, the worst affected of the three, wandered restlessly around the circular glass prison in which he found himself trapped.

At last he ceased his meanderings not far from Jinny's seat, and stood with his left arm folded across his chest, right elbow supported on his left palm, right hand in front of his mouth. Ahead of him he could see the main runway, and beyond that a double security fence, a road, some fields. Dusk came insidiously. Neon lights flickered on and he winced. The tinted glass made everything seem gray. His whole world was dissolving into grayness. . . .

"Simon." Jinny's voice was urgent. "It's in."

A white Boeing 747 bearing the insignia of China Airlines was gliding to a halt on the apron, its black-painted nose only a few feet away from them. Lennie brought more coffee and they stood in silence, looking at the plane.

Li Lu-tang was one of the first to come through the gate. He stared about him for several moments before spotting the Young delegation. He nodded at Simon, then turned away and deliberately sought a chair on the opposite side of the pod.

Jinny placed a hand on Simon's arm. "Good luck," she murmured.

The passengers' lounge was crowded now. Most of the chairs in Li's vicinity were taken, but by placing bags on the seats on either side of him, he had managed to reserve some privacy.

Simon dumped one of the bags on the floor and sat down. Li pointed at the departure board above the gate where the China Airlines plane was parked. "Forty minutes on the ground, that's all."

"I know."

"Were you followed?"

"Yes."

"Who by?"

"I'm not sure. Mainland, probably."

"Where is he?"

Simon discreetly pointed out the Chinese businessman, who had changed seats in such a way as to be able to keep both Simon and Jinny under observation.

"When does your flight leave for Hong Kong?"

"Ten minutes after yours." Simon hesitated. "You have the . . . package?"

"Yes. It's stowed on the aircraft. It stays there until just before departure. Then you can collect it, in exchange for your own"—Li's lips formed a sardonic smile—"parcel."

The two men inclined their heads toward each other, ensuring that the words they murmured would carry no farther. "You understand the deal, Lu-tang? I wouldn't like there to be disappointments later."

"Nor I. It goes like this. You're going to deliver the scientist who developed Apogee—"

"But mainland China gets all that you get; I'm merely placing you both on an equal footing."

"We accept that. In return, we give you back your son—who wasn't a very obliging guest, incidentally."

"He told you nothing, in other words."

"I didn't say that."

"You didn't have to." Simon allowed pride to show, just for an instant. "If Mat had talked, you wouldn't be sitting here."

"Believe that if you like. But be careful when you get him home. He has a violent nature."

"What are you talking about?"

"Ask him. Time's short. Where's this man Luk?"

Simon hesitated, trying to fathom what was behind Li's cryptic words. Then he flicked his forefinger. "Sitting next to my wife."

"Good. The changeover will take place by the snack bar, opposite gate forty-four. That gate's halfway between my plane and yours. The two candidates will take seats next to each other, while the principals inspect. Then, simultaneously, they'll get up and—"

"No. I have to keep Luk's transfer a secret from the mainland as long as possible."

"So?"

"So I've arranged for a double to take Luk's place on the Hong Kong plane. It's essential that no one has an opportunity for the kind of inspection that your proposal involves."

Li's face hardened. "This is a bad time to start fooling around. We came in good faith—"

"Surely you see the danger I'm in? I've no alternative." Simon's voice was harsh with self-condemnation. "I need insurance."

Li Lu-tang sucked in his lips. "All right, agreed. I'm going back on the plane. We'll meet there, at the gangway."

"I'll tell Luk to change places with his double. Our side'll be ready to deal in five minutes."

"You'd better be. But if anything upsets us . . ." He trailed off with a nod at the plane, a palely visible image viewed through glass by the half-light of early dusk. Watching him go, Simon felt a stab of pain above the heart. So near, so very near. Mat was on that plane. For another thirty minutes he'd sit there, within mere feet of his parents. Then he would go. Unless, unless . . .

He returned to where Jinny sat, with Lennie hovering over her like a bodyguard. "All right," he muttered. "You're on. Goodbye, thank you, good luck."

Lennie picked up his cabin bag, walked down the stairs to the toilets, and let himself into the second cubicle from the wall. He scratched quietly on the partition. As soon as he heard the answering tap from Fong, he pushed his bag beneath the divider and received an identical one back. It took him only a few moments to change, stuff the clothes he'd been wearing into his new bag, and leave.

Standing in front of a mirror, he shaved off his mustache with an electric razor, removed his spectacles, and inserted contact lenses. Then he retreated into another cubicle and sat down to wait.

Meanwhile, Li had returned to the ticketing desk at the top of the China Airlines gangway, looking for Simon. A gong echoed resonantly through the pod, followed by three announcements in Japanese, Mandarin, and English: first call for the China Airlines flight to Taipei.

Simon ran across to him. "We've only got a few minutes left," he said.

"I *know*!" The gong sounded again. "And that's calling the Hong Kong flight." Li gnawed his thumb, and saw that he'd made the cuticle bleed. He pulled himself together with an effort. "I'm going to bring your son up front, into the corner of the gangway, so that you can see him from the boarding desk. Then Luk surrenders his pass and gets ready to go on the plane. They'll cross at the gate."

"I don't like it."

"Take it or leave it."

The gong sounded for the third time. "China Airlines flight three-zero-nine to Taipei, final call."

"All right. We go with it."

"Then *move*!"

Simon ran down to the men's room, whistling. The tune was recognizable to at least two other occupants of the toilets. Fong Mun Wah exited at a brisk pace, one hand raised to adjust the unfamiliar spectacles he was now wearing, closely followed by Lennie Luk.

Simon grabbed Lennie as he reached the door and whispered, "Go to the gate, give up your pass, and wait for my signal. But make damn sure that plane doesn't take off with Mat on it. If they try a double-cross, do anything, throw a fit if you have to—but stop that flight!"

Fong was the first to surface in the pod. He strode quickly to the Hong Kong gate, hat pulled well down over his eyes, and kept going all the way down the tunnel to the plane. Jinny followed him. Simon kept well ahead of Lennie, who deliberately hung back.

Simon marched swiftly up to gate 43, went to one side, and

peered down the sloping corridor. What he saw made his heart contract. Mat was just visible in the angle of the telescoping gangway, with Li Lu-tang. His face was pale, his eyes blazed as if he had a fever.

Lennie approached the China Airlines gate. He presented his pass, stopped, and turned. Simon waited another second, then nodded. Lennie trotted down the gangway, out of sight. Mat gazed after him, a look of stark disbelief on his face. Only then did Li pitch him into his father's outstretched arms.

"Are you all right, Mat?"

"I'm all right." He spoke very slowly. "I'm fine now."

"Mother's waiting for you."

"Why's Lennie getting on that plane?"

"Tell you later. Come on; the flight's closing."

"He mustn't!"

"Come *on*!"

As they approached the Hong Kong gate, Mat mumbled something.

"What?"

"I said . . . Li Lu-tang. He's not what you think. Lennie shouldn't be on that plane!"

They took their seats. Jinny reached out to press Mat's hands between her own before wiping the tears from her cheeks. "Never mind Li, you can tell us later," Simon said.

"No! It can't wait! You have *got* to get Lennie back!"

They began to taxi. Mat looked out of the window and saw a white plane jet reach the end of the runway, spotlights illuminating the China Airlines insignia on its tail. "*Christ!* Dad, *listen!* Li Lu-tang isn't working for the government. He's a member of the Formosan independence movement. And he's going to use Apogee to buy power from the Kuomintang."

"*What?*" For a moment all Simon could do was stare at his son, aghast. Then his eyes flashed to the airliner already gathering speed along the runway. Its stern sank down, the delayed roar of its engines penetrated the quiet cabin . . . then it was up.

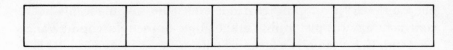

TWENTY-NINE

Fong Mun Wah was bored. He'd been kept hanging around Hong Kong for two days now, with nothing to do except read girlie magazines and occasionally help out with the more tedious aspects of office routine. After Seoul the food was just great, and some of the chicks hanging their tails around HQ were really something, but shit! A man could get wet rot on the brain like this.

Fong found himself a virtual prisoner.

The car came at eight o'clock and took him to the office via a different route each morning. At half past six in the evening the chauffeur turned up again and ran him to the block of flats in Mansfield Road where Ducannon Young kept a safe house. And there he stayed, under the eye of a housekeeper, until eight o'clock next day.

They'd given him plenty of money, but what was the point if you couldn't spend it? And there seemed to be no end in sight.

Until now.

Today had been different right from the start. Fong arrived at the office and was waiting for the elevator. The doors slid open.

He moved forward, but before he could enter the car, a Caucasian came out and did a double-take. "Hi, Lennie. It is Lennie Luk, isn't it?"

Fong Mun Wah froze. This wasn't supposed to happen. Your double hasn't worked or lived in Hong Kong for years, that's what he'd been told; there'll be no problem. . . .

"Uh . . . no. That is . . ."

"But you remember me? You must remember me."

"Sorry . . . late." Fong fled into the elevator just as the doors were closing. The last thing he saw was the *kuai-lo* standing in the lobby with a puzzled look on his face. He briefly thought about reporting what had happened, then forgot the incident.

At last six-thirty came, but the driver did not. The office emptied, leaving Fong alone with nothing to do. Six-thirty-one. Thirty-two. Thirty-three . . .

He glanced again at his new Cartier: nearly five minutes late. The watch sat well on his wrist. Third Uncle on mother's side had one just like it. Fong remembered Third Uncle with a smile. He'd bought a new place in Aberdeen not long back and sent his nephew a photo of it. Forty minutes away, no more.

He looked at his watch again, hesitated one last time . . . and bolted.

He crossed over Queensway via the overhead walkway and descended the stairs to the bus shelter north of Admiralty Gardens. As he joined the line his eyes swept the throng of commuters and were suddenly arrested by the sight of two people staring at him. Fong quickly turned away. He didn't like to be stared at, it was bad joss. What business did strangers have with him?

But when next minute he resumed his survey, they were still there. A man with one arm, *tew neh lo mo!* Fong shuddered. And as if that wasn't enough, a *kuai-lo* as well. The same foreign devil he'd seen that morning. *Shit!*

Fong rapidly walked away; but the two onlookers were faster. "Hi!" said the devil, planting himself squarely in Fong's path. "We didn't have a proper chance to chat this morning." His eyes narrowed. "You *do* remember me, don't you?"

"Uh . . ."

"Haines," said the stranger with a genial smile, holding out his hand. "Rod Haines."

At about the time Haines and his one-armed companion were buttonholing Fong Mun Wah, Assistant Commissioner Reade strode into the living room of the Youngs' house at Repulse Bay and said, "We're going on a little trip. You too, I'm afraid, Mat."

"My God! Is this how you normally—"

"There's a patrol boat waiting in the cove and we're already late. You'd better find Jinny and tell her you don't know when you'll both be back."

"I resent this intrusion." Simon sounded bleak. "Mat's only just recovering from the most godawful experience and I'm not in the mood for—"

"Well, you'd better get yourself in the mood, then, because if I have to arrest you, I fucking well will!"

"You've got a nerve, talking to me like that in my own house!"

"I'm ready," Mat said. "I need a change."

Peter Reade, struck by his tone, gave him a sharp look. "Come on, then. *Both* of you . . ."

Simon and Mat followed Reade's flashlight beam down a flight of steep wooden steps to the cove below the house, where a police cruiser was moored to the pier. The moment they set foot on deck the boat sped away, leaving Round Island on the starboard bow before setting a southeasterly course for Bluff Head.

"Are you having us tailed, Peter?"

Simon had to shout above the noise of the engines. Reade glanced irritably at the helmsman to see if he'd heard, and drew Simon aside. "Do you seriously think my men haven't anything better to do?"

"So the answer's no?"

"The answer's no," Reade confirmed. "I realize that when someone like you kicks Red China in the teeth he's got his worries, but—"

"Well, somebody has Jinny and me nailed down tight. I can tell you exactly what they look like."

"It's not us. Don't get paranoid."

"Paranoid! If your best employee was in the hands of the Taiwanese government—"

"And who put him there? Eh? *You* did! Do you realize what we're facing in this colony tonight? Well, *do you?* Military intelligence reports a massive buildup on the Fujian coast: planes, tanks, amphibious landing craft, the lot! If they're going for Taiwan, it'll make the Allied invasion of Normandy in World War Two look like a child's pool party; and Hong Kong's got a bird's-eye view, all right. The best seats in the fucking house! And you expect me to worry about missing staff. . . ."

"All right, you've made your point. Where are we going?"

"Sung Kong."

"Where the hell's that?"

"It's an island just this side of the Waglan light."

"But that's miles away!"

"Ten miles." Reade glanced over his shoulder to where Mat was sitting. "Is he okay?"

"What do you think, after the horrors he's been through? We only got him back two days ago, he needs rest, not this nonsense."

"Only he looks as though he might . . ." Reade's eyes wandered back to Simon's face, ". . . break something."

"I wish he would. Whatever's bugging him, he needs to let it out."

"Has he told you what happened yet?"

"Some of it." Simon looked away. "Don't ask."

The journey did not take long. Soon a large black landmass loomed up out of the darkness. Reade turned to Simon. "There's an inlet on the northeastern side—excellent cover."

"Cover for what, exactly?"

"We have a shy visitor."

The boat rounded the northern tip of Sung Kong and eased itself slowly into a narrow channel, while two crewmembers scanned the coast through night-glasses.

"There," murmured one of them, pointing.

"Right." Reade's face was somber. "Take us in, please. I want her brought alongside, but don't make them nervous. They're touchy and they'll be armed."

"Armed!" Simon stared through the night, trying to see what had attracted the crewman's attention. Suddenly he saw it: another boat, completely darkened, riding gently at anchor beneath a rocky overhang. As they slid closer two men appeared on its deck, their white uniforms showing up faintly in the gloom, and deftly fended off the Hong Kong police boat. Seconds later the two vessels lay moored alongside each other. A plank was shunted across the narrow gap between their rails.

Reade beckoned Mat over to join him and Simon. "By coming here, our visitor's put himself in grave danger of having his throat slit. We may have to leave in a hurry. If we do, no questions, over the side we go and off. Have you both got that?"

"I guess so," Simon said. "But it had better be important, because if—"

"It's important."

They scrambled along the plank onto the deck of the mysterious craft and were ushered down some stairs into a spartan cabin. There was only one other occupant. He stood at the far end of the room, hands behind his back. Seeing the visitors enter, he said in English: "Good evening, gentlemen. Please take a seat."

For a moment or two Simon couldn't bring himself to believe the evidence of his own eyes. Then, "Borisenko," he muttered.

The host smiled. "Krubykov. That's my real name."

"Major General Krubykov," said Reade, standing at Simon's shoulder. "Of the KGB."

Simon sat down heavily. "My God."

"You are surprised. Of course."

"I'm outraged."

Krubykov turned his head slightly. "You, I think, are Matthew Young?"

Mat gave a curt nod as he sat down.

"But . . . but how did you *get* here?" Simon asked.

"We have a carrier in the South China Sea," replied the general, taking his own seat. "And I must be on it within two hours, or risk becoming a very exposed castaway. So can we please get down to serious talking? About the war . . ."

"War!"

"Mr. Young, let me explain the position. Sometime within the next few days, I cannot be more precise, Red China intends to invade Taiwan, first taking out the defenses on Quemoy and then proceeding across the straits to the main island. In order to do this, they'll be using Apogee, something you may assume I know about. And we have to stop it."

It took Simon a few moments to collect himself. "You know about Apogee? How?"

"We had two sources. Moscow and Beijing made a high-level, ultra-secret pact—"

Simon pounded the table. "I guessed it!"

Krubykov lit a cigarette. "Information was exchanged, pursuant to the pact. Reference was made to Apogee—not much, but some. We learned more from our second source. Until recently we've been backing an organization called Our Formosa Now—you've heard of it? Good. One of OFN's top men recently cracked." The general turned to Mat. "You had dealings with someone called Wu Tie-zi, yes?"

"Yes."

"Trust him?"

"Not much."

Krubykov nodded his agreement. "Wu fled, taking his wife with him. He was on his way to New York. He was terrified. It wasn't hard to get him to talk; he came to us, not the other way around."

"Wu was your contact?" Simon asked.

"One of them. If OFN succeeded, he was due to become

Minister of Armaments—that's what kept him tied to them for so long. But he was scared; oh, was he scared!"

"Why?"

"If you realized who's behind OFN—"

"Li Lu-tang."

Krubykov made no secret of his surprise. "You already knew that?"

"I found out." It was Mat who spoke. "He boasted of it openly."

"But you, Mr. Young, didn't know?"

"Not until my son told me. The only reason I didn't make trouble when Mat disappeared was that I thought I couldn't fight the Kuomintang, the government. If I'd known for one second that Li . . ."

"Don't blame yourself. Li took great care to conceal his true loyalties."

"He wasn't the only one! We managed to make a contact inside Li's organization, a woman. She never so much as hinted he was working for anyone other than the Kuomintang government."

"Mei-hua may not have known.' Mat sounded surly. "Or she may have been terrified out of her wits. Had you thought of that?"

"All right, Mat . . . sorry. Whichever way, it's not important. But Li *is* important. The power he wields is incredible!"

"Why say that?" Krubykov asked. "He's very high in Taiwanese intelligence—ranking number four."

"But he doesn't control everything. His power is patchy," Mat said.

Simon turned on his son in surprise. "You seem to know a lot about him."

"I've been thinking, these past few days. Li had a lot of influence, but he wasn't in total charge, not yet. That's why he could get a few air force friends to organize an attack on your Learjet, at night, away from land, but he couldn't risk having Qiu arrested in front of the world's press. He couldn't afford to do anything too public, for which he might have to account to the Executive Yuan."

"That fits."

"I think so. He had some luck, too. He could use that customs prosecution, which we brought down on our own heads through carelessness, to have us shut down. But if it was left up to him, he couldn't have brought the case himself."

"You may be right," Reade interrupted. "It tallies with what we already know. But I wish you'd told me about Li before, Simon."

"Sorry. Mat was ill, I was worried out of my mind, and"—

Simon shot a troubled glance at his son—"to be honest, I was trying to get some verification before I came to you. It does sound a little . . . well, far-fetched."

"Yes." Reade shook his head. "My God, what a risk Li took in letting Mat go. When you think how many things he gave away . . ."

"He had no choice, Peter. Once he knew he wasn't going to get the Apogee technology from Mat, what else could he do but make an exchange?"

Krubykov rapped on the table. "Can we proceed? Li's important, yes, but he isn't OFN's only agent. They long ago planted a mole in the Ducannon Young organization." He paused. "His name is Haines."

A soft sigh escaped Simon's lips. It seemed to go on for a long time. Krubykov smiled, making his face look cruel. "Your security officer in Taiwan. Yes."

"That figures," Mat said quietly.

"What's that?" the general asked.

"I mean that a lot of things fall into place, once you know it's Haines. Dad, do you remember the night Lennie first told me about Apogee, and Garrison Command busted us?"

"Of course."

"Haines knew Lennie wanted to see me about something important; he knew I was going down to Hsinchu later on. He made phone calls after dinner." Mat nodded, as if he'd checked his reasoning and was satisfied. "He must have been tipping them off. Only of course, it wasn't Garrison Command. It was Li's men. That's why they didn't risk taking anything away with them; I always thought that was odd."

"Very likely," Krubykov agreed. "Haines told OFN all about Apogee, what he knew of it, many months ago."

"Did Wu tell you that?" Simon asked.

"Yes. And that Li was holding Matthew Young on Quemoy. Now. Haines arrived in Hong Kong yesterday. We lost him at the airport."

"But . . . he's got no business being here!"

"Oh yes he has," Mat put in. "Quarterly review."

"Of course!' Simon's eyes opened wide. "Just a minute—the lookalike! Fong Mun Wah. I've told him to show up at the office because I want to throw the mainlanders off Lennie's scent. And if Haines is in Hong Kong . . ."

Mat followed the train of thought. "He might run into Lennie's double."

"What are you talking about?" By now Reade was manifestly angry. "What's all this about a lookalike?"

Simon rapidly explained the ruse he'd used for the change-over at Narita. Krubykov's frown deepened as the story progressed. "I see," he said, when Simon had finished. He turned to Reade. "If Haines should meet Fong in the office . . ."

Reade stood up. "I need to use the radio."

Krubykov spoke a few sentences into the phone, then told Reade, "Someone will escort you to the radio room."

Reade left. There was a long silence in the stuffy cabin. Simon rubbed his eyes, trying to throw off the bleak implications of what he'd been told. "Haines, of all people," he muttered. "One of my oldest friends recommended him to me.

"That means he's very good, then, doesn't it? As a spy." The Russian extinguished his cigarette and went to open the porthole. A stink of rotting seaweed mixed with stagnant water seeped into the cabin. As Krubykov returned to his seat, he studied Mat from under his eyelashes. He'd seen expressions like that before; experience told him he'd be wise to keep the Englishman in view at all times. Krubykov would have given a lot to know what had put that look in Mat's eyes.

Reade came back. "Simon, I'm sorry, but it's bad. A few minutes ago, George Forster rang Central and reported Fong as missing—seems his driver got stuck in traffic and the boy'd gone by the time he arrived."

"*What!*"

"I've put out a full alert, priority one-A. Fong's got family here, they'll be on the computer. If he's still in Hong Kong, we'll find him."

"Haines?"

"Nothing."

Water lapped against the boat's hull, but otherwise it was perfectly quiet in the cabin. Krubykov lit another cigarette. "All right," he said. "We've got more urgent priorities. Let me tell you why I requested this meeting. The Red Chinese realize you've double-crossed them by handing over Luk. This means that they've been compelled to bring forward the schedule for their invasion, before the Taiwanese air force can find out what Luk knows."

"You sound so *sure!*"

"I am. We sent a flotilla to monitor the southeast coast of China. The commander's confirmed there's a huge buildup in progress."

"Wait a moment." Simon raised a hand. "OFN isn't the government of Taiwan, it's bitterly opposed to it. So if OFN's holding Lennie, how can Taiwan's air force benefit from his knowledge?"

"Because OFN intend to barter Apogee in return for political power."

Simon turned to Mat. "You were right about that, too, then. Krubykov, is that something else you got from Wu?"

"Yes."

"But then why are you involving *us* in this?" Simon's voice was harsh. "What do you want?"

"OFN has to be stopped. You can help us do that. No one else can."

"I'm lost! Why do *you* want to stop OFN? What on earth can I do to help?"

"The Chinese are planning to make use of Apogee in an invasion of Taiwan, that's obvious. The Beijing-Moscow pact I mentioned earlier was always bedeviled by problems and now is at an end. Therefore, the Chinese know they can't rely on us to support them; the reverse is true. If the U.S. sends the Seventh Fleet to prevent the invaders getting a foothold . . . it's war."

Simon stirred uneasily. "Surely Beijing must know that?"

"Yes—but they think it could be a risk worth running. Red China's been looking for an excuse to take over Taiwan for many years, yes?"

"Yes."

"Well, now it's about to get one. OFN plans to assassinate the President of Taiwan. That's another thing Wu Tie-zi told us. The second he dies, Taiwan will fall apart. Then OFN makes its pitch. It'll offer to provide the government, what's left of it, with Apogee, with the means to defeat an invasion by the mainland, right?"

"Yes."

"In exchange for political power."

"Yes."

Krubykov spread his hands. "What more could mainland China want? There's an insurrection on Taiwan, civil war looms. They come in to restore order, kick a few asses."

"And America would think twice before being seen to interfere. . . . But OFN must have allowed for that?"

Krubykov's eyes broke contact with Simon's. "Who knows, they've demonstrated they can be pretty stupid."

"But—"

"Can't you see the attraction of it all, from the Red Chinese point of view? A public service, that's what they'd say: 'We're invading Taiwan merely to tidy up a little local difficulty.' " His face darkened. "No, thank you very much! Once the mainlanders get control of Taiwan, they'll be able to exclude the Soviet fleet from the Pacific and Indian Oceans. Fine, as long as the Moscow-Beijing pact lasted, but that's off now." He banged on the table with both fists. "So it has to be stopped, before OFN gives the mainland its excuse to act! The Soviet Union is mobilizing against mainland China, in case worse comes to worst. But full-scale mobilization takes more time than we have. Which is where you come in, Young. You can move quicker than we can."

"*Me?* You're getting ready to turn China into a nuclear frying pan, and you expect me to press some switch and solve your problems? Tell me, Krubykov, just what am I supposed to have that's more impressive than a billion megatons of plutonium?"

"Not patience," Krubykov said through gritted teeth. "Not that! If you'd only listen, instead of shooting off your mouth at every opportunity . . ."

Simon sat back in his chair. "Get to the point."

"We want you to expose Haines, Li, Wu, the whole OFN hierarchy. Name names. Do it *publicly*. The Kuomintang moves fast, when it's of a mind to; they'll put down Li and his gang within the hour. Then no assassination, no excuse to invade. Which will mean no invasion."

"The mainland might still go ahead and chance it."

"They might, if they thought all they had to fear was United States intervention. But now they know there's more to it. We're about to terminate their pact with us, which will leave them out on a limb. If we can also prevent the assassination of the Taiwanese President, we're going to rob them of a legitimate excuse for interference as well. That's one problem too many. They'll balk."

"But why should the Taipei government listen to me? I'm just a businessman."

Krubykov guffawed. "Yes? You think they'd listen to us, per- haps—to the KGB? They'd laugh in our faces! But you've got a son who was their prisoner. He was *there*! He can identify everyone connected with OFN who ever mattered."

Simon nodded; it made sense to him. "That's part of it," he said slowly. "But you're not telling me everything, are you?"

"Do we really need to prolong this discussion?"

"Oh, I think we do." Simon distractedly ran his hand through his hair. "You've been making use of OFN for your own ends, and now you can't manage your creatures. The thing's running out of control."

"I never said that."

"You didn't have to. Why else would you be here"—Simon

[325]

gestured at Reade—"with your head in his noose? And there's something else, too, something you shied away from earlier."

"What?"

"I still can't for the life of me understand why OFN should risk provoking a Chicom invasion by killing the President of Taiwan. No, there's more, there's more . . . but I can't . . ." His hand smacked the table. "Yes I can, though. Of course I can." He smiled at Krubykov. "Wu Tie-zi told you something else, didn't he? OFN is going public! It's going to advertise the big Moscow connection . . . how much help you've been, natural allies, and so on." He was grinning now. "By God, yes! That's it! How much help you've *been*—past tense. You're pulling out, and they know that."

Simon swung around in his chair until he was facing Reade. "Don't you see it? This lot, the KGB, they've been monkeying about with the Taiwanese independence movement—arming them, I shouldn't wonder. OFN feels so confident of its Russian allies that it's even prepared to risk an invasion by killing the President. Why not? Moscow can always send a few divisions. So mainland China has to come in to keep the peace, finds herself met with *Russian* guns loaded with *Russian* bullets. . . . Moscow sees which way the wind's blowing, can't rely on the pact with China, gets frightened and backs off, OFN's riled. . . ."

"I think there's more to it," Mat said quietly.

"What?"

"Moscow backs off, OFN's riled. That's what you said."

"So?"

"So I was thinking . . . Li said something about . . . negotiating with other interested parties."

It suddenly became very quiet in the cabin.

"There's a mistake I always make here," Mat went on. "I keep thinking Apogee's just a weapon. It isn't. It's a commodity, something that can be bought and sold."

"You're losing me."

"It's kind of complicated, Dad. But keep thinking in terms of buyers and sellers: Apogee in exchange for something else."

"Go on."

"I can think of two parties who might be interested. There's the Russians, but they're pulling out. Which leaves . . ."

"The United States." It was Simon who finished the sentence. "Li sells Apogee to America as the price of its support; that means the Seventh Fleet *will* intervene; Russia loses her Pacific sea lanes; America and Red China have Apogee; the Soviet Union doesn't. . . . Oh yes, General. I see. At last I really do see." The expression on Simon's face as he turned to his son was one of profound awe. "That's . . . brilliant."

Mat said nothing.

"In terms of the balance of power, it would make Reagan's Strategic Defense Initiative look like a peashooter by comparison. Now then, Krubykov." Simon's voice became brisk. "OFN has to be discredited as soon as possible, yes?"

"Yes."

"And to do that, I need first of all to expose Haines—no, correction, Reade here needs to *find* Haines." Simon mused. "What do you think, Peter?" he asked, swiveling around. "Do we believe this guy here?"

"Difficult. But yes, I think so. All our own material backs him up, as far as it goes. And he did come here. It was a hell of a risk to take."

"Mm." Simon turned back to Krubykov. "What have you got in the way of hard evidence that I could use against Haines?"

"There's a dossier. Remember, Wu Tie-zi cracked; he told us a lot about him."

"Right. Then there remains just one question. What's it worth?"

Simon heard Reade's sharp intake of breath and ignored it. Krubykov grunted. "What is it worth—to prevent a world war?"

"Oh, I'm not responsible for the war. You are. You've got yourselves in a position where the other two superpowers may end up with Apogee, but you won't; that *has* to be worth something. I betrayed Red China and I'm likely to find myself ruined as a result. And I'm fed up with being manipulated by the world's intelligence services. This time they can pay for the privilege and be damned! So what have you got to offer?"

"I really don't—"

Simon cut Reade off in midsentence. "You shut up." But when he turned back to Krubykov it was to see the Russian reach into the breast pocket of his jacket, and he froze.

Krubykov's hand emerged holding not a gun but an envelope that he now pushed across the table to Simon. The Englishman opened it and took out a long letter. He read through it quickly and looked up. "This is a guarantee."

"Yes. In effect, the Soviet Union will underwrite any losses you suffer as a result of your decision to double-cross Red China."

"You know what'll happen if you fail to honor this? Apogee will go to the United States."

"We shall honor it. Look at the signatures; the Politburo stands behind that letter."

Simon placed the document in his pocket. "There's just one more thing. Why did they send you to this meeting, General? Any underling would have done."

"Perhaps. But I'm known to you." Krubykov's eyes glinted. "It was thought that you would . . . remember me. That you would listen to me, when you might not have paid attention to anyone else."

The two men stared at each other for a moment longer; then, simultaneously, they smiled.

Simon stood up. "I'm ready, Peter. Krubykov, have you got that dossier on Haines?"

"Here." The Russian produced a cardboard folder. Simon took it, skimmed through a few pages, and slammed it shut. "Good night, General."

They scrambled back over the side of the police patrol boat and made for the bridge. As they slowly reversed away from the Soviet craft, Reade turned to the captain. "Have you identified her yet?"

"She's a Pchela-class hydrofoil. Nippy little ship."

"Let's get going, then."

The radio came alive. Reade donned the headphones and picked up the mike. Mat used the opportunity to take his father aside. "There's something we didn't discuss back there."

"What?"

"Lennie. He's been left to rot on Quemoy." Mat's voice was flat. "Are you going to stand for it?"

"What can we do?"

"We can get him out, that's what."

"How? You and I aren't equipped to—"

"No. But that pet monkey of yours is. Where the hell's Qiu?"

As the patrol boat nosed out of the inlet, swinging around on a course that would take them back to Hong Kong, Reade removed his headphones and smiled wearily at Simon. "Haines has surfaced. He and another man are being held on a charge of murder. I'm sorry . . ." In the final second before the turbines exploded into maximum revolutions, drowning out all other sounds, Simon heard Reade say, ". . . but Fong Mun Wah is dead."

THIRTY

"How did you find this place?" Qiu couldn't help shivering as he stared at the damp walls, the filthy concrete floor.

"We played here as children. The garden backs onto my parents' house."

"It looked weird on the outside."

"Japanese-built. We used to pretend it was haunted and scare ourselves half to death." Lin-chun leaned forward to plant a kiss on his mouth. "I was worried about you. When I heard your voice on the phone just now, I . . . I . . ."

"I know. How do you think I felt when they told me you'd been on the *Golden Eagle* that night?"

She clasped his hands between her own and gave them a squeeze. "Don't. It's over. I survived. Now, you must be hungry."

"I haven't eaten since morning; it's nearly midnight now. Can we risk a light?"

"As long as we stay in the cellar."

They ate the picnic she'd brought, not speaking much. When they'd finished, Lin-chun said, "Tell me."

Qiu rested his back against the wall with a sigh and outlined what had been happening since they'd met in Singapore. "Cheong reported the rescue mission's failure to Simon Young," he concluded. "For twenty-four hours after that, nothing. Then Li made contact. He wanted to deal."

"What kind of deal?"

"An exchange: Mat for Lennie Luk. Young was prepared to negotiate; I wasn't. I know these people. They'll double-cross him. We quarreled. I haven't seen Young for three days."

"But why did you come here, to Taipei? It's so dangerous."

"I told you in Singapore I'd come back. I had to see you."

"Do you think anyone followed you?"

"No, I telephoned your parents' house, then came straight here from the airport."

"Oh my dear . . ."

"Things are getting serious, aren't they?"

"Yes." Lin-chun sighed. "There's a curfew. Radio and TV keep broadcasting warnings—nothing definite, just a plea for everyone to be alert. But nobody's fooled. The invasion's coming."

"It must be frightening."

"Oh, that's not the worst. We've been hearing shots, late at night. My secretary's got a cousin out at Wulai. They're building some kind of internment camp there, she says. We have practice air-raid warnings every night."

"You know that soon it'll be impossible to leave? That's why I'm here, to take you away."

"Did you really come just for that?"

"Yes. Don't cry . . . I've made arrangements. Before we quarreled, Simon Young agreed to offer you a job in one of his companies."

"But my parents won't leave. They're frightened, yes, but they've got nowhere else to go. We aren't rich people. We—"

"Quiet!" For a second Qiu held his body in perfect stillness while he listened; then he pounced on the flashlight, killing it with a flick of his thumb.

"What's—"

"Hush!" Qiu pulled Lin-chun toward him and laid his lips against her ear. "A board creaked. Is there another way out?"

When she shook her head he grabbed her shoulders and signaled with deep pressure that she was to remain still.

He tiptoed across to the wall and used it as a guide, feeling his way to the foot of the stairs. If he strained his hearing he thought he could just detect the echo of a distant siren.

He was on the point of returning to Lin-chun when the sound that had disturbed him earlier was repeated, and he knew for sure they were no longer alone inside the house.

Qiu placed a foot on the lowest step, hesitated, pushed himself onto it. Slowly he lifted his other foot high and brought it down next to its fellow. One.

There were eight steps leading up from the cellar. He had automatically counted them as they arrived, unconsciously obeying a rule instilled in him during his long training. Someone was up there, seven steps above his head.

Someone? Many someones?

Qiu put his right foot down two steps above the one he was standing on. He pressed lightly, feeling for weaknesses in the board, but it was sound. Then he raised his left foot, using the wall to keep his balance.

There was a door at the top of the stairs. Had they left it open or shut? Qiu couldn't remember, and for a moment he nearly panicked. He had been taught to remember things like that *always*!

Ajar. The door had been left ajar.

Another two steps: more than halfway. Yes, that's right, he was replaying memory in his head, like a film, and now he could see clearly, the door opened inward, it had been left ajar. But he couldn't see anything. The newcomer must be operating without lights, just as he and Lin-chun had done.

Qiu levered himself up two more steps. This time the wood gave slightly beneath his foot and he quickly lowered it one tread, content to halve his rate of progress in favor of preserving silence.

Whoever was in the room above didn't know what to expect. If the intruder realized that the cellar contained only two unarmed people, one of them a woman, and if he himself had a weapon, he would already have attacked. So he wasn't armed. Or he was armed, but didn't have any idea of the strength of the opposition. Or maybe it was just some derelict, looking for shelter for the night. . . . No! A tramp would have made more noise.

A cat? A rat?

Qiu lifted his right foot again and placed it two steps upward, avoiding the tread that had creaked before. His brow came into contact with the edge of the door and he went rigid.

The next phase was going to be difficult. He dared not pull the door open wider, in case the hinges squeaked. Could he edge around it?

Somehow he managed it, without losing his balance. Immediately in front of him, perhaps twelve paces away, was a square window quartered into four panes. At first he didn't understand what he was looking at: a gray blob contrasting oddly with its surroundings. Then, slowly, the blob began to assume a hard outline with edges and he realized what it was.

Why did the window have a soft center?

The thought formulated itself just like that, unedited: a window soft in the middle. He ran through all the possibilities. There could only be one answer. Some obstacle stood between him and the outer wall of the house.

A siren sounded in the distance, and almost at once a bright gleam danced across the window as the searchlights hoisted themselves skyward. It lasted less than a second, but that was enough to delineate the shape of a human head obstructing the point where the four panes of glass met to form a cross, so that for an eerie instant Qiu imagined himself to be looking through a telescopic rifle sight at the silhouette of a man.

"Elder Brother . . ." The syllables drifted across the quiet room, and every nerve in his already taut body seemed to stiffen.

"Who are you?" Qiu said.

"My name is Gu." There was a pause. "Five Dots Gu."

Watery light had begun to ooze through the window, carving human figures where before there had been only blackness.

"And that's all?"

Lin-chun shook her head wearily. "I can't remember anything else. I've told you so often."

"But you understand," Qiu said softly, "why we ask you these questions? Why it's important for us to know?"

"Yes. I've told you *everything* I can remember Mei-hua saying about Quemoy. And I've given you the sketch map she drew for me."

"Please forgive me, Elder Brother," Gu said, turning his head a fraction toward his superior. "But Miss Shan has been most helpful. We're in danger of repeating ourselves. And she's tired."

"I know." Qiu continued to gaze at Lin-chun for several moments longer, while the light outside slowly and steadily intensified into full dawn. "I know," he repeated, and stood up. "What time does curfew end?"

"Five forty-five," said Lin-chun. She too rose and Qiu took her hand.

"You must go home now," he said. "Act normally. Don't bother to pack more than you have to."

"All right."

"You'll want to say a special goodbye to your parents this morning. Resist the temptation."

"You sound so . . . brutal." Her voice was low.

"It's not a time to be soft. As long as you're sure you want to come."

Her eyes slid sideways to Gu. "Do you believe the things he's promised?" she whispered.

"Yes." His features remained lost in shadow, leaving her with only the merest impression of how he looked after a night without sleep. "I trust him."

"Then . . . I'm sure."

"Go now. And hurry!"

As soon as she'd left, he returned to squat in front of Gu. "You've been brave, coming here."

"Not so brave." Gu spoke with quiet diffidence. "I just waited for Miss Shan to act. She came here, I followed her, then it was easy."

"Do you know how Beijing traced her?"

Gu coughed. "I gather Mr. Ng tape-recorded certain . . . exchanges between you and her, in Singapore. An address was mentioned."

The bedroom had been bugged! Qiu colored and turned away to hide his embarrassment. "Five Dots," he said, not quite meeting the man's eyes, "you've more to tell me?"

"Please excuse me, but in front of the miss . . . I hope you understand."

"Yes. Tell me now."

"Let's go back a little. You do see why I was sent?"

"I think so. Controller Sun knows that as a result of my . . . my connection with Shan Lin-chun, I have extensive information concerning Q-4, where Li's now holding Luk. So the exchange did take place, then?"

"Yes."

"Hm. Sun wants to have my information so that he can make use of it."

"He wants *you* to make use of it. We must have Luk."

"Must?"

"The invasion of Taiwan may have to be postponed indefinitely." Five Dots ignored Qiu's gasp of surprise. "Young has

[333]

surrendered Luk to the Taiwanese; Apogee has fallen into enemy hands. A direct attack is therefore considered inadvisable. But there *is* to be an assault on Quemoy."

"To get Luk out?"

"Before he tells them anything vital, if he hasn't already— exactly. He's to be taken to the mainland, where he'll work for the rest of his life."

"Does he want that?"

"Luk's wishes really don't matter. What matters is that you organize the mission to Quemoy. Only you have the necessary knowledge, coupled with the required expertise, to bring him out."

"I know that."

"Therefore, all sanctions against you are rescinded. You're clear about the offer that's been made to you?"

"The guarantees concerning my wife and child?"

"If you succeed in sending Luk to Beijing, your wife and son will be restored to their former positions and given the choice of residing where they please. You'll be free to go. No one will come after you."

"Yes, yes, your exposition was most clear. And I've accepted."

"But you've not yet had a chance to accept the real offer that's being made to you."

Qiu turned around sharply. "What's that?"

"There's a little more to it." Gu laughed in his modest fashion. "Simon Young has betrayed the People's Republic; he's given away secrets that weren't his to give. Sun has decided that Young must be punished."

Qiu eyed Five Dots intently, trying to delve beneath his smiling, shy expression. He liked this man, who struck him as an excellent soldier. "What's that got to do with me?"

"You must first go back to Hong Kong, as planned. When you get there—"

The door to the room clicked open and both men spun around.

"I came as fast as I could," said Lin-chun. "Please hurry. I managed to stop a cab, but the driver won't wait."

Qiu turned back to Gu. "Later," he mouthed; and the other man nodded.

As they got into the taxi Lin-chun said, "International Airport, please. Departures."

"Better hurry! You hear the radio this morning?"

"No, what—"

"Airport's closing at noon. All flights out fully booked; no more incoming flights at all."

Qiu leaned forward in the backseat. "Then move!" he rasped, and the cab shot away from the curb.

Early-morning traffic was heavy. The streets seemed to be filled with nothing but armored personnel carriers, jeeps, and ten-ton trucks, all competing for priority. Suddenly the driver jammed on his brakes and stopped under the arm of an MP. A convoy sped across the intersection: first came a crimson, open-topped car with white crests on its doors and pennons on each front fender, containing an officer and two NCOs carrying flags. Then a large black car with tinted glass flashed by, closely followed by a jeep full of soldiers.

"President," the cabbie muttered as the MP waved him on. "Going to the hills."

It took their taxi over an hour to crawl up Chien Kuo Road South to the freeway turnoff. As they accelerated through the outskirts of San Chung, the music coming from the radio gave way to an announcement. Lin-chun listened intently, then turned to the driver. "The main north-south highway's closing?"

"Yes."

"But why?"

"Must be for the air force to land." The driver switched off the radio, his face drawn. "You got a seat on a plane this morning?"

"Yes," Gu said quietly. "Confirmed reservations."

"Okay. I'll drop you off as near as I can. But I was at the airport yesterday and I tell you, you'd better have your elbows ready."

He wasn't exaggerating. The double line of cars extended back almost a quarter of a mile from the departures building. They paid off the cab and walked the rest of the way. Qiu took Lin-chun's arm. "What was all that about closing the highway?"

"There are six places where the road can be converted into military landing strips. They take away the central divider and—"

"Of course." He spoke tersely, unwilling to pursue the line of thought.

They virtually had to fight their way into the terminal. The only thing visible above this bedlam was the computerized departures board showing flights in great yellow letters. Four were scheduled to leave within the next two hours; the rest had been canceled.

"The Cathay desk's to the left," Gu shouted. "You can't see a thing in this crush."

Nearby a woman shrieked and Qiu hastily looked around,

thinking it might be Lin-chun. But it was a mother whose child had slipped from her arms and was lost somewhere in the crowd. She became hysterical, battering with her fists on the chests and backs of those nearest. A few were sympathetic and tried to help, but one man turned on her, his face contorted in fury, and slapped her hard. Lin-chun raised her hands to her cheeks in horror.

"Don't look," said Qiu. "Come. *Come!*"

"I'll pay the airport tax," Gu gasped. "You stand in line for check-in."

Somehow they managed to force their way to the front of the crowd. Gu joined them at the last moment and smashed the tickets down in front of the ravaged clerk. As they rode up the escalator to departure level, Qiu turned back to see only a forest of heads, upraised arms, angry, frightened faces.

"You're gate two," Gu said to Lin-chun, handing her one of the boarding passes. "We have to use gate three: aliens."

They took up position in front of the booths. The lines moved slowly. Armed infantrymen directed severe, questioning looks at everyone. As they moved farther down the hall, Gu nudged Qiu's arm. "There's no time left, I must tell you now before the girl rejoins us."

"Be quick, then."

Gu laid his mouth against Qiu's ear and started to whisper.

Lin-chun was already waiting for them as they came through into the customs area. She smiled at Qiu, then she looked more closely and her smile died. "What is it?" she exclaimed, clutching his sleeve. "You've gone as white as death!"

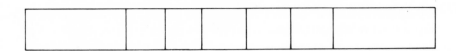

THIRTY-ONE

The video image steadied, became clear: a nighttime street scene with an ambulance in the background, and a police car's red roof light dominating the first few seconds of tape. The picture quivered again; then the car drove away and Radio Television Hong Kong's logo appeared in a corner of the screen.

"We put it on all the early-morning news programs," said Reade. "There's the body. Look! That's Haines in the background, they're taking him away . . . surgeon . . . barriers, there was a crowd. . . ."

"What time did it happen?" asked Simon.

"About seven P.M. . . . Ah! That's Mai, the killer . . . it's coming up now, coming . . . There!" Reade froze the frame. "Top left quarter of the screen, front row."

"The woman in the red jacket?"

"That's right. Mah-jongg agent, from Sun's executive unit. We've had dealings with her before. There's your tail, Jinny, or one of them, at least. That's why you've been feeling so jumpy these last few weeks."

"But . . . why?"

"That woman told me they've had orders to track everybody in Ducannon Young who matters, ever since Mat was abducted. Her job was to watch Haines. Look, we'd better get going; we're on in two minutes."

Reade led the Youngs out of his top-floor office at Central and down the corridor toward the interview suite. "Sun's kicking himself," he muttered to Simon. "His people came in just too late."

"What really happened?"

"Haines has admitted he thought Lennie'd escaped from Quemoy, or perhaps given Li the slip; he couldn't get instructions because Li's gone missing. Apparently the boy panicked and tried to make a run for it. Mai knifed him, going for a flesh wound, I guess, and got it wrong. Pierced a kidney. The medics think Fong may have had a weak heart. Anyway, the shock finished him off in the ambulance."

"Shit."

"I know. Try not to blame yourself."

"He'd been told not to go out alone."

"Now *look*!" Reade stopped short of the door to Central's largest interview room and turned on Simon. "Get a grip on yourself. I need a performance and a half out of you."

"I know." Simon rubbed his forehead. "I'll manage."

"It's not you I'm worried about so much. Mat's the star of this thing." Reade eyed Mat closely. "Are you *sure* you're all right?"

"Don't keep asking that."

"Sorry. But there's a lot riding on you at the moment. And to be frank, you look . . ."

"I look *what*?"

"Doesn't matter." Reade took his arm. "Remember," he said quietly, "the single most important thing they have to hear is how Li Lu-tang confessed to being OFN. I don't care what else you say or don't say, just as long as you put that across. Got it?"

"Got it."

"Let's go, then."

The room was filled to capacity, with many reporters standing in the aisles. Reade and his party were met with a blitz of exploding flashbulbs. The assistant commissioner was already rising to his feet when a uniformed sergeant ran up to lay a sheet of paper in front of him. Reade scanned it and placed a hand over the microphone. When he bent to whisper to Simon, his face was jubilant. "Haines has cracked. He's implicated Li, he's singing like a dawn chorus!"

Simon clutched his hands together in a triumphant gesture

while Reade turned back to the microphone. "I won't waste time on introductions. There's a prepared statement being distributed now, but it's long, so I'll summarize. Li Lu-tang, a senior member of Taiwanese intelligence, has for many years been working for the independence movement known as Our Formosa Now. Unknown to his employers, he kidnapped Matthew Young, who's sitting beside me, and held him prisoner on Quemoy. The purpose of this . . ."

But the purpose was lost in a surge of reporters. Only Jinny, from her vantage point beside the podium, noticed how one man at the back slipped away, clutching Reade's statement. . . .

Qiu and Lin-chun got to the Ducannon Young Building at the same time as Simon's party. The two of them raced up the steps a short way in front of a human tidal wave. From the safety of the foyer they looked back to see Reade and the Young family squeeze inside with the help of two janitors. Then the doors slammed shut, leaving the press to hammer on the glass in vain.

"Quick," said Simon, grabbing Qiu's arm. "Mary just called me in the car. Minister on the line from Taipei."

As the elevator ascended to the top floor he briefed Qiu on the press conference. He barged through the doors before they were fully open and thrust his way into the boardroom, where Mary Street was waiting with the receiver in her hand. "Minister for Trade," she said tersely. Simon threw himself into a chair, breathing deeply. Then he snatched the receiver from his secretary. "Young."

"I heard you'd been exchanged for Luk," Qiu murmured to Mat.

"Did you?"

Qiu, hearing the coldness in Mat's voice, directed an inquisitive glance toward him.

While Simon waited for the minister to come on the line he looked from face to face, suddenly registering one more than he'd expected. "Diana!"

His daughter sat in an armchair by the far window. She was dressed formally in a tailored raw-silk jacket and had a suitcase beside her. "Hi, Da."

"When did you arrive?"

"Couple of hours ago. I was on my way home, but there aren't any westbound flights out of Kai Tak."

"My fault." His expression became less genial. "You mean you were leaving without even saying—"

But suddenly the line clicked and Simon raised a hand for silence.

Diana plucked her brother's sleeve, nodding toward the passage. At first he was reluctant, but she persisted. They went only as far as the first empty office. As Diana shut the door, Mat gravitated to the window, where he stared out moodily over Victoria Harbor.

"Bean Sprout . . . what's wrong?"

"Nothing." He turned away from the glass and slouched to the nearest chair. "Why do you ask that?"

"Please don't talk to the table."

"Oh, for—"

"It's just that if you talk to the table I can't hear what you're saying. I wasn't trying to be difficult."

His smile conceded her point, though not immediately. "Sorry."

Diana moved away from the door until she was standing over him. "Mother told me what a hard time you had. I—"

"Yeah, yeah. Thanks."

"You can fool everyone. Except me."

"Look, if you've got anything to say I wish you'd stop blathering and say it, only I want to go back next door. Right?"

"I'm not leaving for London until you tell me what happened."

"What do you mean, what happened? I got kidnapped, taken to Quemoy, beaten up."

"And?"

"And!" Mat exploded. "What else do you want—the color of the blood on the sodding walls?"

"There's more." Diana's voice was calm. "I know there's a lot more. Have you looked in a mirror lately? Your eyes . . ."

"What's wrong with them?"

"They're round and they're small. Like pinpricks. You don't open them properly. And your face has sagged. It makes you look reptilian. Yes"—the image pleased her—"you're like some kind of malevolent lizard, crouching on a rock."

Mat stared up at her. Then he stretched his lips; perhaps he thought he was smiling. "You really want to know what happened on Quemoy?"

"Yes."

Mat told her.

When he'd finished, Diana said nothing for a while. "He was lying, of course. Li would have killed Mei-hua, whatever you said or did."

"I know."

"You do?" Diana was surprised. "I thought that's what was ripping you apart—not knowing."

His head twitched impatiently. "I've thought about it. All the time. I don't sleep, you know, I . . ."

"Go on."

"I never found out how Li knew the escape had been brought forward. For a time I thought Mei-hua betrayed me, that it was all part of Li's plot."

"And wasn't it?"

"No."

The words *How can you be sure?* sprang to Diana's lips and died there. Mat must have seen her expression, however, for he grunted and turned away. "I know. She was a great actress, she could have been faking terror; maybe it was their last ploy to make me talk— 'tell us what you know or we'll burn your lover alive.' "

"Well . . ."

"No. Maybe I'm a fool, after all she'd done to me, but at the end I trusted her. She *did* change. I have to believe it."

"Have to?"

"Of course! The alternative's that Li really didn't mean to kill her." The look he gave his sister was indescribable. "One of the guards she thought she'd fixed talked to Li. Something like that. But it wasn't her."

Suddenly Diana understood the meaning of faith.

"No, that's not the worst part. The worst part"—Mat stood up and once again made for the window—"is that I killed the woman I loved."

"But you were being merciful."

"Was I?"

"If you believe Li would have burned her—yes." Diana came to place her hands on his shoulders. Mat whirled around, gripped her wrists, and flung them off. Sweat poured down his forehead; he was gasping. Diana stood stock-still while the violence communicated itself to her through his hands, along her arms. A wrong word, a false move . . .

Diana waited until she was sure the fit had passed, and every nerve in her body seemed to uncurl. "Sometimes we all kill things . . . people . . . we love." Mat heard the catch in her voice and looked up. "It's . . . for the best. That's what we tell ourselves, isn't it? For their sake, for ours . . ."

"Don't cry."

"Not crying," she choked.

"Because if you do . . . I . . ."

The noise Mat made when he broke down was dreadful. For a second Diana wanted to cover her ears in an effort to shut out that terrible howl of grief and self-hatred. She reached down inside herself, searching for curative words . . . but found only an empty place. So she hugged her brother's shoulders until he stopped shaking. It was the only thing she could think of.

When at last Mat looked up she could see that some of the evil had gone—not all, but enough to guarantee that more could and would follow.

"I understand," Diana said, "about the killing. You don't have to explain that to me."

Mat wiped his face several times. His hands were still twitching but he seemed calmer now. "How can you know? How can anyone who hasn't—"

But along the corridor Simon was shouting, "Mat! Where are you?"

"It doesn't matter. Look, you must go and I'm off now."

"But you can't go yet."

"I have to. You'll be all right. Call me sometime."

"Diana!"

"Go on, Mat. Da needs you."

They returned to the boardroom in time to hear Simon issue orders to George Forster. "Contact Cheong To right away. Tell him we need the *Golden Eagle* for another trip to Quemoy. Offer him anything!"

Diana picked up her case and went to plant a kiss on her father's cheek. "Adventure playtime, is it?" she said, and her voice was bored. "You men . . ." She turned to her brother. "Look after yourself, Bean Sprout. Take care. I'll be at the house until there's a plane." She walked stiffly away with a smile at Lin-chun, and was through the door before finishing the sentence.

"Diana!" Simon rose to his feet. "Diana," he repeated forlornly. He removed his glasses and mopped his brow. For all his energetic talk, he looked utterly drained. "All right, Mat, pull up a chair," he said, at last accepting that his daughter wasn't coming back. "The Minister of Trade didn't have much time, but this is the picture he gave me. They got to the President in time to stop the assassination; he's safe. Next: you're in the clear."

"Me?"

"Remember the court-martial, when you were supposed to have been tried for the murder of that man in the sauna? Li had a photograph implicating the Minister of Justice. He planted it in my plane. It was a clever fake. Wu left a letter before he fled. He's told them where to look for the negatives."

"Why on earth should Wu do a thing like that?"

"Fear. Krubykov said he was terrified. Or insurance—maybe he's hoping to be allowed back someday. Who the hell knows? Next, they've confirmed what Haines told Reade, that Li's disappeared. The Taiwanese think he must be on Quemoy somewhere, but they aren't wasting time looking for him. All their military resources are currently being diverted to Quemoy. They're expecting the Reds to come tomorrow night at the latest."

"Any news of Lennie?"

"No. The minister's sending a telex to the commander of defense forces on Quemoy. That's the best he can do."

"Best! It's fuck-all!"

"Wait, listen. They've authorized us to go to Quemoy ourselves. On the *Golden Eagle.* We've got free passage through Taiwanese waters and permission to land, but no guarantees beyond that. Strictly at our own risk."

"Who's going on this expedition?" Mat asked.

Simon pointed at Qiu. "It's perfect! He's got the training, he's got the guts—"

"You're really going?"

"Yes."

"You'll need help. I'm coming too."

"You are *not!*" shrieked Jinny. "Are you out of your mind? Simon—tell him! He's ill. He's sick, he needs rest and care and—"

"He says he's going."

"I forbid it," Jinny said.

"Please, Ma." Mat put his arms around Jinny's shoulders. "Lennie's my best friend. He volunteered to take my place. I have to go."

Jinny stared between her two men, both children, both equally stubborn, and she could not understand what was happening to her, or why they were doing this. "Please don't," she whispered to Mat. "Please!"

Reade took advantage of the flare-up to murmur in Simon's ear, "Qiu'll never make it in time. It's three hundred fifty miles to Quemoy from here, and that's by the most direct route, along the coast. Cheong daren't go that way; the Reds would spot him within minutes."

"Shit, that's right. No, wait—he can detour out to sea, come in from the east."

"Well, I'll clear it with the Hong Kong harbormaster, but that's as far as I go."

"All right. Where will you be if I need you?"

"Shuttling between Government House and Central. But try not to need me. We've problems of our own."

Jinny, seeing Reade getting ready to leave, managed to attract her husband's attention again. "Simon, Mat can't go. Make him see!"

Simon fidgeted indecisively. Jinny determined to make one last appeal. "Simon . . . you're stretching me beyond what the gods meant me to bear. I've done so much, I've fought for you, I've . . ."

But Simon had had enough. "He wants—no, he *needs*—to go. *Let him!*"

Jinny looked between father and son a moment longer; then, without a word to either of them, she stalked from the room in Peter Reade's wake.

Back in the boardroom, Simon poured himself a glass of water. The strain of the recent quarrel showed on his face. "Qianwei—what's your next move?"

Qiu did not answer immediately; instead he turned to Linchun. "Would you please leave us for a moment?" he said softly. "This shouldn't take long."

When the door had closed behind her, Qiu sighed. "My next move? You ask that question as if I had options, when in fact they've all disintegrated. But I still have unfinished business up north. . . ." He nodded toward Kowloon and the Chinese mainland.

Simon made an effort to concentrate. "Your family?"

"Yes. Sun's proposed a bargain, through an intermediary. Your expedition coincides exactly with his wishes. I'm instructed to bring Luk out. If I succeed, I'm at liberty to go where I like, work for whomever I please. Also, I can be divorced."

"What about your son?"

Qiu's gaze fell. "One cannot have everything."

"Why's Sun decided to do this?"

"So the Taiwanese don't get their hands on Apogee."

"That's all?" Mat interjected. "That's the whole of the deal? We don't have to hand Lennie over to Sun?"

"No."

Mat was on the point of speaking again, but Simon cut him off. "I don't understand why it has to be you. Anyone could lead a mission like that."

"No. I'm uniquely placed. I know a lot about Q-4, and then there's Mat—who's here, with me, not in Beijing with Sun. Mat, do you remember how you got as far as the *Golden Eagle* that night?"

"Vaguely. A guard led us through caves to the sea."

"Mei-hua made a sketch map of those caves, which she copied and gave to Lin-chun. Here." Qiu peeled a sheet of paper from his wallet. "Where once you came out, the pair of us might go in."

"I don't know," Simon said. "It's risky."

Qiu chuckled. "You think Sun doesn't know that? He doesn't seriously expect me to come back. That's why the deal was made to look so sweet from my point of view; he believes he's never going to have to honor it."

Mat subjected him to another stare, but kept quiet. It was Simon who broke the silence. "Sorry, but if it's that dangerous, I'm siding with Jinny. I can't let Mat go. I didn't think before."

"How are you going to stop me?" Mat's tone was light; he intended no quarrel.

"I'm assuming if I ask you not to go, you won't."

"Don't assume. Especially since you were on my side a minute ago. You know what? You're starting to sound unreliable."

"But be reasonable! Surely you must see—"

"What I see is that I'm going to Quemoy with Qiu. And if I'm lucky enough to come face to face with Li . . . I'll kill him."

Simon was silent for a moment. "What do you want me to say, that I respect your principles?"

"No!" Mat banged both fists down on the table. "I want . . . I'd like you to try and understand why I'm going. But if you can't—well, then that's too bad. And now, if you'll excuse me . . ." He darted a final strange look at Qiu and left the room. To his surprise he found Diana and Lin-chun talking quietly in the corridor, but Mat was in no mood for further confidences. He pushed past the two women into Mary Street's office, slamming the door behind him.

Meanwhile, George Forster was on his way back to the boardroom. "Cheong flatly refuses to have anything more to do with Quemoy," he said as he closed the door.

"Shit! What did you offer him?"

"He said it wouldn't matter if I offered him everything in the Bank of China's vaults. No deal."

It was Qiu who broke the ensuing silence. "Mr. Young, why don't you contact Cheong personally?"

"What good would that do?"

"Maybe none. But if you offered to come on the expedition yourself . . ."

"Me? What use could I be? I'm a middle-aged, unfit, short-sighted businessman—"

"Who knows Cheong better than anyone. You once told me

he owed you many favors. Favors are personal things. If you show him you're prepared to risk yourself, your own life even . . ."

"It might work," Simon said slowly.

"And there's something else, too. You know Li Lu-tang from way back. If we can only find him, you'll be the best one to do the talking."

"Talking? It's a shootout or nothing, isn't it?"

"Who knows? In a situation like this, every ally helps."

"It's worth a try," Simon said at last. "I'll speak to Cheong myself."

They went out through Mary Street's office to find Mat in there replacing the phone. "More problems?" Simon said testily.

"No, I don't think so." There was an awkward silence while Mat frowned at Qiu, as if trying to make up his mind. "Just arranging a little travel insurance for us, that's all." His face cleared. "What are we waiting for? Come *on*!"

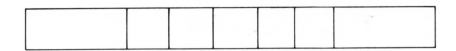

THIRTY-TWO

Sun Shanwang's first impression, on entering the Chairman's office in the Great Hall of the People, was that he had never seen this room look so gloomy. An air of melancholy permeated the tenebrous sanctum like smog. The Chairman sat behind a huge desk, a cigarette held just in front of his lips. When he caught sight of Sun he did not wave as usual; instead he slowly stubbed out the cigarette like a man giving up the habit at the last of many attempts and said, "What's the time?"

"Six-thirty, Chairman."

"In the morning?"

"In the morning, yes."

Sun began to clear away some of the papers that littered the floor. Every so often a red light in the receiver of one of the Chairman's five telephones would wink for a few seconds, then die for want of attention. The Chairman used the spittoon and cleared his throat.

"The General Secretary of the Soviet Communist Party has booked a call for half an hour's time." He gestured toward a set of double doors opposite the fireplace. "I've got the Politburo in there. We've been in session since dinner. I'm supposed to tell them something positive." His snuffle was without humor. "I wondered if you knew what the Russians were going to say to me."

"Best guess?" Sun shook fifty or so pages headed *Left Stroke: Command Logistics Fujian* into a semblance of tidiness. The two men allowed their eyes to meet, and exchanged tired smiles. "Yes," said the Chairman.

"They're going to terminate the pact formally, as a prelude to calling on you to cancel the invasion. If you resist, they'll remind you that the Americans are sailing for Taiwan, the Pentagon's on purple alert, and the UN is nerving itself to call a meeting of the Security Council. If we go ahead now, we'll be alone."

"Where have we gone wrong?" The Chairman's question was more than rhetorical; he reminded Sun of a child who'd been hurt for reasons beyond his comprehension.

"There were too many leaks." Sun looked unhappy, aware that leaks were his department. "And not enough honest exchanges of information."

"Yes." The Chairman sighed. "Well, at least now we know the answer to the question 'What would the Americans do?' "

"Forgive me if I sound presumptuous, but I never thought they'd stand by and let it happen. I have to know whether the invasion is to go ahead."

"Why?"

"Because I'm trying to think what's best to be done about Luk. As long as he's in Taiwan he's a threat."

"You mean he could show them how to defend themselves against the weapon he devised?"

"That's right. He *must* be neutralized."

"I thought you'd sent Colonel Qiu to get him out?"

"He's on his way now, with the Youngs. But to be frank, I don't believe there'll be any survivors of that mission—which doesn't trouble me as far as Qiu's concerned, but it still leaves Luk. If the invasion's to be canceled, I'll have to try to think of some other way of making him harmless. We could mount a raid on Quemoy from Xiamen, across the bay, or we might—"

"When must you know?"

"The invasion's scheduled for tonight, so . . ." Sun calculated. "By noon."

"You'll know before then, I promise. A moment ago you said 'no survivors.' " The Chairman's face was troubled. "And that includes Luk?"

[348]

"I'm afraid so."

"He's a gifted man—hard to replace. When I think of the investment in our future he represents . . ."

"I know. But if he's killed, at least the Taiwanese won't benefit from him."

The red telephone nearest the Chairman emitted a trill. He looked at it without apparent emotion. "Moscow. We can discuss this more profitably in a moment, when we know the worst." He picked up the receiver. "I'll take this in private."

As Sun came out of the Chairman's room he ran into Chief of Staff Wang, who managed a smile. "I'm glad to see you, Controller." Exhaustion had stamped itself on the marshal's face like a wasting disease. "What's happening, do you know?"

Sun shook his head. "Moscow's on the line now."

"Ah! It's the end, then."

"You think so?"

"Yes. Once they abandon us, we're finished." Wang was silent for a moment, then composed himself. "We can't keep this invasion on hold much longer. Things are starting to disintegrate down at Quanzhou. Qi's on the verge of dementia."

"What's wrong?"

"His planes are—"

A lieutenant came up and handed a folder to the Chief of Staff. "Dispersal reports," Wang muttered, taking a pen from his top pocket. "All . . . right." He signed his name at the bottom of the last sheet and tossed the folder to the officer.

"Waste of time," Wang said gloomily to Sun. "As I was saying, the planes are arriving and we don't know what to do with them. When I last spoke to Qi he had the First Airborne Wing stacked over Nanan and wanted to know if he should land them. And I couldn't say!"

"What's gone wrong?"

"Our original plan—"

The same lieutenant ran up. "Commander land invasion on the phone, sir."

"Tell him to wait." Wang turned back to Sun. "Our original plan was that they'd land, refuel, and be in flight again before they were detected. We always knew the Yankee Keyhole satellites would spot them on the ground, but as long as we got them in the air and over Quemoy within minutes, no problem. But if I can't get authorization to commence the next phase—"

Another officer approached and saluted. "Sir, field commander amphibious landing craft wants to know—"

"Tell him to fuck off! *Ai!* These . . . *people!*"

"How many planes are we talking about?" Sun was aghast. "Are they still up there?"

"Fifty F-9 Fantans. Yes! And they take up a lot of space. We need to get them back up fast. But without orders—"

The door to the Chairman's sanctuary opened a crack, revealing his secretary. "You two!" he called. *"Now!"*

They went in to find the Chairman sitting with his hands folded in front of him on the desk blotter. He stared into space, oblivious of the entrance of the newcomers. Tonight, he was old.

As Sun approached he heard the Chairman mumble some words. "Excuse me?"

"I said, do not forget, we should never forget . . . there is but one China. . . ." The old man swallowed, looked at his hands. "And Taiwan is part of it." His head shot up, the somber mood shattered. "It seems the rebels are free to go their own way a while longer," he snapped. "All right! But you can still teach the Taiwanese a lesson, Wang! *Do it tonight!*"

Mat leaned over the rail of the *Golden Eagle,* gazing at the sea. The water in the inlet was stagnant with coffee-colored froth and strips of tangled weed washed up and down by the swell. He found its unpredictable eddies almost hypnotic.

Simon laid a hand on his shoulder. "All right?"

"Mm. Funny, I was wondering the same about you." Mat turned to rest his back against the rail. "You looked bushed back there."

"Hot, that's all."

Mat looked at his father and somehow he doubted it. "You'll feel better when we're on the move again."

"Yes."

There followed a long silence, which Mat ended by saying, "I've been thinking."

"What about?"

"Haines. Mei-hua."

"I see." Simon hesitated. "You don't mind talking about it?"

"Not now."

"What happened? Why the change?"

"Something Diana said. Doesn't matter." Mat shook his head, ruling a line under all that had gone before. "Haines was the one who introduced us, you know. He kept a database of Taipei nightlife; she was on it."

"She?"

"Mei-hua. He made it look so accidental, that day we met. He knew I loved her movies, said he'd introduce us. No one likes feeling he's been used, does he?"

"Of course not."

"I wanted it. Sometimes you do. . . ."

"Wanted . . . ?"

"To be used. That's the only explanation I've got for my behavior. She dropped enough hints, said I wasn't right for her, I ought to go out with other girls. Conscience, I think. Something like that, anyway."

It was the first time Mat had spoken of Mei-hua to Simon since he'd told his father how she died. Simon couldn't think what to say. "You'll get over her," he said, and at once felt asinine.

"Yes. That's bad though, in a way. Who was it said dead people have to die twice: once in the flesh and then in the hearts of those they leave behind?"

"I've never heard that."

"Die in the hearts of those they leave behind . . . who loved them." Mat's voice sounded gentler than at any time since he'd left Quemoy.

"Isn't that what you want—to forget?"

"Yes." His control wasn't perfect; he averted his face. "But it's hard."

On the deck behind them, Cheong adjusted the dial of his transistor radio and the fragile father-son dialogue was corrupted by static, then: ". . . BBC World Service. The news. Senior officials in Beijing today denied that the recent concentration of troops in the southeast of mainland China was linked to an invasion of Taiwan. Army sources confirmed that the buildup was in preparation for an exercise in Fujian Province that had been scheduled for months. At the United Nations headquarters in New York, non-aligned countries have been lobbying in favor of a resolution calling on China to withdraw. . . ."

"You can turn it off now, can't you?" said Simon, angry at having his conversation with Mat disturbed; but Cheong impatiently raised his hand.

". . . Fears expressed yesterday in Hong Kong . . ." The signal wavered and began to fade. ". . . In London, the Foreign Secretary had talks late last night with the American ambassador . . . formal protest . . . orders to the Seventh Fleet. . . . Latest reports of storm damage in southern Italy . . ."

"Shit!" Cheong switched off the set. Simon and Mat dragged themselves away from the rail and flopped beside the others.

The five of them—the Youngs, Qiu, Cheong, and Uncle—lay under an awning at the stern. There was no breeze. The midday heat and humidity were at their peak. Cheong had decided to carry fuel, rather than large quantities of water, so they were rationed to one pint of liquid per man, every four hours. Enough for survival, but not for comfort.

"Where are we, anyway?" Mat asked wearily.

"Just south of the Pescadores," Cheong replied.

"How long are you planning to stay here?" Simon said, and Cheong turned his weird, mirrored eyes on him with a look of fury. "Why? Got any better ideas?"

Mat felt as if he'd heard a match strike in a bone-dry forest, and swiftly intervened, "No, he hasn't."

Simon glared but said nothing. He uncorked his water bottle and took half a dozen sips, waiting for his temper to cool.

Uncle collared a pair of binoculars and staggered upright. He examined the horizon, passing from one side of the boat to the other to complete the sweep. Mat addressed him in his best Cantonese: "Can you see any more smoke?"

When Uncle shook his head, Mat turned to Cheong and, using English this time, asked, "What do you reckon it was?"

"Don't know."

"There are several naval bases at Shantou," Qiu said thoughtfully. "Frigates, mostly—Kiang Nan class. They make a lot of smoke."

"Can you outrun them, Mr. Cheong?"

"Sure thing. But better they don't see us, hey? So we stay here a bit. Maybe go far as Pescadores this afternoon. Then see."

Cheong produced a toothpick and methodically set to work, every so often casting an eye at the horizon. Simon's head lolled forward onto his chest and he woke with a start. The awning shielded them from the worst of the sun, but the air on deck was the texture of steam and as painful to his sinuses. He longed for the boat to be under way, so that the rush of its passage might bring relief from this terrible heat and he could sleep. He felt more tired than he could ever remember.

Mat examined him without seeming to. He was worried about the old man, and as he formulated the phrase, he realized that the words were no longer just a synonym for *father*; they had become a literal description.

Cheong followed his gaze, then caught Mat's eye and rose. After a moment, Mat followed him up the ladder onto the bridge. Cheong seemed to want to talk but didn't know how to begin.

"Your father okay?" he said after a while.

"I think so. He's not cut out for this. Nor am I."

"Sure he can handle it?"

"I'm not sure, no. But you insisted he come."

"I know him from way back. Don't know you. Not yet. But . . . you're tougher than your father."

"I'm younger, that's all."

"No. Father was never that tough."

"Look, he's fit, right? If you could try not to quarrel with him . . ."

"Okay, okay. Listen. You got a gun?" Mat shook his head. "Think you should."

Mat rubbed the back of his neck, stuck for a response. "Dad and I don't know how to use those things. We'd do more harm than good."

"No—easy to learn." Cheong pointed to a brace of clips set in the bulkhead. "For my gun. Stow it below, most days. Need it in my business. Six in the hold."

"Jesus! And you go in and out of Hong Kong with those things?"

"Yup. Got a few friends in port. No problem."

"It's a death sentence if you're caught."

"Not caught. Not going to be." Cheong subjected Mat to another hard look and made up his mind. "We all take one. Even the odds a little, yes?"

Mat stared at the deck. When he raised his eyes to Cheong's face, it was to meet those reflective circles of black-rimmed light, and he felt ripples of gooseflesh. "You really think we're going to need them?"

"You really want to go to Quemoy?" Cheong jeered.

"You'd better show us how to use them, then."

"I will, I will." Cheong slid off the chair. "I'll sleep one hour now, maybe more, then I'll show you. You keep watch, ah? You and Uncle? Don't trust that Qiu, and your father isn't enough awake."

"Sure."

"And don't let Qiu out of your sight, y'hear? He's trouble. Shouldn't be on this ship!"

"He's all right."

"So you say." Cheong opened the door to the bridge and crossed the companionway into the day cabin opposite. "Going to be a long night," he said laconically. "I rest now."

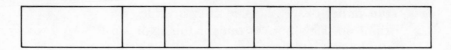

THIRTY-THREE

The *Golden Eagle* hove to with all her lights extinguished. A full moon cockleshelled the black water, illuminating its currents as they flowed and counter-flowed—a sea eternally at war with itself. Simon listened. The sound of an outboard motor was his first indication that their presence had been noted.

Another craft came alongside. The next moment, a dark shadow was climbing up the ladder. "Hello," Simon called softly from the stern. The shadow spun around and ran aft.

"Simon Young?"

"Yes, here. Also my son. There are three other men on the bridge; one of them owns this ship."

"My name is Tsai. I'm a captain in the Taiwanese military police. Quemoy's commander-in-chief, General Lo, has detailed me to accompany you."

Mat moved forward. "Zi-yang."

"Mr. Young."

Quemoy was in total darkness; they could not see each other.

The silence endured for several moments. At last Mat said haltingly, "I'm glad you're here."

Zi-yang made no reply. Both of them were remembering their last encounter, but words did not seem an adequate way of communicating such shared recall. Simon cleared his throat. "Can we get going, please?"

"Where do you want to go?"

"The northwest coast. Nanshan."

"*Zhidaole.*" Zi-yang went to the side and spoke to the cutter's captain. "They'll radio for clearance," he said as he returned to where the Youngs were standing. "But you're taking a terrible risk, I must tell you."

"Why?"

"Because we're convinced the Reds are coming tonight. So there's no equipment and no men to spare—except me."

Simon nodded. "I'll get us under way. Be back in a moment."

He returned to the bridge and almost at once the *Golden Eagle* began to move, leaving the cutter to make its way back to shore.

"Zi-yang," said Mat. "Why are you here?"

The officer sounded embarrassed. "General Lo decided to send me. He knows the whole story now."

"What *is* the whole story?"

"I was seconded to Li Lu-tang, at Li's request. I had no idea what that man was really like, I—"

"I believe you. Go on."

"After Mo's . . . execution, Li arranged for me to be court-martialed. But when nobody appeared to present the case against me, I was sent back to Q-4. I found it locked, and the telephone link was dead."

"What did you do?"

"I went back to base. My commander reported the closure of Q-4 to Garrison Command, and General Lo heard about it. There was no news of Li. Then the minister telephoned him from Taipei with news of your coming. The general questioned me. He thought I was the best person to send."

"Did you tell him everything that had happened?"

"Everything."

There was a long pause. "You know what we've come for?" Mat said at last.

"Yes. My orders are to help in any way I can."

"When were you last inside Q-4?"

"Two days ago."

"Was everything normal then?"

[355]

"It seemed so."

"Did you see this man Luk? He's about five foot six, mustache—"

"I didn't see him, but he may have been there. I checked the roster. There was only one prisoner, no name, just the usual number code. When I asked about him, they told me he was connected with the Apogee project."

"You were told, you say. By whom?"

"The duty officer."

"You didn't see Li?"

"No."

Simon came down from the bridge to rejoin them. "I'm glad you could come, Captain. Do you know the caves underneath Q-4?"

"Yes."

"That's where we're headed. We're going to get in that way."

"Impossible! Two days ago they wired off the bay and laid mines out there."

"Shit! You mean there's no way in from the sea?"

"None."

"Goddamn! I'd better tell Cheong To."

As Simon disappeared, Mat faced Zi-yang. "Look. You'd better know that one of the men on this ship is a communist cadre. His name's Qiu Qianwei; he's a colonel in the People's Liberation Army."

Zi-yang stepped back. Mat, sensing his alarm, hastened to reassure him. "Qiu works for us now. His only concern is to help my father and me."

"Is he armed?"

"We all are."

Neither man spoke for a while. "Your father should have told me about the Chicom at once," Zi-yang said at last.

"I agree, he should. But we're here to rescue a friend, if we can. We're a very small sideshow. One Red colonel isn't going to change anything."

"Maybe not." The captain analyzed his situation in silence. "You surprise me," he said eventually. "You're so calm."

"Why shouldn't I be?"

"*Why?* After all you endured here . . . doesn't it affect you?"

Zi-yang peered through the darkness at the Englishman, but could see nothing of his face. When Mat spoke, his voice was harsh.

"Will you tell me something?"

"If I can."

"Was Mo Mei-hua the one who told Li about our escape plan being brought forward?"

"No."

Zi-yang found a hand gripping his arm above the elbow, gripping it hard enough to make him wince. "How can you be sure?"

"I thought you knew. The argument—"

"What argument?"

"With Li. Before Mo was . . . Li and I were quarreling, remember?"

"Yes."

"I asked him why he was so angry with Mo, when she was on our side. Like you, I assumed she had . . . I'm sorry."

"Go on."

"Li told me she'd disobeyed orders. The captain of the fishing boat took fright and talked."

Zi-yang waited for a reaction, but none came. The *Golden Eagle* rounded the northernmost point of Quemoy and reduced speed.

"We're nearly at Nanshan." No response. Zi-yang raised his voice. "Mr. Young, please! We need to make some decisions!"

But still Mat was silent.

"I'm worried about this Colonel Qiu," Zi-yang muttered. "The Reds will come soon." He peered at the luminous numerals of his watch. "Midnight . . ."

Over on the coast of Fujian, a single flare soared upward. As it reached the pinnacle of its arc, the night became a white sheet of searing sound.

Twenty-four mainland shore batteries opened up simultaneously. For several seconds Mat's mind was a blank. Then, slowly, conscious thought returned. He was flat on the deck, that was the first thing; beside him, the captain lay on his stomach, hands clasped behind his neck, lips drawn back to the gums.

Disorganized images impressed themselves haphazardly on Mat's retinas. Blinding flashes blotted out his normal vision, then faded away to leave shrinking purple patches behind his eyelids. Smoke clogged his nostrils and lungs, making him retch. Flames crackled. Whistling, never-ending whistling, that sundered his eardrums . . .

Then Quemoy's batteries began to return fire, and at once Mat found himself back inside his cell, with a metal bucket over his head and people banging on its sides. Temporarily he seemed to lose consciousness. He clapped his hands to his ears and prayed for the noise to stop. But instead it intensified.

Seventy seconds after the first shell landed there was a brief lull. Mat became aware of Zi-yang kicking him. He staggered up, his head still pounding, and ran forward after the captain. A glance over his left shoulder was enough to show Nanshan in flames. As the *Golden Eagle* moved inshore, her spotlight sweeping the beach, Mat dazedly saw the remains of a barbed-wire barrier. "The mines!" Zi-yang bawled in his ear. "The shells detonated the mines."

They reached the top of the ladder. The barrage opened up again. Two shells bracketed the *Golden Eagle,* putting her almost on her beam ends. Mat and Zi-yang were flung back into the dayroom. The ship righted herself, searchlight pointing heavenward. Now a machine gun added its clatter to the blitz of sound assaulting Mat's ears, and he guessed that the Taiwanese were trying to shoot out Cheong's light.

Cheong changed course in a violent maneuver that was almost instantly corrected. Left, right, more right . . . he took evasive action as if he'd been practicing for this all his life. Mat's head exploded with pain—the roar of the engines, the crash of shell after shell erupting around them, automatic fire, there was no end to it.

Flares. Suddenly the two Chinas were competing to light up the night. For an instant they shared a common target: the *Golden Eagle.* Cheong pointed his ship at the coast of Quemoy and opened the throttle wide. His light pierced the surrounding darkness like a silver sword. Two plumes of water shot up into the air ahead of him, sending the vessel reeling to port. The wave lifted her up so that Cheong suddenly found himself looking at the stars; then she dipped, her screws whined against empty air, and the ship plunged down a sheer mountainside of water, heading for the rocks.

Somehow, through it all, Cheong managed to stay in his seat and keep hold of the wheel. As his beam steadied he caught a fleeting glimpse of what he'd been looking for: a narrow, V-shaped cleft in the cliff immediately ahead of him. He tore the throttles back, made a swift course correction, and pointed the *Golden Eagle*'s nose toward the center of the opening.

Another shell exploded somewhere astern. Water poured over the bridge, momentarily extinguishing vision. As the flood sluiced away from the glass, a shock wave hurled the boat through the V, into a cave. The *Golden Eagle* rocked wildly, coming within an inch of the granite wall before the sea exhausted itself in a last pump that spattered the rear of the cavern and rebounded to meet the ship head-on. Her prow reared up, fell back. Then it was over.

The clamor of the shelling reverberated strangely through the granite hall, but it was fainter here than on the open sea. Mat slowly came to his senses. He saw his father stretched out on the floor of the dayroom. "Are you okay?"

Simon opened his eyes with a groan. "Where . . . are we? Oh God . . ." He lifted his head and peered about him. "You all right?"

"Yes. You?"

"Think so. Why are you whispering?"

"I'm not. I'm shouting."

"Jesus! The noise. Can't . . . hear. Buzzing . . ."

Mat checked himself for damage. No bones broken. Apart from his ears, which appeared to be stuffed with cotton wool, he was unharmed. As he helped his father up, a disturbingly loud blast rocked the *Golden Eagle* and a mass of rock splinters showered down into the cave. The two men ducked, then slowly stood upright and crossed the narrow passage to the bridge.

Qiu was leaning on the control console by the forward port. Mat joined him. They couldn't see much in the single beam of the ship's light: seething, oil-dark water, jagged edges of what looked like slate, some of it interleaved with a coppery, reflective mineral, and at the farthest extremity of the cave, a crude flight of stairs leading up into darkness.

Cheong was mopping blood from a gash on his forehead. Every so often he'd pause to stare at the gore that soaked his handkerchief. As he saw Simon appear in the doorway he nodded toward the second chair.

Uncle slumped with his head lolling over the backrest at an impossible angle and only a yawning hole where his Adam's apple once had been. When Simon moved forward, something crunched under his feet; he looked down to see that a sheet of glass had shattered, blown inward by the blast from one of the shells. "I'm sorry," he muttered.

"Yeah. So'm I."

"We're leaving," Qiu interrupted. "And we need the guns."

Zi-yang stirred restlessly, upset by the thought of Qiu being armed. Cheong seemed similarly affected, but finally he nodded. "In the hold."

"Show me."

A few moments later Qiu and Cheong reappeared carrying FC-180s and spare ammunition clips. Qiu dumped his burden on the table. "Is that all?" he asked Cheong.

"What do you mean?"

"I mean—do you have any more arms aboard?"

"No."

"I hope you're telling me the truth."

Cheong looked ready to snap some reply; but then he caught sight of Qiu's expression and the words never came. Qiu gathered up all but two of the guns, walked to the side, and dropped them overboard.

Cheong went wild. "You got no right—!"

"I intend to leave this place standing up and with my eyes open, so I've every right. You!" He eyed Zi-yang with manifest hostility. "What's your name?"

"Tsai Zi-yang."

"You know the way?"

"Yes."

"Then you'll go first. But *I* command! Understood?"

"I won't take orders from a Red."

"You'll do as you're told. I want your pistol. *Now!*"

Zi-yang saw that the muzzle of one of the guns was suddenly pointing at his stomach. Reluctantly he unbuttoned his holster and placed it on the table.

"Good. Simon, stay here with Cheong To. Mat—you come with us."

"Are you sure? I'm worried I'll only hold you up."

"I need firepower! And eyes as well. Two men to lead, one to follow up the rear. There's no one else fit enough. Ready?"

For an instant Mat hesitated, remembering the things that had happened to him here, and they all saw it.

"I'll go," Simon said tersely.

The smile Mat gave his father was warm with understanding. It took them both back to a far-off time when to be Simon Young's son meant more than just claiming succession to a commercial conglomerate. But the smile also had something of that steely quality people use when they want to soften the exercise of power.

"It's my fight, Dad. Thanks."

Simon looked at Mat and for the first time accepted in his heart that he'd grown to manhood.

Qiu tossed Mat the other remaining gun. The touch of metal, with its rich smell of oil, jolted him back to the present. Qiu's laugh dispelled any lingering sentimentality. "Know how to use it?"

"Cheong To showed me earlier."

"Good." Qiu darted a final glance at Zi-yang. "Remember, Tsai . . . I'll be watching you. Every step. Now *move!*"

The three men clattered down the ladder to where the dinghy was stowed and soon had it in the water. Moments later they were heading for the stairway at the back of the cave, paddling along the path lit for them by the *Golden Eagle's* spot.

"Do you remember any of this?" Qiu asked Mat as they scrambled ashore.

"I'm not certain. It was dark in here that night, all we had was a flashlight. Mei-hua . . . Mei-hua relied on the guard to lead the way. He seemed to know it blindfolded."

Another loud boom rocked the *Golden Eagle,* making her light flicker and dance. A few stones plopped into the water, but that was all. "Come on," Qiu muttered. "You—Tsai! Go first; then you, Mat. I'll be right behind."

When the *Golden Eagle's* light finally disappeared around a corner, the darkness that enveloped them was total. Sometimes the crash of a particularly well-directed shell penetrated their ears, but the deeper into the rock they progressed the quieter it became, until eventually all they could hear was the sound of each other's footsteps and the thumping of their own hearts.

"Fuck!" Mat's hand had slid off the rock wall and was thrashing about in space. "There's a split in the path."

Zi-yang stood with his head to one side, listening. He licked his finger and held it up. "Air current coming from . . . *that* direction."

At once the floor began to angle steeply upward. Progress, already slow, became snaillike. They'd been going for about five minutes when Zi-yang felt his way around a corner and instantly plastered himself to the wall. In the second before he pulled Mat back, the Englishman had time to look over his shoulder and see a faint orange glow shimmering up and down.

"What is it?" he breathed.

"Torches."

"I remember them. We must be getting close now."

Qiu had narrowed the gap between them enough to hear his last words. "Li's torture chamber?"

"Yes."

Qiu released his safety catch. Mat did the same. The aftermath of noise seemed to linger in the tunnel for a long time.

They crept forward until they could see the nearest torch, flaring and spitting on its bracket, with only darkness beyond its narrow ambit. On the edge of the circle of amber light, Zi-yang paused. He waited several seconds, flexing his muscles; then he bounded forward, spinning in midair as he did so and coming to land at a crouch in the protective darkness on the other side.

Mat advanced, waited a moment until Zi-yang waved the all-clear, then followed the captain's lead. He landed awkwardly, knocking his gun on the stone slabs that paved this part of the tunnel complex, and for long moments they held their breaths, awaiting reprisals.

But reprisals did not come. They were alone in the tunnel.

Zi-yang signaled them onward. About twenty feet ahead of them was a turn, faintly illuminated by a torch around the corner. Zi-yang sidled along the short wall of the approach to the bend and risked one glance. Another length of tunnel stretched out in front of him, lit by three flambeaux.

They repeated the earlier exercise, leaping from stepping-stones of gloom over pools of light. As they passed the third torch they heard a faint echo of voices and stopped.

"Sounds close," Mat whispered in Zi-yang's ear.

"It's distorted," the captain replied. "The tunnels are like that. Those voices might be near or far." He clicked a tuneless rhythm with his tongue. "I recognize this. Halfway along the next corridor there's a junction with the passage up to the prison level."

"That's where we're going?"

"Yes. Unless . . . I don't know what those voices mean. It's almost as if someone were in the museum."

Qiu came up silently and nudged Zi-yang, making the officer start. "Keep moving. I'll stay with you for a while."

The three men proceeded slowly, backs against the wall, until they reached the intersection Zi-yang had mentioned. The sound of voices grew louder as they advanced, until at last Mat could distinguish two speakers. One voice was scarcely audible, but the other was loud enough to enable him to identify its owner as Li Lu-tang.

Mat's stomach muscles tightened in a spasm of fear. But only for a moment. Then the rage that now perpetually hovered on the borders of his self-control reasserted itself. "Let's move," he muttered.

They crept past the junction and on, until eventually they were standing in the circular chamber that led to the gates of exquisite view. Mat eyed both doorways. "Which one?"

Zi-yang shook his head. "I don't know . . . the echo confuses me. But I think . . . that way." He pointed to the opening on the left.

"I'll stay behind you," Qiu whispered, withdrawing into the darkness.

The displays were lit. As Mat passed the first, he turned his head and quickly looked away with a shiver. The figures in "hell" seemed preternaturally real, larger than life. Memories crowded in with a rush, and for a moment he faltered.

The sound of conversation rose and fell. Now Mat could hear other, softly spoken Chinese voices and he knew they must be getting very near.

They continued to advance, drawing level with another display. This scene portrayed a woman suspended upside down in a harness being lowered into a clear-sided tank full of piranhas, while two armed guards looked on. A glance at the stage was enough to remind Mat that it represented a Uruguayan torture; the flat, vaguely Mongolian features of the guards, far from untypical in South America, did not strike him as odd.

He took another step.

Resonance of automatic fire, smell of cordite, Zi-yang crashing back against him, falling to the ground: all were concentrated into a microsecond. As Mat rolled sideways he caught a glimpse of the "Uruguayan" who had fired. Live guards, two of Li's marines. Of course. *How stupid can you get?*

Where was Qiu?

"Bring them here!" Mat heard a familiar voice say. A guard dragged him to his feet and hauled him to the next display, where Li Lu-tang was waiting.

"The other one?"

"Captain Tsai, Controller. He's wounded."

Li was standing at the front of one of the recesses. It contained no exhibit. A table had been set up against the back wall, with Apogee spread out along it: two screens, two printers, disk drives, telephones. The lighting here was brilliant: four spots on each of three metal tracks. Lennie Luk stood at the far end, gazing down on Mat with an expression of horror. Two other men, scientists perhaps, were seated in front of the screens, obviously terrified.

"What's that?" Li gestured to the FC-180 dropped by Mat, and a guard handed it to him. Li examined the gun critically before leaning it against the side wall of the recess. "We have Apogee now," he said quietly. "Luk has cooperated. These two gentlemen have sufficient understanding of the principles involved to counteract its radio guidance system."

"Too late. The invasion's beginning. We were shelled on the way in."

"Yes. You would say that."

"It's true!"

Where was Qiu?

"Even if it were true, it wouldn't alter my plans. I have the

[363]

bargaining counter I need. Taiwan will be saved—if not by us, then by new-found allies who will flock to acquire Apogee." He turned briefly to the guards—"Keep Luk covered"—before addressing Mat again. "Why did you come here?"

Mat said nothing.

"Tell me how you came here!"

When Mat still refused to speak, Li nodded at the guard standing nearest him. The man worked in silence, but he was thorough, and before long Mat slid to the floor with a groan.

"All right, enough!" Li stood looking down on Mat for a long time before he spoke again. "The Japanese were accustomed to enforce their rule severely, here in Taiwan. For fifty years . . . they used to make examples of those who dared oppose them, particularly within the family. They executed my father, in front of me. Their purpose was to make me remember it. And I did remember. I can see his execution now, as if it were yesterday."

He drew his sword from its scabbard. The scientists sat transfixed, deep in shock.

"I propose to make an example of you, Young." He raised his sword and beckoned the marine who had beaten up Mat. The man marched two paces forward, raising his gun. Li tensed as he prepared to execute the sword-stroke that would signal the end.

Mat's mouth was as dry as sandpaper. In the next few seconds he was going to die. There were no ifs; life had run out. His ears filled with torrential, rushing noise. Over what seemed a great distance he heard a burst of rapid fire and felt his knees give way.

But it was the marine beside him who tumbled forward and lay still.

For an instant, nobody moved. Then the second guard darted for his Browning. Jumbled thoughts raced through Mat's brain: Qiu must have crept up behind them, why didn't he fire again, what was Li doing? *Why didn't Qiu shoot?*

Then he saw why.

When Qiu fired, Li had leaped to one side. Now he stood behind Lennie Luk's chair, the sword upraised only a little way above the prisoner. "Drop the gun!" he grated. "Or I'll cut his head off."

Mat turned to see Qiu walk forward into the light, gripping his FC-180.

"Drop it!"

Qiu halted, but still kept hold of the gun. Mat guessed he was calculating distances, times, odds. . . . *What if he hit Lennie instead?*

Li's teeth ground, a vindictive smile curled across his face. His tongue darted over his upper lip. Mat saw the muscles flex. The blow was coming. Any second now . . .

Li would have to strike hard and fast to beat Qiu's finger on the trigger. There must be no hint of warning. Suddenly he flicked the sword up, striving for momentum. In the same second, Qiu fired. His aim was wide and Li, elated, lifted the blade higher.

Without stopping to think, Mat flung himself forward in a rugby tackle. Li saw him coming and flinched. He stepped to one side; Mat stumbled and fell. Li, now torn between two victims, decided to dispatch the nearest: Mat. He slashed back and up, extending himself to full height in preparation for a chopping stroke.

The sword-point embedded itself in the metal slot of a lighting track immediately above his head. The bulbs flickered wildly. For a moment the whole length of the blade glowed a magical shade of blue. There was a flash, a shriek, a tongue of flame in a cloud of black smoke; and so Li died, collapsing to his knees, very slowly, as if to worship.

The lights restored themselves. The second guard's hand was on the butt of his pistol. Mat, on his knees by now, dived for the FC-180 that Li had left propped up against the wall. As he landed he rolled over on his back, pulled the stock into his stomach, and fired between his outspread legs. He missed. The guard turned, pistol cocked. Mat pulled the trigger again. This time his aim was true.

Mat threw down the gun. He was trembling so badly he couldn't move. He knew that if he tried to stand his legs would collapse beneath him. Lennie ran forward through wreaths of smoke to lift him up.

"Help me . . . please." Zi-yang had crawled to the edge of the stage. Qiu looked down at him, eyes glinting. "You are hurt," he said unnecessarily.

"Leg . . . Lot of . . . blood."

"You'll have to make it to the boat." The colonel pulled roughly on Zi-yang's arm, making the injured man grimace with pain.

"Get away from him!" Mat was surprised to hear the venom in his own voice.

"I was only—"

"Leave him! I'll do it."

Mat knelt down to arrange Zi-yang's arm around his shoulders. The captain looked at him and for the first time that night saw a smile extend as far as his eyes.

They went back the way they'd come. Lennie removed one of the torches from the wall to light their path, but Zi-yang's injury slowed them down and it seemed a long time before they once more found themselves on the flight of stairs to the inlet.

They knew they'd nearly reached their destination when the shelling began to sound menacingly close. Qiu was in the lead. He turned a corner and there lay the ship, just as they'd left her, riding high in the gentle swell of the cave. The dinghy had to make two journeys. Mat was last to go aboard. He helped Zi-yang to the dayroom and made him comfortable with Lennie's assistance; then he went to the bridge, where he found his father and Cheong.

"We got him!"

"Well done." But Simon's face was haggard.

"We have to go. The Taiwanese will be coming soon. Apogee's up there, somewhere."

Simon stared at him. Mat had endured so much, yet as the night progressed he seemed to become stronger, more in command of himself, than his father could ever remember. Simon felt old, adrift. At last he made a weary gesture. "Yes."

Cheong took the captain's chair and started the engines. Simon slid onto what had been Uncle's seat, Mat standing at his shoulder. Slowly the *Golden Eagle* began to ease her way backward. They were nearly at the open sea when someone behind them said, "You will set a course for Xiamen. On the mainland."

The two Englishmen turned. Qiu stood in the doorway, holding a key in one hand and his gun in the other. His field of fire was uninterrupted; he had everyone covered.

"I've locked the renegade in the dayroom with Luk." Qiu tossed the key and pocketed it. "Do as I say."

But Mat reached across Cheong to kill the engines. "Why?" he asked.

"I don't want a discussion, I want a passage to the mainland." Qiu's face was pasty. "Start the engines!"

"I want to hear why."

"It's no business of—"

"It's *exactly* our business! You made a deal with Sun, didn't you? But not the one you told us about."

Qiu gazed at Mat, wondering what lay behind his smooth, enigmatic expression. "I'm to deliver you to the mainland," he said vacantly. "My obligations end there."

"Me, my father, and Lennie?"

Qiu said nothing.

"Lennie's to work for Beijing; we're to be shot. We'll be reported as killed in action, no doubt. So those were Sun's terms. I wondered why you insisted my father come on this trip; now I know."

Qiu examined the young Englishman through half-closed eyes. He was missing something obvious; either that, or Mat would make a remarkably good actor. So confident . . . "You're to be punished," he confirmed.

"And the punishment for treason is death, yes, I know." Mat turned to his father. "You betrayed them by sending Lennie to Quemoy."

"I had no choice, I—"

"You could have chosen to sacrifice me, or not." Mat smiled. "I'm glad you decided not. But now we do have this problem. He has the gun. I left mine in the caves."

It was Qiu who broke the long silence. "Sun proposed a deal. I . . . couldn't refuse."

"Let me see if I can figure it out. You're to deliver Lennie Luk to Beijing and hand us over to the authorities. In return, you can have a divorce, Lin-chun, *and* your son."

"Not bad."

"And you believe Sun?" Mat was incredulous. "You've always been sold to us as an experienced agent, no fool. Yet you—"

"Yet I have to *try*! Don't you understand? I have to go back and make a deal, something that'll stick." Qiu couldn't take his eyes off Mat's face. He wiped his forehead a couple of times. "I want to be able to go home," he said at last. "Live in Beijing, with Lin-chun."

"How did you know?" Simon breathed.

"Not difficult," said Mat. "The deal described to us in Hong Kong was impossibly one-sided. Qiu got everything in exchange for nothing. You didn't see that, because you've dealt with them for so long you've become blind. Sorry."

Simon stared down at the deck. "I . . . I trusted them."

"Yes." Mat turned back to face Qiu. "There's no need to justify yourself, Colonel. You can't have Lin-chun."

For a moment Qiu didn't understand what he was saying. But then Mat pulled something from his pocket and held it up for the cadre to see. "Shan Lin-chun's passport, courtesy of Peter Reade." As Qiu stepped forward, Mat flung the passport through the shattered window into the sea.

"Your Miss Shan has just become a stateless person." Mat smiled. "So sorry."

"You're a fool!" Qiu controlled his temper. "Bits of paper are irrelevant."

"Perhaps. But Reade's detention order isn't. I've arranged for Lin-chun to be held in Hong Kong as security for our return; the British still run the place for a few years yet, you know. She won't get out unless she's sponsored by my father or me. And if you can't produce either of us to Reade . . ." Mat caught his father's eye. "That's the travel insurance I arranged, back in the office."

By now Qiu had lowered his gun. Mat tried to read the expression on his face but found it impossible. "I don't think you should feel too badly about this," he said gently.

"Why?" Qiu's voice was hollow.

"Because your heart was never in Sun's bargain, was it? You and my father aren't exactly friends, but you didn't want to hand him over. Too many obligations on both sides, I'd have thought. Too many *favors.*"

Qiu remained silent.

"And even if you did hand him over, would you trust Sun Shanwang again? Do you remember what you said back in Hong Kong—Sun didn't expect you to return from Quemoy, he was never going to have to honor this deal? That bit was true, wasn't it? So put down the gun, Qianwei."

"There's one point you've forgotten." Qiu slowly raised his eyes to Mat's face. "My son. I can't give up my son. Not without going back, making one last attempt."

"Last attempt is right! They'll shoot you."

"I'm useful to them. They won't be in a hurry to liquidate someone who knows the things I know. Anyway, it's a risk I have to take."

"Why, in God's name?"

"Because I could never feel safe, no matter where you sent me. Sun would find me. And those I love."

"No. The British intelligence service would fit you out with a new identity. You'd be in London within hours; Sun couldn't touch you there."

"That only shows how little you know about him."

When Mat did not respond, Qiu addressed Cheong. "Start the engines."

"Hong Kong?"

"No . . . Xiamen."

Cheong looked at Mat. To the cadre's surprise, he nodded reluctantly. "Xiamen."

Mat was thinking furiously. Somewhere in all this there had to be a deal, an angle no one had thought of. Think leverage, he told himself; think *pressure.*

As Cheong brought the *Golden Eagle*'s prow around, Mat said casually, "Of course, you needn't give up your son."

Cheong throttled back.

"What?" Qiu barked the word, suddenly a man who longs to be convinced.

"If you come back to Hong Kong with us, we'll tell Sun that unless he sends you the boy within forty-eight hours, we'll give Apogee to the United States in return for an indemnity against any lawsuit or countermeasures the Red Chinese bring against Ducannon Young."

"No!" Simon's voice was raw. "We have a contract with these people. They're our future, our one last remaining market. *We can't do that!*"

"We?" Mat sounded disdainful. "In your pocket you have a document from the Russian Politburo that already protects us against China. If we marry it up to an American indemnity, I'd have thought Ducannon Young would be fairly well placed to survive, wouldn't you?"

"You'd really do that?' Qiu's voice scarcely carried across the cabin.

"If it's a straight choice between that and you taking us to Xiamen for execution—yes."

"You can't, Mat. I won't let you."

Mat studied his father for a long time without speaking.

"There has to be another way, son. We have obligations toward these people."

Mat extended an arm toward Qiu. "They sent him to kill you. Was that one of *their* obligations?"

"I let them down."

"*Let them down?* And before—when they sent men to kill our house servants, ruin our companies, destroy us—had you let them down then? You've done everything in your power to help them, ever since I can remember! No, Father." Mat spoke bitterly. "No."

"So you speak for the companies now, do you?"

"You know I don't. Not while you're alive. I can't dictate to you. But perhaps I can persuade you. I've shown you what these people are like, *really* like. This man Qiu represents how far they'll go to eradicate their opponents. So now, Father. You're the boss. You choose."

When Simon did not answer, Mat turned back to Qiu. "Ducannon Young will honor the commitment I've outlined. You have our—my—word."

But still the cadre hesitated. "Even so . . . Sun Shanwang might not comply. If he gives me back my son, my freedom, what guarantee does he have that I won't betray China's intelligence secrets to the West? The risk is incalculable."

"No," Mat said. "The risk is small. A handful of military dispositions, gossip about the Politburo, they're nothing compared to Apogee." He smiled. "You know the only relevant question, you know it perfectly well. Who do you trust more—Sun Shanwang . . . or us?"

Qiu's eyes clouded over, his brain refused to work. The decision was stark. He looked at Simon. "Mr. Young? Is what your son said true—you would honor such a bargain?"

Simon did not meet Qiu's eyes; instead he stared at his son. When Mat's face remained implacable it suddenly came home to Simon that his life resembled nothing so much as a game of chess: he'd been allocated time in which to make his moves, cramming them ever more swiftly into a diminishing span; but one day soon the clock would stop for him and then he would be obliged to rise from the table, leaving the board for another. . . .

Across what seemed a vast distance he heard Mat say, "Cheong To—get us out of here."

As the *Golden Eagle* began to edge forward, Qiu allowed the FC-180 to fall on the deck.

"Unlock the dayroom, Qianwei."

The colonel obeyed like an automaton. Mat saw Zi-yang emerge, and beckoned to him. "How are you, Captain?"

"Okay. Luk helped bandage me up."

"What do you want to do?"

The officer scowled at Qiu. "Please leave me somewhere on the coast; I'll find my way back to base."

"Very well. Lennie . . ."

"Yes?"

"We're going to Hong Kong now. I really don't want to do this, but I must: I have to give you a choice. You're not happy, I've known that for a long time." He gestured at Qiu. "His task was to take you back to Beijing with him, to complete your work on Apogee. Is that what you'd have wanted?"

"No. Of course not. But . . ."

"But you won't be coming back to Ducannon Young." Mat smiled at his friend. "All right."

"You understand?" Lennie was astonished. He turned to where Simon still slumped in his chair. "Mr. Young—what about you?"

"It's Mat's responsibility," Simon said heavily. "If he doesn't mind . . . I don't."

"But you're—"

Simon raised a hand and turned away his head.

"Let's move before they start shelling again." As Mat spoke, they heard a shrill whistle in the distance. He swore. "Too late."

"Like hell it is!" spat Cheong. While they were talking, he had slowly navigated the *Golden Eagle* as far as the mouth of the cave. Now they cleared it; and Cheong brought the ship's nose around until she faced due south. The Chicom gunners were aiming high; their shells pounded inland before exploding with a roar that was only slightly muffled by the hills. The new barrage lasted less than a minute. In the lull that followed, Cheong swept inshore and managed to drop Tsai off on the beach near Nanshan.

Mat stood at the stern, reliving the memory of that day when he and Zi-yang had picnicked on the sands.

"Mr. Young, you are a strong man."

Mat gazed down at him, feeling his chest tighten. "I won't forget you, Zi-yang. *Tsai-jien.*"

He was about to give Cheong the order to run for it when the captain pointed to his left. "Look! They're switching on the underwater floods!"

Mat saw great pools of light explode beneath the surface of the sea. Three, four, five . . . a whole string of lights, dispelling the shadows that edged the shore, until the whole west coast was a shining ribbon of white.

The eerie silence was shattered by a machine gun.

"They're preparing for the Reds' assault craft," Zi-yang shouted.

Mat lifted his head. He thought he could hear faint sounds, high up and far, far away. A distant droning . . .

He wheeled around, looking up at the cliffs. Grayness had begun to dilute the nighttime gloom. He scanned the four quadrants of sky as the murmur grew steadily nearer. Where was it coming from? East? West?

The machine-gunner opened up again and soon was joined by one of his fellows. They began to fire steadily, tiny columns of water spurting to mark their aim . . . and now the first rays of the sun speckled the placid surface of the channel separating the two Chinas, carving out a highway of brilliance to make them one.

"*Go!*" Mat screamed. Cheong punched the twin throttles forward, launching them into a desperate race for the south and safety. The second shells of the dawn barrage whistled overhead to land with a roar of destruction in the cliffs high above, pounding the dignified inscription "Do not forget when you were last in Ju" until only the character for "Ju" remained. But already the *Golden Eagle* was far along the coast, outrunning the bombardment that poured down on Quemoy like a presage of the ending of the world. A last plume of spray licked the starboard bow, one final zigzag, and the boat was streaking through into blue water.

The hum in the distant sky grew ever louder, and now it was clear that it was coming from the east, from Taiwan. Tsai lifted his hand to wave before removing his helmet and wiping an arm across his forehead. "*Feiji lai-zhe,*" he said to himself as he replaced the helmet; and a smile stole over his worn face.

The planes were coming.

GLOSSARY

Aiya!	Chinese exclamation denoting surprise
Baba	Father (Chinese); also, nickname of the former head of the mainland Chinese Secret Service
Cempedak	Jack-fruit tree
Chedi	Thai temple dome
Chicom	Abbreviated term for "Chinese Communist"
Chingai-de	Darling, dearest (Chinese)
Dacha	Russian country house
Durian	A strong-smelling, thorny fruit with custardlike pulp, found throughout Southeast Asia

Executive Yuan	One of the five branches of the Taiwanese government, akin to a Western cabinet
GRU	Soviet military intelligence
Guo-yu	"National speech"; the Mandarin spoken in Taiwan
Klong	Canal (Thai)
Kuai-lo	Derogatory Cantonese for male foreigner
Lalang	A coarse grass found in the Malayan peninsula
Li-shu	Old-fashioned style of Chinese calligraphic script, now obsolete
Mah-jongg Brigade	Another name for the Central Control of Intelligence, mainland China
Middle Kingdom	Ancient name for mainland China
Soi	Lane (Thai)
Taijiquan	Chinese system of exercise; shadowboxing
Satay	A Malay dish of skewered beef, lamb, or chicken broiled over charcoal, usually eaten with peanut-flavored sauce
Tew neh lo mo	Cantonese obscenity
Thangka	Type of Buddhist scroll made from linen or silk
Tsai-jien	Goodbye (Chinese)
Tuk-tuk	Enclosed motorcycle taxi (Thai)
Vykhodnoi	Day off, rest day (Russian)
Zhidaole	Understood! Got it! (Chinese)